To most of the known galaxy he was a legend without a
face, and to the rest a face without a name.

But luck and disguises had finally given out, and a Na'id
squadron was in fast-closing pursuit of his ship, *Liberation*.

He was staring out the viewport without really seeing, when
a pattern of lights appeared out of an unexpected quadrant.
And a slow sick horror penetrated the blank space inside
him.

> *Na'id?*
> Could he possibly be *surrounded* by Na'id ships?
> But it was not a Na'id ship.
> It was worse. . . .

JERUSALEM
FIRE

R. M. MELUCH

JERUSALEM
FIRE

DAW BOOKS, INC.
DONALD A. WOLLHEIM, FOUNDER
375 Hudson Street, New York, NY 10014

ELIZABETH R. WOLLHEIM
SHEILA E. GILBERT
PUBLISHERS
www.dawbooks.com

Does Jerusalem stand?
    —Traveler's question

I don't understand Jews.
    —Shad Iliya

Christians, Mohammedans, and Jews, peoples who placed
revelation before reason . . .
    —T. E. Lawrence, *Seven Pillars of Wisdom*

Idolatry is worse than carnage.
    —Koran

Thou shalt have no strange gods before me.
    —Decalogue

To whatever name you pray, God hears and answers.
    —Na'id tenet, adapted from the *Bhagavad Gita*

The human Deity hath many names. No god ever told us a
name to call. Perhaps we are being snubbed?
    —Roniva

I don't understand Jews at all.
    —Shad Iliya

PART ONE:

Alihahd

1. No Blaze of Glory

THE CAPTAIN WAS a notorious rebel runner. He was called Alihahd. This was his last run.

He had no real name, only a Chesite word, alihahd, which meant "he left." He had no country, no planet, though several including Chesa claimed him. To most of the known galaxy he was a legend without a face, and to the rest a face without a name.

He was very tall, lanky. His long arms were gnarled like the ancient olive trees of Earth. He had the punished look of one at war too long. A dignity of bearing saved him from being gangly.

His eyes were splendid, expressive in their depth. His features were strong and regular, but he was too drawn to be called handsome anymore.

He'd lived over half his natural life span, which was much older than he'd ever expected to get. He was not surprised that it was to end now.

Luck and disguises had finally given out, and a Na'id squadron was in fast-closing pursuit of his runner ship *Liberation*. Alihahd had begun loading his refugees into *Liberation*'s twelve emergency shuttles. They would need to make the rest of the journey to the free planet New Triton without him.

Alihahd and a handful of volunteers would stay in the mothership to lead the Na'id on a chase in a false direction until overtaken and destroyed. Or, should the Na'id try to board the *Liberation*, she would self-destruct to cover the absence of her passengers and shuttles.

Alihahd stood motionless on the command deck, one large and knobby hand at his belt, one fist on the console, knuckles down as if he'd punched it and frozen there. He could overhear sounds of orderly flight drifting up from below where refugees spoke in whispers and shuffled in steadily moving lines onto the emergency craft.

He heard an air lock close, lock. The life bay thumped open. A shuttle detached and moved silently to the port side of the mothership where four other loaded shuttles were grouped in the bright oasis of the *Liberation*'s docking lights, waiting to depart all together in a convoy when the last of the shuttles was boarded.

Another air lock closed. Locked.

That was six.

The mind counted without passion. Alihahd hadn't thought that the end would feel like this. He was feeling nothing.

He had planned for this contingency a long time, down to the clockwork details. The actual crisis was so like the countless times he had run it in his mind that this seemed just one more exercise.

He was fundamentally alone in this, without friends or lovers. There was no one aboard who honestly knew him as a man. To his passengers, and even to his crew, he was a distant, unfailing protector come from nowhere without selfish motive to spirit discontented subjects away from Na'id rule. His history was a blank but for a hint in his beautiful, correct voice. He would slip into high prose at times, and everyone supposed he was fugitive royalty, but his cosmopolitan accent didn't say from where.

He kept himself remote. There was a too-gentle way he moved his hands, suggesting a tender nature—or hiding a violence that dreaded all but the lightest touch lest he destroy.

He was staring straight out the viewport without really seeing, when a pattern of lights appeared out of an unexpected quadrant, and a slow sick horror penetrated the blank space inside him.

Na'id?

Could he possibly be, he wondered, *surrounded* by Na'id ships?

But it wasn't a Na'id ship.

It was worse.

A ghostly white image of a derelict sailing ship glided into view on the waves of a nonexistent sea. Misty at first, the frosty glow took the shape of an ancient brigantine, its shredded jibs straining from the bowsprit on fraying ropes, its topsail a fluttering rag on the splintered yard. This ship was the last sight of many a Na'id crew. "*Marauder*," Alihahd breathed without voice. The *Flying Dutchman* of the stars.

A chill ran up Alihahd's back, pricking at the hair along his spine and his arms. His thick lips twitched, then he resumed his habitual stone face.

The *Marauder* had once been only a legend, for centuries the terror of superstitious travelers. Someone in recent years had made the *Marauder* real and used it to destroy ships of the Na'id empire.

Marauder's long tradition had fixed it in popular memory as a childhood fear that never went away. On sight, it was instantly recognized and instantly feared. The *Marauder* could scare a victim to death before firing a shot.

But the eerie brigantine was only a projection. Alihahd knew the real ship must be nearby. He found it. It hovered outside the periphery of the *Liberation*'s sphere of light, painted black and difficult to see, its surface albedo nil, giving the impression of something not there. The backdrop of stars allowed only glimpses of its clawlike angles. It looked like a nightmare.

The spectral hologram was the announcement: *You are next*. It was the lurking ship that carried the guns.

Many horrified people fired at the hologram. Then died.

Alihahd wouldn't be thrown by the unreal—though he'd been accused of the tendency. He kept his eyes on the black ship.

He should've been relieved to meet the archfoe of his enemy—

—except that his own ship bore Na'id markings. *Liberation* was disguised to travel in Na'id space as a Na'id vessel, so how could the *Marauder* know that it wasn't?

The command deck had become still. His crew looked at Alihahd the way they always looked at him—as if he could perform miracles. He could see a ghost of his own reflection in the viewport—a rangy, underfed man, old beyond his years—and he wondered what it was they saw.

He was conscious still of the unwary shuffling of refugees below deck.

On the *Marauder*'s blank surface appeared the ragged outline of mandibles opening to a red furnace within. The thing was about to open fire.

Alihahd moved to his ship's transmitter, intending to get out an order for the six waiting shuttles to scatter and run. At least one might escape. But he froze at the switch—not from fear or indecision, but from instinct.

He drew his hand away from the switch—and braced for the fire when his instincts proved wrong.

But the *Marauder* didn't fire. It held its position and observed, as if sensing something not right, something different, maybe curious as to why a sound vessel was being evacuated. Or maybe the *Marauder* had instincts, too.

An air lock closed. Locked. A shuttle detached, oblivious to the threat. Shuttles had no viewports.

Still the *Marauder* watched.

Alihahd moved his hand back to the transmitter. He masked out the shuttle channel, and opened all others. In what code did one attempt contact with the *Marauder*?

He decided on a voice message. "Alihahd," he said. He did not know if the *Marauder* understood the Universal tongue, but maybe he would recognize the name of his enemy's enemy if nothing else. "This is Alihahd. We are not — *not*—Na'id."

He paused.

There was no movement on the command platform save for the silent shifting of panel lights that washed pale red and green across bloodless faces, some of them terribly young.

There was no acknowledgment from the *Marauder*. But neither was there an attack.

The phantom ship menaced with its red maw gaping, a ticking bomb to be defused before the caprice of a moment turned the decision. There had to be a way to get through. With every second, the *Marauder* could imagine deception in a blinking bow light and open fire.

Without taking his eyes from the viewport, Alihahd spoke to his bridge crew in a quietly urgent whisper. "Close that hatch."

They scuttled across the deck to obey, sealing off the hatch to the shuttle bay before someone could come up and catch sight of the shimmering sails of the ancient derelict and scream its name.

The command console had lighted up all over with hailing signals from perplexed shuttles, which could detect but not see or identify the presence of an extra ship near them. They could only tell that the configuration was not Na'id.

Alihahd clicked off all the demanding lights with his long fingers and glanced at the chronometer. The Na'id — real ones—would be closing in soon. Six minutes.

He leaned straight-armed over the console, glowering at the black ship, his mouth drawn taut. His dusky face darkened. He lowered his chin and glared. The gaunt muscles of his arms stood out in high relief as he grew angry over a sudden suspicion. An instinct.

The bomb was not ticking. It was chuckling.

Alihahd touched the transmitter again. "I think you are reading me, *Marauder*," he said in a sharp voice that made his crew gasp and cringe and brace for explosions. "I also think you know Universal. So understand this: A Na'id squadron is due here to destroy us in five minutes Earth standard. Now I have to assume, since you are playing the *Dutchman*, that you also mean to destroy us, but if you want me to grovel for my passengers' lives, you will have to inform me soon or forfeit the pleasure to the Na'id. But then you would have to break your precious silence, would you not? For myself, by you or by them, I will be equally dead. I don't very much care. So please either shoot, talk, or go away. Or you may go to hell, where I am bound with or without you." Then he added crisply, "Do you want me to repeat any of that?"

Again the *Marauder* gave no acknowledgment—except to pull away and vanish.

The crew stared at Alihahd with reverent, startled wonder. He had pulled off the required miracle.

No miracle, thought Alihahd. He had lived long enough to know the smell of a player of deadly games.

An air lock closed. Locked.

That was eight.

There was still time. The boarding continued smoothly, the refugees unaware that the ghost ship had brushed so close and passed them by.

The last shuttle was loaded but not launched when Alihahd saw glances and nods pass between the muscular crewmen to either side of him. Alihahd backed out from his spot in between them to look at them—one then the other—straight into their guilty eyes. The rest of the bridge crew froze like dogs caught chewing the carpet. There were too many people on the command platform.

"What? What is this?" Alihhad spoke levelly, even gently. "Is this a mutiny?"

There was another exchange of glances. Whatever it was, they were all in on it. If they had turned against him, he was alone.

The handsome crewman to Alihahd's left shifted his weight, pushed an auburn curl off his forehead, cleared his throat. "Please, sir," he said. "Get on the shuttle. You don't have to die. Let us take the ship by ourselves."

After a grim, intimidating pause, Alihahd shook his head and said gravely, "You know better."

"We intended to force you," the crewman said softly.

For a moment Alihahd was too surprised to react. Not that they should conceive of such a plot—his crew were addicted to dreams of daring valor—but that they still, even faced with his disapproval, seriously intended to go through with it.

The mind assimilated this new development without the body giving sign of the panic quailing at his core. Alihahd maintained his perfect outer calm—it maintained itself out of habit—while inside he was struggling to hold his guts in. Only his fragile dignity was still keeping his crew at bay. There was really nothing else to keep them from laying hands on him and ingloriously dragging him down to the loading platform, depositing him in the last lifecraft, and shuttling him away to safety.

There was not one of them he could best if it came down to a physical pull, grab, and wrestle. They had chosen their beef for this task, knowing he would object for all he was worth. He was taller than the tallest and had the bone structure to match the strongest, but he hadn't the flesh. Age and abuse had taken much from him. He felt suddenly exposed and powerless in their midst, nothing useful within his grasp. He was clad in a pocketless red tunic, a holsterless belt, and rubbery-soled deck boots that would not even let him deliver a convincing kick.

And his mutinous worshippers were determined to save

him against his will, at the cost of their own lives. They would stumble over each other to be first in selfless heroism—they had learned it from him. They wanted to be like him. Now he had to confront these heroic monsters of his own creation.

But in their bright-eyed enthusiasm—which they had *not* imitated from him—they oversimplified, overstepped, and overlooked, and did not realize that even selflessness had its selfish reasons, and Alihahd would not be turned.

He preserved his quiet poise, making no quick desperate motion that would bring them all lunging toward him at once. Liquid eyes cast a spell, and he cloaked himself in his lordly mystique, too stately to be touched.

But awe was a feeble barrier against a dwindling count-down. The chronometer read three minutes. Someone needed to act quickly or every one of them would fall to the Na'id.

With deceptive casualness, all his apprehension contained, Alihahd walked across the deck—ten steps was suddenly an eternal length—passing between two mutineers, to reach under the command console and take out a gun hidden there. He pointed the gun to his own temple, and said, "Very well, then. Force me."

By the time any of them even thought about stopping him, it was too late to do anything. The crew continued to stare—now completely stumped.

Alihahd gave them a few long seconds to realize defeat, then said, "Move. We are running out of time. You will jeopardize everyone with your ill-timed heroics. The thought is not unappreciated, yet it remains very foolish."

The crewman who had spoken for the others moved first, backing off. And because there was nothing else to do, the rest returned to the duties of the original plan of evacuation—Alihahd's plan.

Alone, Alihahd held the gun close across his chest, one hand around its barrel, trying not to shake and trying to hold inside what must remain inside.

They were going to admire him to death, his crew. They

wanted him to live. But at what cost? He pictured himself aboard the shuttle, staying apart like a leper, meeting no one's eyes, reaching haven, and answering the question, "Where is your crew?" He felt sick. He knew this feeling. He breathed with his mouth open as if there were no air left in the ship. A slickness filmed palms that never sweated. He did not relinquish the gun until the last shuttle was launched.

The little fleet of twelve shuttles separated from the mothership, moved off, and disappeared. Alihahd turned off the bright docking lights and leaned back against the bulkhead, his head back, hands loose at his sides. From here there were few decisions, and few mistakes that could bring worse results than success.

An odd elation came over him along with the first peace of mind he could remember.

He put on his spacesuit, secured himself into his seat at the ship's controls, and waited. One minute.

The countdown was still at thirty seconds when blips appeared on the computer tracker with simultaneous visual contact. Six ships of metallic blue sublighted for attack, their hulls ablaze with the red twin symbols of Galactic Dominion/Human Supremacy.

The computer pilot engaged, and the *Liberation* shot away past the Na'id ships. The stars disappeared.

Before leaving the squadron behind in the sublight universe, Alihahd had recognized the flagship, *Jerusalem*.

I am being chased by Jerusalem. He found that thought horribly funny. Horribly.

Alihahd knew who commanded the flagship *Jerusalem*. That man was not a mindless destroyer. General Atta"id would try to catch Alihahd if he could. A high price had been put on Alihahd's head—something the Na'id did not do as a rule, but how else to combat someone they could not recognize on sight and who left no tracks and tripped no alarms? And, in the end, the price had done it. Alihahd's fall had come through no mistake of his own. He had been betrayed.

How fitting.

Six ships they sent after him. They had greatly overestimated him, the reputation grown bigger than the man. They thought him capable of anything.

At length the pursuit ships became visible again, gradually closing the million-mile gap their second's hesitation had made between them. They came into range for weapons. None of the ships flew directly behind the *Liberation*, fearing what might be dropped back in its wake. They never guessed that the rogue ship might possibly be unarmed. Their caution threw off the accuracy of their fire, and the *Liberation* was able to lure them farther and farther away from the shuttle convoy.

Alihahd had made no pretense to his volunteers of having the slimmest hope of getting away. If he could have done without his crew, he would have. He wished they were not with him. Did they expect another miracle?

I told you this was suicide. And—do you guess?

I want it.

The first close salvo came from the flagship. The next would find its target.

Alihahd touched the intersuit com switch at his throat and gave an order. "Brake."

There was a click in his headset. "Braking, sir."

The engines reversed. The chase ships overshot and disappeared, and the stars returned as the *Liberation* dropped back into sublight.

The end came in an instant.

Lights, sound, pressure, gravity—even the vibration of the ship's engines—suddenly ceased. Arms and legs flailed with the outrush of air. Stomach jumped. Muscles contracted. Alihahd felt himself come off his seat, pulling against the straps, and he hit the self-destruct switch in the dark.

Nothing happened. He clutched the console with both hands, swallowing, his eyes wide and sightless. He wondered if he had been blinded.

In a moment, when everything was abolutely still again, he reached down, unlocked a catch, and swiveled his seat around.

And he saw stars where the hatch and most of the deck should have been.

No.

He turned on his headlamp. The command platform with him on it, had been sheared clean off. The great bulk of the ship *Liberation*, with the engines, was gone.

One by one, the crewmembers who remained turned on their headlamps. They were three. They stared at one another in shock, waiting for the circling sharks to board.

To Alihahd, it was a nightmare of nightmares—one of the few things that could go wrong. The thought of facing Na'id mortally terrified him. He knew they wanted him very badly. The only alternative now was suicide by vacuum, which also terrified him or he would have done it long before this.

But the Na'id did not board. They were not circling. They were nowhere to be seen, and it took some moments to realize that when the *Liberation* had broken in two, the Na'id had chased after the other part.

There came a blue-white flash in the distance like a quick nova. That would be the *Liberation*'s engines exploding.

Minutes passed. Half an hour. The Na'id did not come back, and the surviving rebels knew they had been overlooked—left alone, without power, light-years from anywhere.

This was not what they had expected at all. They were supposed to have been in that nova, making a statement for the Resistance. The *Liberation* had made the statement without them.

Here was no end in a blaze of glory. Rather a slow and cold grave.

A creeping feeling of smallness grew in the quiet, noth-ing between the four small human beings and the incon-

ceivable vastness of space. The gaping breach in the deck let
the emptiness in.

Alihahd did not look at the others—knew they were
looking at him.

At last, because he had to, he steeled himself to turn and
face them. He nodded. He held out no hope to them. They
accepted their fate. All they wanted was his approval.

He turned away.

He could not tell if their scrap of ship was moving. The
stars did not appear to move. Nothing did. At least they
were not spinning.

After a time, the crew began to talk in short, muted murmurs through the suit intercoms. A voice, click, silence. Answer, click, silence. An attempted joke, click, silence. A long
pause. A voice, click, silence.

Alihahd was still mercilessly alert. It would be a while
yet until their air ran out. And in the silence his thoughts
moved in. He was aware of what was left to him. Endless
dark, endless void, a floating tomb, the stars' indifferent
steady light.

There was some comfort in knowing that he had made
his last mistake. He had discovered he had a tremendous
capacity for being wrong.

And he was never in a position to be wrong. He was one
of those who always rose to the top. Leadership came easily
to him. Power fell into his hands. He need only stand somewhere and a line formed behind him.

The problem with power was that one's mistakes became
catastrophic. Alihahd lived in perpetual fear of a false step,
perpetual regret of past false steps. He wondered if he
would be better off blind drunk in an alley.

There was an alley in old Cairo on Earth he knew. He
never should have left.

He found himself in vacillating prayer to a God he did
not rationally believe existed; first asking to live, then, realizing he did not actually want to go on living, he would re-
cant and start over—not that Anyone was paying attention

either way. The idea of a benevolent, prayer-answering deity went against logic. Alihahd usually avoided thinking about it. But adrift in the eternity between the stars, it seemed a natural thing. The line between logic and illogic thinned and snapped.

He thought seriously of all the nonsensical religions, impossible to believe. They even found each other absurd.

The Na'id were much more sensible on that score. They combined rational and humanistic bits of many religions—which, of course, was unacceptable to all of them. The devout still died by the millions for their dogmatic and antiquated doctrines.

Alihahd had read their books—a few used the same one—in an effort to understand their people. He found words now in one, words spoken in a garden.

It was easier to pray in borrowed words. Alihahd was not adept at talking to God in his own words—he did not know what to say—and these fit his changing mind.

He remembered the garden. There had been much blood, none of it his.

Old skeletons rose. A lot of blood. Flame and smoke billowed. A summer day. A woman in a boat. God was suddenly near, very real, and it scared him.

Reality unhinging, time uprooted, space frayed and folded. He was going to panic.

Why had he picked those words connected with that place? His galloping heart shook his whole body.

The others were sleeping, and he was alone. With God.

Stop.

He held on to the armrests of his seat. They were hard and substantial. Only the ship and the stars were real, and all this other stuff was nothing but panic, pure panic. Just a man going mad inside his spacesuit. He tasted salty beads on his upper lip.

Stop thinking. Hallucinations lurked round the edges of the light from his wavering headlamp.

Circulating air in his suit cooled the sweat on his heaving

sides. At this rate his oxygen would run out first of the survivors.

His hand trembled, uncoiled his suit's life cable. He hooked the cable to his seat, then unstrapped himself and made a floating prowl through the remains of the bridge and found a stashed container of wine. He returned to his seat and drank himself into a stupor—so that he would not notice when he passed out for want of air.

2. Iry

WHEN ALIHAHD WOKE, he was in a strange place—a spaceship—and he was no longer in his spacesuit. The air pressure was less than he'd kept *Liberation*'s but was still safe.

He was lying on a deep-colored carpet spread over a hardwood deck. There were straps around his head, his shoulders, and between his legs, and for a terrible moment he thought he had been captured and bound. But he sat up and found that his limbs were free, and that the ship was not of Na'id design. The strap around his head held a tubed mask to his face. He was breathing pure oxygen. He lifted the mask and sniffed the ship's atmosphere. It was depleted of free oxygen, poisoned with carbon dioxide, and unbreathable. He fitted the mask back to his face.

The other straps made up a harness that did not fit at all well with Alihahd's tunic. He fumbled at the buckle and was going to take it off as soon as he figured out how, but his wine-dulled mind was easily distracted and shifted to something else.

What caught his attention was the damage. This ship had been in an accident. Or battle. There were signs of fire and buckling in what he hoped was not the outer hull. The overhead lights were flickering, cold and blue. Electrical burns, scorched metal, and ozone censed the cabin, whose mahogany fittings were charred. Frostily tinted lamp covers lay shattered in pieces on the black-fringed carpet.

Beside Alihahd, his three crew members lay sleeping—or drugged. Closest to him was the athletic spokesman of the mutineers, his muscles smoothed in unconsciousness. Long lashes grazed his youthful cheek. His name was Neal. Alihahd lightly brushed an auburn curl out of his face with the back of his hand. *I could kill you for what you tried to do to me.*

Next to him was the *Liberation*'s engineer. Yuko, her petite form curled up like a puppy, her little mouth drawn down into a frown as in a bad dream. Her black hair was clipped so short it stood on end. Bleached into it behind one ear was a white pentagram. Yuko was a witch, she said, but Alihahd had never seen her magic work. She was a better engineer.

Beside her was a pale youth whose name Alihahd didn't remember. He was also fitted into a harness.

And there was a fourth person. Alihahd hadn't noticed him immediately because he had stood apart, unmoving in the semidark. He'd looked like an empty spacesuit set ceremonially to one side like a suit of armor. The viewplate was opaque one-way glass and Alihahd couldn't see the face. This would be the owner of the ship.

The stranger was tall, very tall, clearing even Alihahd's height. He—Alihahd assumed it was a man from his imposing frame—stood dead still, observing in silence, arms at his sides. Alihahd rose to his feet and stood up straight—the oxygen tube barely reached—facing the stranger who was equally still and unspeaking. Alihahd wasn't accustomed to looking up at people, and he hadn't realized that it could make such a difference. The dimensions of the ship were slightly big as well and gave Alihahd the vague, uncomfortable impression of being a child again at the control and beck of others.

Behind the visor he sensed a familiar stranger—someone he had never met but knew as if he'd always known him. He was an adversary.

Alihahd didn't try to communicate. If the ship's master wanted to talk, he could talk first, and he could say who he was and why he had taken the *Liberation*'s survivors aboard. Did he know whom he rescued? Was this a rescue at all? The man could be a jackal of war, a slave trader picking up Na'id leavings. He could be a Na'id private citizen who had found what appeared to be a Na'id wreck and had rescued what he thought were compatriots. He could be a neutral from uncharted space.

Or was this the master of *Marauder*?

How to know?

The ship spoke much but answered little. Its large dimensions were either a custom design for a tall man, or the standard of a tall race. It was an expensive craft, fitted out and detailed with somber luxury in colors of wine and gold, rose, amber, black, and deep brown wood. There were no nationality or planet markers anywhere in sight, and the man himself was totally obscured in his steely gray suit.

Alihahd gazed steadily at the smoky visor, trying not to look as weak as he felt. His head throbbed. He tasted stale wine.

At last the man turned away and beckoned with a slow wave of his hand for Alihahd to come with him.

Alihahd hesitated, limited by his oxygen tube. The tall figure retreated down the corridor without looking back and disappeared through a hatchway. Alihahd took a deep breath, held it, dropped his mask, and followed.

Alihahd stepped through the hatch into the ship's control room. Two great iris-apertured viewports were wide open on either side.

Stars. There were stars. The ship was traveling sublight.

The pearly white river of the Milky Way cascaded across one viewport. The vast glowing galactic hub filled the other.

Bright in the foreground shone a single yellow sun.

Alihahd drew closer to the port and looked down.

The ship was orbiting a moonless planet of muddy-green continents and blue seas. The equator was wreathed in thick white clouds that spiraled and thinned to the north and south. Even from this distance Alihahd could see mountains. A permanent haze of vapor steamed off the ocean's surface.

The ship's master drew Alihahd's attention to the control console, where he traced slowly on the smooth surface with his forefinger in Roman characters—symbols used by many languages, including Universal—a single word and question:

IRY?

A thrill of discovery awakened in a mind Alihahd had thought too jaded for wonder.

Iry was one of the lost worlds. There were many places known in the First Historical Age that had been lost after the Collapse. But this one was a fantastic place. Not everybody was convinced that Iry had ever existed.

Yet here was a living planet, beyond recivilized space, its yellow sun hidden in the Great Rift where it was supposed to be, and it looked right.

The Eyes of Iry stared back at him, two impact craters peeking clear of the shroud of clouds. He couldn't see the encircling River Ocean, but the computer diagram on the ship's screen said it was there beneath the clouds.

The computer diagram also revealed this to be a peculiar little solar system in keeping with the myth of one sun, one planet, and no moons.

This last was the telling point. In Alihahd's experience, one was an extraordinarily odd number of planets for a normal yellow star, and there were few mid-sized worlds anywhere orbited by no moon at all.

Alihahd looked up to the ship's master and answered with a downward nod, which would tell him yes if this man understood nods. Then Alihahd left the cabin to return to the makeshift contraption that was his oxygen mask. This ship wasn't designed for guests or for emergencies.

It wasn't a slaver either. Slavers didn't pick up anything

they couldn't sell. This ship couldn't even get itself to a familiar port.

Iry. The name summoned visions of Itiri warrior-priests who lived on mountaintops, attended by familiars. They flew on wings with the eagles of Iry. Itiri warrior-priests journeyed on quests between the stars, armed with their magical double-curved swords that never dulled. Legends always had their special weapons. It was required of them. For the Itiri it was the double-curved sword.

Of course, the Itiri were beautiful: humanlike, tall and fair, golden-haired and emerald-eyed—a distinctively un-Na'id concept of beauty.

The legend was popular outside Na'id circles. It dealt with what the Na'id dreaded and insisted could not exist—a superior sapient species.

But if the Itiri were anywhere near as prodigious as their reputation, where were they now and where had they been hiding for the two thousand years of the human Dark Age? Truth was that when Earthling ships had ceased to fly, so did the Itiri, which told Alihahd where the stories were coming from—human imaginations. He didn't believe in the Itiri's superhuman exploits any more than he believed that Atlantis had developed atomic power.

For him the great significance of the stories about Iry's natives was not that they gave any insight into Itiri nature—Alihahd believed they did not—but that they suggested the planet itself—the core of the myth—was habitable.

And for the first time he realized that he was going to live. He was too numbed to know how he felt about that.

He held his breath and rejoined the ship's captain in the control room.

The ship had started a slow descent. Alihahd felt the added tug of the planet's gravity and the ship's resistance as the brakes cut in. He could tell by the way the ship was going down that she was not an in-atmosphere vehicle.

They were entering twilight, descending on the night side of the world. The creepingly slow landing would use all the ship's reserves, but the battered vessel was not going to take anyone anywhere again. When Alihahd left this world, it would be in another ship—or never.

He glanced at the stats on the computer screen. They read in Scientific, a specialized language even more universal than Universal. The figures told him the planet was smaller than Earth and heavier, its density 7.19. It was .9 astronomical units from a sun whose spectrum was strong with heavy elements. The planet's atmosphere was oxygen-rich and contained more inert gases than Earth's, but not enough to be a problem. Pressure at sea level was three Earth atmospheres.

Already Alihahd felt hot and heavy and crowded. He started again to take off his harness, but a silvery-suited hand closed on his wrist and stopped him.

The contact startled Alihahd, and he looked up at the opaque faceplate in surprise.

The strong hand slowly let go of his wrist. The grip hadn't been tight, but it had been powerful, and Alihahd was not at all sure he could have pulled free had he tried.

He retreated from the control room, paused at his oxygen mask to breathe, then went searching for and found the head. The ship's owner was male. He also owned a cat or a ferret or some small pet. There was no one else aboard, no room for anyone else. For all the sense of space in the moody corridors, it was a small ship.

The fittings were rich, heavy, and dark with gilded borders. The ambient strength, even arrogance, of the place was disconcerting.

Alihahd returned to his oxygen mask and sat on the deck. Had he been alone, he would have stolen into the engine room to see what kind of equipment the generators were loaded for. The number of exterior leads would tell quicker than anything what this ship was about. He suspected he knew. He wanted to look for a lead to an exterior hologram projector.

But laws dissolved in outer space, and a ship's master

was its god. There was nothing to say that the dark stranger could not put Alihahd and his companions right back where he found them.

For the crew's sake, Alihahd stayed where he'd been put—on the short leash of his oxygen tube.

As he watched his dozing comrades, he became convinced that they'd been drugged. He heard the engines complain, more and more as hours dragged by. Then tension gave way to tedium and at last he slept.

A star fell out of the sky.

Five tall slender figures stood with the sentinel, silhouetted against the star field out on the eagle ridge, gazing up.

It was a new star. It hadn't been in the sky the night before. At twilight it gleamed in the Red Geese like a nova, but then it slowly slipped out of the Ring of constellations and down toward the River Ocean beyond the horizon.

The Fendi, Roniva, turned to the younger aghara beside her with a wave of her night-colored hand, a black glitter of onyx flashing on her forefinger. "Go thou. Take thine fire kin and see. And take thou one from the fire clan of the carnelian serpent. Take Arilla."

She met a quizzical look. "Fendi?"

"Someone who knows of humankind. Thou may need." Roniva turned away, her thin, hard arms crossed. *Naedenal*, the night wind, moaned down the cliff face in a cold gust to become lost and voiceless in the deep ocean of air in the valley. "I sense. I sense."

"Humans?"

Roniva murmured assent. Her black gaze swept the wide heavens. "After such a long time. . . ."

Alihahd was still asleep when he heard a crashing. The deck heaved beneath him, and he was catapulted into empty air.

He woke falling. He gasped in air, icy-cold and sharp, not pure oxygen. He opened his eyes to bright blue all around him. The ship was gone. He was in Iry's atmosphere.

And dropping like a rock, headfirst, eight kilometers up, the air so cold it burned and sliced like knives. His tunic flapped wildly in the wind. His heart galloped, skin prickled. There was a sweet-sour taste of fear in his mouth, a roaring in his ears, nauseous terror in his throat. The oxygen mask was still strapped to his face, its disconnected tube whipping madly at his ear. He saw the dizzily closing ocean far below tracked with white, saw sky and white clouds and morning sun until his eyes teared shut. And he went down, faster and faster, trying to scream.

Then he felt a yank at the harness straps as if grabbed from behind and above, and he was righted, swinging suspended under an expansive white canopy, floating down at a gentle speed. Had there been anything at all in his stomach, he would have thrown up.

The pounding of his heart subsided slowly till he was left with only the ashes of fear, a dull lump in his stomach and a flat taste in his mouth. His skin was icy. He took off his useless mask and let it drop.

He looked up at his parachute. He had never seen one before. It seemed a primitive thing. He wondered what had triggered it to open and guessed it had to be his speed. His hands sought the harness straps and gripped them, trembling involuntarily.

He looked down. A silvery glint on the water still four kilometers below had to be the ship. He was drifting quickly away from it. Seeking a way to steer, he tugged at the risers and managed to guide himself back without setting himself into a spin.

Another parachute blossomed below him and to the windward. He looked for others, but remembered with sinking sickness that only one of his companions had been harnessed.

The ship had not been equipped for guests or for emergencies.

Then he caught sight of a long thin line plummeting

straight down. At least one other person had acquired a parachute while Alihahd had slept.

A bad one. Alihahd watched, mentally screaming as it hurtled down and out of sight. It never opened.

The only other things in the sky were the circling birds. The enormous creatures already clustered around where the fouled parachute had gone down, while others glided around in lazy arcs on broad wings.

Scavengers.

Alihahd looked up again and clutched the risers, this time in anger and horror. If only he had known. He was wearing a parachute, and others weren't. He should've given his to someone else.

He could already hear the question always put to a surviving captain. *Where is your crew?*

He tried to make his hand release the clasp of his own chute, but it wouldn't move. He had a hideous survival instinct for someone who shouldn't be alive.

He closed his eyes hard, grimaced, and tensed back his neck. He felt as if someone were driving nails into his skull.

Does it never stop?

He opened his eyes and looked down at the blue ocean. It was much closer now. The air had become very warm, then hot, and the wind was heavy like a current of water. He could make out some definition in the craft on the water. It wasn't the *Marauder*. And, closer, he could see it was not even a spaceship. It was a seaplane. He couldn't find the spaceship anywhere.

Surface winds across the sea swept him swiftly away from the seacraft so he couldn't see it anymore. He was aware of the dark moving shadow of a bird above his chute, and he wished he were armed.

Descent seemed very fast during the last few meters. He hit the water hard and plunged under. The parachute billowed down over him like a wide compass on the water's surface. He bobbed up, but the parachute draped over his head and clung closely without space for air. He tried to breathe through it, but it drew in, impermeable as plastic, suffocating him. He pushed up on the fabric, but it only formed a vacuum and sucked up the water with it.

Head ringing, lungs hurting, he fought to get out from under the canopy, but there seemed to be no end to it. Heat built up behind his eyes. He saw black and red. He thrashed, tried to breathe, took in water, coughed on reflex, and gasped in more water.

Strength and even fear left him at once and he began to sink in a druglike torpor.

Thought he was dying. Thought he was dead.

Suddenly there was light above as the chute ripped away. There was a splash and a column of bubbles from something plunging into the water beside him, going down and shooting up. A myth closed powerful hands under his arms and heaved him up. His head broke surface. A fist pressed under his rib cage. He expelled water in a violent rush, coughed, choked, spat, and finally drew air.

When the whirl of bright-dark colors blinked clear, Alihahd was staring into the green, kohl-smeared eyes of an Itiri warrior-priest.

Alihahd couldn't speak. He opened his mouth, squeaked, then coughed.

Unconcerned with its own improbability, the myth disengaged Alihahd from the parachute harness with agile hands and pulled him clear of it. The Itiri encircled Alihahd's upper body with a long hard white arm and swam toward the ship. Dazed, Alihahd let himself be dragged. Saltwater and the heat of the air hurt his eyes. Steam was rising from the painfully bright glittering water, searing his brine-inflamed lungs with each breath.

The ship was the one he had seen from the air, a primitive aluminum seaplane afloat on pontoons. Alihahd smelled fossil fuel, tasted it on the water, the back of his mind making note that this was not the product of a space-age civilization.

As they drew near the plane, a wave came over Alihahd's head and set him coughing and gasping again. From above, two hands seized his armpits hard enough to hurt, heaved him out of the water, and sat him down heavily, a dead weight on the hot metal pontoon.

On the plane were a few more aliens, climbing over the wings and fuselage. And there were two wet humans on the pontoons—a boy spitting up, and a man.

When Alihahd could breathe again, he grabbed one of the tall, lithe humanoid aliens. Green eyes turned to him curiously. Alihahd thrust up two fingers, gesturing urgently at the humans, then to the ocean. He croaked, "Two more. There are two more of us."

Alien eyes seemed to register comprehension. The Itiri parted from him. Alihahd continued to speak after him as if the alien could understand, "I saw one go down with a parachute that did not open."

A voice behind Alihahd said in Universal, "That was mine."

Alihahd turned. Water trickled down a strand of hair plastered to his forehead and ran into his eyes. He brushed the wet hair off his lofty brow and blinked at the man.

"It opened, then?" said Alihahd.

The parachute must have opened. Obviously. The man was alive, not smashed into the water's surface at terminal velocity.

But the man said, "No." He pointed up.

There was an eagle.

Alihahd shaded his eyes and squinted up at the bird. From below, it appeared dark until it passed out of the cloud shadow. Then the sun struck its back, and its plumage burst into all the shades of fire.

It was fully large enough to carry off a man.

Alihahd remembered the shadow over his parachute and the Itiri dropping out of the air to rescue him. The immense birds were not scavengers after all.

Alihahd looked again at the humanoids. They looked

just like all the impossible stories said, creamy white with golden hair and brilliant green eyes. All six of them were two meters tall with long, lean, hairless bodies. They moved with a grace Alihahd considered the province of the animal kingdom. But then these were not humans. They had the physical fascination of big cats and fine Arabian stallions: beautiful, powerful, and frightening like cats, creatures that could prey on human beings.

The Itiri eyes were elaborately lined with kohl like Egyptian tomb paintings. The single female was squatting atop the plane, balanced on the balls of her feet. She faced into the wind, her arms resting on her knees, the image of a hawk ready to take flight. Gold tassels bobbed from a wide gold band across her forehead. Evenly spaced scars welted her fair cheeks. In a sheath at her side she wore a long double-curved sword.

Alihahd jerked his gaze away.

At least she didn't have wings.

The seaplane rose high on a swell, then settled into a horizon-swallowing trough as the wave rolled under. The sea had looked calm from the air.

Alihahd groggily regarded the Itiri warrior-priest on the pontoon with him, and he spoke, rhetorically as much as anything, as some people talked to their cats or some drunkards to their pink elephants. "What men are you? What woman is this?"

He was astounded to get an answer in kind. "We are such as thou see."

Alihahd jerked back. The elephants were not only pink, they were talking to him in his language.

The alien warrior crouched down before him. Deliberate scars and smeared eye paint marred his high cheeks. There was intelligence in his green eyes. His expression, if Alihahd could read alien faces like human faces, was benign, a little whimsical, and Alihahd sensed that his elephant was laughing at him.

Alihahd spoke again with a feeling of the High Absurd.

"Then I am dead, for Itiri warrior-priests are nothing more than the dreams and hopes of despairing souls."

The Itiri cocked his head quizzically, then replied with an equal sense of absurdity, "If I were born of thine desperation, I could not say. Though I could swear I remember existing before I found thee drowning. All the same, we are now."

Alihahd raised his brows. He had read enough of the old histories to decipher the dialect. He nodded. He had to admit this was all real — the planet, the eagles, the swords, and the warrior-priests speaking archaic Universal as it was spoken before the Collapse some two thousand years ago.

His head felt very thick, his ears caving in. The atmosphere was oppressive, too much pressure, too much oxygen. He was dizzy, hot, and sick.

The Itiri started to rise. Alihahd caught his arm. "Others," he said. "There were two others."

"We continue to look," said the Itiri and nodded up at the soaring eagles.

The birds wheeled high over the water with slow turns on the heavy sea breeze.

The warrior-priest climbed atop the plane's wing and waved the eagles farther downwind.

Alihahd turned to see who had already been rescued.

The boy was standing on the pontoon, clutching the airplane strut in both white-knuckled fists and staring out to sea. He was very slender, clad in light-blue space coveralls. Alihahd couldn't think of his name.

"Are you hurt?" said Alihahd.

"N-n-no," said the youth, trembling. His brown face had paled. His brown eyes were wide and white-ringed. His appearance was unremarkable except that there was nothing particularly Negroid or Oriental about him. Even his skin color was still within the confines of the broad spectrum known as White. He looked suspiciously pureblooded Caucasian. It might explain what made him a rebel.

The Na'id Empire espoused a doctrine of dissolution of

all barriers that could splinter the unity of humankind, be they cultural, religious, or—most visibly—racial. The Na'id despised persons who carried recessive genetic traits. The persistence of recessive traits was a symptom of isolation from the general gene pool. Recessive traits needed to be reinforced in order to perpetuate. If individuals of all kinds mingled freely, recessive characteristics would diminish and die out. People like the boy were symbols of elitist rebellion and disunion.

"Vaslav," said Alihahd, remembering.

The youth perked up at the sound of his name in Alihahd's voice, and he beamed to be known by his leader.

Alihahd had a memory for names, but this young man was not memorable, and, in truth, Alihahd couldn't say whether the name was first, middle, or last. He could not for the life of him recall the lad's other name or names, so henceforth he was simply Vaslav.

The other human survivor was mixed-blooded, older, striking. He was also wet. The eagle that caught his failed parachute must have slowed but not completely stopped his fall to the sea. He was sitting on the pontoon, emptying water from his rawhide boots one at a time.

His dark, red-bronze skin stretched taut over a lean, imposing frame. His wedge-shaped face narrowed wolfishly toward his chin. Soft lips curved slyly at the edges beneath a neat mustache. His cheekbones, very high, seemed to crowd his eyes and gave the effect of a permanent squint when actually he didn't squint at all. His brows arched sharply over almond-shaped eyes. The eyes were really very beautiful—like one of those angels who was asked to leave heaven—the whole face astonishingly demonic. His wiry, graying copper hair was pulled back and tied at the nape of his neck. He wore a russet bandana twisted into a headband across his forehead. Two bright gold loop earrings pierced through one ear, making him look like a pirate or a gypsy.

Gentleman pirate, it would seem. His kid leather vest was lined with gold.

He wore a rawhide redingote that fell to midway down his thighs. He possessed the air of one unrepentantly self-confident as if he were someone of importance. Even sitting down he moved with a kind of swagger. There might have been no one else aboard the seaplane. All his attention went to pulling his sodden leather boots back on, acting as if nothing was wrong in the world except that his clothes were wet.

His gun was a self-customized, crazy-looking thing with a wood handle and a long stabilizer that jutted out like the barrel of an old projectile weapon. He wore the gun at his belt toward his right side, grip forward, as a right-handed person would wear a sword.

Once finished emptying his boots, he drew from his waistcoat a white-gray meerschaum pipe fitted with an amber mouthpiece. Its bowl was carved into the figure of a fox head. He fished out from his coat pocket a mess that used to be tobacco. At this, Alihahd had to smile.

Tawny eyes slid sideways to Alihahd. The man returned a slow, wan smile.

Alihahd's thickened brain realized this man was not one of his volunteers. For one, Alihahd would've remembered if he'd ever seen him before. For another, he was too tall.

Their eyes met and held. Menace and amusement lurked in the orange-brown tigerlike eyes.

This was the rescue ship's master. And Alihahd was still wondering: friend or foe?

He was dressed like a civilian but looked old enough to have been retired from military service if he was Na'id. He was obviously a private citizen now, but of where? From his style of clothing he was possibly a native of Eridani. But Eridani was a Na'id possession now, had been for fifteen years. Whose side did that put him on?

Alihahd couldn't ask him to fly his colors without showing his own first. These were cautious days, and the correct answer to a stranger's inquiry of "Who are you?" was either "Why?" or "Who are *you*?"

Alihahd couldn't know if it was safe to speak his own volatile name. At its very mention that crazy weapon with the notched handle could come whipping out and shoot through his heart.

There were worse fates.

Alihahd couldn't wait for the man to drop a clue. He needed to know now.

He looked dead into the tiger eyes. "Alihahd," he introduced himself. "Captain of the late runner ship *Liberation*."

"Hall," said the stranger. "Harrison White Fox Hall of the late ship *Nemo*."

And Alihahd knew hardly more than he had before. The name wasn't Na'id. But if Hall had been a conscript from Eridani rather than a volunteer, he wouldn't have an honorific name. He hadn't reacted one way or the other to the name Alihahd.

Then what did the ship's name signify? "What is Nemo?"

"In Latin it means 'no one,' " Hall said like a beginning, as if there was more to be said.

Alihahd was already alarmed. He knew what Latin was—a dead Earth language from the First Historical Age, the time before the Collapse. The Na'id were peerless in their knowledge of mankind's ancient history. A Latin name was a Na'id enough thing. Alihahd braced himself should the second half of Harrison White Fox Hall's answer be accompanied by the draw of his weapon and arrest in the name of the Na'id Empire.

Hall continued, "In Greek, it means 'I allot.' "

That was curious. "Allot?" *Allot what?*

"Nemesis," Hall said. "What is deserved." He glanced away toward the horizon. His voice changed pitch, and he tossed the last line away as if unimportant. "Revenge, if you will."

He looked back to Alihahd, and understanding passed between them. Alihahd knew enough. Nothing more need be said.

"Mr. Hall." Alihahd finally nodded in greeting.

"Captain." Harrison White Fox Hall returned the nod, conspicuously avoiding the false name Alihahd.

Alihahd saw Hall taking another hard look at him.

Alihahd cut a fine figure: rangy, thin as though from dissipation, his dark red tunic stuck to his gaunt frame. He spoke and carried himself like aristocracy—profoundly weary aristocracy, at once proud and sorry as a tattered flag.

He knew what it was Hall watched with those long stares and intensity bordering on venom. Alihahd's "name," his tunic, and his swarthy coloring were all appropriate to the planet Chesa. But his features were wrong—tall flat forehead, straight Nordic nose, fine hair—they were pure Caucasian. The mixture made him look very very Na'id.

Their gazes had locked again, and they tried to stare each other down. The boy Vaslav, standing over them, looked from one to the other, aware that something was going on beyond what he could see. Neither man was going to break away.

Till an eagle alighted on the aircraft, its great wings and tail fanned in braking, its talons outstretched. It screamed.

Its landing rocked the plane on the water, and Alihahd grabbed a strut to catch himself. As he pitched far over the edge of the pontoon, a whalelike head rose up from the sea, and Alihahd was suddenly face-to-face with a black-and-white sea creature. A barrage of delphine clicks and squeals sounded from its blowhole. When the plane settled, a warrior-priest knelt next to Alihahd on the pontoon, and leaned over to listen to the whale as if its noises were actually intelligible. The Itiri turned his head to Alihahd. "Two, didst thou say?" He held up two nailless fingers. "This many? Thy companions are dead."

Alihahd hung his head. He had already known. "Very well, then," he said to the warrior. "We are in your hands."

The Itiri waved the whale away and stood up. The eagle launched itself with a push that bobbed the plane like a toy on the water. The warriors shouted and whistled to one another, climbing into the fuselage, readying the plane to depart this place.

Eyes downcast, Alihahd became aware of rawhide-booted feet standing at his side. He looked up. Hall had risen and was offering a hand. Alihahd hesitated. He didn't want it. The unease he'd first felt on meeting the spacesuited stranger returned. He could stand up by himself.

But in some parts of the galaxy to refuse a man's hand was ground for murder.

Alihahd took the offered hand, and Hall pulled him easily to his feet.

Hall climbed inside the plane with the Itiri. Alihahd started to follow, but noticed Vaslav hanging back, staring forlornly at the waves.

The boy appealed to Alihahd, stammering, "But. . . ."

Neal and Yuko, Alihahd thought. He'd failed to retrieve his dead.

He put a hand on the youth's shoulder. "It's as good a resting place as any," he said with comfort and sureness he didn't feel.

And to soothe the boy's mind, he spoke a few words over the souls beneath the waters though he was certain they could find their way to their God without him.

It was the first of the Red Geese when Alihahd, Harrison White Fox Hall, and Vaslav came to the Aerie. The journey took several hours in the slow way of primitives aboard a noisy vibrating craft kept aloft by propellers and piloted without a computer. The hulking machine lurched into flight and climbed slowly, shuddering. The heat and pressure of the air lessened with altitude, and Alihahd felt better, though he was still plagued with the mistrust of a starman staking his life on an antediluvian transport that felt and sounded as if it would rattle apart.

The Itiri spent the entire journey in a separate compartment, leaving the humans in the cargo hold.

Fine by Alihahd. He had never liked aliens.

Harrison White Fox Hall took off his wet coat and rolled up one of his shirtsleeves. He drew his notch-handled gun and inspected it for saltwater damage.

Alihahd was not going to ask if the notches represented humans or aliens.

Now Hall sat on the deck by a porthole, one elbow resting on one knee. He seemed to be enjoying the view.

A man who decides who lives and who dies. Not even a pretense of regret. When Hall's ship was in danger, Hall had placed the available parachutes on himself and the other captain, the last people who should have been saved, and he stayed cavalier through the entire harrowing ordeal.

Alihahd felt anger. And envy.

The plane hit an air pocket. The metal box jumped and dipped. Alihahd closed his eyes and waited for the crash he thought was coming.

When it didn't happen, he opened his eyes. Hall was looking at him.

A ghost of a smile glided beneath the graying mustache. "Not afraid, are you, Captain?"

That was provocation. Hall wanted a fight. And he wanted it with Alihahd. The boy Vaslav didn't interest him.

Alihahd wouldn't have it. He would take a fall before he would be baited into defending himself. Self-respect, he had none. Honor was long gone. There was nothing to defend. Hall ought to know that about men without names.

He swallowed the insult. "Maybe I am."

He could tell that Hall wasn't sure if he'd won the confrontation or not.

Hall distractedly drew his pipe, took it between his teeth and reached into his pocket for tobacco. Finding his pocket empty, he suddenly became conscious of what he was doing and put the pipe away.

Alihahd had disturbed Hall's perfect understanding of the universe.

Avoiding a challenge was not a thing to do where Hall was from. It was cowardly. Yet Hall couldn't call Alihahd a coward—not under the circumstances in which he'd found him.

Alihahd had admitted fear outright. On Eridani, a man did not back down from a challenge like that.

Unless he was very very sure of himself.

And it occurred to Hall that Alihahd just didn't care what Hall thought of him. The accepted insult wasn't surrender. It was dismissal. Alihahd's regard for Hall was so slight as to nullify anything Hall might say to him. Alihahd probably didn't even realize what he was doing, the insult more complete for being sincere and uncalculated.

Hall had never been so thoroughly put down in his adult life.

Hall was amazed, about to be angry. Then a slow hunter's smile crept onto his lips. He laughed, a low grumbly sound.

Alihahd looked at him. Hall winked a stalking tiger's eye.

The captain was an enigma: brave and frightened, strong and weak, assured and uncertain, serene and haunted. Nothing about him was clear or unopposed by some other trait.

And Hall realized it could only be that his elusive captain was two people. And one was not real.

The one without a real name.

The airplane abandoned the coast and turned inland to cross a mountain range.

"Good," Hall said. "I can't swim."

"I suppose I cannot either," Alihahd said. "I drowned once before."

"Only nearly, it looks like," Hall said.

Alihahd didn't elaborate. He gazed out a porthole.

The land was stark and impassable save by air. Unable to clear the towering peaks, the plane wove a path between mountains.

Vaslav watched their passage with one hand clapped

across his mouth, his eyes round with dread. He hadn't stopped trembling. He lowered his hand. It fluttered like an indecisive butterfly. "Will we be here the rest of our lives?"

"I do not know," Alihahd said, his words slow and distinct, for the boy was new to the language. "The natives did not learn Universal in total isolation. That much is certain."

Vaslav craned back his head, perplexed. "They're speaking *Universal*?"

Alihahd smiled. "Of a sort."

The plane stopped once to refuel on a lonely plateau, then continued over the rugged land on its solitary winding way. They'd lost the eagles long ago.

At last the jagged peaks gave way to a sudden, startling cradle of relative flatness, a wide fertile plain in an open valley ringed by high mountains where eagles flew. Squares of green-and-gold cultivations checkered the fields and crept up the feet of the enclosing mountains on terraced slopes. A long thin veil of a waterfall spilled from one of the massifs and fed a river that twisted through the valley in a lazy course lined with willowlike trees and neat, pretty, little houses built of broad, woody reeds that had been carved and shaped, perched on stilts. The houses were roofed with varicolored reeds upcurved at the eaves.

The plane landed in a warm, dusty meadow of brown grasses. The warrior-priestess named Arilla came back to the humans' compartment and let them out to the summer village of Kaletani Mai.

Alihahd dropped down from the plane and took a few unsteady steps on the first solid ground he'd trod in a long time. The sky was clear blue. The smell of ripening fields drifted to him on a mild breeze.

The villagers came running out of the fields at the aircraft's arrival, and Alihahd backed up against the plane in the face of the noisy, barefoot onslaught of short stocky aliens who panted like dogs and chattered in a strange tongue. But it was a benign rush, aimed at the warrior-priests more than the humans, who were a mere curiosity.

The villagers were short and bulky like big gnomes—as draft ponies to racehorses next to the six tall, slender warrior-priests. Their skin was brown or white. The color changed as the aliens stood in full sunlight or shadow. All of them had light red hair and black eyes. Their kind were called ranga. The tall, fair warrior kind were called aghara. They looked like two different breeds.

Looks deceived.

The babbling, smiling ranga surrounded the laconic warrior-priests, who answered them tersely in an incomprehensible language. There was a lot of talk—questions, answers, directions, arrangements, acknowledgments. Vaslav listened closely, as if he might actually pick out patterns in the noise.

Alihahd eased away from the throng and retreated to the far side of the airplane. Under the shade of the wing, he leaned on the pontoon, his head resting on his arms.

Harrison Hall had taken off exploring on his own.

Vaslav came under the plane wing with Alihahd. Alihahd lifted his head and rubbed his brow. "Yes, Vaslav."

Vaslav's eyes were darting this way and that, taking in the alien trees and crops, the charming village, the blue sky. He was furtively smiling but unsure if he ought. He looked to his captain for the proper reaction. Alihahd did not look happy.

"Are—are we safe?" Vaslav asked.

"I see no evidence for alarm," Alihahd said. "Go walk with Mr. Hall. I swallowed too much brine, is all." He motioned the boy away with a weak wave of his hand.

Vaslav's smile spread to a beaming grin, and he bounded away to catch up with Harrison Hall.

Alihahd covered his eyes with his hand. It was the mark of a great leader to be a consummate liar. Alihahd was scared to death. But why ruin the boy's image of an idyll—especially when he just might be right? Alihahd kept the worry to himself. That was what leaders were for.

The complete alienness of the surroundings weighed on him. He felt ill. He needed distance.

He stooped to crawl underneath the body of the plane. He sat down with his head leaning back against the rough treads of the tail wheel, and shut his eyes.

He found comforting familiarity in the sound of wind in leaves, the smell of chlorophyll and dry grain fiber, and the rubberlike tire at his back. He could almost imagine this to be one of Earth's far-flung colonies, and the alien voices just the chatter of slaves.

Yet darker visions invaded his illusion. He knew what experiments the Na'id performed on live aliens, on parts of them.

And humans were the aliens here.

He bided an indeterminate while beneath the plane, and began to think he'd been forgotten. The day grew hot, and he had no ambition to move. The sun was directly overhead.

He listened to the buzz and chirp of reptilian birds, dozed off and on, studied his sheltering plane with its wheels and pontoons, and decided it was a stupid design for an aircraft.

Harrison White Fox Hall returned from his prowl, his dark red-bronze face burned a deeper red. He eased himself under the plane with Alihahd. Vaslav crawled in after him.

"Didn't get too far," Hall said. He took off his bandana, loosed the knot, and retied it around his head. "Some industry behind the hill where the river curves round. Hardly impressive. This seems to be state-of-the-art technology." He patted the metal belly of the amphibious craft above their heads.

Alihahd groaned, his hopes of ever getting off-world fading. Yet he hadn't realistically expected more.

Hall stretched out his long legs. "My dear Captain, there are worse places you could be marooned."

Alihahd turned to look at him directly. "With worse company?" he asked sincerely. He didn't mean the aliens.

Hall grinned, took Alihahd's head in his hands, and kissed him on the mouth. "Possibly not," he said.

"I thought as much," Alihahd said. Many cultures sent people to the grave with kisses. And as Hall lowered his hands, Alihahd grasped one of his wrists—the one with the sleeve not rolled up. Alihahd's fingertips touched something hard, the hilt of a hidden dagger strapped to Hall's forearm.

Both men froze, the same question on their minds. Should they attempt it, which of them could draw and use one of Hall's weapons first?

Vaslav coughed nervously.

Alihahd turned his head. Vaslav was confused. Vaslav couldn't see the dagger, couldn't see Alihahd's and Hall's thoughts, which were so transparent to each other. He couldn't reconcile their actions with any antecedent action, their words with their silken tones. He could only figure he was having a severe translation problem.

"Poor Vaslav," Alihahd said and let go of Hall's wrist.

The tall warrior-priestess Arilla came again, bearing thin-skinned fruit, green leafy stalks, and coarse flat bread. She placed them in the grass under the airplane. "For thee and thee and thee."

She saw their hesitation. "Not to worry," she said. "It is safe for humankind." She didn't say how she knew.

With little appetite, Alihahd took a bite of the bread, then pushed everything away with an unsteady hand.

Arilla told him he was bony. Alihahd could not be persuaded.

Finally Arilla beckoned, her bracelets jingling and sliding up to her elbow. "Come, if thou wilt not eat. We are not home yet. This is only the Lower Aerie."

Lower Aerie? They were three and a half miles above sea level. "There is an Upper Aerie?" Alihahd asked, climbing from under the plane to join Arilla in the open sunlight.

"There." She pointed upward.

3. Island in the Sky

HIGH ABOVE THE PLAIN towered the forbidding peaks of a great mountain, its twin summits separated by a deep narrow crevasse, as if a god had taken a cleaver and sliced the single mountain in two. Where the two peaks slanted away from each other in the misty distance, Alihahd could see tiers of stone arches on both sides of the fissure.

"There is a foot bridge," said Arilla. "On one side stands the Aerie. On the other Haven. Both together are also called Aerie."

The mountain was block-faulted, its south face a barren granite palisade with the Aerie an inaccessible citadel at the top of the sheer rise. Itiri planes couldn't fly that high. Even Iry's heavy atmosphere thinned at such heights. It was six miles above the sea.

"How can anyone possibly get up there?" Alihahd asked.

"We are going to walk," Arilla said.

"We are?"

"You are going to fly." She guided the humans across the golden field to the foot of the twin mountain where a balloon was prepared.

Alihahd liked this method of transportation less than he did the seaplane.

The balloon rose slowly, smooth and soundless on a warm anabatic current, the wind the Itiri named *eaninala*, the day wind.

Then a sudden gust swept the balloon toward the cliff face. The mountain loomed large and filled the view. A glitter of quartz. A rock wall with the shadow of their fragile basket growing on it.

Then the shadow of an eagle.

There came a tug and a change of direction.

An eagle had seized a ring at the end of a long rope attached to the balloon and was towing it back into the rising air current.

There were more eagles just above them, scouting the winds to find where the eddies flowed.

Vaslav leaned over the edge of the basket to try to see the birds. "Are they yours?" he asked the warrior Stasa-yxan, who had come with them in the basket.

"The talassairi belong to no one," said the warrior.

The boy was abashed. He didn't talk well. He had only been using Universal for a few weeks. He was sorry he had tried to say anything.

Harrison Hall was relaxed and merrily sinister—even as they were swept toward the rocks—the only one of the humans who seemed untroubled.

It began to grow cold, and Stasa-yxan gave the three humans black cloaks to wear.

The air thinned. The balloon spread out. The countryside diminished into a sunny haphazard checkerboard whose straight rigid boundaries had been forced to curve with a winding river and to scallop the rising ground into flat stepped concentric levels outlined with blue-gray stone retaining walls so that the whole scene looked as if an orderly pattern of red and brown and green and gold squares had melted and run together.

Stasa-yxan frowned at some part and murmured as if making a note for himself, "Blight."

The others saw nothing. The fields looked healthy.

Alihahd had been silent this journey, lost in a brooding sulk, until Vaslav glanced his way, did a double take, and pointed, his mouth open but lacking the words to explain.

Alihahd blinked back to awareness and looked down at himself. His cloak had turned from black to white. "Is this thing alive?"

"Thou mindest not the cold as much as thy companions," said Stasa-yxan. "Thy thoughts are elsewhere."

Alihahd pulled the now-white cloak around him and huddled bleakly in the bottom of the woven-reed basket. "How appropriate."

The balloon rose to a level jut not far below the bald pate of the western summit. Alihahd climbed woodenly out of the creaking basket and jumped down to the rock shelf, landing weightily on his feet to find himself standing on an island in the sky.

High. So high. Above was nothing but cold sky and bright sun. The air was dry and thin, and everything appeared distinct in the harsh desertlike light.

Low furry plant life crept all the way to the tops of the mountains. Even on the nearly barren rock summits some life still clung, a tatter of grass, a patch of lichen.

Stasa-yxan led the way on a footworn twisty path through moss and creepers to the colonnades of Haven. The path leveled and straightened to a paved walkway called the Ledge Path, from whose base the five levels of Haven rose up in columned tiers, each higher level set farther into the slope. The little city in the sky gleamed in the bare light, the columns, arched doorways, and lancet windows intricately carved, latticed, fretted, and inlaid with gemstones and leafed with metal.

Across the narrow crevasse that separated the twin peaks, Haven's twin, Aerie, glittered in near mirror image, so that the terraced hollow between the summits formed a titanic natural amphitheater split down the middle.

Curious red-haired ranga poked their heads from the archways of Havenside to peer at the human strangers. There was no movement or curiosity from Aerieside.

A bridge spanned the crevasse where it narrowed to twenty feet across. It was a single-person footbridge made of wooden planks and rope, with knotted handrails. At its mooring Stasa-yxan stepped aside for Alihahd. "Thou first."

A wind moaned up the fissure and the bridge swayed.

Alihahd watched it swing.

Stasa-yxan fastened a safety line to Alihahd, but it provided no feeling of security. If anything, it made him feel worse.

For being six miles above sea level the winds were light here. They should have been roaring through that narrow abyss as in a wind tunnel.

They could always change.

Stasa-yxan nudged Alihahd. The short span was suddenly very very wide, becoming wider the longer Alihahd stared at the knotted fiber ropes and the wooden planks.

Somewhere beyond the sheltered hollow a wind howled.

Because there were no choices, Alihahd grasped the rope guides and stepped out, not looking down. He was midway across, poised over empty space, when a voice sounded from behind him on Havenside, calling long and tonal, a muezzin sound of repeated ritual.

"Erika! Ameeerrrrika!"

Alihahd turned his head with a start. He could not have heard what he had heard.

Sudden and startling as a splash of water, a child appeared running down a mountain path like a hardy little goat. "Coming!"

A human child.

She was bundled in a long heavy dress, wide-legged trousers, thick cloak, and leather boots. Black hair spilled down her back to her hips. Baby-fat cheeks were red and round. Her black eyes had lights within.

Alihahd felt his interest spark, and was so shocked by it he had to clutch for the bridge ropes and catch his balance. He was not sure how old the girl was, but knew she was not old enough for any man to be looking at her the way he was—especially him.

And you, he was thinking to his prick. *Never mind that.*

It had a mind of its own, and its timing was awful. He considered himself too old. It should by rights be dead. He'd honestly thought it was. He just wanted it to leave him alone.

When was the last time you rose to any good occasion?

This had less to do with the girl than it did his present danger. It was a sad state of affairs when it took proximity to death to excite him. He held his white cloak fast around him and growled inwardly. He continued across the bridge, disdainful of the long drop—courting it, in fact.

Safe on the other side, he turned to look again, but the girl Amerika had disappeared into one of Haven's many rock chambers.

Did I dream her?

Human. His emotions raced. Not for the girl this time, but for what she implied.

Space travel.

Trying not to hope too much, Alihahd unhooked his safety line and let it drop back to Havenside so the others could cross.

As he waited, slowly, subtly, the aura of this side took on life and strength and pressed itself into his consciousness. He knew without being told that this side of the Aerie was home to the warrior-priests.

The Aerie was silent, in repose. Like a monastery, it breathed feelings of age, space, and power, as if God were actually more manifest here than other places. Mosques, temples, and cathedrals gave Alihahd the same impression and always left him uneasy—places built for the God of the People of the Book.

The sun had passed its zenith, and the first direct light of day was arriving now on Aerieside. The warm rays lifted steam from the shade-dank rock, and furtive vapors trailed low across the cold blue-gray stones and spilled out between the pillars of the shadowy arcade, then faded in the thirsty air.

The priestess first appeared like a vision at the end of the colonnade. Backed in the sunlit frame of the farthest arch, she came striding up the columned arcade through alternate light and shadow, sunbeams catching on clouds of rising mist that swirled around her feet with her advance and rolled outward in her wake. She moved with a purpose, flow and force in her walk, sharp as an arrow in flight.

As she neared, she took on lines of reality. A sheer blue kaftan billowed out behind her, its long full sleeves slit from shoulder to cuff so her arms showed through thin and ropy with sharply defined muscles. Her tough, weathered skin was blue-black. Her coarse black hair swung down, long, straight, and thick, from a glossy topknot and was knotted again at the end. She wore a white flower behind her ear and a double-curved sword at her side.

She turned and passed under an ornate archway aglitter with topaz and chrysoberyl to an inner chamber.

And when Alihahd's companions had crossed the bridge, Stasa-yxan led them to the same monumental archway.

Alihahd paused at the entrance, then walked in.

The chamber was a great nine-sided room with polished wood floor and high domed ceiling of gold. Mirrors set in the tall window jambs shot sunlight up to the ceiling, where it diffused and spread softly, and the chamber glowed in warm golden light.

The golden dome unsettled Alihahd.

Two more warrior-priests flanked the inner doorway. Tall and strong as the others, they seemed somehow smaller in this chamber: not so sure, not so proud. And Stasa-yxan changed as he passed under the arch. He seemed to shrink and become meek in this place.

But it wasn't the chamber itself that affected the warriors. It was the figure at the far end.

Enthroned in a wide ceremonial seat on a dais behind a low lattice barrier was the dark warrior-priestess. Her eyes, trained on the doorway, were black and bottomless, fierce and benign. Her daunting presence filled the room.

She was jet, head to toe, a melano color phase, like a panther. Broken red scars blazed on her sharp cheekbones. She sat with one elbow propped on the armrest, her body curved to the side, one bare foot folded underneath her on the seat. A great snowy owl perched on the tall carved back of her throne.

Stasa-yxan bowed in the universal gesture of respect. "Azo! Fendi!"

The Fendi returned a light nod.

"It was a starship that fell out of the sky," Stasa-yxan said. "These survive."

"Are they human?" the Fendi asked. Her dialect was clear—almost modern.

"They are," Stasa-yxan said.

The Fendi raised hairless brows. "Human starships fly to Iry again. How long has it been?"

"Fendi, I know not."

The Fendi smiled at Alihahd. She spoke, eyes on him, words directed at Stasa-yxan. "It has been a while."

Two thousand years it had been.

Alihahd spoke. "So long we forgot you were real and not a dream of ours."

The warrior-priestess smiled wider, baring white teeth.

Alihahd was puzzled. It had been two thousand years since an Earth ship came to Iry, yet....

He heard pattering feet on the path outside. *Amerika.* He knew her step already. She was no dream.

"Fendi. Was that not a human girl I saw?"

The Fendi nodded to Stasa-yxan. Stasa-yxan answered for her.

"It was," the warrior said. "We have several guests here. But she did not come on her own ship. We brought her."

Then they do have interstellar capabilities! Hope leaped to full life.

The Fendi spoke again, musing to no one in particular. Not to the humans. Not directly. "So Earth finally decides to remember us."

Her tone was nonjudgmental. She considered the development neither good news nor bad news, only interesting fact.

Birds were flying in the chamber's spacious dome, flitting in and out of the tall windows. They were little black birds like swallows. One flew near the Fendi, and she absently snatched it out of the air with lightning grasp without even turning her head, nothing moving but her arm. She petted its head with one long finger, then tossed it back into the air, unhurt—all as effortless and unthinking as a person might bite his nails.

The snowy owl blinked a slow blink.

At last the Fendi asked, "They are not of these new humans—the Na'id, they are named?"

New? Comparatively, Alihahd supposed. Na'id colonization had been spreading for the last century and a half. The empire had conquered a large part of the known galaxy in that time.

"No, we are not," said Alihahd. The question was for him even though she'd directed it at Stasa-yxan.

"They are not here to assert human supremacy and— what is the other slogan?—galactic dominion?"

"No," said Alihahd. "We were shot down by Na'id." Then he remembered that he was not actually certain of what had befallen Harrison White Fox Hall's ship and realized he'd been answering for the man. He rephrased, "The boy and I were, anyway."

The Fendi's eyes slid to Hall. Stasa-yxan spoke to Hall for the Fendi. "And thou?"

"*We* were," Hall affirmed.

"Tell them to stay in peace, then," the Fendi said, finality in her voice. Alihahd sensed dismissal.

And he felt panic. *Stay?* He needed to get out of here, and soon. "Fendi," he said quickly. "I cannot stay. If you have a starship and could give me passage, I will give you anything you ask. I can pledge a great deal. Only tell me what you want."

The smile disappeared. The eyes flashed. Her head snapped toward Stasa-yxan. "Say to that one: Thou camest. We did not bring thee. We are not for hire." Her alien accent thickened in anger.

Alihahd immediately backed down. "I am sorry. I am already in your debt."

She smiled again. "Art thou a Fendi?"

Stasa-yxan made a noise in his throat. The Fendi had forgotten to speak to the human through her intermediary.

She hadn't forgotten. The Fendi stood, pushed her warrior attendant aside, and descended from the stepped dais. She moved around the lattice barrier.

Alihahd was struck speechless for a moment. What a bedraggled thing he must look; he had just insulted her, and she asked if he was her equal.

"I was," he said.

"Thou hast a people to whom thou must return?"

"Yes, Fendi," said Alihahd.

She reconsidered—seemed to.

"When one of us next leaves Iry, thou mayest go also," she said. "The physician may be next. Till then we can take you back to Lower Aerie. Most of our human guests are there. Winter drives them down. Only *niaha*—three—humans stay up here. Amerika, Layla, and Montserrat."

"When will the next ship leave?" Alihahd asked. Why had she mentioned winter?

The Fendi frowned. The snowy owl clacked its hooked beak.

"It could be long. It could be tomorrow. Like death," she said.

Whether the last words were statement or analogy Alihahd couldn't tell. The Fendi was displeased, and her warriors were frightened.

She ascended to the dais again. "My name is Roniva."

That was a signal to go—for the second time—and they'd best obey. She didn't want their names. She would learn them in time if she cared to.

The owl glowered from its perch on the back of the throne.

The young warrior, Stasa-yxan, motioned the guests out. Alihahd started to leave. He glanced back once, and forgot what he was going to say. His back hadn't been turned for more than two seconds.

The snowy owl was gone.

It was a long hall, its shadows very deep. Alihahd had come this way still seeking an escape. The labyrinthine passageways of Aerieside led him up rock-hewn stairs spiraling up a mammoth newel like a ziggurat, and he was wheezing by the time he climbed to the top. There was oxygen enough in the air. He simply couldn't draw it in. Blood pounded in his head.

At the end of the long hall shone a turquoise door. It was open. A shaft of sunlight fell into the dark corridor from the chamber.

A voice called to Alihahd from beyond the door. "Ave."

It was the girl Amerika.

Then came a male voice. "Peace be upon you."

"And upon you peace," Alihahd answered, curious. He approached the massive door. Its ancient mosaic was faded from long standing in the dry air.

Inside he found a warrior-priest, the girl, and an eagle. The eagle cocked its head sideways and regarded Alihahd with one onyx eye, inhuman intelligence in its gaze.

The girl stole shy glances at Alihahd from beneath long black lashes. Her dark skin deepened color in a blush.

The elderly Itiri beckoned Alihahd farther into his chamber with a white, spidery hand, his drooping skin jiggling with his motions.

The cave with its stuccoed walls was small, clean, and lined with racks and racks of herbs and delicate blown-glass vials of swirling colors. It was a physician's chamber. Even with the clutter, the room was airy, its woven mats fresh. Swallows trilled at the tall windows.

"Thou art ill," the physician said from his worktable.

"No. No, I am not," Alihahd said.

The physician wrinkled his brow in doubt. He said to Amerika, "Healthy humans appear thus?"

"No," Amerika said.

"Thy temperature is high," the physician told Alihahd, and Alihahd wondered how he could tell.

"How is it you speak Universal?" said Alihahd, drawing attention from himself.

"It is the language between the stars," said the Itiri physician. "Is it not?"

The way you speak it? "It was. Two thousand years ago," said Alihahd.

The physician made a motion with his head that was analogous to a shrug.

"We knew you would be back." He rose from his worktable. "Rest thou. Our air is thin to thee. Keep thee here and rest." He moved toward the door.

"What would be my chances of leaving Iry within the week?" Alihahd asked, and quickly added, "Seven days."

"Oh," said the physician without excitement as he was leaving. "None."

All in a wave, sickness rose in Alihahd's throat. His vision blurred and he reached for the wall, suddenly too dizzy to stand. There was no chair, so he sat on the floor.

When the spell passed, Amerika was kneeling at his side, biting her lower lips, afraid to touch him.

"It is nothing," Alihahd said.

Amerika sat back on her heels, unconvinced and unhappy. She was a lovely child, smelling clean of sunlit air, grass and leaves, and the woolen scent of her cloak.

The eagle in its corner stretched out its neck and lifted

one wing to peck at a bare patch of skin. Amerika snapped her head around and cried, "Not to do that!" And the eagle stopped. Amerika turned back to Alihahd.

Alihahd gave a pale smile. The girl was a provincial. She spoke Universal in the peculiar dialect of the Itiri. She must have learned the language here, not on her backward home-world Solea.

Her necklace placed her. The necklace was a polished chain carved from a single block of petrified wood, each loop an unbroken circle. The chain had been placed on her as a baby and could no longer be taken off over her head. The chains were customary to certain Solenense tribes. That Amerika still wore it meant she had never fallen into Na'id hands. The Na'id habitually cut the repressive symbols from the necks of all the young Solenese girls. That she still wore it signified that she was a virgin.

"A Solenese healer?" Alihahd said. "Is that not un-usual?" Solea had no medical technology.

Amerika tried to hide a bashful smile, but it glowed in her eyes and on her cheeks. "Who told thee I was of Solea?" she said playfully.

"You did." Alihahd looped his forefinger through the chain at her throat.

Amerika's skin warmed against the back of his hand, and she blushed very dark. Alihahd let the chain drop.

He got up and smoothed his tunic. He moved to the door.

Suddenly plaintive, Amerika said, "Why must thou leave in seven days? This place pleaseth thee not?"

The way she said it made him sound ungrateful for wanting to go. He turned at the door. "Do you know, child, only hours ago I believed I was dying, and I expected nothing else. I know I am fortunate to be alive and to be here. But now that I am here, alive, and I find these people have starships —"

"Thou wantest to go home," she finished for him with a downturn in her voice, a litany of disappointment.

"No," Alihahd said. "I can never go home."

Amerika brightened. "Then stay thee here."

"I have no choice, it seems."

"Why so eager to go nowhere?" she demanded.

Alihahd couldn't explain, not without touching the past, and not without telling a child that the prospect of living could be infinitely more terrifying than dying. So he excused himself and left.

The warrior-priest Jinin-Ben-Tairre wrapped the felt cover around the ancient tungsten-plastic blade and replaced it in its scented wood chest, closed the lid, and fastened the polished brass catches. He had heard the eagles arrive earlier with Universal-speaking newcomers. Ben-Tairre had not gone out to look. It was his practice to avoid off-worlders. He preferred to maintain ignorance of things that lay beyond the planet he fiercely loved—or even of things beyond the Aerie—since the time he had first walked the fire and become a warrior-priest.

He stood, straightened his clothes, and secured his cloak with a short length of chain across his broad chest. Then he turned and bowed to his Elder. The hanina's hood was up. The old woman had ceased speaking for the day. The younger warrior withdrew and set off for his own chamber, muscles flowing in his powerful thighs with each stride, his winged familiar fluttering at his shoulder.

Long rays of the sinking sun reached the far wall of the arcade. Ben-Tairre walked through the colonnade, stepped down to the Ledge Path, and came face-to-face with one of the newcomers. Thunderstruck eyes met his own, and both men stopped dead.

The newcomer was a tall, gaunt human with straight Nordic nose and clear deep-set eyes in a swarthy, long face.

Jinin-Ben-Tairre's shock passed to fury. His eyes blazed and he walked swiftly past. Who had spat this being at him? Laws of hospitality forbade him striking the stranger's head off. The warrior's fury doubled at his own inability to choke down hatred. He did not go to his own chamber, but kept walking.

Alihahd turned to watch the retreating figure incredulously. If a hallucination, it was vivid.

The warrior was human.

A swift breeze swayed the bridge unsettlingly as Alihahd crossed to Havenside.

He found Harrison White Fox Hall and Vaslav at dinner in the dwelling of the human woman Montserrat. The cave was large, warm, its walls hung with red-and-amber tapestries. A kettle bubbled on the hearth.

There were two women inside. The pale, nervous, petite woman in a red dress was Montserrat. She kept her rusty wiry hair cut very short except for long bangs that nearly obscured a red chevron tattooed on her brow. She gave up her cushion at the table as Alihahd came in, and she fetched another for herself, her brown eyes downcast all the while. Hall called her Serra.

The second woman was as small, looked tougher, and was wearing a hide jerkin and trousers. She was cleaning a jeweled dagger and scowling at Harrison Hall, her lightly freckled nose wrinkled in disdain. Straight brown hair was pulled off her heart-shaped face and braided back with a leather thong. Her brown eyes were lined black like an Itiri's. She wore a small beam gun holstered under her left arm but seemed to favor the dagger in her hand. She was Layla, a Nwerthan mercenary. Alihahd could spot those right away. Modern worlds customarily recruited and trained the primitive Nwerthans in warfare because they fought like the very devil and seldom asked why.

Both women were not much older than thirty years Earth standard.

Alihahd bid a proper Universal greeting to them, then spoke to Hall. "I saw—" And he stopped, doubting what he had seen—a powerfully built young warrior-priest with golden skin, brown-black slanted eyes, a heavy jaw, flat nose, and short black hair. He'd borne the symbols of a warrior-priest: the red broken scars on his broad cheeks; a white flower at his belt; a signet ring on his forefinger, though his was on his left hand. His right hand was gloved in black and didn't look real. His knife had been sheathed left-handed. Red rags were tied around the highly arched insteps of his small feet which were scarred as if by fire.

A bird had ridden on his shoulder—a real bird, not an avian alien. It was a kestrel.

There was a power in the young warrior, and a horror-branded depth in his dark eyes that looked murderously at Alihahd. He had walked past Alihahd as if past an urn of ashes.

Alihahd decided that he was certain of what he'd seen. "I saw a warrior-priest," he told Hall. "He was as human as you and I."

"Jinin-Ben-Tairre," Layla said. She sheathed her dagger at her belt and placed eight dainty rings from the table onto the short, tapered fingers of her rough-lined and callused little hands.

"Is that a name?" Alihahd asked.

Layla assented with a nod. "It means 'The Warrior's Feet Are Burned.'" She spoke Universal with the studied precision of a second language.

"The Fendi said there were three humans on the Aerie," Alihahd said. "Why am I counting four?"

"Because Roniva will not speak his name. And because Jinin-Ben-Tairre is not human anymore," Layla said.

Alihahd found the idea of a human trying to be alien offensive. "He pretends he is not human so that makes him not?" Acid had crept into his deep voice.

"If Ben-Tairre thinks something is so, it is so," Layla said. "You will see. He has a familiar."

Alihahd remembered the warrior's kestrel and Roniva's disappearing owl. "What are they, the familiars?"

"I do not know," Layla said. She crossed one dun-booted

foot across her opposite knee. "I do not think the Itiri know."

"Are they alive?"

"They do not eat," Layla said. "I do not think they breathe."

"They disappear from one place and appear somewhere else in an instant," Serra added haltingly in a low voice that went to breathiness and slight feminine gravel. Her hands fidgeted over her teacup. Serra's skin was pale brown, without sun, her eyes unlined. Her small nose had once been broken, and there were scars on her pretty face. Someone used to hit her.

"From where did Jinin-Ben-Tairre come?" Alihahd asked.

"He has no past," Layla said. "He killed it. He locked it in a box and burned it. It is dead."

Serra spoke in a near whisper. "Old ghosts have a way of catching up with you in the safest of places."

"I guess that bears keeping in mind," Harrison White Fox Hall commented. He turned his eyes to Alihahd.

"And what are you?" Layla challenged Alihahd. "You look like a Na'id."

The boy Vaslav had been letting the others talk. Here he spoke up in defense, proud and indignant, "He is not a Na'id! He is Alihahd!"

Layla's jaw dropped in surprise, showing crooked white teeth. "I know you," she said. Alihahd flinched. Layla's attitude changed to deference. "You fight Na'id."

"I do not fight them. I run from them," Alihahd said.

"You are much too humble," Serra whispered.

"No. In point of fact, I never met them in battle," Alihahd said. This point was important to him.

"But you are a great man," Layla said. "Everyone knows you made the Na'id leave Chesa."

The liberation of Chesa had been Alihahd's first and most notorious feat. It had made his "name." By means of false orders from nonexistent admirals and generals, false intelligence reports, bogus replacement troops, fabricated computer records, suspicions cast left and right so that no one talked to anyone else, and all manner of deceptions, Alihahd had systematically tricked the Na'id into abandoning an entire occupied planet. A full standard month passed before someone realized that anything was wrong.

"An exercise in vanity," Alihahd said. "They came back. There was no point to it beyond letting it be known that I could do it."

When the Na'id reoccupied Chesa and demanded of the natives who was responsible for this incredible plot, they replied, "Alihahd," which in their native tongue meant, "He left." And so he was known ever after, an elusive force with a formidable knowledge of the Na'id chain of command, codes, and way of doing things. He'd spent the rest of his shadowy career throwing the system into chaos and providing means of escape for unwilling subjects of the Empire.

"You are not eating," Serra said.

"We ate at Lower Aerie," Alihahd said. From the corner of his eye he saw Hall scowl at him. "Have you anything to drink?" Alihahd asked. He'd barely touched his tea.

"If you mean alcohol, there is none." Serra shrugged. "The Itiri don't seem to make any."

Alihahd dismissed the thought with a pass of his hand. His head hurt.

The sun was setting. The only light in the cave came from the hearth. It had been a long day—days. Alihahd had lost all sense of time since the *Liberation* had broken apart.

He stared futilely at the bowl of stew cooling in front of him. He couldn't eat.

Amerika came to the door, and she peered in. Alihahd could see half of her, one bright black eye, one half of a coy smile, one baby-fat hand hugging the doorjamb.

Hall was speaking to him, "Did you find a way off-planet, Captain?"

"No," Alihahd said and closed his eyes. "We are trapped here."

Layla uncoiled from her cushion. "Then let us find a place for you." She was looking at Hall. "You are not staying in here."

"There is a chamber," Amerika piped cheerfully from the threshold. "Sit thee down, Layla. I shall show them."

"Whose chamber?" Alihahd asked.

"Thine," Amerika said.

Alihahd turned to Serra. "Why are we being given everything? Whose chamber am I taking, and who is giving it to me in return for what?"

Serra smiled for the first time, color in her pale brown cheeks. "It is the way of hospitality. Travelers must have what they need. If the cave is empty, you may have it. No one gives it. Nothing belongs to anyone anyway."

"Is this the law?" Alihahd asked.

"Not law. Virtue."

"Then what consequence if you are not hospitable?" Alihahd asked.

"Then you are a bad person," Serra said.

Alihahd didn't understand the world. He'd never been so lost, forced to conform to alien ways. "Is there anything I should be sure to do or not do? Am I likely to commit a crime in ignorance?"

"No there aren't any laws. Only for the warrior-priests. A guest would have to be very evil for harm to come to him. You're safe here," Serra said.

"Safe from the Itiri," Layla said, her eyes on Hall.

No, I am not safe, Alihahd thought. *I must leave this place very, very soon.*

"Come with me," Amerika sang and waved the men outside with her.

"And do something with their clothes," Layla called after the girl. "They stink."

The night was clear. There were no lamps on the paths, for the starry sky was bright, shedding light equal to several full moons.

An albino Itiri sentinel crouched at his post on the dawn

ridge, his face washed silvery blue in the cold light. Red eyes watched over the peaceful valley, while distant yellow fire-lights winked back from the little village far below.

Small black shapes darted through the air over the Aerie—swifts—catching winged bugs swept up the chasm on rising air currents.

Alihahd stopped on the windy path. Across the chasm a figure lurked in a dark archway. Starlight gleamed off a naked sword blade slanting down from a left-handed grip.

A man without a past was a dangerous sort, Alihahd knew. He stood out of the edge of the cliff path and faced the shadowed figure across the abyss, the wind in his hair, his long arms hanging at his sides from his wide, straight shoulders in weaponless, tired readiness until the dark figure and the sword withdrew again into blackness.

Alihahd walked on.

The cave where Amerika led them was clean, with a fire already burning in its hearth, and three separate piles of bedcovers set on the expansive chaff-filled mattress that would have been big enough for six people. The girl had been busy. Amerika stirred the coals in the hearth. She darted out again like a swift. "Good night. Good night."

Alihahd peeled off his tunic, pulled off his flat-bottomed deck boots, pounded out a place on the uneven mattress, and lay down.

Vaslav took a place against the wall behind which sounded the trickling of water. Vaslav huddled against the warm stone and was soon snoring softly.

Hall walked out to water a bush on the mountainside, then returned and undressed. His dirk he kept with him. That and his gun and his fox-head pipe. He gave up his other things to the little ranga male who came into the cave to collect their clothes and spirit them away.

Hall's trim body took on a burnished sheen in the fire-light, muscular and taut for his age, deep-chested and wasp-waisted. A few age spots dotted his shoulders. His hair, loosed from its tie, was streaked heavily with steely gray.

Hall settled under a pile of bedding on the other side of Alihahd from Vaslav.

The glowing coals in the hearth shifted and settled. Outside, night birds sang.

Alihahd shivered. This place was barbaric. He could have been in New Triton by now. His emergency shuttles should have arrived there by this time. He could hear them telling the other rebels, "Alihahd is dead."

Alihahd wished he were.

He sensed Hall was still awake. Alihahd turned to him.

One tiger eye was open and watching. "A touch xenophobic, aren't you, Captain," Hall said.

"I was never known for my love of aliens," Alihahd said shortly.

"The Na'id call rebels *alien-lovers*," Hall said. Alihahd was a notorious rebel indeed.

"Does not necessarily follow," Alihahd said.

They were speaking in near-whispers, reluctant to disturb the quiet. Except for the birds, they seemed to be the only beings awake in the world.

Hall propped one bare arm behind his head, the brindle fur cover across his deep chest, his gaze directed toward the ceiling. Hearthlight picked up copper flecks of beard stubble on his cheek.

Hall was a hunter and a controller. The more elusive and powerful the quarry, the more interesting the capture and control. Alihahd would not be controlled.

Hall sighed and went to sleep.

Alihahd shivered. He couldn't seem to put on enough covers. He'd never felt the cold before. This cold came from within.

He fell asleep shaking.

4. Circle Circle

HARRISON WHITE FOX HALL awoke the first morning, pushed the blankets from his face, and breathed in the cold sting of mountain air. The fire was dead. He reached out a bare arm from the warmth under the covers to rest atop the frosty fur.

Some small light came from outside. It was almost dawn. The boy Vaslav was still asleep, quietly snoring. Alihahd had already risen and gone.

On the corner of the wide mattress Hall's clothes had been returned to him, neatly folded, clean, dry—and cold. He threw off the blankets and jumped out of bed onto the icy granite floor, naked and barefoot. He was quickly dressed.

A clay jug of water stood near the hearth. Hall broke the iced-over surface with a silver ladle and shaved the copper stubble from his face with the straight edge of his dagger, which was still warm from being sheathed against his forearm. He hadn't taken it off.

Vaslav, like most space travelers from more modern worlds than Hall's, showed no trace of a beard.

Outside the air was piercing fresh. Painted streaks were

spreading in the eastern sky. A few bright stars still glim-
mered in the indigo west. Then a bright shaft of light spilled
over the eastern mountains and splashed across the peaks.
The valley below lay still in shadow. The sentinel on the
dawn ridge opened his arms in salute to the sun as it
climbed over the edge of the world.

There were no clouds anywhere, and Hall could see for
miles—mountain after impassable mountain beyond the
isolated terraced valley with its waterfall spitting rainbows
into the air in the morning light. The day would be fair.

Hall stretched, feeling the mountain cold in his bones.
He could see summer far below in the still-shaded village
Kaletani Mai, but pride refused to let him go there. The air
was only slightly thin to him, coming from Eridani as he did.
He could survive up here.

The Aerie stirred. Hall watched the white ranga come
out of their caves and turn dark in the sunlight. They were
funny, cherubic little people, always cheerful, and a bit stupid. They were of one breed with the tall, slender enigmatic
aghara. That's what Serra said. It was difficult to believe.
Polymorphism in the extreme, Hall thought. The majestic
aghara were actually the rare children of the chubby
gnomes, and the Itiri warrior-priests were what the aghara
kind spent their lives training to become.

Hall watched a few warrior-priests summon aghara children from out of the ranga caves. Youthful scarless faces of
the uninitiated appeared in answer to their masters' call,
and the young cheelas crossed the bridge to Aerieside to
run with their masters over the mountain.

Hall followed one pair for a while, but he couldn't keep
pace. So he dropped out of the running and walked alone
along a swift-running brook where black birds with serrate
beaks and oily feathers dove into the water seeking crusta-
ceans under the rocks of the streambed. The winds were
fast out here beyond the Aerie. Hall's face was stung red.
He unrolled his bandana and tied it on his head to keep the
buffeting from his ears.

He strayed from the beaten track through a stand of scrubby, distorted would-be trees that fringed the sun-bleached rocks of the ridge. The hunter in him was drawn by a trail of footprints crushed into moss still exhaling strong fragrance as if recently done. Someone had strayed this way before him—someone who wore shoes. Possibilities were limited.

And in an isolated depression where the air was still, sheltered by a curving rock wall and carpeted with long low-lying grasses, he found Alihahd seated on a rock, his elbows on his knees, his head bowed, his hands trembling. At Hall's approach he looked up, pale, beads of sweat on his face. Then his watery gaze returned to his feet. Hall jogged down the rocks into the low space and drew closer. He stood a moment in observation. This wasn't altitude sickness. "Alcoholic, Captain?"

Alihahd looked up in helpless self-surprise. He drew a wavering breath, licked his salty wet upper lip, and tried to steady his hands. "I would have said no." But his shaking hands held out before him defied him.

Hall watched curiously, weight on one foot, the other foot angled in. "You're not seeing snakes, are you?"

"No. No snakes."

Alihahd hung his head and closed his eyes. Hall climbed back out of the sunken area and left him alone with his misery.

Vaslav stumbled into Serra's cave late in the morning and squinted at the green breakfast Serra set before him.

A little while later Alihahd showed up, looking wounded and fragile. Serra took a separate kettle from the fire and poured an herbal brew for him. It smelled medicinal. Alihahd looked at Serra dubiously.

"Mr. Hall said you were sick," Serra said.

Alihahd's eyes shifted to Hall. "Mr. Hall said that, did he?"

Hall took his empty pipe from between his teeth and

gestured with it to the cup of tea on the table. "It's a mild sedative."

Alihahd spoke stiffly with an edge in his voice. The words were, "Thank you, Mr. Hall." The tone said, *Back off, Mr. Hall.*

"You look pale," Serra said.

Alihahd's brows rose over deep-set watery eyes. "I imagine I will look much paler before long," he murmured.

Alihahd took to bed and stayed there, wretchedly ill. One by one his deadly secrets were beginning to slip away from him into open air for all to see, hard as he tried to lock them down.

He couldn't stop the Itiri physician from coming to examine him. The Itiri had to know if Alihahd had the plague.

Alihahd crouched back against the wall in drunken fear of the alien and in real fear of the examination—or rather the verdict of the examination. Alihahd had been afraid the alien would step back and declare, "He's a drunk." But the aged Itiri merely announced that he had never seen this particular malady before. He rubbed his withered jowls in puzzlement and muttered about inoculations and quarantine.

A low chuckle at the door made him turn.

Harrison Hall rocked back on his heels. His eyes were merry crescents. "Oh, it's not plague," Hall said.

From the bed, Alihahd's liquid eyes fixed accusingly on the tall satanic figure in the doorway, awaiting betrayal.

But Hall said to the physician, "It's a poison."

"Will he die?" the physician asked.

"I think not," Hall said.

"O God, why not?" Alihahd moaned and tried to vomit.

He writhed at night with horrid dreaming and rasping breath, trying to draw in enough oxygen from the air that seared his throat raw as he gasped at it.

The ranga moved a mass of potted bushes and leafy plants into his cave to replenish the oxygen and moisture in the closed air.

Alihahd lost track of day and night. He knew only twilight and darkness and his own agony. Hall had moved out and sought shelter elsewhere.

From a nightmare Alihahd awoke, thrashing and sweating and shivering under the rough blanket. He turned over in the dark to someone there — Vaslav sitting on the edge of the wide bed keeping vigil, his youthful face angelic with devotion in the infinitesimal light.

Alihahd lay on his back, gasping, his hair a matted snarl, perspiration and tears beaded on his haggard face and trickling down its deep furrows. He reached up a feeble hand — he could only lift his arm from his elbow — and touched Vaslav's cheek with the back of his fingers. In a deep, croaking voice he said, "Vaslav, do you love me?"

The boy's eyes flew wide. He sputtered, choked, stumbled over an aborted explanation, and stammered out, "Yes."

Alihahd's strengthless hand dropped back on the bed. "Then please let me vomit in private."

Abashed, the boy stuttered a flustered apology and left. Had he a tail, it would have been between his legs.

Alihahd curled up and wrapped his arms around his abdomen.

He woke at late dawn to a cold waft of fresh air in his stuffy chamber. Long slanting sun rays streamed in from the doorway, its hide cover blown slightly agape. The bushes in their trough at the far wall of the shadowy cave leaned toward the light, stretching out their leafy branches. They seemed to be straining.

Then one pulled itself up by its bipartite roots and walked out.

Then all the rest of them, save one, unearthed themselves and pattered out in a herd.

The last one tugged itself free and ran out with a hasty *whap whap whap* of roots on the floor.

Alihahd pulled the covers over his head, delirious.

At midday, Alihahd woke again, lifted the covers, and peered out.

A trail of dirt was strewn across the floor from the empty planter at the far wall to the door.

Alihahd pulled the covers back over his head.

He swore the bushes would be back next time he looked.

He looked again when he heard Amerika's darting foot-steps and sweet, scolding commands, "Get! Come back, you little monkey!"

And a stampede of slapping roots.

He lifted the blanket to see Amerika chasing a bunch of errant bushes back into the cave. They fled before her, dodged into the dark place, sank their roots into the trough, and became very still.

Amerika gave a single nod of satisfaction, wiping her hands on her skirts, and went out.

Alihahd laughed till he threw up.

And steadily, as days passed, he grew more pale—almost white—and his eyes became blue, and the roots of his hair emerged blond. When finally he sat up, washed, and dressed, he was perfectly fair.

Hall was surprised—and a little amused. "You're a nazi!"

"Don't—" Alihahd began too loudly. He caught himself and finished softly, "—call me that, if you please."

Hall shrugged his big shoulders. "Isn't that the Na'id word for your kind?"

"It means more than blond-haired and blue-eyed. Do not call me that."

Hall shrugged.

The coloring was rare now, but not as rare as the Na'id would like. Still it was far too conspicuous for a man trying to move in Na'id circles without attracting attention. The way Alihahd looked now, he could not pass for a Chesite or a Na'id. The bogus Na'id captain was bogus indeed. "A white Na'id," Hall chuckled.

"Do not call me that either."

"Sorry," Hall said. He was aware of the full implications of that epithet and knew it was a bad one.

Serra stared at the new Alihahd. She didn't say anything.

She sat down on the bed, drew a skinning knife from its sheath in her boot, and proceeded to cut off his hair down to the blond.

Vaslav was thunderstruck by the change. "Are you really Alihahd?" he asked in doubting distress.

A cut lock of black hair fell down Alihahd's face. He brushed it off his knee. "I am the only Alihahd there ever was," he said, changing the words slightly. "Alihahd was never quite real."

The hero the boy believed in, he was not. There was no hero Alihahd.

White and shorn and still very weak, Alihahd ventured outside alone. Everything startled him, as if a filter had been lifted from his senses, and for the first time in over a decade he received the full assault of the world around him, so aware of life that it was painful.

He climbed the path on trembling legs, his hand out to steady himself on the cliff face, bracing himself against the wind's push.

Even his own hands were strange to him now—pallid great bony things tracked with bulging blue veins. He was frowning at them and at the blond hairs of his white forearms, when suddenly a warrior dropped down from the next level onto the path before him.

A flat and handsome yellow face with smoldering eyes.

Blinding sunlight on a naked blade.

Jinin-Ben-Tairre.

Alihahd didn't move as the sword turned, the blade gliding in a silken pass from Ben's massive shoulder and into another ready position. Ben was naked to the waist, and every clearly defined muscle in his arms and broad chest showed flexing and flowing, one with the weapon. Ben made no sound, not even the rustle of clothing. He wore only satiny black trousers and the red rags on his scarred feet. There was a carnelian ring on his left hand, and the black glove over his right hand. The warrior circled slowly.

Alihahd didn't dare turn. He did not know what laws

bound an Itiri, but knew there was nothing to stay this bastard warrior from killing him here and now if he so chose. Alihahd waited for the sword to split his skull from behind, an old chant running through his brain:

Circle circle, dance of death
Once she cries, twice she lays
A wreath about his youthful head
Thrice she flies, for nothing stays.

Full circle, Ben stopped before Alihahd. Alihahd felt naked with his true face exposed. He was more gaunt and drawn than before, his hollow cheeks deepened. Marked crevices were chiseled from his nostrils to the corners of his mouth, and his forceful bone structure showed beneath emaciated flesh. But most revealed were the luminous blue eyes, sunken in their orbits. Their gaze penetrated with a daunting power that had been masked before by the darker pigment.

Ben's sword changed hands, left to right, and he reached out with his left hand—the ungloved one—to Alihahd's white face. Alihahd tightened, anticipating pain, but felt only the light brush of short fingers on his chin.

Ben withdrew his hand and left.

Alihahd stood, still frozen in place. Sun tingled his fair skin. The wind was cold on his short-sheared scalp. Finally Harrison White Fox Hall came and took his hand like a child. "Come on, Captain." Alihahd looked at the dark red hand, then looked at Hall's laughing face.

"Are you laughing at me?" Alihahd asked.

"Yes," Hall said.

And since there was no intelligent answer to that, he said, "Oh," and let Hall guide him back to the cave—laughing.

Gunshots reported and echoed through the mountains in the early morning.

That will be Mr. Hall.

Alihahd stepped out of his cave. Shadows were very long. He followed the sound, stopping every few hundred feet to rest and breathe in frosty clouds.

The gun's reports led him to Harrison Hall, poised on a mountain spur with his crazy-looking notch-handled rifle. He was shooting clay pigeons that Vaslav hurled out from a higher ledge.

Alihahd made his way to Hall's side, his approach loud enough, his tunic red enough that he wouldn't surprise the gunman. Hall was hitting every bird, some several times when the fragments were large enough to bother with.

At last Vaslav called down, "That's it." The boy opened empty arms, having run out of clay birds.

Hall turned his head to Alihahd for comment.

"Impressive," Alihahd said.

Hall put one foot up on a rock and rested the butt of his gun on his sloping thigh. "Not my usual kind of target, but—" He finished with a shrug.

"What do you usually shoot?"

"Whatever's blue and glows in the dark."

Na'id uniforms and Na'id ships were electric blue with glowing red insignias of Human Supremacy/Galactic Dominion.

"I was shooting the real birds this morning," he told Alihahd. "Our hosts didn't like it."

"Do you ever miss?"

"Never."

Vaslav clambered down from his high ledge and came to them puffing. His cheeks and nose were wind-bitten. He looked healthy. A few days' primitive life had done him good, shedding him of his spaceship pallor.

Eight days. Alihahd had sensed the days were long here—30.96 standard hours, said Vaslav, who wore a standard chronometer around his wrist. It seemed time for a tentative evaluation.

Alihahd propped his foot up on the same rock as Hall

and leaned in, casually conspiratorial, one arm across his knee, a carefully magnetic gesture, and the other two men automatically leaned in for a private conference.

"What do you think of them?" Alihahd asked quietly. "Our hosts." Himself, he was not sure. He'd been in bed most of the eight days. These two had seen more than he.

"Too passive, if you ask me," Hall said.

"That is bad?" Alihahd asked.

"They have an army up here. I may be able to shoot the birds, but Roniva catches them in her bare hands without looking at them. I've seen their swords cut through tempered steel, and I hear you have to walk through fire to become a warrior. They're all crack shots, and from what I've seen, it's not too much to guess that they could totally annihilate the Na'id's Great Human Army if they put their minds to it."

Alihahd couldn't argue, even though he estimated only a thousand warriors on the Aerie by highest count. He wondered if there were many more. He shuddered at the words *totally annihilate*.

Given the proper technology—which, fortunately, the Itiri lacked—Alihahd didn't think there was much the Itiri couldn't do.

"But what do they do?" Hall continued, then answered his own question, "Sit up here and protect the birds."

He raised his gun and centered a winging swift in his sights. He didn't pull the trigger, just said, "Bang." And Alihahd knew the bird had been spared—no luck or maybe about it.

Hall lowered the gun. His tawny eyes glittered with ferocity. His lips curved beneath his gray mustache without a trace of softness.

Alihahd paused. "Whom did you lose?"

The eyes flickered to his, then looked away to the sky.

"Everyone."

5. Does Jerusalem Stand?

THE DATE WAS THE NINTH DAY of the Red Geese, year of the Ship in the Opal hexade-cade. So said Vaslav. It was all mush to Alihahd. But, cast outside the stream of human events and beyond the relevance of human calendars, he ought to get used to it. Layla had been here on the Aerie seven Earth years. Serra had been here fifteen years, Ben seventeen. God knew when Alihahd would ever leave. He could die here. He was convinced that Ben-Tairre meant to kill him, though Amerika said not—it would not be virtuous. Alihahd didn't place much faith in the human-turned-alien's virtue. The man hated him.

Alihahd heard the wind brass tapping in the swift gusts outside the cave where the humans had gathered.

"What is the date?" he asked Vaslav. "The real date."

Vaslav glanced at his wrist chronometer, "Tenthmonth nine. It's 0935 hours on the meridian."

The year would have been 5856 CE were anyone still using the Gregorian calendar.

Earth's civilization had reached its height long ago, in the third Common millennium, with an interstellar technology and human colonies flung across the Milky Way. At its peak the delicate balance had crashed, and civilization itself imploded in a galaxy-wide political and economic collapse that threw humankind into a dark age for two thousand years, a time when no ships would fly. Colonies, cut off from each other and left to their own resources, lost their technology, their ties with Earth, their count of years. Many forgot Earth and each other altogether.

In their isolation—after the anarchy and struggle for bare survival was over—the colonies tried to piece together what they had lost. The old learning was reclaimed imperfectly and at different rates in different fields and in different places. Some worlds remained sunken in total savagery. One built to an atomic age and did not make it out. But most worlds progressed.

And, finally, a few tentative starships traveled out again at the middle of the fifth millennium. The Dark Age was over. But the travelers were hardly Earthlings anymore. They had their own worlds, their own cultures. Earth was some faraway cradle of civilization, if remembered at all—

Except on one colony which remembered well where it came from and why. The planet was Mat Tanatti—Land of Praise, Land of Glory.

The colonists of Mat Tanatti had begun as a large group of discontented idealists on Earth in the third millennium. They had gone forth in self-exile to an uninhabited world to start a new culture on a base of equality undivided by artificial boundaries of nations and languages and antique faiths which the modern world had left behind and which turned brother against brother against sister.

The pilgrims named themselves *Na'id*, which meant *praiseworthy* or *alert* in the dead Earth language they took for their tongue of naming names.

And since they had already isolated themselves before the Collapse came, they weren't drawn down into it. No lifeline was cut, and Mat Tanatti was the one world that never fell. The Na'id kept their civilization, their history, and their purpose.

The end of the Dark Age found them successful beyond all prediction in creating a unified people. But the pessimists were justified in their insistence that Man must have his hatreds and prejudices. The Na'id stressed their humanity—as opposed to aliens.

The end of the Dark Age found the Na'id with the most advanced technology in the galaxy. They took it as a sign that their ideology was right and they were duty-bound to reunite their long-lost human brothers and sisters, and to free Earth from alien influence and wrong-thinking.

There had been no peace ever since. There was always fighting somewhere, and the biggest battles were not with aliens but with their own kind, the humans who didn't want to be united—not after two thousand years, and not under Na'id domination.

In professing tolerance of all human creations and culture, the Na'id encountered a dilemma: Were they to tolerate intolerance? Most religions included more than one tenet which ran counter to Na'id thought. The Na'id couldn't allow anyone's provincial ideas to infringe on the rights of others.

So they accepted all religions, with modifications, cutting out all portions that gave one segment of humanity superiority over another.

But the Word of God would not be picked apart so easily, and the Na'id movement met its major obstacle in the power of religion and the vehemence that met any attempted change.

Race was another sensitive point to the Na'id, but more quickly, if superficially, solved. The Na'id had never actually learned to live with and enjoy mankind's natural variations. There were always vague suspicions that one race was smarter, stronger, healthier, better than another, and a vague terror that the suspicions might be right. So their method of eliminating prejudice against racial differences was to eliminate the racial differences—to mix all the races and make humankind into one homogeneous mass. Ethnic purity became equated with elitism, and the Na'id would not tolerate it.

The Na'id fought their own kind to absorb them into the fold. They raped the pure races and stole the children to save them from narrow teachings. Brotherhood became assimilation, and supremacy leached in besides. Forbidden to hate one another, the Na'id channeled their hatred toward aliens. Humankind needed someone to dominate, someone on whom to blame the bloodshed, someone to be the common enemy against whom all humans could unite.

So began and continued the great crusade to save humanity and to liberate the homeworld, Earth. The fighting had gone on for well over a hundred years.

"Does Jerusalem stand?" Serra asked.

That was an old question. For a long time it had been the first question asked of any space traveler upon arriving anywhere.

The seat of the three major monotheistic religions, Jerusalem became the most important city on Earth. To the resistance it was a symbol of freedom that must never fall. The Na'id knew the value of symbols, and they were determined to have Jerusalem—for its impact on rebel morale and for its place in human history. The Mother City of Humankind, they called it.

The Holy City lay under siege for a hundred years, and humans everywhere, who had never seen Earth and never would, whether they belonged to one of the three faiths or not, asked of anyone who might know, "Does Jerusalem stand?"

The question was seldom heard anymore. Everyone knew the answer.

"You do not know?" Alihahd asked Serra.

"I had heard," Serra said. "Layla told me. I thought it was propaganda. Is it true, then?"

"Thirteen Earth years ago," Alihahd said.

The fall of Jerusalem had been a turning point in the

war. The Bel had all but declared total dominion of the known galaxy in his Jerusalem Address, expecting the rest of the resistance to shrivel up and for holdouts to fall in quick succession to his unstoppable general, Shad Iliya, the White Na'id.

Shad Iliya's army had never lost a battle — though most of the battles Shad Iliya ever fought had been on backwater alien worlds. The general had been long kept a half-hidden embarrassment because of his un-Na'id coloring. He'd only been brought into the open as a desperate attempt to end the hundred-year siege of Jerusalem.

Easy victory in the Holy City had made Shad Iliya's name and assured his infamy for a good part of forever. Instantly, Shad Iliya was the greatest hero/villain in the universe next to the Bel himself. No one doubted that the rest of humanity would fall to the man who had taken Jerusalem. Na'id morale had never been higher, nor rebel prospects lower.

Then Shad Iliya died. It was very soon after the historic victory. God/Jehovah/Allah consumed him in a pillar of fire, said the believers. The Na'id accused rebel agents of assassination. Rebels not of the faiths claimed that the Na'id got rid of the White Na'id themselves. The general's first lieutenant suggested it had been suicide, but no one listened to him.

The timing of his death made Shad Iliya a convenient demon by whom rebels could summon curses and frighten children. His was the face seen in the mirror in the dark. Being white helped to make him eerie. It also made his name a good insult for rebels to hurl at people who looked like Alihahd did now with his ghostly pale skin and white-golden fuzz of hair growing back on his shorn head.

But even with the death of the great general, the fall of Jerusalem remained a devastating blow to resistance. The mere speaking of it dampened the spirit of all in Serra's cave.

Amerika turned on Hall and Alihahd as if they were

negligent gods. "Could you not save it?" She beat the shoulder of the nearest one—Alihahd—with her little fists.

Alihahd rested his chin on his hand and looked forlornly heavenward with his large expressive blue eyes. He was very thin from his illness. He drew in a breath as if to speak, then exhaled without saying anything. He changed expression and finally spoke one word, hard. "No."

"How was it taken?" Layla demanded, crouching on her hassock like a hunting animal, her hair braided back with leather thongs. Layla was the combat soldier of the group. "What strategy?"

Alihahd answered in a dull, reciting voice, "Hand-to-hand. On the ground."

Amerika was confused. Hand-to-hand was the only kind of battle she had ever known. "Are not all battles so?"

"No battles are fought hand-to-hand these days," Harrison Hall told her. "We have much more efficient ways of doing each other in."

Yet superior weapons and modern technology couldn't win the war, as the Na'id discovered. Shad Iliya had revolutionized modern warfare by taking it backward—to people with guns.

"Infantry will always win the war," Alihahd said quietly as if thinking aloud. "But it's a lost skill. The only way to beat a good infantry is to destroy their entire planet. Or come in with a better infantry."

There was a somber pause.

The distant eerie sound of the wind brass on the eagle ridge intruded into the quiet. The arrhythmic tapping of the whip ends kept the humans inside, warning them that the winds were fast.

"How goes the conflict now?" Layla asked.

There had been no news at the Aerie in a long time. Even old information would be news here.

"Not well," Alihahd said. "But we've had no crushing reverses since Jerusalem."

"The Na'id lost several of their best leaders," Hall added. "Besides Shad Iliya."

"Did you kill him?" Layla asked.

The question startled Hall into a smile. He tilted his head and played at the two gold earrings in his one lobe. "Not I."

"I tried," Alihahd said.

Hall turned to Alihahd, his smile broader. "Did you really? I tried to kill the Bel."

"How is it you failed?" Layla demanded.

Alihahd leaned his head back against the wall. "Diverse reasons. None of them good." He put his long knobby fingers to the bridge of his nose and closed his eyes. "It is in the nature of our side to be inefficient. When the ultimate goal is disunity, you cannot have an efficient organization. Our side has a seedy lot of heroes. Myself. The *Marauder*." He cracked his eyelids and stole a peek at Hall, who gave no reaction to the name. Not a lash flickered out of place. Alihahd dropped his hand from his brow and sighed. "Decisive action is rather difficult when all factions of the Resistance are at cross-purposes. For my part, I am not trying to overthrow the Na'id empire, only loosen its grip on the unwilling. I haven't the right to decide how humankind shall or shall not be governed simply because it might be within my power to do so."

Hall laughed.

Alihahd frowned. "Did I say something funny?"

"Your flights of eloquence are precious, Captain."

"I am glad I keep you amused, Mr. Hall," Alihahd said. He was, he thought, not good for much else at the moment.

Talk of the past had made him introspective—something he tried to avoid—thinking of who he was, what he had become, and what was left to him now. He wanted to get back into space and do his work as Alihahd, the rebel runner.

Or, now that he thought of it, did he really want to return to that life—ever? The possibility of not wanting to do so shocked him. He was conscience-bound to want it. But it was out of reach. Running from responsibility was one thing. Being thrown from it was new. He got to his feet and walked to the doorway, where he leaned against the rock jamb to gaze across to Aerieside. The rock walls shone pink in the sunset.

He couldn't leave. The old way of life was far away.

A shadow fell across him. Hall had come to his side. Alihahd breathed, "Can I possibly be free at last? Can the albatross have fallen from my neck and I be truly allowed to forget?"

Hall took his pipe from between his teeth. "You can't hide from the past, and there's no permanent haven. The past will come looking."

Alihahd turned from the door. Hall's words were ominous.

The opal eyes of the fox-head pipe glittered unevenly. One was cracked.

Alihahd should have known Hall would champion the past. Those who lived for revenge never forgot.

"What are you thinking of?" Hall asked.

Alihahd leaned back against the rock, his eyes wide, his hands gently, too gently, tracing the grooves in the wall behind him. "My death," he said darkly.

Then he looked up. His face changed. His eyes became clear and his voice blithe. "I was to have been taken alive by the Na'id. I was imagining General Atta"id explaining my death to the Bel. That is all."

Hall gave a wicked smile that was not a smile. "I fear the honored general Atta"id will explain nothing. The honored general is recently deceased."

"Ah," Alihahd said, a lament. He scowled at Hall. *Marauder.* That was never spoken between them. "I regret. He was a good man."

"You mourn your enemies, Captain?"

"I would mourn any good human."

"You've been impersonating the Na'id so long you're beginning to smell like one," Hall said.

"Not everything the Na'id believe in is wrong," Alihahd said. "Part evil isn't necessarily all evil. People who hate cannot see that." He was looking squarely at Hall.

Hall smiled and appealed to the others as his jury. "What is one to make of this? One of the Na'id's most devastating adversaries does not hate them."

"Make of it what you wish," Alihahd said wearily, fingertips to his forehead. "I don't hate anyone. I am so very tired. . . ."

In the muted light before sunrise, in the hour of the eagles, a warrior-priest wearing a yellow robe stepped outside and swept away the debris that had collected in the windpockets on the path overnight. The dawn was the last of the Red Geese. The sun would move into the house of the Twins at the solstice later in the day.

Alihahd sat in a thicket of leatherferns. His eyes were shut, his nostrils catching faint scents of dark green alpine growth, dusty rock, and dry earth in the thin air.

Earth?

Soil, he corrected himself.

The last of the fog had lifted from his mind, and his thoughts ran swift and clear. The heartsick weariness that had hung on him for so long was leaving him tentatively as if he were afraid to give it up. It had so long been a part of him that it hardly seemed natural to be without it.

When you are who I am, there is no such thing as a safe place. He needed to keep that in mind.

A flutter of wings very close made him open his eyes. A bird lighted on his bent knee.

Its heavy, seed-cracking beak parted. *Cheep!*

Alihahd watched it without moving, not quite sure how he felt about being perched on. The bird cocked its scaled head sideways, robin-style, to see him out of the eye on the side of its head.

Cheep.

"Alien," Alihahd croaked at it like an insult.

Cheep.

The bird refolded its wings and shrugged its little shoulders like a man adjusting his coat.

Alihahd guessed he'd been judged an adequate perch.

Chi*reet!* The bird took flight with a flurry of wings and a rattling scolding *trrrrr* as Amerika came bounding up the path holding up her long skirts with one hand above the grass-stained knees of her wide trousers. An empty basket swung on her arm. Burrs clung to her woven cloak that was striped in wide bands of blue and violet. She gave Alihahd a radiant smile as he sighted her. Her cheeks and nose were rosily wind-bitten.

She told him that Ben-Tairre was inviting him on a hunting expedition with his party today.

She took Alihahd's hard gnarled arm in hers and led him to where the hunters were gathering. Harrison White Fox Hall was there. He had words for Alihahd's tunic as Alihahd strode down the slope.

"If my knees were that bony I wouldn't wear a dress."

Alihahd smiled wryly. "I do not wear it for you to admire my legs, Mr. Hall. Who invited you?"

"I invited myself," Hall said. He'd also invited Vaslav, who stood behind him like a small pale shadow. "Should be great sport."

Alihahd lowered his voice. "Though I am not sure of the game here." It was folly to take up this challenge, like following a predator into its lair. Ben-Tairre didn't carry himself like a man making peace.

Ben equipped Alihahd with an Itiri weapon, a beam gun called a taeben, "warrior's eye." Like the never-dull tungsten-plastic swords, the taebens were products of a technology far beyond Iry's. The taeben Alihahd was given was a ronin's. It could be triggered by any hand, whereas the warrior-priests' weapons were keyed to their owners' use alone. Alihahd was told about the animals of the mountain, what to watch for, what to watch out for.

Alihahd was going to watch his back.

The hunting party was Ben-Tairre's fire clan of the carnelian serpent, and five young warrior-priests of the fire clan of the opal sword. They started out on foot down the green-cloaked north slope of the mountain and descended all the way to the timberline where wind-tortured half-trees grew along the ground. Far in the distance ahead loomed the next taller peak, the Guardian.

Alihahd shot at nothing. It was all he could do to keep up and pretend it was easy. And when the hunters stopped to reorganize, Alihahd went apart to rest behind an escarpment. There he could hang his head, bending over, hands on his knees, breathing hard.

Harrison Hall found him there. He leaned carefully against the glittering crag, crossed one leg over the other at the ankles, and regarded Alihahd curiously. "Captain?"

Alihahd spoke very quietly. "I am not doing well, Harry." It was the first and last time he spoke the man's given name.

Hall looked down at the bowed blond head. "Unhealthy posture," he said. "Your lungs can't expand."

"If I stand up, I shall pass out," Alihahd said.

His watery eyes focused on the contorted timberline trees. He began to feel like one of those stunted shapes twisted along the ground. He could see the direction of the prevailing winds from the trees' eastward flagging, but anything actually broken broke southward. It would seem there was a violence that came out of the north.

Loud crunching footsteps made Alihahd straighten up. Vaslav joined them along the scarp. "They say there are berinxes in the area," he said.

"Berinxes?" Alihahd looked to Hall. "Those have the teeth?"

Hall nodded.

And at that moment there came a noise from above, high on the rocks, with a trickle of dislodged sand and pebbles. All three spun with weapons raised, but Alihahd immediately pulled back his own and reached over to hold Vaslav's hand from the trigger.

It was a predator up on the rock outpost—one with slanted coal-dark eyes and a small mouth twisted into a hard contemptuous line in his flat-boned, coldly handsome face. "We are moving again," Ben-Tairre informed them and moved away.

Vaslav drew in a wavering breath and rejoined the hunters.

Hall waited for Alihahd. An insinuating smile crept beneath the mustache, as if he'd caught some secret Alihahd let slip.

"What?" Alihahd said to the smugly knowing look.

"I don't care what you say, Captain, you've been in combat."

Alihahd was much too quick at turning and aiming—as a thing done so often it became reflex—and he was much too good at *not* shooting never to have seen battle.

Alihahd frowned at the weapon in his hands. "Not against Na'id," he repeated and he hiked after the Itiri hunting party.

By the time they started home again, racing their shrinking shadows, Alihahd was lagging behind. He stumbled, skinned his knees on the gravel slope, and didn't get up.

"Shall I carry thee?" Ben asked.

Alihahd stiffened. "No, that is all right. Thank you very much," he said with such a tone of offended aristocracy that it made Harrison Hall laugh.

Ben-Tairre made a pointed gesture of looking at the sun. At this pace they wouldn't reach the Aerie in time. The noonday sun was lethal. Nothing stirred at midday, not even the chitinous lizards with reflective scales. The Itiri were anxious to beat the sun home.

So Alihahd was left behind. The hunters found a sheltering cave where he could wait out the noon hour and continue the journey alone after the deadly time was past.

A lizard crawled off its sunny ledge and went slinking into a dark crevice in the rocks.

The croaking of a reptilian crow split the thin air.

A burr of insects shivered in the heat.

Then there was no sound of anything that was living.

Nothing moved.

Shadows shrank to nothing.

Air sizzled. Brown grasses withered.

Outside the cave was a blistering glare—like the sun on a Mediterranean strand.

The sky boiled. Rocks hissed.

He remembered the sun on the Mediterranean Sea. He thought back farther, to the last time he had been completely sober—thought clearly about things best not remembered.

He curled his knobby thin legs up and hugged his skinned knees as if he were cold. His mind was clear and there was nowhere to hide.

Vaslav paced the north ridge, waiting for Alihahd's return. Hall came out once to stand at his side, coat drawn back from his wasp waist, fists on his narrow hips, empty pipe between his teeth, earrings gleaming against his deep red-bronze skin.

The weather had changed. There was no sign of the captain.

The red flags were out, warning that the winds were picking up and it was ill-advised to go beyond the Aerie's sheltered amphitheater. The shadows had lengthened before the clouds cast them over. The Itiri were flocking home.

Pack beasts honked and gurgled. Itiri voices hushed. Birds stopped singing. The beasts sniffed the air.

Broadside, a pack beast was an ungainly bulk. Face on, its enormous body was an aerodynamic wedge that could withstand a three-hundred-mile-per-hour gale.

All over the mountain the beasts stood aligned toward the north, facing the mountain Guardian.

A cloud. A shadow. A cool breath.

Alihahd woke from a dreaming half-sleep. He wandered

from the cave. He had lost track of time and he could see no shadows. The sky was a white slate.

High, high above came the faint echoes of the clashing wind brass and voices that carried even to this distance: "Off the bridge! *Shandee!*"

Alihahd climbed up to a rocky prominence and gazed up toward the sound, curious.

From over the lofty mountain peaks a swelling cloud loomed and rushed down. The swift wall of gray darkness seemed fast even from far away. It had to be moving in a torrent.

Alihahd was mesmerized by it, like the black cloud over Jerusalem that had come and engulfed him and blotted out the light, everything.

So, frozen, dull, and disbelieving, he stared at this storm that roared like a rocket rain. Its speed was unreal, like a jet stream.

Or *was* it an actual jet stream? He was five miles above sea level.

And then it occurred to him he ought to be running back for cover. But—as at Jerusalem—it was too late for him to go anywhere. The winds were here.

He started for the cave in the last seconds left to him. He jumped from the rocks with a cold spray of sand and grit. He fell hard, pain exploding in his shoulder and shooting in fiery spikes through his body and behind his eyes. He rolled.

He stopped rolling, and opened his eyes to search for the cave, but saw a figure over him, cloaked in storm clouds.

Jinin-Ben-Tairre.

A yank on both arms brought a blaze of pain. Alihahd was lifted like a rag doll. He fell against Ben's body that was almost too hard to be flesh. The blast of wind hit like a truck. They were thrown, flying into sudden still darkness.

Alihahd folded over in pain on the rock floor of the cave as *Shandee* roared past.

At length Alihahd lifted himself onto his knees and looked up.

A moving wall of gray wind thundered past the cave entrance. It appeared as if they were in a speeding vehicle. Outside was a blur. Inside was still.

And Ben was there, snorting. His face looked burned, his broad flat cheeks scored by flying grit. He shook debris from his hair. Upon catching blue eyes directed fixedly his way, he stopped.

Alihahd simply gazed, cornered, his long limbs drawn in and folded to fit the cramped space, his big frame ill accustomed to bending into unaccommodating places. He lacked Itiri grace but was not without his dignity. It never failed him.

He held his one shoulder at an odd slope. His thick lips turned down, furrowing deep frowning lines into his long face, his brow pinched.

Ben moved smoothly to his side and grabbed Alihahd's arm with a twist and a hit and a flash of blinding pain. Alihahd roared and turned to strike with his other hand, until he realized that the pain had suddenly abated as quickly as it had come, down to an aching throb, and he could move his right arm in its socket again.

He wasn't grateful. Anyone who pushed him into harm's way could damn well pull him out and not expect thanks for it.

He withdrew as far as he could to wait out the storm, squared off opposite Ben-Tairre.

Why not just lose me to the wind? Alihahd thought. It would've been a human enough thing to do.

But this being was trying very hard not to be human. He'd been born among humankind, had once answered to a human name. But it wasn't what he wanted to be.

Alihahd could see the struggle inside—a man who was two people—and Alihahd knew the feeling well.

He slumped back against the dank rock wall, rueful at

the situation—caught here, prisoners of the storm, hating one another. *All four of us*.

Ben spied the corners of a sardonic smile, and his head turned a quick hawklike fraction in suspicion. He wouldn't like to think himself a source of humor.

Dark-eyed gaze bored into Alihahd, but didn't penetrate. Alihahd was well practiced at being opaque.

I am older than you. My armor is thicker. Though you are not doing badly for yourself, warrior-priest. I still see a human boy. You hate me.

Alihahd coughed, deep honking spasms that shook his aching shoulder. Then he sat back again, drained, guarded, his blue eyes heavy-lidded.

You hate me. Hatred is fear. But I really cannot see what you fear.

Alihahd was two meters tall, fair and blond like a warrior-priest, but haggard, bone-weary, old, the ruin of a once great man. He let his head tilt to one side.

You fear me? He smiled again. *I am the one defeated here.*

When the winds lifted, Alihahd couldn't walk. He was sick, and weakness forced him to take a humiliating ride up the mountain on the back of a shaggy pack beast.

His illness went on for days, and this time he didn't recover. His breath rattled. He didn't want to leave the lordly inhospitable heights of the Aerie as most humans did, but he realized this place was going to kill him, and finally he asked to be taken down to the summer village Kaletani Mai.

With a cloak wrapped around his emaciated figure, Alihahd retraced the twisting trail to the waiting balloon and climbed, subdued and unhappy, into the woven reed basket.

Harrison Hall came to see him off at the ledge, the place where they had first landed on the Aerie, seemingly a long time ago. He faced into the wind, his redingote open to the breezes that tugged at the moored balloon. He clenched his empty pipe between his white teeth. All the sinuous lines in his dark red face molded into one of those lovely demonic smiles that revealed absolutely nothing. He was sorry to see his adversary get away from him, fallen to another opponent.

Alihahd looked back, bitter. "I don't lose well," he said quietly.

Hall nodded imperceptibly.

Two ranga unfastened the balloon's ropes and threw them to the pilot. Eagles guided the balloon as it lifted off the rocks.

Hall took his pipe from between his teeth. Nodded. "Captain."

"Mr. Hall," Alihahd said.

Jinin-Ben-Tairre was alone in the training hall. Its great wide windows were flooded with sunlight that reflected a honey glow on the butterwood panels. The worn wooden floor was pitted and scarred with sword grooves. Ben knelt, sitting back on his bare feet, his head bowed on his heavily thewed neck, his eyes shut. He tried to clear his mind, think of nothing.

His even breaths deepened, but not into the peace of sleep—deep in anger. He tried to calm his thoughts. Darkness kept stealing into his mind. Angry, suppressed thoughts rose into the clear space. He needed to banish them altogether—the dragons he had never really slain, merely pushed aside for a time.

He opened his eyes, stood, crossed to the sword chest, and took up his blade, *Da'iku*. He glided it through all its possible moves, then began to visualize attackers and cut them apart. They came by twos. He killed by twos. More moved in, all sides. His ivory-gold skin glistened, his black hair matted to his head. His mechanical hand whirred. Invisible necks severed and heads tumbled. Ben rolled, stood, kicked, slashed. Attackers reeled back. He drove straight down with the blade and kicked straight back. He wheeled and cut the air. Movement became random, precision muddied in his savagery.

"Careless, careless, careless," Roniva said from the arch-way.

Ben came to a standstill in the center of the chamber, perspiration streaming down his sides. He blinked sweat from his eyes. He hadn't even heard her come in. His training, his awareness, failed him. *Did she see it?*

Had to.

Such slips could be fatal when one had powerful enemies waiting.

"How may I serve thee, Fendi?"

"Thou hast hurt my guest," Roniva said.

There was danger when a Fendi spoke face-to-face. Direct speech from the monarch was reserved for certain messages which brooked no intermediary. Roniva hadn't spoken to Ben-Tairre since the day she had become Fendi of the Aerie. This moment had been long in coming. Ben knew what this meeting meant. Time had come. *Setkaza.* Legend called it dance of death. It was an ancient right to be invoked when there were no more options. Declaration gave one leave to kill at any time—and opened oneself to being killed at any time by one's declared opponent.

"Thou hast killed my cheela. Thou hast killed my son. Thou hast driven away my guest," Roniva said, the whites of her eyes flashing in her ebony face. She wore a long flowing tunic of shimmering green. It left bare and free her thin whipcord-sinewed arms. Her hand was on her sword hilt.

"He is evil," Ben-Tairre said.

"I wanted him *here!*" Roniva cried as she drew her sword in a furious arc and jabbed its point into the floor. She stepped back from the blade, her fists at her sides, her voice a strained tremulous quiet. "From this moment we are bound in setkaza, thou and I. Look to thine own resources, Wolf, for thy days are numbered from today."

PART TWO:

Ben

6. Wolf at the Door

Gregorian Year 5839 CE

IN THE YEAR OF THE TOPAZ GATEWAY, in the days before Roniva became Fendi of the Aerie, a small stowaway was found aboard Xanthan's spaceship when the young warrior returned to Iry after a year's journey among the stars.

"*Azo!* What hast thou brought to us, Xanthan?" Roniva said as her warrior cheela stepped from his ship into the yellow grass of Lower Aerie.

"What have I . . . ?" Xanthan echoed in puzzlement and turned back to his ship.

A starved, wild-eyed boy stared out through the hatchway at the sunlit village Kaletani Mai and the towering mountains.

"By the fire of my making!" Xanthan exclaimed, and the boy pulled back with a start.

Roniva advanced to him. Her swordbelt jingled with her stride. Sunshine cast a blue sheen on her hair. She leaned in and sniffed at the boy, who drew down into a wolfish crouch. He smelled bad. "What is it?" Roniva asked.

Xanthan stammered. "I—I meant not to bring him. He is a human being. One of the Earth breed."

The boy emerged from the ship cautiously to crouch in the warm sunshine. His ribs stood out in high relief under translucent sickly yellow skin. Coal-dark eyes smoldered deep in his skull-like head. He snarled at Roniva and ran past her to throw his stick arms around Xanthan's waist and locked his fingers together. Xanthan placed his hand gently on the boy's dirty black hair.

Xanthan was lovely, his tender eyes soft green like the sea, his flaxen hair braided into a crown, his skin smooth and unaged. The boy was in love.

Roniva pressed the back of her forefinger to her lips, speculative. Her onyx signet left a fleeting imprint of a sword there when she took her hand away again. "What doth it call itself for a name?"

"I know not. I found him in a trash heap. I fed him and let him go," Xanthan said.

Xanthan *thought* he had let the child go. He bowed his head to meet the oddly shaped dark eyes at his waist. "What is thy name?"

Sunlight glistened on the bright edges of Xanthan's clean golden hair. It made a shining corona around his angelic face. The boy gazed up at the face and clung fast to his silence.

"Doth it speak?" Roniva asked.

"He hath a voice. I have not heard him to speak."

Xanthan had heard the boy yowl and snarl and screech.

"Perhaps it hath no mind," Roniva suggested. Her arms jangled with enameled bracelets as she reached out to touch the boy's head. He snarled and bit her hand.

Roniva jerked back, flashed anger, and smacked him down the nose with her open palm.

His face turned up, cold and twisted, into a vindictive mockery of a smile. He'd known she was going to hit him. But he'd got her first.

The Elders who had come behind Roniva agreed they had never seen anything that untamed, that dangerous.

"Shalt thou kill it, Xanthan?" one asked. "It is distorted."

Roniva licked her punctured hand. "I will kill it."

The boy, without letting go of Xanthan's waist, skittered around behind the warrior and peered out with a pinched glowering face.

"Ah, it understands," Roniva said. "It doth have a mind, if not a name."

One of the other Elders spoke. "Then we cannot kill it."

"It is a *guest*?" Roniva cried.

"How can it be else? Xanthan brought it here."

The stinking little creature thrust the lower lip of his small mouth at them, angry.

Roniva leaned forward, her hands on her knees so her eyes were level with his. "Thou art vicious, and I shall call thee Wolf for lack of a name."

"What is to be done with it?" an Elder asked.

Xanthan reddened. "I brought him. I shall take care of him."

"It will die on the mountain," Roniva said.

Another said, "Leave it here with the ranga. They will feed it. The rest is for its own devices."

The other Elders agreed. And that was to be the final word on the human boy, Wolf.

No one counted on him following Xanthan up the mountain.

When the hungry, frenzied, mangy-haired thing peered over the rock at the top of the snake path, a ranga woman screamed and dropped her water jug. Clay shattered, water splashed, and the ranga woman ran on stubby legs, shrieking that she had seen a monster.

A crowd gathered to see the monster. Xanthan pushed to the fore because he had an awful feeling that he knew what he would find.

His skinny foundling, hands and feet torn and bleeding from the climb, crawled over the last step onto the Ledge Path. The boy searched the staring faces and picked out his ivory-and-gold god Xanthan from the throng. The boy's dark eyes were wide in abandonment and asking why. He couldn't understand what he'd done to be left behind.

And the boy didn't know why all these other beings had come out onto the terraces to stare at him. They gazed at him in hushed awe. He didn't know what he'd done.

What he had done was to begin turning into a warrior-priest.

Aghara children came to the mountain by instinct. Drawn to the Aerie like spawning salmon on Earth. They answered an impulse to be with their own kind. From all parts of the world they hunted the hidden valley and climbed the mountain to become warrior-priests. Or die trying.

Xanthan blurted out before thinking, "I want to make him a warrior-priest."

"That?" The voice was Roniva's.

The boy scratched his runny nose. His hand left a smear of blood there.

Xanthan looked up to the second level where Roniva stood. "He hath the heart."

"Thou mistakest madness for courage," Roniva said more gently.

An Elder's hand came to rest on the nape of Xanthan's neck. "A human child, Xanthan? He will die."

"He doth not want to die. I will not let him," Xanthan said.

"He will endure not the ordeals. At best he will bore."

"Then let him bore," Xanthan said, feeling utterly alone. He thought his was a natural decision. What great foolishness did the others see that he did not? "Let him fail for himself and return to his own kind of his own choice. He came here like a warrior cheela."

As he was speaking, everyone turned away, and Xanthan's blood turned cold, knowing who approached. The crowd parted.

The berinx padded through the parted way on heavy paws with lowered head, its fanged jaws agape and drooling. It stopped in front of the Earth boy, shook its brindle mane, yawned wide, and sat with a woof like a real berinx.

"Where is thy master, Chaulin?" Xanthan asked in weary ritual.

The berinx snarled. *Thy master also.*

The Fendi came slowly in his familiar's wake. He wore his naxa cloak thrown over one straight shoulder, its chain passing under his sword arm. His cloak was always black now. His wispy hair was too thin to be bound. He held himself strictly erect as one who begins to feel gravity too much.

Eyes like hard green glass chips fastened their gaze upon Xanthan, then upon the little Earthling.

The Fendi extended his blue-tinged, fragile-looking hand. The boy made to bite it, but, quick as a katalin's wing-beat, the aged Fendi closed his grip on the boy's lower jaw and held it unyieldingly.

He turned the child's head first to one side, then the other, examining his face, his yellow skin, his exotic eyes sunk deep in his hunger-stark skull.

Finally, the Fendi released the Earthchild's jaw with a slight firm push that prevented the creature from snapping at his withdrawing hand.

The Fendi turned slowly to pat the head of his fanged berinx. He talked to it. "If he climbed up the mountain, then he can climb back down in his own time." The Fendi's hard glittering green eyes slid to his youngest warrior-priest. "Xanthan, he is thy cheela."

Xanthan stared, blank, for a long moment, then smiled and looked to his new cheela in joy.

The boy knew the meaning of smiles. Something good had happened. Lovely Xanthan was happy. The boy started to return a wan grin gapped with missing baby teeth.

Then his eyes rolled back, and he crumpled to the path in a dead faint.

7. Wolf by the Hearth

5839–5850 CE

XANTHAN CAME TO THE BEDSIDE in the ranga cave and watched his sick cheela. Asleep, the child looked even younger than he actually was. His closed eyes were smoky-ringed in his starved face. He took up such a tiny corner of the wide mattress.

Then the eyes opened, dark like a ranga's and slanted like no other creature's in the world. The boy blinked sleepily.

"How is it with thee, Earthchild?" Xanthan asked.

The boy's black brows lowered at the name Earthchild. His tiny bow mouth curved down so hard his chin puckered. His little fists balled, and he sat up and spat in hatred of his own kind. He made it clear he was not an Earthchild. He bit his upper lip and glowered at Xanthan.

"Be thou then no more an Earthling," Xanthan said. "Only let go thine hatred."

The boy fell back on the bed, exhausted.

"I have something for thee," Xanthan said. He held up a closed hand.

The boy uncurled his scrawny claw fingers to receive the blue gemstone Xanthan dropped into his palm. The boy brought it up close under his eyes and watched the stone move with his pulse.

"Lapis is thy courage and thy will," Xanthan said. "That is one. There are eight. When thou hast eight, thou wilt walk the fire."

The boy grabbed Xanthan's ring hand and pulled it to him to inspect the warrior's carved signet stone. "That comes ninth." Xanthan smiled. "Not till thou art a warrior. That is for my clan—the topaz twins. We walked only two years ago. I am a very new warrior."

As he was speaking, a white bird appeared from nowhere and alighted on Xanthan's shoulder. The boy gave a startled cry. Unperturbed, the dove preened a snowy wing, puffed up its ruff, and rearranged its long plumed tail. "My familiar," Xanthan told the child. "That comes tenth—I know not from where."

The boy frowned dubiously.

"This creature I have named Asha," Xanthan said. "What is thy name, my cheela? I need something to call thee."

But the boy wouldn't speak. His hand clamped shut over his gemstone, and he retreated under the covers.

"Please tell me," Xanthan said. "Or they will call thee Wolf."

The boy nodded, his native gesture of approval. His lips were pursed, his brows knit, but not unhappily. Wolf would do fine for a name.

The first thing Wolf needed to learn, if he was to be mute, was the way of silent speech. There were many signs and attitudes in use, so he could go a long way without speaking. And it was well that he spurned the chatter of little birds and ranga. Eagles and warrior-priests soared silent and alone. A warrior-priest didn't disturb the silence without a reason.

Wolf was soon healthy again. Flesh covered his ribs, and his skin turned from sickly yellow to an odd but vital sun-darkened brown gold.

Once Wolf was fit, Xanthan began to tap on his door in the mornings.

"*Sae duun. Sae duun*, cheela."

The boy was always outside on the first tap. Then Xanthan didn't need to tap at all. Wolf was awake ahead of the dawn and listening for Xanthan's footsteps. Xanthan would approach with soundless tread, and still the boy was outside.

For the first year he did no fighting, but learned to fall and jump and listen and feel and see and breathe. He had already had a great deal of martial training among humans. It was obvious in the way he used his inner strength and the way he moved—not sticklike and unnatural in the usual human fashion.

In the first year, Xanthan was learning as well, discovering the oddities of his small charge.

Xanthan woke, the first time of many times, in the dead of night in his solitary cave on Aerieside to find Wolf asleep, curled under the blanket at the foot of his bed.

Xanthan lifted him by his shoulders to face him.

Sleepy eyes blinked back.

Xanthan's white skin was smoothed cold like marble in the dim starshine that spilled into the cave. His warrior's gemstones gleamed darkly in the polished rock wall. Xanthan told the boy his place was across the way at Haven with the ranga.

The boy shared a cave with eight male ranga, as most aghara did while they were children. The ranga lived in heaps. Warriors lived alone. Wolf cared for neither arrangement. He wanted to be with Xanthan.

Xanthan would wrap a cloak around Wolf and send him back to Havenside, except when the wind brass sounded. Then Xanthan would either carry him across the swinging bridge himself, or let him stay, breathing softly at the foot of the bed.

The next surprise came on a cool and breezy day in what passed for summer on the mountain when Xanthan took his cheela hunting runner-birds.

Xanthan soon spotted a trail, and he trotted over the ridges and down the gullies and inclines in pursuit, his cheela dogging him faithfully.

Then the trail split, a bird and mate. Xanthan told Wolf to take the low trail. Xanthan would climb the steep rocks. And Xanthan bounded up the treacherous rise. The boy just stood in the ragged brown grass, bewildered. Xanthan stopped on his rock perch, perplexed and annoyed. "Follow thou, before it fades!"

The boy turned a complete circle, searching for something fading.

Xanthan became cross. "Art thou blind?"

As soon as the words were out, the young warrior recalled something spoken once of humans being blind. He leaped down the rocks and rolled in the grass at Wolf's feet. He jumped up. "Come thou with me."

They abandoned the hunt and returned to the Aerie. Xanthan sought his own master, Roniva.

"Azo!" Xanthan saluted the Elder with his sword fist on his left palm. "Hanina, knowest thou of humankind?"

"I know some small thing." She strolled across the cave and ran her fingers through Wolf's hair. It was coarse and black like her own. Wolf had learned by now not to bite everyone who tried to touch him. "Ask thou," she bid her warrior.

"Are humans somehow blind?" Xanthan asked.

"Heat blind," Roniva said. "Infrared they cannot see. They see one octave only. The lower frequencies are invisible to them. To thine wolf, this cave is dark."

Xanthan was numb with shock.

"Knowest thou wherefore I opposed thee, cheela-nu?" Roniva said as Xanthan began to realize how difficult a task he had taken upon himself in this human cheela. A cheela needed every sense and every strength and skill he had to become a warrior-priest. "I wanted not to see thee break thine heart." Roniva drew her saffron shawl around her and stepped out of the cave into the wind.

Xanthan turned to his cheela and took his glowing hot face in his hands. The boy must have some other strength somewhere, something only humans had. Xanthan sensed it pulsing between his hands, knew it as he knew some part of his spirit would transcend death, knew it without having any reason to believe. The boy had to have something else. He must.

Because Xanthan, like all warriors, could not fail and live.

It was Roniva who taught Wolf to write and to count in the Itiri way. "It uses its left hand," she said to Xanthan. "Mark thou on that?"

Xanthan had noticed. The boy would carry a sword in his left hand. "It—" Xanthan began, then caught himself. *It.*

Roniva smiled with white teeth and admonished, "I trapped thee in my circle, Xanthan. Be thou more careful."

"Yes, hanina."

"And feed it." She squeezed the boy's arm. "It needs to be fatter."

"I fear the winter," Xanthan admitted.

Roniva demurred. "Not if it be fat. I wish I were built like thine creature. Its stock cometh from mountains. Look thou at it. How short its fingers and toes. How flat its face. How thin and small its lips. How short it is. Its blood has less a journey from its heart and will not cool. See the fold of fat over its eyelids. Those eyes will never freeze, nor that flat nose. Its stature looks as if it will broaden if he grows. I would spend my winters easier had I that build and those fingers and toes." The tall, lithe warrior-priestess felt the cold quickly in her long tapered extremities if she didn't bid her heart to work faster. "He hath mountain eyes like mine. Dark eyes burn not in the light at these heights where the air is too thin to blunt light's cutting edge."

Xanthan blinked his kohl-lined green eyes. "He."

"Cheela?"

"Thou said he."

"Ah." Roniva spread her long spidery fingers. "I am weary of thine savage. Take it with thee and go."

Wolf survived the winters well, and in the year of the Topaz Beacon, Xanthan began to teach him to fight with his open hands.

Days were idyllic on the mountain, and, with no other humans around him to remind him, Wolf started to forget, truly forget, what he was.

Then, in the year of the Topaz Serpent, humans were brought to the Aerie. They'd been found drifting in space without power, victims of a war humankind was waging across the stars.

Wolf hated them.

"But they are thy kind," Roniva said.

Wolf motioned a negative. He would not be human.

"The girl, perhaps?" Xanthan said. "Thou wilt need a mate someday."

No. No. No.

And to Wolf's bitter glee, the humans couldn't endure the cold winds on the rugged mountaintop. All but one of them retreated to the mild climate of the Lower Aerie, so Wolf did not have to look at them.

Only the one named Montserrat stayed, a timid woman, full grown, who kept to herself on Havenside.

Wolf wouldn't hurt her. Such would violate his emerald. He took out the stone and gazed into its clear green crystal whenever the hatred boiled up inside him. The emerald was for kindness. Wolf had been given the gemstone for his generosity to the eagles. The boy had an affinity for the talassairi.

He still didn't talk. He howled if he was hurt or left alone. He still came to the foot of Xanthan's bed at night—so stealthily that the warrior sometimes didn't waken. All those practices came to an end in the winter of the Topaz Serpent.

Wolf was given his own cheela-cave on Havenside. It was a small solitary chamber, a proper home for a warrior in training.

Wolf hated it worse than he hated the cave full of ranga males. He spent little time in it.

But he had no choice come winter, when, on the eighth of the River, Shandee returned for its annual maraud, and all activity came to a standstill and everyone took to his home as the deadly jet wind raged through the mountain peaks nonstop for twenty days.

Wolf had never spent twenty days alone before.

The forsaken pleading in his eyes when Xanthan shut the door on him to seal his shelter haunted Xanthan back to his own winter prison.

Shandee howled. Or was it the boy? Sometimes Xanthan could hear both and thought his heart would break.

After five days he heard only Shandee.

At the end of twenty days, in the abrupt silence of the winter wind's leaving, Xanthan burst from his cave in a flurry of snow and sailed across the bridgeless crevasse with a running cat's leap to dig out his cheela from the pilcs of blown snow.

The cave door opened with the cracking of ice.

Xanthan saw nothing at first in the dark cave, then perceived the heat aura of the solitary figure in the corner. Wolf was alive. But he didn't move, or whimper, or fly into Xanthan's arms. The boy was silent, his eyes open. He was there, but not there, lost somewhere inside himself.

Xanthan hugged him and cried, "Come back. Come thee back."

But Wolf stayed rigid through the nightfall, and Xanthan carried him back to Aerieside on the new bridge, set him at the foot of his own bed, and waited. The boy didn't curl up there. He'd always curled up. He stared at the ceiling.

Xanthan caught him up, held his stiff unyielding form,

and cried on his black hair. "Oh, little Wolf, what hast thou done to me? Who ever had such a stupid cheela?"

"I am not stupid."

Xanthan was shocked out of his tears. "What sayest thou?" he whispered.

Calm eyes riveted to his, and Wolf spoke distinctly. "I am not stupid."

Xanthan couldn't speak. The boy was perfectly composed. "I will drink now," he said, and Xanthan gave him water. Then Wolf said, "I will eat now."

And when he was fed, he returned to his lonely cave and slept.

He never came to crawl into Xanthan's bed again to sleep at his master's feet, and Xanthan was very sorry for that, the last gentleness gone from the child. Wolf had been taught to stay by himself, and Xanthan wondered if it hadn't been a mistake.

Wolf now cherished his solitude with a vicious fervor. Patience he also acquired. It was a weird and unworldly kind of patience, not like turquoise at all, and he took hurt without sound. This wasn't the peace of eagles. This was fire in the mountain.

He was a different Wolf ever after, grown, with an Itiri warrior's reserve and dignity. The ranga said Shandee was still on the mountain and that it lurked within him. They sensed something odd in his kind of quietude.

And the eagles were afraid of him.

In the year of the Topaz River, Wolf was taught his first weapon. It was a sword, the tungsten-plastic kind. "When thou wilt walk the fire, this will be thine," Xanthan told him.

Wolf ran his palm along the flat of the ancient blade, his dark eyes alight.

Xanthan's white bird trilled on its perch over the lintel by an inset ruby rose.

"Why do we not teach a sword to wield itself?" Xanthan posed the question to his cheela.

Wolf scowled. He pulled at the cuffs of his rough-woven cheela's tunic. He'd outgrown another one. "Because it is impossible," he said.

"No," Xanthan said. "Had we want, we would find a way. Thine answer shows a want of thought. Topaz is wisdom. Thou hast it not."

"Then I don't know why we don't teach swords to wield themselves," Wolf said.

"Because a sword hath no virtue," Xanthan said.

Wolf wore his virtues on a leather thong around his right wrist. He had four: lapis for courage, emerald for kindness, diamond for honor, zircon for modesty. Xanthan closed his hand over the bracelet and squeezed Wolf's wrist. The stones bit into his brown flesh. "Keep these little stones in mind when thou hast thine own sword," Xanthan said.

He showed Wolf a few simple moves with the sword and let him practice until his wrist and forearm tired. Then Xanthan brought him the felt cover in which to wrap the sword and replace it in its scented wood chest.

Wolf's eyelids fluttered uneasily at the covering. "The Gurkha never sheaths his kukri unblooded."

Xanthan asked, "Art thou one of these Gurkha?"

"There is one in my ancestry," said Wolf. "My brother owns a kukri. There is much blood on the blade."

"It's a foolish custom," Xanthan said, enclosing the tungsten-plastic sword in red felt. "How is one to practice with one's actual weapon? Thy Gurkha brother must have many scars."

Wolf was about to speak and suddenly frowned, as if catching himself at something forbidden. "I forget," he said.

In the year of the Topaz Veil, Wolf was taught his last weapon, the taeben. The Itiri called the beam guns "eyes" because the taeben were useful and powerful, and they lured their users into letting their other talents atrophy. Relying solely on a taeben was seductively easy.

"A gun is a coward's weapon," Xanthan said. "Any child

can kill with a gun. It is also thy most powerful weapon, not thy sword. The sword is art. The sword is discipline. The gun is life and death."

Wolf had handled guns before and became quickly expert. He was also quick to put the taeben aside and polish his other skills. He didn't like the weapon. Guns were too human.

As the short years passed, Wolf was becoming a young man. His frame broadened as Roniva had predicted, and his muscles filled out with great strength and un-Itiri bulk. He stretched hard to keep his form sleek. Bulging thews were for Earthmen.

And toward the close of the Topaz hexadecade, more Earthlings were brought to the Aerie, refugees of the human war. They were surprised to find a human cheela among the legendary warrior-priests, and the young women thought him breathtaking. Wolf was disturbed and confused, and he kept his distance from them, which made him all the more attractive.

He stood on the highest level of Aerieside, glowering across the crevasse, his head held high, his disdainful slanted eyes directed downward. He wore only dark trousers, a sash belt, and a wide red band across his forehead to keep his human sweat from his eyes. His arms were crossed defensively over his bare chest. And the girls peered up at him from the lower level of Haven and giggled.

"What is wrong with them?" Wolf said.

Xanthan crouched beside him on one knee, his sword planted point down before him like a staff. "What is wrong with thee, cheela-nu?" he said. "Thou art bright as plague fever."

Wolf's heat aura glowed vividly about him to Itiri eyes. "Be this something human?"

Wolf burned more brightly still. And scarlet blushed down his neck and chest. "I am not human," he said.

Xanthan considered the young females across the way.

They were a varied group in color and size. Xanthan didn't know what was the desirable standard for humans. Itiri came in two basic types only—the tall, slender, blond, green-eyed aghara, and the short, stocky, red-haired, black-eyed ranga. Humans came in all sorts. "Thou findest none of them an acceptable mother for thine child?"

"No. I am Itiri."

"Thou canst not give child to an Itiri woman," Xanthan said.

"Then I will have no mate," Wolf said. "I need no children."

"Thy choice," Xanthan said.

In the year of the Carnelian Sword, to begin the new hexadccadc, Xanthan embarked on a trek with his cheela on foot across the mountains to visit outlying ranga villages and show Wolf there was more to Iry than one mountain and one valley. They were gone for four years.

When they returned, Wolf would have been twenty-one years old by Earth count. By Iry count, he was thirty-four. Onto his leather bracelet Wolf had added turquoise, which was patience, topaz, which was wisdom, and sapphire, which was control and strength.

At nightfall, Xanthan came to Wolf's chamber and sat at the foot of his bed. Wolf rose in puzzlement.

A cold wind of coming winter moaned outside.

In the almost dark, Wolf could see his master's beloved face, soft eyes, and golden hair braided into a crown. Angels looked so in the dim early memory of gentle times when Wolf was still a baby and carried a human name.

Xanthan pressed a pebble into his hand in the dark. Wolf held it up to see fiery-colored flecks within a milky white blaze. The colors shifted in the hearthlight. An opal, which was integrity, soundness, and wholeness. The gem was his eighth. The last. His training as a cheela was over.

Xanthan bowed his beautiful head, his face happy, sad, proud, and troubled. "When the spring cometh, the fire is for thee."

8. Wolf in the Fire

THE PLACE OF FIRE was open to the sky. Its hearthstones had been laid into a level breezeless garden court where its flame burned upright, though the slopes beyond it were blasted by stiff winds that bared the rocks. Sharp crags isolated the fire garden. It was a difficult approach from whichever way one tried.

Wide, flat squares of marble checkered the courtyard, alternating red and black. Leathery plants circled round about the sanctuary or trailed inside it on tendriled vines. At one side of the square an ancient spring still bubbled to life from time to time. Heat from the water flowing hidden within the rocks kept the snow from sticking here.

The tiles at the center of the courtyard were discolored where flames had licked and where sooty feet had trod.

In the year of the Carnelian Beacon, on the first of the Sword, only one cheela was walking. That was not proper. But the one was expected to fail.

Not to taint the fire for others, Wolf would go alone.

The Elders ringed the court. Painted kohl lines extended

in flowing curves from their eyes and drew lashes down to the broken red scars on their cheeks. They wore eight jewels in their hair with their Elder's stars. Their swords lay unsheathed across their knees as they sat cross-legged on the marble. Their familiars crouched, perched, or sat to their left sides.

The warrior-priests who were not Elders sat with their fire clans. There were no ranga here. This was the one place ranga couldn't go. But no fretful mother and father would be hovering in the snow at the sanctuary boundary this time.

Wolf gazed into the flames. His trousers were rolled up and tied below his knees. Around his head he wore a red band. Around his neck he wore a thin leather strip which he would untie on the far side of the firepit.

A walk through fire. Easily done if done at all.

Xanthan waited on the far side with his own clan of the topaz twins. He was angrier than Wolf had ever seen him, upset that his cheela's walk was to be solo, that no celebration was prepared, that everyone was already trying to forget this day.

Wolf tried to catch his eye. *Watch this!* But Xanthan couldn't see through the wall of heat above the fire.

Wolf tossed back his head. *I am Itiri. I shall not burn.* And he stepped into the fire.

He smelled it before he felt it. Pain and utter shock arrived at once.

Wolf leaped from the firepit and fell to the marble tiles hard on his knees. He dropped over onto his side, writhing in pain, digging his fingers into his thighs as if to cut himself off from his charred, oozing black-and-red feet.

Repulsed and embarrassed faces were turning away.

Wolf ran, scrambled, from the place of fire, out of their sight and into the snow. He tumbled down a jagged embankment and landed in a drift.

He buried his face in the icy snow, breathing fast, the pain inside greater than the searing throb of his burns that racked his body and made him tremble and sweat in the cold.

All his agony and shame couldn't change what happened. And it happened over and over with every blink of his eyes, branded into his mind.

Ice melted on his feverish skin. With a will born of extremity, he blotted out the physical pain. It was not there, so he gave it no mind. No mind at all. Nerves brought pain pulses to tap at his brain and found the gates locked fast.

He rested, breathing, trying not to think. There was only one thought.

Clouds moved in, closing up the sky. The snows would return.

After an eternity, Wolf tore his red headband in two and wrapped his ravaged feet in the rags. Then he hiked the tortuous blowing path back to Aerie.

On the high terrace he caught sight of a tall slender figure dressed in plain brown, hooded, arms folded into wide sleeves. All Wolf could see of her was her blue-black feet. Roniva was in mourning.

Wolf was puzzled. She would not be mourning him, so who? Who was dear to Roniva?

Wolf's heart caught.

No. What had to be could not be. Wolf forbade it. No! NO!

Roniva's hooded form moved like a shadow, retreating from his sight.

Wolf stumbled to her at a hobbling run. She didn't stop for him. One did not speak to the hooded, but Wolf fell to his knees as he reached her and he cried, "Where is my master?"

Roniva's eyes were hidden, the hood pulled far forward. She continued away, soundless.

Wolf clutched at the hem of her long sleeve and held fast. "Where is Xanthan?" he screamed.

The hooded figure stopped, withdrew a spidery hand from her opposite sleeve, and pointed a long black finger to the bridge, where a ranga woman was weeping and yanking out tufts of her red hair and tossing flowers, gems, and pretty things into the crevasse. Wolf knew her. She was Xanthan's mother.

Roniva pulled her cloak out of Wolf's numbed grip and walked away with spectral steps.

Wolf crawled down the terraces to the bridge. A whining snarl squeezed from his tightening throat as he grasped the ropes, and Xanthan's mother fled in terror.

Wolf dragged himself onto the bridge and clutched at the scattered flowers she had left. He whined at the pretty flowers, tears coursing down his cheeks. "Why? Why? Why?" He collapsed in sobs.

He couldn't see downward. Tears blurred everything in that direction. He tried to look over the edge where Xanthan had gone, where Wolf was supposed to go now. He was expected to jump.

Just as he'd been expected to fail.

In sudden fury he was on his feet. Crushed blossoms fell off the knees of his trousers. He ran from the bridge and away from the Aerie on wounds that felt nothing as the spring snow began to fall.

Warmth came late to the Aerie. The snows quit in the mountains and true spring came at last, without Xanthan, and without Wolf. It was assumed that Wolf had gone off alone to kill himself in his own way. The season passed in fleeting brilliance.

The valley was still cloaked in summer when autumn crept quickly over the mountain. Seasonal grasses turned red and gold. Desiccated plants crumbled to ash. Winged keys and clouds of tufted seeds drifted and tumbled in the brittle wind. Eaglets flew. The berinxes left the high slopes, and a sharp burned-wood smell hung in the air. Burrowers went into hibernation, and Itiri stocked their caves with food. Soon Shandee would be upon them again.

He appeared over the summit on scarred feet after a cold rain, come like a dark spirit, changed.

He was taller, his chest deeper, the youth fully a man. The leather thong of a fire walker was still tied around his thick neck. He stood above the Aerie.

The berinx padded up the high trail, its thick brindle coat catching burrs, its long tongue hanging from the side of its heavy jaws. It woofed at the rogue cheela.

"Where is thy master, Chaulin?" Wolf said.

The Fendi's familiar couldn't snarl its ritual answer: *Thy master also.*

The rogue cheela had no master. Wolf ought not to be here.

He ought to be dead. The berinx didn't know what to say. It scratched at its mane in distracted confusion, then vanished. The burrs from its fur fell to the ground.

The Fendi came slowly up the path the berinx had taken. The Fendi's glass-green eyes were narrowed to slivers against the drying air. Moisture came hard to old eyes. Withered hands held thick cloaks around his slight, once-powerful body.

Wolf crouched before the monarch in an attitude of humble favor and asked to walk the fire again.

"Never done."

The answer wasn't the Fendi's. It was the Elder Roniva who spoke. She stood behind the Fendi and placed another cloak over his head and shoulders.

"Never done because never tried," the Fendi said, his voice a whisper in the thin air. "Never asked. No one ever lived to try again. It was not because of a law."

"Natural law," Roniva said.

"If natural law can be broken, it is the law, not the violation, that is wrong." The Fendi beckoned his berinx. It appeared at his side out of the air. The old man scratched the beast's ruff. "I must consult the archives," he told his familiar. "Something must govern this matter."

* * *

The Great Chamber was a nine-sided place with a great gray stone dome, tall lancet windows, fluted pilasters of colored granite, and opalescent white alabaster fittings. A fire blazed in the hexagonal firepit set into the floor of honeycombed red tiles. Black smoke sooted the high dome.

For a second attempt to become a warrior-priest, requirements were three. For the first, the cheela must combat a full warrior-priest and win. The volunteer for combat was Sentalla of the fire clan of the topaz twins.

Smell of deadly intent hung close and tense in the wide chamber. Wolf tested his grip on his sword. He crouched on a black hexagonal tile across the Great Chamber from his warrior foe. Wolf's black hair was cut short, out of his eyes and off his ears. His wrists and right forearm were wrapped in leather. The soles of his feet were rosined to keep him from slipping on the stones that had been polished to a glassy sheen.

Wolf had nothing to lose here. He was, to his own mind, already dead. All from now was gain, and he was free. He had only to let himself do what his self knew to do. Anger he had locked away in some deep part of him. An angry warrior defeats himself in combat, Xanthan had told him.

Sentalla had a personal grudge in this battle.

At the command to begin, Wolf swung his sword and sprang across the floor with a screech, but Sentalla had already fled his place on an oblique line and turned to slash at Wolf's flank. Swords met with a dull clash, then strained crossbar to crossbar. Both pushed and sprang back out of sword's reach to circle more warily now, having failed at their first shock tactics.

They stalked, feinted, shifted feet. Sentalla's sword switched hands. Wolf charged in with a yell. Sentalla parried, countered, was blocked, and danced away.

Wolf screamed again, leaped, slashed.

Sentalla sidestepped, placing his blade into Wolf's flying path.

Wolf batted the sword away with his own, turned in the air, and landed facing Sentalla.

Sentalla danced lightly back and circled. He had done really nothing yet, watching. He was nearly ready. He had seen enough. His jade-green eyes took in all of his opponent at once.

His beloved Xanthan had always said that his fire brother used his eyes too much.

Wolf circled behind the blazing firepit and disappeared from Sentalla's view behind its rising curtain of heat.

Sentalla approached the pit cautiously, eyes darting both ways, ready for whichever direction Wolf might reappear. Sentalla circled the firepit silently to his left, but Wolf circled also, staying exactly opposite him across the pillar of heat.

Among the spectators, Roniva bolted to her feet and stood like a quaking statue. She could see that Sentalla didn't know—Xanthan had never told him—that Xanthan's cheela was half blind. *Heat blind*.

The odd thing with this blindness was that it left no veils before Wolf's eyes. The heat barrier over the fire was only opaque to one of them. Wolf couldn't see the heat. He could see *through* it. Roniva wanted to shriek a warning. It wasn't her battle.

Sentalla, he can see you!

The fire crackled and spat up sparks.

Wolf crouched to leap, neither left nor right, but straight over the firepit. Few warriors would risk a blind attack. For Wolf it wasn't blind.

He sprang.

Wolf appeared out of the wall of heat, silent, and suddenly *there*, blade slicing. He turned at the last instant to smack Sentalla across the midriff with the flat of the sword hard enough to stagger the warrior.

"Stop!" the ancient Fendi cried, and his berinx appeared between the combatants to divide them. "That is a victory."

Sentalla was winded and scored with two long curving

red lines across his belly. Had Wolf not turned his blade, he would have sliced Sentalla in two.

Wolf blinked soot from his eyes, slightly dazed, victorious. He didn't move from his place.

Someone came to take the sword that was not yet his from him. Wolf's short fingers uncurled slowly from the grip, reluctant.

"Thy mercy does thee credit," an Elder said, wrapping the sword in felted cloth and taking it away. It was the first thing anyone had deigned to say to him directly since his return.

Wolf lowered his eyes and bowed his head.

His hair was singed, the edges curled up in thin coils that broke off with a touch. A black hand reached over to brush him off. It was Roniva. She sniffed at the burned stench. "Very resourceful, my cheela's cheela. Making a virtue of handicap."

"Hanina," Wolf acknowledged.

Roniva was dressed all in black bedizened with diamonds. She ran her hand across the shimmering stones. "But where are thine?"

His diamonds, she was asking. His honor. She meant he should have suicided for honor's sake instead of subjecting everyone to this insanity when he should know he could not succeed. Should not have succeeded if he were a true Itiri warrior-priest.

"My honor is that I cannot know defeat," Wolf said.

Roniva clamped her teeth and lips tight. The thought, the possibility was daunting—the existence of a thing that never breaks, that could come crawling out of the lowest gutter and prevail.

The Itiri had never conceived of a mythical phoenix. Such a creature didn't exist even in Itiri dreams. The tasks to reach his goal were impossible.

And Wolf was a third of the way there.

Wolf piloted an airplane to the primitive side of the planet where rain forests grew thick and ranga hadn't produced an aghara offspring in so long that the idea of tall blond warrior-priests wasn't even in their memory.

For his second trial Wolf had been given a labor. All the Elders had conferred and at last bid him bring the claw of the leopard of Ma-pall-mo.

So Wolf came to the village Ma-pall-mo, the Springs, where the chameleon-skinned ranga were dark most of the day in the bright equatorial sun and white at sundown. They were afraid to venture into the jungle anymore, day or night. They gathered where Wolf came to land, awed by the flying machine and its pilot, a tall man who remained dark in the dark.

They said the gods sent him to kill the leopard.

Silly superstitious ranga.

They told Wolf, "We black our skin with coal in the dark so it does not see us. It smells us.

"We mask ourselves with jungle herbs so it does not smell us. It hears us.

"Now the gods send you dark and odd-smelling and silent as the leopard itself."

"I was sent to kill the leopard," Wolf said in their own tongue. "But not by the gods."

But the ranga insisted the gods had done so, obviously, because he was here.

"I don't even know what the leopard is," Wolf said. "Tell me about the leopard."

"The Claw! Watch out for the Claw!" one cried.

"What kind of claws?" Wolf asked. "How many claws?"

"One claw. Silent it comes," another said. "It comes in the dark with its claw."

"Sometimes you smell it come. You don't hear it until it is upon you, then it paralyzes with its voice and then claws you to death. In a group of hunters maybe one of you will escape and tell the same tale."

"The Claw! The Claw! Look out for the Claw!" one cried, and all the others made him be quiet.

"What does it look like?" Wolf asked.

They looked to each other. None of them could answer. "Has it ever been seen?"

"No," they all said. "Not by any who lived."

"This is not helping." Wolf's small mouth curled in exasperation, but he couldn't be angry with the ranga. They were like children. They plucked nervously at their red hair, seeing him displeased. There were some very thin-haired villagers in Ma-pall-mo. *I must slay this leopard, or they will all be bald.*

"What does it smell like?" Wolf asked.

Someone dashed away at a waddling run and came back bearing a torn rag on the end of a stick so as not to contaminate it with his own musky smell. "It smells like this."

The scent on the rag was very faint. The short hairs rose on the back of Wolf's neck.

He knew the smell.

The jungle was black as sundown without stars, a verdant hell, dripping heat. Darkness training let Wolf move without sight, silent and loud at intervals. He wanted the leopard to come to him.

He heard the leopard at a distance—not its footfalls nor its passage through the dense spongy vine nets of the rain forest, but its quiet panting in the heat. The leopard couldn't sweat.

Wolf had become still. The leopard fell silent. It could neither see nor hear him but had caught his scent, and Wolf could tell it was puzzled. It had never smelled an Earthman.

Wolf crouched in an acania thicket, ready to move, holding a dagger in his left hand, waiting for the leopard to attack or flee.

Then it came, screaming an Itiri death cry, with a whistling of a double-curved sword that tore into the acania thicket.

Wolf was no longer there.

The leopard hadn't been expecting one of his own. He was not prepared for any skill, any threat to himself. He had been very reckless. Now there was a dagger in his gut, thrusting up through his diaphragm, and he knew too late that this strange-smelling creature was an Itiri, too.

Wolf buried the warrior's body in the jungle so the villagers couldn't do anything abominable to it, and he took the tungsten-plastic Claw back to the Aerie.

He threw the double-curved sword at the feet of the Elders.

"What would it have cost thee to tell me what I was hunting?"

The Fendi picked up the sword and passed it to Roniva, who bowed her head. "No one told *him* what was hunting him," she said.

Wolf bristled. "Was that not neat and clever—to have one distort kill another? It matters not which wins. Maybe they will kill each other if you are very lucky. You must have been very proud and pleased with that idea!"

"No joy. No satisfaction. And not lightly decided," Roniva said, holding the flat of Claw's blade to her cheek.

The tender gesture was alarming. Wolf's mouth was suddenly too dry. He tried to swallow. "Who was he?" he demanded in dread.

"No concern of thine."

Another cheela of hers? Or—but that was hardly possible.

Aghara women were almost always sterile. Aghara children were rare enough—one out of one hundred thousand births—but an aghara born of an aghara? Wolf had never heard of such a thing.

Yet Roniva wore an eternity flower at her belt. She had a mate. Sterile women did not mate.

Someone say I did not kill her child! Wolf thought wildly. But no one was answering him. "Thou hoped I would lose," he said.

"I hoped he would not lose," Roniva said with altered emphasis. "Thy losing was merely the other edge of the same sword." She passed Claw back to the Fendi—it was no longer anyone's weapon—and she sadly walked away.

And so Wolf had come to the last trial. As ever, a walk through fire.

The objection was raised. "There is a full clan this year. He must wait."

A fire clan could be two, three, five, or seven. There were five for this clan of the carnelian serpent.

Then one died. His cave was opened after the twenty days of Shandee had passed, and the cheela was found frozen, nine days gone.

The time of fire was coming soon. A decision needed making. The would-be clan was now one short or one too many, and Wolf was waiting.

"This could be a destined thing," the ancient Fendi said. "Ask of the carnelian serpent if they will take this cheela for their fire brother; otherwise, they must say which of them will stay behind."

The four cheelas said they would take Wolf as their fire brother.

"He could taint your fire," Roniva warned. "He hath already failed. You may yet be a clan of four."

"We will be five," said the girl cheela, at that time known as Mardeia. "Let him walk with us."

Wolf, at the edge of the firepit, gazed through the wavering heated air and smoke to the hooded figure cloaked in brown who waited for him on the far side with a bare sword. Failure in a second attempt meant death. Roniva would make that happen. She also made certain that Wolf didn't bathe his feet in ice before coming to this place of fire.

The other four cheelas had already walked. Now they looked back for him to come through the fire and join them, the four nameless warrior-priests of the carnelian serpent. They had shed their cheela names in the fire and had not yet been given new ones. They untied the leather thongs from around their necks and waited for Wolf to make them whole.

Go to them.

Wolf relinquished conscious control, released everything—

Let go. Let go. To win, let go.

—and cast his fate to an inner voice. The body is limited, Xanthan had said, the mind hath no limits.

Wolf set one foot into the fire.

The ring of Elders and warrior-priests rustled uncomfortably. This would be painful to watch. They had seen it before. A cheela ought to have the grace to spare them from this pain. This one was putting them through it twice. The Fendi should forbid it.

Wolf stepped with the other foot onto the coals and became lost to their sight, shrouded in heat.

Into the forge. To be burned or created.

Heartbeats paced off creeping moments. Smoke curled to the sky.

Wolf reappeared on the other side as from a mist, his face visible first where the heat dissipated, icily serene. He advanced over the coals and stepped out of the pit, unscathed.

The mountaintop erupted into a clamor of war cries, crashing wind bronzes, rattling daggers, and stamping. All the warriors were on their feet at once, and the ranga echoed from down in Haven with jubilant yells and beating on metal.

The new warrior joined his brothers and sister, and he turned, not smiling, no happiness on his face, not even pride—only vindication and some kind of revenge.

He tore off the old leather circlet from his neck and threw it into the fire.

It was a clean fire, and all the others danced through it.

The brown-cloaked figure stood alone at the edge of the fire court, her eyes flashing, thin nostrils flaring. The sword trembled in her tight grip.

The rest of the mountain was in joyous uproar, the din reaching way down to Kaletani Mai. Only Roniva and one new warrior were silent—and only until white hands tugged on broad yellow-brown shoulders and beckoned him from his dark visions. "Dance, fire brother."

The words, like an enchantment, charmed away some of the black spell that lingered about him, and he danced with the others.

A wayward breeze blew smoke through Roniva's hair spilling from her hood, and she wished she were ranga to believe in protective spirits and to make a warding sign. She wondered what name would be given this being that had just been made from the fire. She was shaking.

What have we wrought here today?

9. Wolf at the Ramparts

5851–5856 CE

JININ-BEN-TAIRRE THEY CALLED HIM, the Feet of the Warrior Are Burned. A point of awe, the name carried a sense of overcoming the insurmountable. To a strong people with a stony will there came a point where they would break instead of springing back. This warrior had no such limit. The name was who he was.

Roniva approved of the reference to his burn scars. But Ben was a rare name, conferred on few—Warrior. There was only one other Ben alive on the mountain. This great honor seemed to her a mistake.

The girl Mardeia became known as Arilla, named for corundum, the virtuestone of strength. The other warrior-priests of the fire clan were given good names also, and the ranga foretold that one of these five would be Fendi one day.

With the glowing red tip of a firebrand they burned the dotted warrior's lines into each other's cheeks and pressed herbal ash into the wounds so that they would heal red. A ranga artisan fashioned their signet rings, serpent intaglios carved into polished carnelians set in platinum. The artisan chattered about Ben-Tairre's "ranga hands," broad and stubby fingered next to the long, tapered aghara hands. No one had ever made such a wide signet band for a warrior-priest.

Ben was given a book of law and philosophy. He vowed never to take a life without just cause, to fight only his own battles and those of his allies, which were these:

His fire kin.

The talassairi, the eagles.

And the mandesairi, the whales.

And he was given his sword. Ben Christened his *Da'iku*.

He shed his drab cheela garb for warrior's finery. Warrior-priests were peacocks except during the days of restraint, the somber days between the wind Shandee and the new year's fire.

He climbed to the top level of Aerieside to stand on the cold ramparts with his fire kin, a pride of young lions, flush with the newness of their arrival. Jinin-Ben-Tairre, once a wolf that had come to the door for warmth, took his place with them as a warrior-priest.

A thin layer of cloud brushed the top of the mountain with gray gauze. It meant the winds were calm.

Jinin-Ben-Tairre looked to his fire kin. Two familiars had appeared while his head was turned, a white binaya for Arilla, and a red snake for Aliathan. Ben muffled his own pain. He had resigned himself a long time ago to the fact that he could not have one, any more than he could ever hope to have heat vision or green eyes. Everything he could control he had won. He had walked the fire. He had a sword, a fire clan, and a name. That would have to do.

Not to be unhappy in his brothers' and sister's joy, he started down the terraced slope of Aerieside.

Suddenly there was a keening *scree* and a burst of talons and feathers in his face. He ducked down, and *Da'iku* flashed a cutting sweep through the air.

The bird disappeared at the advancing sword's edge, then blinked back into view as the blade whistled through its completed arc.

A familiar.

Ben-Tairre stood up from his crouch and sheathed his sword. The little brown hawk fluttered around his head and screamed at him.

Whose?

The familiar alighted on his shoulder and squawked in his ear.

Comprehension arrived with a rush of surprise and emotion.

Mine.

"What is that supposed to be?"

Roniva blocked Ben's path in the arcade. She appeared severe, hard, and angular as an eagle. Her black hair was pulled back and hanging straight from its topknot. Her whip-thin body was robed in plain dun but for all her bright enameled bracelets, anklets, and toques. Her black eyes narrowed critically at the bird perched on Ben-Tairre's shoulder. "Well?"

"My familiar," Ben answered.

Roniva's expression soured as if to say, *I know that.* "What is it supposed to be?"

"A kestrel, I think," Ben said.

"An *Earth* creature?" she said as if it were the ultimate insult.

Ben didn't mind the form of the creature. At one time it would have upset him horribly that his familiar should take the form of an Earth creature. Enough now that it was a familiar and it was his. It was an indelible stamp of legitimacy. No one had expected a familiar to appear for him. Now there was no doubt that he truly was a warrior-priest. "It only appears so," he said.

"My Xanthan's familiar had not talons and a hooked beak," Roniva said in reproach.

The kestrel was screeching in Ben's ear. "Knowest thou what it sayeth?" Ben asked.

"Thou wilt need to decipher its noises for thine self,"

Roniva said. She'd meant to be short with him, then decided to say more. "It is a primitive language. The first sound out of it will be a verb. The mode and tense thou knowest not and it will tell thee not. But I can tell thee it will almost always be a command. These beings are not informative. Thy familiar will spend most of its time giving thee orders."

Screee, said the kestrel.

"Another thing," Roniva said as the bird batted Ben's face with its wing. "They are not known for their patience."

Ben pursed his lower lip over his upper lip and furled his brow for a thoughtful moment. At last he said, "Can I give him back?"

It was the first time he'd expressed anything like humor.

"Certainly," Roniva said, taking her leave of him. "Discover from where he came and thou mayest return him."

That was a no. No one knew where familiars came from.

Ben drew his sword and turned it in the light which streamed in shafts between the pillars of the arcade.

The blade would cut stone. Handed down for countless generations, still it was honed fine.

"Thou art not my familiar," Ben said to the kestrel.

The kestrel squawked.

"Thou belongest to my sword."

The bird turned its head from him and preened its wings, noncommittal.

"I know I'm right," Ben said.

Ben sheathed *Da'iku*. He moved swiftly to the other edge of the arcade. He leaped lightly, barefoot, onto the balustrade. He hugged a jewel-encrusted pillar, and leaned out to gaze down into the chasm cleft into the mountain between Aerie and Haven. Xanthan's grave.

"O Xanthan, one *can* teach virtue to swords," he whispered.

The kestrel bit his ear.

"Rather, swords will teach," Ben said.

His eyes burned as he stared into the crevasse. He shrugged off a ruby-inlaid armband and hurled it down the void. He swallowed the thickness that rose in his throat, made a fist, and swung impotently at vacant space. "Wherefore is it too late to tell thee anything!" he hissed without voice. His voice failed him entirely. "Couldst thou not wait? Thou didst not know thine cheela."

Tiny claws were digging into his shoulder. A trickle that could have been blood or sweat traced down his back.

Ben dropped into a sorrowful crouch on the stone rail, his forehead on his knees. He pointed down the abyss without looking and told the bird, "Get thee down there. Get thee down and tell him."

Piercing talons released their hold without a rush of wingbeats. Then the kestrel was simply gone, and Ben was alone.

He doubted the kestrel would give any message to Xanthan.

Ben lifted his eyes to peer over his own knees and spoke, muffled. "Would that thou wert alive to forgive me. . . ."

In the year of the Topaz Triquetra, the Fendi sent Jinin-Ben-Tairre starward in an ancient ship called *Singalai* to live awhile in the world outside.

"I shall not revert to my blood," Ben vowed, anticipating the reason he was being sent on this quest.

The Fendi patted the head of his shaggy berinx and echoed Ben's claim. "He will not go back to them." The words suddenly sounded overly insistent to Ben's own ears. And the Fendi told the berinx in the next breath, "Then he shall know—for certain."

The Fendi read hearts and minds as most people read the stars and the seasons.

Hard, glass-chip eyes of brilliant green shone eternal fire within the mortal confines of his papery translucent lids. Wispy white hair wreathed his eggshell skull. The Fendi's physical form looked as if one day soon it would be spirited away on a dry autumn wind with the rest of the season's ashes of transitory life.

A figure of awe and wisdom, the Fendi was not one to whom brash declarations should be made. Ben backed down to a humble silence.

The Fendi scratched the brindle ruff behind his berinx's ears. "Let my warrior stay because he is an Itiri, not because he knoweth humankind not."

Ben dropped to one knee and touched his forehead to the floor in final acceptance and farewell. "Yes, Fendi."

Two years abroad revealed nothing to sway Ben's already fixed mind, and nothing to endear humanity to his estranged soul. He found the human war still raging, just as he'd left it, fought in the name of supremacy of a savage, vulgar race. If any change had occurred, it was a widening of the already enormous gulf between expressed human ideals and actual human deeds. There were good people incapable of reaching lofty goals naively set, and there were evil people who perverted the expressed ideals to their own ends. Bungling and avarice took their toll on everyone humans touched. Good intentions did not an empire make.

Human greed was especially stunning to Ben, coming as he did from a place where the concept of ownership was loose. Physical things were used on Iry. To own a thing was an oddity and a privilege.

And among humankind, Ben lost one of his only possessions. His sword.

Contempt had made him careless. The idea that someone would actually take *Da'iku* from him was inconceivable. He could not believe it was gone.

The blade was shipped to another planet, sold at a bazaar, and was in the hands of a new owner by the time Ben caught up with it, led by his shrieking kestrel.

The sword's buyer watched in mute astonishment as first a hawk appeared from out of the empty air and scared his prized white Arabian mare, then a young man with almond eyes and scarred feet walked into his garden and seized the reins of the gold-caparisoned horse, and made her stand still. The mare came to a stamping halt, panting under her heavy ornaments in the damp oasis.

The elderly man's bushy eyebrows rose and disappeared under his kaffiyeh as Ben unstrapped the newly purchased sword from the mare's saddle, drew the blade, and cast the gaily tasseled velvet sheath to the ground. The warrior turned the double-curved blade in the light before his exotic eyes, then whistled it through a helix in the air. Then he walked away with it.

The old man did not interfere. His leathery skin pinched in frowning crevices around a beaked nose and deep owl eyes. He picked up the discarded red velvet sheath, watched the warrior retreat barefoot through the white pillars of his paradise, and he breathed a baffled oath: "Al*lah?*"

That night, while he slept under the desert stars, a pinprick invaded Ben-Tairre's dreams. His mind sludged upward to thick consciousness, never clearing to alertness. His limbs moved as through water, and he knew he had been drugged.

He fought it—in the wild thrashing way of panic, not the calm methodical way of the Itiri. He hadn't the patience to learn that kind of control, so his fight was the charging of a wounded animal, without the concentrated power of thought to break down the evil inside him. He could only rage against it. He thought his simple will could force anything.

For a second time, it was not so.

He tried to turn back and learn—learn now—a systematic defense against the foreign substance in his veins. Too late.

Feebly he pushed at the ropes on his arm, at the heavy feet that stood on his other wrist and on his ankles, until he was pinned down on the sand and couldn't resist anymore. The drug sapped even his desire to fight. It was so easy just to rest and watch them, as if it were all happening to someone else's body and he was only an observer.

His right arm was held out straight and strapped down

to a wooden board rough with splinters so that he couldn't move but to curl his fingers and make a fist around the biting woven hemp bond pulled tight across his palm.

A meat cleaver appeared before his stupidly curious and uncomprehending eyes—a heavy square blade with a keen edge and a black handle. The steel flashed in the lantern light, a harsh cutting glare—unlike the lustrous reflection of tungsten-plastic.

A great bear of a man with a woolly beard wet his fingers on his thick red lips, wiped them on his long striped coat of green, black, and gold, and gripped the cleaver's stout handle in both his hands. He stepped up to stand over Ben, frowned down at him, and muttered a word. "Thief."

Ben followed the focus of the man's bloodshot brown eyes to his own wrist, and meaning penetrated his drugged thoughts. Fear returned. He yanked at his bonds with a sudden twist of his whole body. Wood and rope groaned. He shifted his pinned weight to try again, but a blue-smocked man sat on his chest.

The man with the woolly beard put one foot forward, swung the blade back and up, and with a grunt and a heave brought it chopping down through Ben's wrist and buried the blade in the wood.

Then men cut his bonds, took his sword, and left him there spurting blood into the sand.

The kestrel brought a physician, who followed the bird as if it were a messenger from God to where Ben lay in shock, holding his veins and arteries shut, and waiting out the drug's effects. He couldn't do more.

The physician sealed the wound, said his bone was not shattered and that he was lucky. The physician had no blood to give the warrior, but said Ben was strong and thought he would recover—*inshallah*—God willing.

Having made it this far, Ben knew he wouldn't die. When he regained strength, he walked back to the oasis and retrieved his sword once again. He cut off no hands, though he was bitterly tempted. He returned to his ship, *Singalai*, and went home.

The ranga fashioned a new appendage for him of jointed metal, padded and gloved to look like a hand.

The kestrel hated it and would not alight on it.

"Where wert thou when they were firing drug darts at me?" Ben said to its angry cries.

The new hand lacked dexterity and feeling. It was good for clutching and holding fast and for striking with great force. Ben adapted. The hand was useful.

But in the darkness, its faintly audible clicks and whirrs, ignored in the daylight, became magnified, a loud and desolate song of loss, like the shifting sands of the desert in the quiet of deep night.

The year of the Opal Sword began a new hexadecade. It was the year the child Amerika came to stay on the Aerie.

It was also the winter the Fendi died.

Ben withdrew to a lonely ledge in the gray twilight to be by himself. There was no order in the world. Ranga were wailing in their caves.

It was a cold day when Ben-Tairre wore boots, a day when breath froze in the lungs and eyes would coat over with ice. All was bleak.

He could not find the sun.

He tried to bring to mind hard green eyes like glass, and the voice of a gentle monarch who had allowed a Wolf to become a warrior-priest.

The Fendi's dying words had been: "Not to make Ben Fendi."

Jinin-Ben-Tairre thought it an incredibly odd thing to say.

There were two Bens on the Aerie. The Fendi must have been referring to the other Ben. Jinin-Ben-Tairre didn't think anyone would even consider making him leader. The Fendi didn't need to make a dying injunction against it. It was like telling berinxes not to fly. So why say it?

"Knowest thou not?" his fire kin asked him. "Because thou hast defeated defeat. Something none of us has ever done. And because thou art not a follower. And because no one is sure what to do with thee."

He hadn't known there were so many on the Aerie who would call his name. The Fendi had known. Jinin-Ben-Tairre agreed it would not be a wise choice.

As it happened, Roniva was chosen.

A small breeze cut like bitter knives. Ben covered his face with the edge of his brown mantle. The soft fabric felt rough and hard in the dry cold.

A hooded figure wended the rocky approach to his isolated ledge with careful deliberate steps on brown-slippered feet. A thin figure set in regal resolve, her back erect but fluid, she was known to Ben even without a glimpse of her jet-black skin.

Ben saluted as she arrived on the ledge, his sword fist over his gloved false hand. "Fendi."

Roniva lifted her hood from her face and her glossy black hair. "Not yet," she said. Breath froze to her lips. A white haze of drying skin chalked her high cheeks. "This is the last time I may speak to thee."

Wind picked up the edges of their mourning cloaks, billowed and snapped them like wind flags.

"What sayest thou, hanina?" Ben asked, his brown-black eyes barely open within epicanthic folds.

"Thou murdered my Xanthan," Roniva said.

"I know."

"Thou art here and my son is not. A poor substitute."

Her son. She had never said as much.

"Thy son was distort," Ben said softly.

"So art thou. Shandee drives thee. Thou art nothing without thine anger. This is my Aerie."

Wintry gusts pierced through fabric like sharpened blades. "Is this setkaza?" Ben asked. He hadn't expected to die today.

"No," Roniva said. "I shall not begin my reign with a

bloodletting. I shall try, Wolf. If I cannot live with thee, I will have no choice. And have thee no doubt who will win."

"No, hanina," Ben said.

They held the peace for less than a year, until the coming of an Earthman in the year of the Opal Ship, the man who came to them under the name Alihahd.

Suddenly setkaza was here, the intent to kill, and Ben lived in perpetual readiness for his fatal combat. It could come at any time. Or he could make it happen, choose the time and place to his own advantage and readiness.

But it was said that he who moved first was lost. Setkaza was a waiting ordeal, a trial of nerves. The one who endured the pressure of death threat day after night after day, had always been victorious. Setkaza could go on for years. It could snap tomorrow.

Ben-Tairre knelt on the floor of the training hall. He touched his forefinger to the groove in the wood where Roniva's sword had stabbed, locking their fate.

Turns of life were an unaccountable whirl. Caprice and sudden death and tragedy, fortune, chance, and destiny made vanity of expectation. There was but one certainty now. The death of a warrior.

PART THREE:

Ashar Ari

10. The Gathering Storm

IT WAS STILL THE FIRST WATCH, the hour of the bells. The air was sharp. The sky was clear and the stars shone in full array. Amerika stopped on the Ledge Path and gazed to the east. She sighed, "The Wellspring is rising already. Oh, Harry, I am not ready for winter."

The Wellspring was a cold-weather sign. The constellation was at its zenith at midnight in the dead of winter. Amerika didn't like to see it threaten on the horizon.

Amerika had picked a bunch of the season's last gay cerulean flowers and tucked them into the bandelette tied beneath her small breasts. She took Harrison Hall's arm and pointed up to show him a blue-white open cluster of stars which the Itiri had named for the flowers.

Iry had no moons, so no months. Instead, the year was divided into sixteen signs, each named for a constellation in Iry's zodiac. The sentinels would announce the beginning of a new sign at whatever hour of day it occurred—the time varied, for the number of days in the year didn't divide evenly by sixteen. There were 171.8 long days in the Iry year. Vaslav, who had a wrist chronometer that kept Earth standard time, said there were 30.97 Earth standard hours in an Iry day. It still made a short year, too short for summer to become actually warm, and, with any luck, too short for winter to grow killingly cold.

Just now it was autumn. The day was the eighth of the Beacon, the sign of an eclipsing binary. Only the constellations on the ecliptic were named. They were the only stars of any use to the Itiri, other than the pole star, but from the Aerie the pole star was always hidden behind the towering mountain Guardian.

The names of the constellations weren't as imaginative as Earth's constellations. Iry's were mostly literal, and, once upon a time, the stellar configurations looked like their names—Hexagon, Crown, Cross—but that had been ages ago. Since their ancient naming, the signs had slipped along the ecliptic and the stars drifted in different directions, so that no sign looked like what it was supposed to be. The Red Birds used to form a spearhead and didn't now. But then no real bird on the planet Iry actually flew in a V anyway, so it mattered little that the red stars formed a disorderly flock.

Harrison Hall sat on the balustrade of the arcade, his back against a stone column. He gnawed on the mouthpiece of his empty pipe. Firelights were fluttering to life inside the ranga caves, warming the doorways. Voices carried more clearly in the night air. Music of two woodwinds in rippling cadences chased each other from two caves on Aerieside. Hall tried to hum along but couldn't predict the alien patterns.

He caught Amerika gazing at the valley. Alihahd had been down there all summer.

Rumors and reports made their way up the mountain upon occasion with messengers and deliveries of food from the valley. The rumors were not of Alihahd, but of Alan James. No one in Kaletani Mai had ever met an Alihahd. They only knew a tall, white, blond man with blue eyes and a big voice. His name was Alan James.

So the captain had assumed another alias, thought Hall. Well, Alihahd wasn't really Alihahd either.

By midsummer, the stories that wended up to the mountaintop were of "the Earth Fendi." Hall roared with laughter. Earth Fendi, indeed. If Alihahd stayed down there much longer, the villagers would have him deified.

Very good, Captain. Very good.

Amerika hung on every word spoken about the man, Alan James. She would grab every courier, every eagle, every traveler who came from Kaletani Mai, and squeeze every tale out of him. Her face was wistful now as she leaned over, her forearms resting flat along the balustrade, and she gazed at the lights of the valley where *he* was. The little girl was missing him.

Then her black eyes shifted to a closer focus, and she pointed down. "Harry, look."

Harrison Hall took his pipe from his mouth and squinted into the dark.

Starlight caught on a movement in the blackness, a figure coming up the steep snake path from the valley to the Aerie. Hall could see no details, just a long-limbed form climbing up with a dogged way of moving.

Only warrior-priests climbed the sheer torturous snake path. But this was no warrior. Hall knew who this was.

Yet it was with a sense of disbelief that he beheld the lank, heavy-boned man appear over the top of the precipice to stand on the Aerieside Ledge Path. Harrison Hall thought of something he'd been told about legends—they always return.

Alihahd strode the path with a relaxed gait, tired but without exhaustion. He reached the narrow footbridge and began his crossing to Haven.

He was halfway when Jinin-Ben-Tairre appeared from shadows and stepped onto the bridge from Havenside to cross in the opposite direction. Their gazes met, and they both stopped.

The bridge swayed.

Ben gripped the knotted ropes. Muscles moved in his powerful shoulders.

His small mouth drew down in a sharp tight frown that wrinkled his chin. His eyes slanted even more steeply with the threatening cant of his brows. He took another step on the bridge, his intent clear without words. This Earthling would have to make way for him.

But a deep voice came from the bridge, very tired, short of temper, and unimpressed. "Move back. I shan't jump." And Alihahd looked away to the side as if annoyed and impatient. He knew what was rightfully his and was not about to be intimidated out of it.

Ben-Tairre blinked, slow to believe Alihahd could actually mean it. But Alihahd was not going anywhere—least of all backward—and slowly Ben-Tairre stepped down.

Alihahd completed his crossing. He walked past Ben without looking at him. It wasn't a gesture of avoidance. It was non-acknowledgment. Ben might as well have been a bush for all Alihahd cared.

Amerika gave a joyful little shriek and ran along Havenside's Ledge Path to meet him. Harrison Hall followed her at a casual walk. Hall stopped a few paces away, his weight on one foot, one hand in his redingote pocket, the other holding his pipe. "Captain."

"Mr. Hall," Alihahd said in his elegant voice. He hadn't changed. Not in that respect.

Hall had to smile. "How did you get up here?"

Alihahd's glance shifted sideways toward Ben-Tairre, and he answered loudly, "I walked."

Amerika clapped her brown, baby-fat hands with a gleeful giggle.

Hall gave a small nod. "Bravo," he said softly.

Jinin-Ben-Tairre turned away from the bridge as if he had never wanted to cross it in the first place, and he mounted the stepped path to the higher terraces instead.

When Ben was gone, Alihahd let some starch from his proud stance, turned his head to Hall, and said, "Have you any conception of how far three miles straight up is?"

Hall chuckled. "Do you know what you just did to him?"

He cocked his head in the direction in which Ben had re-treated.

Alihahd did. Ben's first climb of the snake path was a village legend. "Purely intentional," Alihahd said.

"Are you going into warrior training next?" Hall asked lightly.

"Are you mad?" Alihahd returned. He pictured himself, a forty-eight-year-old cheela. No, he hadn't climbed the snake path in answer to any calling. He'd climbed it to slap Ben's alien-posing face.

"You were saying, you don't lose well," Hall said, picking up the end of their last conversation as if Alihahd had never left and there had been no long summer intervening.

Alihahd nodded and spoke low, his voice tinged some-how with regret. "I don't lose."

He retired to the cave he'd originally inhabited upon com-ing to Aerie. His pile of blankets and furs were still folded on the wide mattress waiting for him. Vaslav's were in a rumpled pile against the wall. Hall's were not there. Harrison Hall didn't sleep here anymore. Alihahd wasn't going to ask.

Alihahd collapsed on the mattress without bothering to take off his boots. The boots were the same red leather ones he'd brought with him, but the thick, flat white deck soles had been replaced. He stretched his arms above his head, gazed at the ceiling, and exhaled long, at ease in his re-claimed territory.

Hall stirred the fire that had been dying in the hearth. Warm light caught the red sunstreaks in his coppery hair and flashed gold from his two earrings. His aquiline profile was outlined in orange-red. He rose from his crouch at the hearth and sat next to Alihahd.

Alihahd was little changed from when he left, still gaunt, spare, but healthier, hardier, and his short-shorn blond hair had grown out to cover his tall brow, the tops of his ears, and the back of his neck. His skin was weathered but still fair. It couldn't hold the sun's color like Hall's. Hall was by now very dark.

Music carried from outside, across the abyss. The wood-winds sang a new tune, sad, passionate, longing—the song of the abandoned or of a captive spirit wanting wings. It disturbed, made its hearers restless. The song made one look toward the stars.

"Do you mind explaining to me, Captain, how you got to be 'the Earth Fendi'?" Hall said.

"It was none of my doing, and all actually comical," Alihahd said. "The ranga started it. They assumed because I was tall and blond and lived alone that I must be the Earthling equivalent of a warrior-priest. It escalated from there. I was a Fendi before I knew it."

Hall nodded. But Hall didn't believe it was the ranga's doing. Wherever Alihahd went, no matter how many times displaced, Alihahd would always lead. He was set apart by the way he talked, the easy grandeur of his carriage, and his lordly silences.

"I have something for you," Alihahd said. He unlaced a pouch from his belt. It was filled with dried leaves. "I am told these can be smoked."

Hall received the pouch as if it were treasure. "I thank you, Captain."

"Do not thank me. If I cannot breathe up here, neither shall you. I give you hypoxia, and may your night vision go to hell."

"Merrily," Hall said, laughing, a deep sound in his barrel chest. His lung capacity was enormous, and never mind that smoke added an equivalent of four thousand feet to the altitude, Harrison Hall would endure.

He withdrew his fox-head pipe from his vest. Both its fire-opal eyes were cracked now, and Alihahd commented on it.

"Serra," Hall said. "She shied it at me."

"She does not like you," Alihahd said.

"She likes me fine."

Alihahd had already surmised that Hall was living with Serra. Hall's move was entirely expected. Eridanin lords were not known for their celibacy. It was only natural that Hall would be sleeping with someone. Just as it was natural that Alihahd be alone.

Alihahd pursed his lips, chagrined on the rare occasions when it occurred to him to think about his isolation. He'd always been a failure at human emotion. The ranga reminded him of it. Ranga hugged each other at any excuse — something he could never do. Spontaneity for him was not there. He'd tried once, inspired by a child laughing. He beckoned. The child frowned and toddled away. Fitting, as Alihahd had a face to frighten children. He didn't try again. It was his way to be aloof. He usually liked his distance. At the same time, he was envious of the ranga, their ability to bc closc. Alihahd had never been at ease when tenderness was expected of him, around pets, children, or women except his wife. His had been an arranged marriage. He would never have married if he'd had to go courting for himself.

Now he was afraid to touch anyone.

He looked at his hands.

Harrison Hall picked up one of Alihahd's hands and laid it across his own open palm. The back of Alihahd's big knotty hand was bruised purple, and the skin was split across the knuckles. "Rough climb," Alihahd said and took his hand back, too quickly.

Hall's lips twitched beneath his mustache. He withheld comment.

The palms of Alihahd's hands were unscathed from his climb.

"I have something else for you," Alihahd said. He gave Hall a small felt bag. Something within clicked together like pebbles.

Hall emptied the glittering contents onto the bed.

"Surely that's a zircon," Hall said, pointing to one of the eight big gemstones.

"Which? No. The pink one is a zircon. The boulder is a diamond."

Hall picked up the diamond and held it to the firelight. "What do you think? Five carats?"

Alihahd shrugged.

"You're worse than an Itiri," Hall said to Alihahd's total lack of avarice or even interest. Alihahd had handed the gems over as if they were pretty quartzes and cut glass.

Alihahd rolled onto his side and propped himself up on his elbow. "The ranga decided I needed those, since I was something like a warrior-priest. Those are virtues."

"Is that what they are?" Hall said dryly.

"No warrior should be without them. The beryl is your hospitality, kindness, and mercy—your 'humanity' if you will," Alihahd said. "The diamond is honor, respect, and loyalty—there is a single Itiri word for all those, and a single stone."

"A single very large stone," Hall said.

"Turquoise is patience and serenity. Lapis is courage. Topaz is wisdom. Zircon is humility and modesty. Opal is integrity in the sense of soundness, wholeness, and the like. The ruby is self-control, or fulfillment of potential, or inner strength. The way they consider certain concepts as synonymous I find quite bizarre. At any rate, there you have them. Please take your virtues and let me go to sleep."

Hall scooped the gems off the bed in his fist. He held them each up to the light one more time before putting them in his pocket. He decided he might keep the diamond. The rest he would hock as soon as he was off-planet.

After all, what use were serenity and modesty to a man who piloted a black ship?

Harrison White Fox Hall and the Fendi Roniva crossed swords. The snowy owl observed from a high perch in the training hall, slowly rotating its round head to odd angles as if on a ball socket, so that sometimes its gaze was nearly upside down. Roniva never spoke a word to Hall. At times she would stop, point at Hall, and bark to her owl, "Again!"

That was bidding for Hall to repeat a technique. Hall

wasn't unfamiliar with swords, but the double curve was unusual—like a yataghan, which Hall never had used. Hall preferred guns and short daggers—though he would have sold his soul for a blade of tungsten-plastic. The technology that had made the nearly indestructible tungsten-plastic swords no longer existed anywhere in the galaxy. Where the Itiri had come by their swords was a mystery.

Roniva demonstrated a series of passes and bade Hall repeat it. The dark woman's appearance was still neat, her hair smooth and tied up, her skin dry. The Itiri did not sweat. Hall was shirtless and his skin was gleaming wet. The bandana tied across his brow was drenched, and his hair coiled into dark, wiry curls stuck to the back of his neck. He repeated the series.

Alihahd stopped in the doorway to watch. He leaned the front of his shoulder on a column, his hands tucked under his belt, his head tilted to one side. Soft clean hair kicked over his tall forehead. There was color in his usually sallow and drawn cheeks. The mountain was not killing him this time around.

Hall omitted the last move of the series, which was to flip the blade under his arm as he turned its edge away from him and hide it behind his back. Roniva snapped to the owl, "Tell him to finish."

"Fendi, if I do that I'll cut off my arm," Hall said. It was a tricky move to do the first time with a live blade.

Roniva let it pass and continued to something else.

Alihahd questioned the wisdom of teaching Hall anything. Someone who christened his ship *Nemo* did not need to know anything more about fighting. Alihahd didn't advocate the training of terrorists. By the time Hall left Iry, the Marauder would be twice as deadly as when he'd come. How could the professedly neutral Itiri possibly justify turning such a being loose on the galaxy?

Or did the Itiri ever intend to turn any of them loose? The thought was a recurring paranoia.

He waited until Roniva wasn't wielding a sword to speak.

"Fendi, you realize, do you not, you could be aiding and abetting an interstellar terrorist?"

Roniva seemed to register the data with a momentary wrinkle of her hairless brows. She gave no comment. She took her leave without a word. The owl sailed out behind her in a sudden silent glide.

Hall picked up his shirt and slung it over his shoulder. He sauntered to Alihahd. "There's a burrower hunt today. You're not going?"

That was sarcasm. Alihahd didn't answer it. "*You* are not going?" he asked. Hall never passed up a chance to hunt.

Hall shook his head. "Layla is. I don't trust Layla behind me with a club."

"I see." Alihahd's gaze dropped to the Itiri sword in Hall's grip. "You are getting to be a very dangerous man, Mr. Hall."

"I always was a dangerous man." Hall mopped the sweat from his body with his shirt, and took off his sopping bandana. "You, dear Captain, could be immeasurably dangerous if I could ever pull you from this Itiri-like pacifism of yours."

Itiri-like? I? That was a curious concept. "I'll not be pulled," Alihahd said.

"Wherefore?" Hall said, imitating Alihahd's high-style, sometimes archaic speech.

"Because I could be immeasurably dangerous."

Were he ever to anger, Hall was certain Alihahd would be lethal. But his flashes of glorious rage never lasted, quickly fading to contempt, indifference, or plain weariness.

"Pity you won't budge," Hall said. "I'd have you with me."

"If it's all the same, Mr. Hall, I would not trust you behind me with a club," Alihahd said.

Hall laughed aloud. "Point taken."

Alihahd turned to go.

Jinin-Ben-Tairre was standing in the exit with a drawn sword.

Alihahd felt a ripple of surprise, and . . . disappointment. Alihahd wasn't much opposed to dying, but he would've liked some advance warning. This was too unexpected, like a bolt from the clear summer sky, just when he was feeling safe. It wasn't fair. The feeling of helplessness in the face of the caprice of the universe upset him more than the actual prospect of dying. *So here it is.* He waited.

Jinin-Ben-Tairre turned the sword hilt outward and tossed it to Alihahd.

Alihahd caught it by the hilt.

Hall raised both eyebrows and drew in his chin like a comment. Alihahd had held a sword before.

Ben's smooth face remained an unchanging mask. Apparently he'd lost the ability to be surprised by anything Alihahd did.

Ben moved like a pacing cat to Harrison Hall and thrust out a broad demanding palm to the sword which Hall held.

Hall surrendered the blade to the warrior-priest and stepped back to the periphery of the practice floor as Ben began to circle.

Alihahd turned slowly, keeping his face and his sword toward Ben. He made no circle himself, only pivoted guardedly.

Suddenly Ben charged in with a stomp of his foot and a shout, the sword whistling over his head and down. Tungsten-plastic blades met with a dull crack. Alihahd deflected the blow and dodged to the side.

Ben spun full around with another attack from the side, and Alihahd had only time to shift his sword to a vertical block, catching the blow straight on, and he staggered back with the force of it.

Would he kill me?

Ben's strokes felt real and unrestrained. But Alihahd sensed that the warrior-priest could kill him anytime he wished. This was nothing but cat-and-mouse here.

Alihahd didn't counter either attack, or even attempt to counter. Time after time, Alihahd's moves remained strictly defensive. He had no desire to attack Ben. This was Ben's game, and Alihahd didn't want to play.

Then Ben backed away to a weapons chest. He put down his sword and brought out a dagger. Alihahd waited, uncertain.

"Captain." Hall's voice came from behind him, and Hall pressed the hilt of his own poniard into Alihahd's hand. Alihahd passed back the sword in return and squared off with Ben again to continue the match with new weapons.

Travesty of a match, thought Alihahd. Ben was trained to be a warrior of the galaxy's legendary killing force. To what purpose was this shadow show being staged?

Ben came at him with an underhand thrust. Alihahd dropped his own weapon and blocked downward on Ben's wrist with crossed hands as he jumped back, curving his lower body away from the blade. He seized Ben's thick wrist and twisted it—like trying to throw a tree off balance—then abruptly shifted balance with a foot sweep. Ben rolled and came back up, still holding his dagger. Alihahd's weapon was on the floor. Alihahd skidded it back to Hall with his foot. The blade was worse than useless to him. One did not use a knife to block a knife, and blocking was all Alihahd wanted to do. In this situation he was better off open-handed.

So Ben changed weapons again. Then again.

Alihahd had broken into a sweat all over his body. It became harder and harder not to attack. They were dueling with sabers now. Ben slashed fiercely, hit hard, leaving himself open for a counter, baiting. Blows rained on Alihahd's blocking blade. They jarred Alihahd's wrists and arms. Crashing metal pounded at his eardrums. Ringing steel kept at him and at him and at him like a goad. He could see the demand in Ben's fierce dark eyes. *Fight me, fight me, fight me!*

Alihahd wasn't even thinking anymore. He moved without conscious deliberation. In another part of his mind, above, serene and removed from all this, he heard a mocking chant:

Circle, circle, dance of pain
One is free. He remains
Who cannot see our circle's edge
Another circle, once again.

A crazy look glazed his eyes, blue with white all around. A hunted way of standing made him the image of a wounded animal, cornered, about to turn and bite.

The spectator, Harrison Hall, straightened from his casual stance. He wondered if Ben knew what he was doing. He was going to make Alihahd turn on him, calling him a fraud, challenging how deep the pacifism truly ran.

Alihahd was angry—or was a better word *mad*? His thick lips drew back from his teeth, and he watched Ben from the tops of his wild eyes. The saber trembled in his too-tight grip. Ben pressed until Alihahd surely must crack.

Alihahd did not.

And at length, when Ben-Tairre himself was sweating and drawing ragged breaths, Ben stepped back, put up his weapon, and left the training hall with an air of curiosity satisfied.

With a shudder and a sighing moan that was half a cry, Alihahd dropped his saber as if it were a loathsome thing. He stared at his own hand.

Only when his breaths began to lengthen did normality return to his face. And all at once his strained muscles untensed, and he looked simply tired.

Harrison Hall picked up the discarded saber, tested its balance in his hand. He gave a nod to Alihahd's proficiency with it and the other weapons. "You're better than you look, Captain," Hall said.

"I was not born this old," Alihahd said. He dropped to a squat, his back to the wall, his forearms on his knees, hands hanging loose.

"Careful what you call old," Hall said. "I believe I am your senior."

Alihahd lifted a hand at the wrist and pointed toward the door. "That man does not like me."

"Oh, I don't know," Hall said. It was hard to tell what Ben was thinking. Hall was only glad that Ben wasn't interested in *him*. "I wouldn't worry anyway," he said. "Roniva is in your camp, and between the two of them, my money is on the Fendi."

Alihahd gave a shrug. "Hypothetical situation."

"I hear not," Hall said. He explained what he knew of the ancient rite of setkaza. Sooner or later Roniva and Ben would fight to the death.

Alihahd shook his head and gave a laugh that was helplessness rather than mirth. "Aliens," he said. He stood. Unfolding his long legs was painful. He took the saber from Hall and tossed it back into the weapons chest in distaste. "I used to be good with these toys of destruction." He didn't like them anymore, the swords and bola and archaic things no one really used anymore but to play at war. He slammed the chest shut and turned away from it. "Too much blood under the bridge between then and now."

"Whose blood?" Hall asked.

"Oh," Alihahd said. "I was speaking in general."

Harrison Hall watched with a hunter's eye. Alihahd was a complex individual. The more he revealed the less he was known. He never spoke of his home: whether he had disowned it, was ashamed of it, or was protecting it. His accent and his manner and his knowledge revealed that he'd been just about everywhere. But his origin was a mystery, until one day Layla, who never had heard of tact or even of civilized rules of conduct simply asked him point-blank, "Where are you from?"

Alihahd hesitated. The frankness of the inquiry precluded evasion, especially in front of Hall. Not to be too obviously secretive, he answered the question. "Earth."

The reply caused a stir among the humans. Although called Earthlings, none of them—Layla, Serra, Amerika, Vaslav, or Hall—was actually from the cradle of humankind, Earth. None of them had even seen it, and they all had questions about it.

Alihahd didn't want to talk about it. "I hardly knew the place myself. The whole world is a perpetual Na'id battlefield. I left shortly after I was born."

When asked where he went after that, he said, "Many places," and changed the subject.

He was certainly aristocracy. His lofty, occasionally tortured way of speaking wasn't an affectation. Alihahd fell into it without thinking. There was something so unassuming in his elitism. And he had a voice that made those godawful speeches of his sound right.

He didn't possess Harrison White Fox Hall's cocksureness. Rather, he had the bearing of a man fallen from a great height, a vestige of pride that persisted like an afterimage once the reality was gone. Instinct for command also persisted, like breathing.

Harrison Hall was a lord, but he wasn't a leader. Men and women did not die for Harrison Hall. He inspired no trust, no desire to march into hell for him or to breathe one's last gasp at his feet.

Alihahd could command that kind of loyalty if he cared to—and even if he did not. And it seemed he did not want it, not from anyone. He didn't want the attention. He didn't want to be followed, watched, or known.

It was obvious he had a past—the kind one does not talk about. But the more secretive he was about it, the more apparent it became that he was not simply hiding from the past. He was running from it.

He stood a paragon, so calm, mature, level, patient, and wise. As with everything that had stood too long, his surface was wearing, so one could glimpse through the cracks and find something else.

He'd developed a series of quirky little mannerisms since his return to the mountain—unobtrusive patterns and rituals that appeared at first glance to be simple habits—a way of ordering objects on his nightstand, of layering his blankets in a certain order and going out of his way to maintain that order. He would clean his teeth with salt twice upon rising, his motions identical both times. He would take twelve steps to cross the bridge, no more, no less, starting always with his right foot. This was more than simply being methodical.

None of it went unnoticed. The weakening of a fleet animal did not escape the watchful eye of the tiger in the brush. Patterns were a snare. The greater the attempts to create order outside, the greater the chaos inside. Something was drastically wrong. Alihahd was trying to lock down the corners of an unpredictable universe that kept curling up at the edges.

But Alihahd wasn't absolutely patterned. There was a wayward independence and disorder in his time schedule. He had no schedule. None at all. Hall never knew when Alihahd would be anywhere—when he would eat, when he would sleep, when he would rise—none of which activity had anything to do with daylight hours and was never the same twice. The lack of schedule just did not fit the other obsessive patterns, and the waiting tiger was baffled—and wondered if he was being baited.

Hall bided his time.

The red flags were out. The winds were fast and no one on the mountain ventured beyond the sheltered oasis of Aerie-Haven. No one climbed the peaks, for *ele-ala*, the wave, would sweep them away. The eagles rode the undulating currents, soaring over the valley without a single wingbeat. A swirled puff of cloud poised over the village, caught in a rotor. The eagles avoided it.

Harrison Hall took refuge in a small cave on the third level of Haven, where he stayed when Serra was bleeding and wanted to be alone.

It was Alihahd's custom to retreat here at erratic times. Hall never knew when. On occasion, as today, their visits coincided.

Hall had a fire burning brightly in the hearth when Alihahd came in. The cave was a small place, its decoration begun a long time ago and never finished. Crumbling stucco on the unornamented wall came off in dust at a touch. The worn design on the other wall was also faded, painted quatrefoils within squares, carved in relief and intaglio on alternate squares.

Hall was in his shirtsleeves, sitting cross-legged on the bed, tinkering with a gadget retrieved from his ship, *Nemo*. The mandesairi, the whales, had found wreckage of his broken ship on the ocean floor and had sent pieces back to Hall on the mountain with the eagles.

"Is it a transceiver?" Alihahd said, hopeful.

Hall shook his head and tossed the black box aside. "Just a gadget." He picked up his pipe and, after a few tries, lit it. He puffed clouds of gray smoke. "I take it there aren't any in the valley."

"Transceivers?" Alihahd said. "None that have the range to contact anyone in civilized spaceways—not within this century at any rate."

Hall waved some of the smoke away. "They really don't seem to give a damn about the Outside."

Now and then the Itiri sent scouts abroad to pick up pieces of someone else's technology, a ship, a weapon, and maybe rescue an alien in peril along the way, then return home, recluse again.

"I do see the purpose in hiding their existence from the Na'id," Alihahd said. "The notorious warrior-priests of Iry are sadly unprepared to fight a modern war. Yet they continue to stagnate. There is no effort to build for themselves. They aren't ignorant, exactly, but there is a decided lack of ambition and want of foresight here. Their folly if they think they can hide forever."

Hall was chuckling, gently, mockingly, fondly, his laughter indulgent as at a clever child. "What?" Alihahd said.

"The way you talk."

"So glad I keep you entertained."

"You know, of course, you're wrong."

"I know this?"

"The Itiri could hide forever," Hall said.

Alihahd had to nod. They were truly lost out here. Na'id ships never came this way, never would. Unless something were to draw them.

Hall set aside his pipe, the fire of which had gone out, and he picked up the piece of equipment from his ship again. "Have you noticed they count in hex?" he said.

"Hexadecimal?"

Hall pulled out a lens from the black box. "Yes."

Alihahd paused in thought. "I suppose I had noticed something odd." He'd never heard an Itiri count past nine in Universal.

"Vaslav figured it out," Hall said. He pulled out another lens.

"What kind of people use hex?" Alihahd said.

"People with sixteen fingers."

The Itiri had ten fingers. Logically they should have developed a base-ten number system.

"Computers," Hall continued his list of answers. "People who use binary."

"Which is to say high tech," Alihahd said. "Which the Itiri are not. They are an odd people." He stopped talking. He'd caught himself, not for the first time, calling the Itiri people. He brooded in silence for a long time while Hall repositioned his lenses. Alihahd looked over his shoulder. "Is that anything that will help us escape from this planet?" Alihahd asked without much hope.

Hall looked at Alihahd. He'd already told him it was not a transceiver. "No." Hall looked into Alihahd's eyes, lifted his hand, and touched Alihahd's cheek with a hot, dry touch. "What an incredible color for eyes."

Blue eyes dropped away from Hall's gaze. Alihahd couldn't meet his gaze anymore. He left the cave with the restlessness of a caged beast.

Hall balanced his projector on his knee and slouched

back against the wall, thoughtful. He hitched his thumbs in the pockets of his gold-weave vest. Hall wanted to leave Iry, too. He had a battle to fight. And if his need was not as desperate, at least his motive was clear, which was more than he could say for Alihahd.

There was no good reason why Alihahd should be anxious to leave Iry and rejoin the crusade against the Na'id Empire. His heart was obviously not in it. He seemed weary of the whole thing. Yet he was obsessed with return.

Hall's reason was simple: vengeance. But what made Alihahd go? It wasn't revenge. Alihahd espoused no specific ideology. He had no real cause, except perhaps freedom of choice. But what did that mean to him? He had nothing personal against the Na'id. He did not hate them. He opposed them but not for himself. Or maybe his selflessness was very much for himself.

Hall sat up straight. He saw it in a flash. There was only one real motive for martyrdom, and it was not devotion.

It was atonement.

You're doing penance.

For what? What had Alihahd done?

Evening passed into early night, the seventh of the Serpent. It was unnaturally mild on the mountain, becoming actually warmer after sundown. There was little movement in the air but for a gentle breeze, soft and moisture-laden.

On the horizon could be seen a black mass blotting out the stars. Then distant lightning lit up the outline of a monstrous thunderhead, its top sheared off by a jet wind way up high. The bolts themselves couldn't be seen—only the flashes of cold light from behind the massif and the muffled report of far-off thunder.

The Itiri were taking off their sword belts and their metal jewelry.

Alihahd climbed to a ledge where two warrior-priests kept vigil. The towering thundercloud menaced in a slow advance from the far side of the valley, its flat top miles above the mountains. The Itiri marked the ominous shape of the thing and muttered.

"How long?" Alihahd asked.

"By morning," they said.

As they spoke, there was a change in the air. Cold, with a downdraft.

Alihahd was aware of another menace, in counterpoint to the storm, on either side of the great rift between the mountains. On the dawn ridge he could see Ben-Tairre backed by the turbulent sky. Always a striking figure, Ben had assumed a dynamic stance, a conscious or unconscious display of power and dominance. His clothing, loosely fit, still showed the play of muscles in his thighs, his heavy shoulders, his hard abdomen. He carried an obsidian blade.

On the eagle ridge opposite—black, hard and sharp as if fashioned of obsidian herself—crouched Roniva. Her long thin limbs, tight-corded and agile, were folded beneath her, catlike, her body hard as stone, fluid as water.

Over them the sky was about to break. The air was electric, charged with premonition so strong even Alihahd felt it—a storm that had been building long before he'd ever seen the Aerie.

Alihahd spoke to the warrior-priests on the ledge with him. "What happened here? What is between Roniva and Ben?"

Emerald eyes exchanged hesitant glances as if the warriors were actually afraid.

And they told him there would be a death tonight.

11. Thunderhead

A STRANGE SOUND ROSE over the Aerie, beginning softly, steadily gaining in strength. It was not a rain sound, but an odd rhythmic swelling of voices in an ever building chant, over and over.

Kaza, kaza, kaza.

Serra came out of her cave. She stepped to the rail of the arcade and looked out.

The sky was dark, starless. A few fluttering torches lit the paths of Havenside. The chant carried eerily from Aerieside, from within the Chamber of the Golden Dome.

Kaza, kaza, kaza.

Serra called in to the others. "Something's happening."

Alihahd joined her at the balustrade. An electric hiss of lightning tracked through the clouds. Then the whole sky lit up brighter than daylight. In the brief weird illumination, the landscape was surreal, blue-white, with jagged edges and black, black shadows.

Alihahd saw Arilla dash along the Ledge Path toward the Chamber of the Golden Dome. She appeared as an impala-bodied white streak. A lightning flash caught her expression, froze it. Fear. An odd thing to see on a warrior-priest.

Harrison Hall spoke from behind Alihahd. "She's Ben-Tairre's fire sister. This is it."

Arilla flew into the Chamber of the Golden Dome and broke through the ring of warriors, but at the inner edge she was caught in the arms of an Elder who lifted her off her feet and stopped her flight. There could be no physical intervention here. Her fire brother was alone in this.

In the center of the ring Jinin-Ben-Tairre and Roniva circled the floor, the surrounding crowd calling on them to break setkaza now, finish it.

It was said that he who made the first move lost. Neither would strike first. But the ring of warriors was intent on breaking one of them. They could not leave this chamber until one was dead.

Kaza, kaza, kaza.

Alihahd came to the jeweled arch. He shifted to see between the heads of the crowd of warrior-priests. Their chant surged like the incessant pounding of a heartbeat.

Kaza, kaza.

Suddenly Roniva's sword was out. She moved to the center of the chamber and stabbed the point of her sword into the floor.

The chant stopped. The ring widened as everyone moved back to the farthest boundaries of the chamber, onto the benches and the stone sills of the tall lancet windows.

Ben and Roniva circled the sword three times.

Someone gave Ben his sword. Roniva pulled hers from the floor, and the final battle began.

Blades flashed. The two swept across the inlaid floor like sidewinding serpents. Spectators fled from their approach. The players owned the space, pausing for no one. No one had the right to be in the way of the fatal dance, which Roniva, having begun it, was fated to lose.

Roniva swung at Ben. With a ringing clash, Ben batted the flat of her sword away from him with his false hand. The awkward thing became for him an extra weapon, and he lunged into Roniva with his sword.

The trick should have caught her, would have, but Roniva was quick and wise to Ben's way of turning his weaknesses. She parried, jumped away, and countered.

A wet sheen glowed on Ben's skin in the unheated chamber. The Itiri would see Ben in a shroud of heat. Exotic eyes that always looked angry narrowed in ferocity. Small, broad feet wrapped in strips of red rags were a burned reminder that Ben did not know how to lose.

Roniva advanced on him, her sword a whistling blur before her, and she pursued him to the wall, where watchers divided and dove to either side. Her strike sheared the curtain from the window and shattered the mirrored jamb with a spray of glass. Ben spun off to the side. He seized the offensive, beat Roniva into a retreat, and backed her to the hearth.

Her sash ignited at the fire's edge. She sprang backward over the pit, arched like a cat, cut her sash from her waist, and wielded it as a flaming bola. It swished in a circle, searing the air, and she let it fly.

Ben leaned far to the side. Before the bola was even on the floor, he was on immediate counter-offensive, swinging his sword at Roniva in a mighty arc.

Roniva's sword was down, Ben's blade driving at her head. In a swift deliberate move, as fast as a sword's sweep but with an eerie sense of slow motion, as if time itself were commanded to wait, Roniva raised her left hand in a gesture of halt and caught Ben's blade on her bare palm.

An edge that could sever tempered steel, the tungsten-plastic should have gone through with no more resistance than slicing air. The blade stopped dead still.

The look in Roniva's eyes reflected a power, a force to stop a starship, a faith to move mountains. It was a borrowed power of the universe. The myths of magic that surrounded the Itiri like rubbish were all there, focused in the palm of Roniva's hand.

Ben took a step back in shock, looked at his blade for blood that was not on it. In that moment he lost the battle.

It was quickly done after that. Ben's feet were swept from under him by a long, lashing kick. Roniva stepped on his sword hand and put her sword point to his jugular. All motion came to a stop.

Arilla turned away and hid her face against the chest of the Elder, Eren-Ben.

Jinin-Ben-Tairre didn't breathe. He waited for Roniva to finish him.

Roniva spoke to him directly. He was next to dead and counted as no one now. "He who breaks a setkaza first loses. Except that not for nothing was I made Fendi of this Aerie. I can break traditional bonds also. Thou wert someone before thou wert Itiri, Jinin-Ben-Tairre. That someone may live, if the Itiri agrees to die and never be seen on this Aerie again." Dark eyes met dark eyes and she asked, "Art thou dead, Jinin-Ben-Tairre?"

Any Itiri would rather actual death to ritual death. But survival instinct would not leave him. "I am."

"Let all be gone," Roniva commanded. "Tell everyone that Jinin-Ben-Tairre has died."

As the warrior-priests filed solemnly out, Eren-Ben knelt by the dead warrior, took his sword and placed it in a wooden chest. He took the dead man's eternity flower from his belt and his signet ring of the carnelian serpent from his finger. The flower and the ring he gave to grieving Arilla.

Jinin-Ben-Tairre spoke softly from the floor at Roniva's feet, for only her to hear: "The corpse requests to be buried with his book."

Roniva's visage was severe and scowling. She did not look down, but hissed through her teeth, "Ben, shut up."

Outside, the sky had split open and rain poured down in torrents. Lightning flashed and roared. The smell of ozone scorched the air.

Jinin-Ben-Tairre stayed sprawled on the floor where he'd

died, until only he, Roniva, and the hanina Eren-Ben were left in the chamber.

And Alihahd. He hadn't gone out with the others and didn't intend to go unless he was told. He stayed in the background in the nine-sided chamber, behind the lattice barrier that stood in front of the dais. No one paid him any attention, though he sensed they were aware of his presence.

Roniva lifted her sword away from Ben's throat, and she melted from her regal pose. She seemed to sway for a moment, and she leaned against the Elder, Eren-Ben, who was quietly there where she needed him, the only other living warrior to bear the name Ben. Eren-Ben was shorter than the other aghara, wider across the shoulders. His pacific eyes were a striking blue-green, wide and fathomless. His ageless face was mild, sad, serene. His hair, a flowing mane as long as Roniva's, was a silvery ashen blond different from the normal Itiri gold. He wore his eternity flower behind one ear, as Roniva did.

Roniva drew away from him as Jinin-Ben-Tairre rose to stand. "Thou art kind," he said to the Fendi.

"No, I am not," she said. "I will not have thy death on my sword to weaken my rule."

"Then may I say thou art wise," Ben-Tairre said.

"Thou mayest, and I am," Roniva said.

Jinin-Ben-Tairre took a few steps as if moving in a body that was not his. It was strange to be dead. The reality was only now occurring to him. All that had been his life was gone. He didn't know what was left. "Who am I?" he said, lost.

"I never wanted thee as an Itiri," Roniva said. "Because thy heart is in the wrong place. Thou wantest to be an Itiri so thou wilt not be human. But thou *art* human. Be thou human now."

Eren-Ben put his arm around Roniva's thin waist and escorted her to the archway, leaving Jinin-Ben-Tairre in the center of the domed chamber like a lonely ghost. He called after Roniva.

"May I have thine blessing?"

It had not been offered. It was impudent of him to ask.

"I should flay thee, Ben-Tairre. Thou art too forward, not to mention *dead*. Be thou gone from my sight forever." She went out.

Ben blinked, shuddered. Thunder crashed.

He barely heard, for the loud rush of the driving rains, the voice of one leaning in through the mirrored jambs of one of the tall windows, barking:

"With my blessing!"

Snow came after the torrential rains, and the cold encased the mountain in ice. The morning brought a fog, and all about the Aerie was perfect white. No one could see past arm's reach, and no one could go outside unless he could walk the paths without sight. Pale eyes went quickly blind in the whiteness.

The sign of year turned to the Cross. The clouds lifted near midnight, and the high winds swept them away. The cold night grew colder.

Around the Aerie the air was still. Overhead, the stars shone bright in a velvet field. Around the rocks a powdery white scattering of phosphorescent blossoms dotted the ground like more stars underfoot.

Alihahd walked alone in the starshine. It was the hour of the meteors, the beginning of the third watch.

Thin air made sounds fainter. Snow muffled them. But the night quiet, the cold, seemed to fine-tune Alihahd's senses. He listened.

Jinin-Ben-Tairre was dead. Or at least gone. Alihahd had seen him descend the snake path toward the valley. Yet Alihahd still felt he was being watched.

At last he stopped on the path, and spoke without turning. "Layla, why do you follow me?"

All was silent, but for a distant wind. Alihahd waited. Then she appeared with a soft crunch of crushed ice. She dressed like a child set loose in a theater's costume storage loft. Her head was veiled like a Muslim lady so that only her brown eyes showed, and she wore a down jacket, kalx-hide trousers, a pair of gloves without fingers, and a gold-fringed shawl which she'd tied around her waist. Her jeweled dagger was sheathed in one dun boot. Her gun was no doubt tucked in her pocket. Always a soldier, Layla was never to be found unarmed.

She came to Alihahd's side. Her head didn't even come up to his shoulder. "Why does one move about at this hour and avoid the sentinels?" she demanded.

Alihahd smiled. He realized he'd been skirting the sentinels' vigilance. "Habit," he said. "Is that not a sorry comment on a way to live?"

The question was too nebulous for Layla, and she made no comment on it.

Alihahd admired and envied Layla—her strength, resolution, and unshakable conviction. Layla was also slightly stupid. Blessed with a simplistic bullheadedness, no profound dilemmas ever disturbed her dreams. She was right. Her enemies were wrong. There were no shades of gray.

Alihahd touched her chin through the Muslim veil. "Do you know what your name would mean in Jerusalem?" he said.

"No," Layla said.

"It means night," Alihahd said.

"I like that," Layla said.

"Better than mine," Alihahd said.

Layla took his arm and walked with him a while. She pressed close to his side, not sexually. She was cold and he was there. She didn't mistrust or hate him as she did Harrison White Fox Hall.

Layla called Harrison Hall a slave master.

"Men and women were not meant to be slaves," Alihahd said. "The Na'id are not without a point in that matter. The class system on Eridani before the coming of the Na'id was wrong. I think even Mr. Hall can see that."

"I think he sees nothing," Layla said. Hall was bad. Therefore, nothing about Hall could be right.

"I think I can understand Mr. Hall better than you can," Alihahd said. "We are both ruling class, he and I."

"You more," Layla said.

"I?" Alihahd said. Layla knew nothing about him. She didn't even know whom he ruled.

"It just sticks to you," Layla said. "Harry insists too much. You do not say anything. You do not need to."

"His empire fell," Alihahd said. "It makes a difference."

"Did not yours?" Layla said.

"No. Not yet," Alihahd gave a sad smile. "It is a tottering tower of cards. It will fall. I may even weep when it does."

"You think the Na'id will destroy it?" Layla asked.

"Yes," Alihahd said. "The Na'id will destroy it in the end."

A sudden bright light flaring in the valley drew his gaze.

The roaring followed, lagging behind the light that had begun its ascent. It blazed toward the heavens to the stars and was gone.

Alihahd stared in disbelief. "Goddamn," he breathed. His shoulders drew back, his blue eyes flashed, and his voice became a rolling roar. "Goddamn."

A starship. A starship had left Iry without him.

He pulled away from Layla with a growl. "Where is Roniva?"

"Do not anger her," Layla said.

Alihahd cared nothing for the warning. He would not be treated so. Roniva had said he would leave on the next ship.

He parted from Layla and crossed the footbridge in twelve steps. Aerieside was black without torches, soulless in its majestic repose. Alihahd filled his lungs. Then, into the imposing silence of the caverns and arcades, Alihahd bellowed the Fendi's name.

The echoes of his wrath faded to the night quiet. The wind moaned in the crevasse softly.

She would not come to him. Damn it, he was going to find her.

A single dim light glowed from within the Chamber of the Golden Dome, the place where Jinin-Ben-Tairre had died. Alihahd went inside, his footsteps loud in the cavernous space, ringing off the nine walls and the high metal dome. The snowy owl loomed over the throne. The rustle of its feathers startled him. The owl's round yellow eyes stared at Alihahd unblinking. Cold gusts blew in the windows and the archway, swirling the leaves in the hollow place. This place was deserted. But *she* was here, even when she was not here. *She* filled this chamber.

Alihahd met the preternatural yellow eyes. His voice tremored with rage. "Where is your master?"

The owl clacked its black beak.

Alihahd didn't hear anything, but he perceived a presence behind him. He turned.

Roniva stood in the archway. "Here is the creature's master," she said.

"Forgive me if I abuse your hospitality, Fendi," Alihahd said bitterly. "But your hospitality is not all you would have me believe."

"Explain." Her brows were drawn together in a pained squint over her eyes.

" *When one of us next leaves Iry, thou mayest go also.'* Whose words are those?" Alihahd said.

"Mine," Roniva answered.

"Then what the hell was that?" Alihahd pointed skyward.

The Fendi's brow smoothed in surprise. Then she squinted again, puzzled. "A ship has left?" She turned her head aside and held up her fist. *"Eho!"*

Her owl appeared on her fist.

"Find," she snapped, and threw the owl into the air. It disappeared. Roniva folded her spidery black fingers and assumed an attitude of waiting. "We shall both know shortly."

The owl reappeared on the throne, crying three notes.

Roniva turned back to Alihahd. "No one left on that ship," she said. She rubbed her temples and moved toward the door.

No one? "Lie to me, Fendi?" Alihahd said.

Roniva halted. A volatile word, *lie.* Alihahd was too incensed to care if he angered a woman who could stop a tungsten-plastic blade with her bare hand.

"It was Jinin-Ben-Tairre," Roniva said, her own anger withheld. "He is dead. He is no one."

"I am no one with whom to try semantic tricks," Alihahd said.

"Not semantics," Roniva said. "To us, he truly is no one. I am not accountable for the actions of the dead. When someone leaves Iry, I will know and thou wilt know. That is all."

Alihahd rumbled, "That is not all!"

"I become wroth," Roniva warned softly. "Not easily done."

"I had not noticed that particular fact," Alihahd said acidly.

"Done!" Roniva cried.

"Easily," Alihahd said.

"Oh, thy tongue is a sharp sword and thou art evil. Ben told me so. I should have let him kill thee. You would both be gone from me now!"

Alihahd was shocked to wordlessness for several moments. Then he continued in a softer voice. "How does a neutral nation justify aiding the Na'id Empire by holding one of the opposition's leaders prisoner here unable to lead?"

"I was aiding the opposition by saving said leader's life," Roniva countered. "Neutral, I should drop thee back in the ocean whence I dragged thee."

"Perhaps you should," Alihahd said quietly. "If I am to be your prisoner."

Roniva threw her arms wide in exasperation and cried,

"Thou took exception to my aiding the opposition by training thy Harrison Hall. Which side art thou on?"

Alihahd threw his head back and gazed up at the tall ceiling that was suddenly too low for him. He cried, "Humanity's! Trying to be!" He slapped his palm against a pillar behind him, and almost laughed at his own uselessness.

"As I am the Itiri's," Roniva said. "Remember thou who I am. May I go now?"

Alihahd gave a bark of pain, frustration, and absurdity. *"Ili! Ili!"* he cried.

"What sayest thou?" Roniva asked.

"I am saying, 'Go. I am sorry. Dismiss everything I ever said.' Why not? I am as no one as Ben." And he ran from the chamber.

Serra listened to the rain falling outside. The fire in the hearth sputtered as drops strayed down the chimney. Harrison Hall rose from the breakfast table and took his rain fur from the peg by the door. "Be careful," Serra said.

Hall navigated the slushy paths pitted with footprints, while on either side of the trail the rain pocked the untrodden snow with wet perforations. He came upon a moody Alihahd, his blond hair wind-tossed, his ears and fair face stung a deep red, his blue eyes half closed in the cold wind. Either from self-torture or neglect, he was not dressed for the weather. From the look of him, he had been out here all night. He looked deep in thought. Hall sensed anger.

They stepped around a spongy euglenoid colony that was creeping across the path, soaking up the rain.

Hall walked along in silence. When they had come at length to the entrance to Alihahd's cave, Hall asked for words. "Captain?"

Alihahd expelled a breath, shook his head, said nothing. He went in.

Hall returned to Serra's cave. Serra, Amerika, and Vaslav were at the table. Hall hung his rain fur on its peg and joined them.

"Mad," he said. "Absolutely unpredictable. He's as regular as the damned weather."

"No," Vaslav said.

Hall frowned at the boy. "No? What do you mean, no?"

Vaslav explained that Alihahd was not erratic at all. According to Vaslav—and Vaslav's chronometer—Alihahd kept a perfect twenty-four-hour Earth standard cycle.

Harrison Hall seized the boy's wrist and stared at his chronometer. "Are you sure?"

Vaslav swore it was so. He didn't understand it, how Alihahd did it, but that was what he was doing. Alihahd rose every day at the same time—on Earth. He went to bed at the same time each Earth day. At any given Earth time of day, Alihahd was to be found in the exact same place. The schedule put him far out of rhythm with Iry's days and nights. Not to be regulated by an alien sun, Alihahd rose and slept as his inner clock bid, no matter the position of the Iry sun.

Hall's smile was slow and evil, breaking into an open grin. His gaze turned aside with glinting eyes, toward the door and the outside where the rain had turned to snow.

12. A Winter Conversation

ALIHAHD WOKE AT SUNSET, just as Vaslav was crawling into bed. Vaslav glanced at his wrist chronometer. The time was exactly 0735 on the Earth meridian.

How does he do it? Vaslav marveled. *I have the clock!*

Alihahd went through his waking ritual with seeming meticulousness, putting on his clothes in habitual order, re-making the bed just so—first the quilt, then the woven blanket, then the brown fur, then the silver fur. He brushed his teeth twice.

Then he went outside without his rain fur like a forgetful old man.

The cliff paths were slick with snow. It fell lightly from the high clouds. No one was about at this hour except the two sentinels, who were easy to avoid. Alihahd's walks had settled into a set pattern that kept him away from others as much as possible.

Alihahd wallowed in his solitude. He didn't feel the cold.

Then a voice split the silence and dragged him out of his reverie. "Why art thou always elsewhere than thou art, Alihahd?"

He knew the voice and was shocked that it should address him directly.

Waiting in shadowed ambush on his accustomed path, alone and unattended, was the Fendi Roniva. Blending in with the black shadow she was barely visible but for her white teeth, the whites of her glittering black eyes, and the broken red scars on her cheeks. She wore no jewels to catch the starlight. Alihahd was so amazed that he had nothing to say.

"Thou livest out of time," said the Fendi. "Be here now."

He wondered what she wanted.

She drew closer and passed a leathery hand over his wet hair. She shook the snow crystals from her hand. "Thou hast little regard for thyself," she said. "That is not good. Thy spirit is not well."

"How may I serve thee, Fendi?" Alihahd said at last.

"Dry thyself. Eat. Wear warm clothes and come to me." She turned sharply and glided across the bridge.

Alihahd had detected a subtle nervousness about her he'd never seen before—something in the stiffness of her shoulders, a thin edge to her voice. Nothing blatant, it was the held-back tension of the brave solemnly facing something dreadful.

Alihahd quickly complied with her wishes. He went to Hall and Serra's cave. The two of them were usually to be found up late.

"Good morning, Captain," Hall said, smiling.

Alihahd frowned.

Serra fed him. Hall gave him warm dry clothes and his own fur-lined parka. Before Alihahd left, Serra slipped a packet of breadcakes into his pocket. "Take. It will be a long night."

Alihahd took her shoulder in his hand. "You know what this is about, Serra?"

Serra kept her eyes lowered as a good Eridanin woman would to a strange man. "I think so." She tied the leather drawstring of the parka's hood under his chin. Her shoulders were as stiff as Roniva's. Her voice had gone husky.

"Am I in danger?" Alihahd asked.

"No. You can walk away. She cannot."

Serra didn't explain. The topic was upsetting to her.

Alihahd left the warmth of the cave. Using the safety line, he crossed the bridge to Aerieside in twelve steps, starting with his right foot.

Roniva hadn't told him where to go, so he went where one always had audience with the Fendi, to the Chamber of the Golden Dome.

Even as he approached, he could see yellow light from its arched doorway and its tall windows, darkened by flitting shadows of people moving inside.

He stood at the entrance and witnessed an odd little ceremony in progress within.

Roniva stood in the center of a ring of *ma-hanina*. She wore only a loose flowing ice-blue shift pinned at her shoulders. Her hair was loose. Her bare arms were crossed over her flat chest. Without all her enameled toques Alihahd could see how very wrinkled was her neck.

A warrior-priest stepped into the circle and emptied a bucket of ashes over her neat, glossy head.

She didn't move against him, only closed her eyes and frowned in revulsion. She uncrossed her arms, all her corded muscles taut. Her body was firm and thin and hard beneath the sheer shift that was no protection at all against the cold.

Alihahd was aghast to see the shift suddenly stripped from her and she was driven out naked into the snow.

Alihahd lunged forward to help her.

Her leathery hands met his as she stumbled. Then her face turned up to him, resigned, and silenced anything he might have said.

All was happening as it was meant to be.

She spoke, smudges of white ashes on her black lips. "I am of an age to demand a companion. Walk with me,

Alihahd." She straightened herself and marched into the winter night.

Alihahd cast an appalled look back at the other warriors now assembled in a row barring the cave entrance and the golden glow of warmth within. Jewels sparkled on their thick robes. Alihahd ran after the old woman with ashes on her head.

Roniva's blue-black skin was mottled in places with wrinkles and scars. Her sagging abdomen was corrugated with marks of childbirth.

Alihahd couldn't contain his anger. "What kind of sadistic and barbarous ritual is this that they should degrade a dignified, elderly woman in this way!"

Roniva gave him a dim smile and spoke to him directly, for she had no attendants anymore. Even her familiar was nowhere to be seen. "Too dignified," she answered. "That is the issue. I am the single most powerful being on Iry. One begins to feel like a deity." She spat ashes from her lips. "I am not."

"And you are aware of it. This is not necessary."

"For them, too." She gestured backward. "One's life is not entirely one's own up here."

They hiked over a ridge. A blast of wind lifted a swirl of glittering snow around them. Roniva threw back her head and howled.

Alihahd was puzzled that she could not overcome the cold. "I have seen you step in fire and stop a naked blade with your bare hand," he said.

"Ah. That was then. Now is now. I am naked and I am cold. How I hate this."

Alihahd wanted to give her his coat. He knew she wouldn't take it. Trying to lift her spirits, he reminded her of her own greatness.

"Not to flatter me," she commanded. "I need to find some humbleness if I am to bear this. How beautiful the new-fallen snow." She frisked away like a colt.

Alihahd thrust his hands into the pockets of Hall's parka

as he followed her. He felt pebbles in the bottom of one pocket and he drew them out. They were the eight gemstones he'd brought to Hall from the valley.

Roniva was delighted. "Give thou to me. Hast thou a zircon? I am in need of a zircon."

Zircon. Humility. Alihahd gave her all eight stones. She fingered them like prayer beads.

Silent a while, Alihahd's thoughts jumped. Then he blurted out, "Why did you kill Jinin-Ben-Tairre?"

"I am getting old," she said.

Alihahd foundered in puzzlement. Wind fluttered the fur lining of the hood that wreathed his face.

"I grow weary," Roniva said. "An Elder is truly an elder, thou seest. I am . . . what is the number . . . one hundred and sixty years old. I could die."

Alihahd was amazed and still confused. "What has that to do with Ben?"

"When I die, they could make him Fendi."

"*What?*"

"Thou didst not know? He is a miracle among us. I had to kill him while I had strength. I'll not have him rule my Aerie. He belongs with humans. I sent him back."

"That could be difficult," Alihahd said.

"Thou meanest because of the Na'id?"

"Among other things," Alihahd said.

"Harrison White Fox Hall tells me much about the Empire," Roniva said.

"I know."

Alihahd had told Hall to stop maligning the Empire to the Fendi. It endangered the better part of humanity should the Itiri ever decide to break their neutrality and go to arms. Hall had replied, "Don't use 'better' when you mean 'bigger.'"

"Alihahd, thou speakest not and thou art the one I would have speak," Roniva prompted.

Know thine enemy. She wanted to know the Na'id.

"In true conscience, I cannot," Alihahd said.

Roniva made a questioning noise. She wanted to know why.

Alihahd admitted, bluntly, "Because they are human and you are not."

The Fendi was not offended. Honesty did not offend.

"I am afraid you will need to rely on Mr. Hall for your information," Alihahd said.

"Thou art a worse threat to the Na'id than is Mr. Hall," Roniva said.

"How do you figure?" Alihahd asked.

Hall was dedicated to the destruction of the Na'id. Alihahd only wanted to break their stranglehold on free humanity and to avoid bloodshed.

"Thou knowest them best," Roniva said.

"I do," Alihahd said. "It has been a decided advantage."

"Harrison White Fox Hall tells me evil things about the Na'id. Tell me something good, canst thou?"

Trapped. This woman always won what she sought. He could hardly *not* answer her, and he ended up telling her about the Na'id.

He explained to her the Na'id ideology, before it had run afoul of itself. Its lofty ideal had been to eliminate the superficial barriers which divided humankind.

Roniva countered, "They oppose color barriers, yet they despise thee for thine color. How is that?"

Who had told her about his color? *Hall.* Damn him.

Alihahd regarded his pale hands. He was sensitive about his strange color. It was difficult to keep emotion from his voice. "This is the color of a pure race. It is a symbol of many evil practices in the past—"

"Thou art not a symbol. Thou art a man," Roniva said. "Thou hast also been brainwashed by thine own enemy."

Alihahd wanted to protest, but he would need to tell her too much. He sighed. He couldn't even reason with human Jews and Arabs. What made him think he was going to make an alien hear sense?

It was comforting to know that all these irrational Itiri

were staunchly neutral and wouldn't set out with their deadly martial skills to threaten the Empire.

All but one dead one.

An evil in their midst. The Na'id conscription base locked in on itself in unknowing terror. Brave soldiers feinted at moving drafts of air. A presence among them like a ghost — there but not there — had them cowering defenseless, because they didn't know what it was. They, the arrogant members of the Na'id conscription force who with laughing pride called themselves Mushabriqu's Press Gang — none of them was laughing now. Something was here. Damn it, something was here.

Without striking a blow, the evil in their midst reduced the entire base to grasping terror. Without striking a blow *yet*.

A voice inside the stalking evil told it to wait. *Thou art one. They are many. Yet they fear thee!*

The Na'id numbers were overwhelming. This conscription force had carried off the able-bodied population of an entire village by force. They must be reduced before they could be fought.

I am the attacker. They defend.

The advantage was in the role chosen. The Na'id could have been a hunting party stalking a lone cornered beast on their own ground. Instead, they let themselves be frightened, become the defenders, shrinking from a killer in the house.

It was a night of fear. Slamming doors, heavy footsteps, a flutter of wings that was here and gone, the specter of a hawk, the shadow of a sword.

Thou canst not slay them all at once.

One had to start somewhere. Strategically.

And, after the long night, just when the soldiers began to feel relieved and foolish, they flung the windows wide, and the gentle morning sun lit the courtyard where General

Mushabriqu hung by his neck from the flagpole beneath the bloody flag.

And so it began.

Night turned to the hour of the meteors. The snow had stopped. The clouds were gone. Under the clear sky, the temperature plunged.

Alihahd warmed Roniva's long toes between his hands. It seemed to him that there was something terribly arbitrary about the physical characteristics of the Itiri and their purposeless dimorphism. The aghara were too tall for the gravity and too fair for the irradiation on the mountaintop.

A meteor streaked across the icy sky. Snow on the ground glinted like quartz flecks, crusty cold underfoot. Starshadows were hard-edged and black. Roniva yawned.

Alihahd took her long-fingered hands and held them inside his coat against his chest.

"This is abominable," he growled.

"Thou mayest go in if thou art cold," Roniva said.

"No." The cold never bothered Alihahd much.

In the east the sign of the Mountain was rising, a random-looking jumble of stars that hadn't formed a double peak in 100,000 years. Dawn was still hours away.

Roniva took up their walk again. One hand slipped into Alihahd's coat pocket as a human lover might do—as his wife used to do when they were young and still pretending to be in love for the public eye.

"Are you not afraid of falling ill?" Alihahd asked. He worried about her in the wind.

"We do not sicken," Roniva said. "Most of us are immune to every disease on this world. Frostbite worries me." She flexed her long fingers and toes. "Disease doth not."

"That's incredible," Alihahd said. "How did your people develop such immunities?"

"We died by the thousands," Roniva said simply. "Those that survived passed down immunity."

"A harsh method," Alihahd said.

"Nature's method," Roniva said. "We try to be at one with Nature."

"Nature is cruel," Alihahd said. "Humanity is compassionate."

"Is it?" Roniva said.

"Kindness is a human trait," Alihahd said. "Which is not to say that all humans are kind."

"True enough that one does not often find kindness growing wild," Roniva conceded.

And Alihahd became disturbed by something that had only gradually crept into his awareness since he had come to Iry—the total absence of physical and mental defectives in the population. He asked cautiously if there were any.

"Oh. Distorts. Of course they happen."

"Where are they?" Alihahd asked.

"We kill them."

"That is inhuman," Alihahd said.

Onyx eyes flashed. "We are not human."

"I tend to forget," he said, bitter. "The level of a civilization is measured by how it cares for those unable."

"Very noble," Roniva said. "Very impractical at this point."

"Humans manage," Alihahd said.

"Is it true that human children are cruel to the deformed and the different?" Roniva asked.

Alihahd's white face colored. "Yes, but—"

"Such treatment distorts the inside. The abused grow crooked. They carry much anger. That distorts others. They distort their own children. The spiral goes down."

"That is cold-blooded reasoning. These things can be overcome," Alihahd said.

"So who told thee we were perfect?" Roniva said. "You have your interstellar wars. Why dost thou begrudge us our private atrocities?"

And who had told him the Itiri were perfect? The legends. He of all people ought to know the frailty of legends.

"Is it true you have to kill someone to become a warrior-priest?" Alihahd asked.

"No. That is not true," Roniva said. But before Alihahd could breathe relief, she said, "Thou must kill someone to be a hanina."

A noise like the beginning of gagging escaped Alihahd.

"Oh, one doth not go out and murder someone," Roniva said. "It is not a thing to strive for. It happens or it happens not. It is no one's goal to be a hanina. It is a burden. When one becomes an Elder, one gains access to the Archives. I know thou thought we had no written records. We do. They are kept in a cave in the desert. One can read things one would rather not.

"Ours is not a shame culture, Captain Alihahd. We have no use whatsoever for guilt upon which some human cultures thrive. The Archives collect much dust."

"There is an ancient shame?" Alihahd asked.

"There is. I shall not jump off the bridge for it."

"Your people do not fear death, do they, Fendi?"

"No. It comes to all sooner or later. Preferably later."

Alihahd gazed at the sky. Another shooting star blazed across the Milky Way. "You must be formidable in war," he said.

"I suppose we would be," Roniva said. "But we have not seen war in several lifetimes."

Alihahd's brows drew together sharply. "How did you achieve that?"

"No nations," Roniva said. She crouched in the snow, tried to make a snowball, but the graupel would not stick together. "It is difficult to organize a war without nations. And thou knowest our attitude toward ownership. Humans kill each other for that handful of stones in thine pocket. We own nothing. So we have no property to protect. The ranga are docile. As for the aghara, we all become warrior-priests. We are strong. Only the weak and frightened must fight."

"*All* the aghara become warriors?"

"Or they die," Roniva said.

"They are killed," Alihahd interpreted.

"The same," Roniva said.

"Why must an aghara become a warrior-priest?"

"When aghara go their own way, war will return to Iry."

"Or when it comes from the stars," Alihahd said.

"Or that," Roniva said.

"You seem to be taking that possibility lightly," Alihahd said. "A few thousand warriors and a handful of antique spaceships will not avail you against a modern fleet. Your people were introduced to high technology two thousand years ago and you've done nothing with it in all that time. Your science is stagnant."

"We have all we want," Roniva said. "Why art thou worried about us?"

"I swear I don't know. I should let you all go to the devil. And you will go, if the Na'id find out that Itiri warrior-priests actually do exist. You wanted me to tell you something about the Na'id. I shall tell you something. They will turn you back into a myth as fast as they can seed your sun with a nova core. Sooner or later."

"I should hate to have to deal with that," Roniva said.

When the eastern sky began to gray, Roniva climbed up the highest rise and waited with open arms for the coming of the sun.

Alihahd dropped to one knee a distance behind her to watch, smiling that the long night was past and she was still here to salute the morning fire. The winds picked up her hip-length hair and fanned it out behind her like a sail. Sun gleamed on her black arms thrown wide. She cried out in the ancient tongue, a sound of exultation, fittingly barbarous to Alihahd's ears. He expected nothing less or else from his savage warrior queen.

She turned to him, and he rose.

She returned to the Chamber of the Golden Dome. The warriors who had driven her out were still there, waiting to envelop her in furs and a jeweled robe when she came in.

They brought her to the fireside and brushed her hair and dressed it in gold-and-tapestry ribbons. Her colored toques were replaced around her neck, and her jingling sword belt looped around her hard waist. A warrior brought her sword wrapped in felt. He bowed all the way to the floor at her feet, unwrapped the blade, and offered it up to her over his bowed head.

She took it in a solid grip, reassured by its comforting weight, and then sheathed it.

"Tell the Earthman the Fendi is grateful for his service," Roniva said to the air. "Tell the Earthman he may go."

No one needed to tell Alihahd to go. He left the cave. This conversation was ended.

Alihahd sat on his neatly made bed, lost in thought. Vaslav came in, unwelcomely energetic and tried to talk to him. Alihahd changed his clothes, folded up the ones Hall had given him, and excused himself shortly. "I must return some things to Mr. Hall."

Vaslav scowled after him.

Alihahd took the things not to Hall and Serra's cave, but to the private cave on the third level. Alihahd didn't want to confront Hall. He wanted to return the clothes and leave. He wanted to be alone, unseen.

But he found a fire blazing in the hearth as if he was expected.

Alihahd let his bundle drop onto the bed. Irritated. Of course he'd been expected.

The fox-head meerschaum pipe had been left behind on the yellowwood table. Alihahd was tempted to pitch it into the crevasse. What would Hall think of that?

Hall would laugh.

Alihahd paced to the fire, stopped, regarded the pipe, paced. Hall was so sure Alihahd would not touch it.

Hall was right.

Alihahd touched the yellowwood tabletop with a gentle

hand. He ought to pitch Hall into the crevasse. That was the real matter here.

Alihahd lightly pressed his palms together and wove his long fingers together as if praying, and he gazed into the fire. Licking tongues of flame reflected in his pale eyes.

He saw his own setkaza.

13. Witch Wind

THE TIME OF YEAR CAME when the wind Shandee would blow for twenty days straight, from the second of the River through the sign of the Wellspring to the seventh of the Veil—nearly half the winter. Caves were stocked with food and water, and denizens of Haven banded together for the long season. All six humans gathered in Serra's chambers to weather the storm. They were sick of each other after a few hours, sick of the walls, sick of the howling wind.

Alihahd kept to his singular schedule and intensified all his little rituals, an illusion of control and order in the helpless confinement.

And he dreamed of being buried alive.

He woke in semidarkness, the edge of a dream fading from his mind.

The sentinel from within her cave on Aerieside was beating out the hour for all the prisoners of the wind. Alihahd counted the bronze clashes. Seven. The hour of the eagles. Predawn.

Alihahd sat up on the wide mattress, finally awake.

He pulled on his boots, first the left, then the right. He went to the back chamber to wash and pass water. Serra's back chamber with its nonporous refuse drain was the reason these caves had been chosen for the humans. Itiri excreted little water. Neither did they sweat.

Alihahd rubbed salt on his teeth, did it twice, spat, and came back to his corner of the bed.

He put everything in its place. He owned four changes of clothes by now, and he stacked what he was not wearing in order under the pillow. He folded his quilt, the woven blanket, the brown fur, and the silver fur precisely, in four folds, and set them on his sleeping place.

There was also a mat on the floor, which was not his but had to be aligned with the crack in the floor or Alihahd was not happy.

In this small area of this particular chamber, things were as Alihahd willed them to be. All the rest was as it fell to random human chance.

When all was arranged, Alihahd stepped back (with his left foot) to inspect his niche, and he saw that Amerika had hung her mirror on the wall.

It had been years since Alihahd had looked into a real mirror and seen more than a ghost image reflected in a glass or a polished metal surface. This was a real, merciless mirror. He saw that the skin of his neck had acquired the plucked chicken texture of old age. Tiny broken blood vessels marked his nose, and rays of new lines etched his face. He'd forgotten how truly unpleasant was the look of white skin on a face—the color ancient Caucasians in their infinite elitism had termed "flesh tone"—not the smooth marble white of the aghara Itiri, but a sometimes ruddy, sometimes sallow translucency that showed tracks of blue-and-purple veins.

Alihahd turned the mirror toward the wall. It became part of his ritual.

On the wide mattress everyone used for a bed, Amerika was now sitting up, her face puffy from sleep and marked with lines from the pillow. Her hip-length black hair had been laced into a single thick braid for the night. She had been sleeping right beside him. He hadn't noticed.

She was looking at her mirror turned to the wall.

"Is it an instrument of sin?" she asked, childish guilt in her lovely black eyes. "I only use it to part my hair and paint my eyes. And I only paint my eyes against the sun. I swear."

"No, it is not sinful," Alihahd said.

"Why didst thou turn it over? So the spirits cannot come out?"

"No," Alihahd said. "Because some faces are better not faced at this hour."

He gazed up at the coffered rock over his head, muttered that he could have been light-years away from here if Ben had not gotten off planet without him.

"He was not to have taken that ship," Amerika said. "The Itiri were upset. He was not to have taken *Da'iku* either."

"*Da'iku?*" Alihahd cried loud enough to disturb the sleepers. Serra stirred under Hall's arm, then her breath evened again. Alihahd faced Amerika gravely and whispered, "*Da'iku*—is that what he calls his familiar? The bird?"

"No," Amerika said. "It is what he calls his sword."

Alihahd was on his feet. He strode to the battened door. He brought his fist against the stone jamb. The howling wind sounded very near on the other side. Alihahd truly felt the walls closing in on him. He needed to run, to find Ben, to stop him.

"*Da'iku* is a Na'id name, is it not?" Amerika said.

Alihahd nodded, his fist on stone.

"Thou knowest a meaning," Amerika whispered, pulling her blanket around her as if cold.

Alihahd faced the door. "It means Killer," he said.

14. A Slow-Falling Star

LAYLA ABSENTLY PASSED her finger through a candleflame, collecting soot on her skin, the warm light flickering across her rough, impish face.

Serra was seated at the table, sewing a shirt for Harrison Hall, and refilling teacups as they emptied.

Alihahd's third cup of tea sat half full and growing cold. Alihahd never finished the third cup. He always drank two and a half cups at a time. Always.

On the floor, Amerika was teaching Vaslav a pebble game.

From the adjacent chamber, Harrison Hall was snoring.

Faintly, from Aerieside, Itiri music spun through the wild wind Shandee's howling.

Layla lifted a pendant on a chain from around her neck and held it out to Alihahd across the table. "What is this symbol?"

Alihahd picked up the pendant from her small palm and rubbed his thumb over the metal face. It was a Na'id cuneiform symbol:

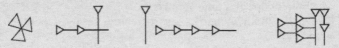

"Where did you get this, Layla?"

"From a dead Na'id."

"Did you kill him?"

"There were many dead on the field. I know not which of them I killed."

"I see."

Layla pointed with her soot-covered finger. "What do the markings mean? Amerika says you know Na'id."

"It's a DINGIR. In this case it means God."

The Na'id had adopted the Jewish/Muslim custom of not depicting God. Christians had a tendency to make God a male Caucasian. The Na'id preferred a deity without form, without color, intangible like the human soul. "This is a religious medal."

"In *this* case it means God?" Layla said. "What other case is there?"

"This mark can also represent a sound in a word—*an* or *il*," Alihahd said. He marked on the table with a piece of chalk:

"There it is pronounced ili—literally gods, but this is a name."

"This is confusing," Layla said, her cheek resting on her fist.

Alihahd pointed to one symbol at a time. "The first mark is pronounced *shad*. It means mountain. These middle two are your DINGIR and a plural sign. The last is pronounced *ya*. It means my. So: Mountain of my Gods."

Serra put down her sewing. The red chevron on her forehead creased. Ignoring the translations, she strung the pronunciations together in order and said, "Shad Iliya."

Layla's brown eyes widened. She pointed at the chalk marks. "That is what this says?"

She scowled at the markings, then methodically wiped them away with the side of her hand. She regarded the resultant smear with satisfaction. In the primitive culture of her origin, to obliterate the infamous general's name was to obliterate the man himself.

Amerika came to the table and looked over Alihahd's shoulder. "Oh. I did not see it. Write it again."

"The same thing can be written a slightly different way—without the DINGIR," Alihahd said and marked on the table again:

"This language cannot make up its mind," Layla said.

"Shad-ili-ya," Alihahd voiced the symbols.

"That cannot be." Serra pointed. "The middle two marks are the same."

"NINI means ili," Alihahd said.

"That is stupid," Layla said, and she erased Shad Iliya from existence again.

"It's an ancient language. It went through several evolutions. Humankind was then only developing the concept of the written word," Alihahd said. He tossed the chalk over his shoulder. "Anyway, it was not my idea to use it."

"It is stupid," Layla said and fastened her DINGIR pendant back around her neck.

Hall stopped snoring in the adjacent cave, and Serra brought him some strong tea.

Talk switched to other things, and Alihahd toyed with a nail, using it to scratch signs into the stone wall, until Layla noticed what he had written:

"What is that?"

"Ashar Ari. Place of Eagles," Alihahd said. "All Na'id planets are called Ashar something or Mat something — Place of this, Land of that."

"You gave us a Na'id name?"

Alihahd put down the nail. "In Na'id culture, to name a place — to give it a Na'id name — is to legitimize it. The name officially recognizes this planet as Place of Eagles — that is to say: place sovereign to nonhuman aliens."

"In that case, I like it," Layla said. "Ashar Ari."

"The Na'id would hate it," Alihahd said.

"The Na'id may go to hell."

Flames raked the sky over the recruiting station, consuming the myriad dead which littered the compound blackened with blood. Mushabriqu's charred body dangled, a grim banner over the blaze, until the flagpole melted and fell. The outrush of heat singed leaves on trees far away.

Beyond the inferno, freed conscript children were running into the surrounding forest.

The killer had been this way before. He knew where to go next.

He boarded his ship, *Singalai*, flew over the flames, and set course for the nearest Na'id reloc center, to kill again.

The caves grew colder. Snow had covered some of the solar collectors outside, and the captives of the storm could only hope it would blow off again.

To make it worse, Layla and Serra were telling ghost stories. Inevitably, they came to the *Flying Dutchman* and *Ma-*

rauder stories. Hall just listened and smiled. He relit his pipe. One of its fire-opal eyes was missing, giving the fox a winking look.

"They say that at the battle for Jerusalem the whole galaxy came to the aid of the Holy City, and all the ghosts of those buried in the hills rose and fought. And they say Shad Iliya saw the ghost of a brigantine ship sail over the city. He died right after that. They say that is what killed him."

"Truly?" Amerika asked, breathless and enthralled.

"So they say," Layla said. "Something got him. It may as well have been the *Marauder* ship."

"I saw the *Marauder*," Alihahd said. He set aside his third, half-finished cup of tea and did not touch it again.

"You never struck me as a teller of tales," Serra said.

"I saw it," Alihahd said.

"I saw it, too," Vaslav said.

Amerika's eyes were huge. "And then you were shipwrecked!" she exclaimed in a whisper.

"Very shortly afterward, yes," Alihahd said. "Though I think I was equal bad luck for the *Marauder*. I believe he wrecked soon after I did."

"How can you wreck a ghost?" Layla asked.

"Because my luck is very, very bad," Alihahd said. "And because this *Marauder* was not actually a ghost. It was a hologram that a pirate used to frighten Na'id ships before he destroyed them. Unfortunately, we two curses crossed each other's paths and that was the end of us."

"Did you see the *Marauder*?" Serra asked Hall.

Alihahd sat forward. He was interested in how Hall would answer that question. Hall said only, "I was on a different ship from these two."

A neat evasion that one—neither yes, I am the *Marauder*, or no, I am not. The man would not be pinned down. He did, however, admit to garroting a Na'id captain with his own hands. He went into graphic, relished detail about it. He had no regret. He waved his hand at the cuneiform Alihahd had engraved into the wall. "It is written in those ancient chicken scratches somewhere, 'an eye for an eye.'" He looked to Alihahd for verification. "True?"

"True," Alihahd said.

If a citizen has destroyed the eye of a citizen, his own eye shall be destroyed. If he has injured the limb of a citizen, his own limb shall be injured. If he has destroyed the eye of a subordinate or injured the limb of a subordinate, he shall weigh out a recompense in silver. If he has destroyed the eye of a slave of a citizen or injured the limb of a slave of a citizen, he shall weigh out half the slave's buying price.

"The principle, I believe," Alihahd said, "behind the law 'an eye for an eye' was, at the time it was written, not that the punishment be severe enough for the crime, but that the punishment not exceed the crime, which was rampant practice in those days."

"You think me excessive?" Hall asked.

"I was not there."

"You think me excessive."

"I think you excessive."

Hall sat up and moved in closer. Low, so only Alihahd could hear, he said, "You didn't tell me you beat a man to a bloody pulp down in the valley."

"It slipped my mind," Alihahd said frostily.

"Why are you so cool toward the idea of vengeance, Captain?" Hall said with oily insinuation.

He was surprised to receive straight out the answer he sought.

"Lest it fall upon me."

The drillmaster enjoyed his work. He had survived yet another summons before the review board on suspicion of excessive and brutal disciplinary measures. He said all the right things, admitted he was often severe with his young charges but only to train them to survive in the field in harsh environments, combating aliens. He said he was strict out of concern for his recruits and that most of them respected a tough master. However, there were whiners in any group. The board found his explanations acceptable. The drillmaster always knew what to say.

In reality, he liked to beat children. Real torture and sexual abuse he reserved for those children already on record as compulsive liars and unwilling conscripts. He'd worked hard to get where he was—to be commander and not the commanded, the abuser, not the abused—and he knew how to preserve his position.

He had been master of the juvenile wing of training section Alpha 4 for twenty-five years. He could handle squealers.

But the last little girl from Qiatte had come across as entirely too credible. She'd been responsible for his latest trip before the review board. It was a pity that her class was gone, moved on to Omonia Station, and he was unable to get back at her.

That whole class had been trouble. Qiatte was a little mining village on a grade four planet. That world turned out some of the most recalcitrant hellions ever to come through this training station. The reloc center always sent the children from Qiatte here. The reloc center had very recently met with a mysterious catastrophe that killed everyone on the base—may they all burn in hell. The drillmaster was glad. He would get no more ungovernable conscripts from that place.

Still unsettled over his inquiry, he soothed himself with food. He ate another honey roll with tearing bites. Then he swiveled in his chair to the water fountain to rinse his sticky fingers.

He turned on the fountain, and the water ran thick red. It looked like blood.

He shut it off, but continued to stare at the red splashes in the basin. Practical joke. Sick one. Someone would hear about this.

He reached back to his desk and pattered around the messy piles of records, feeling for his transceiver.

Suddenly there was a movement and a bouncing clinking as the transceiver arced over his head into the fountain basin.

He grabbed for it, but before he could swivel around to see who had tossed it, a fist closed on his hair atop his head. There came a whistling swish and a current of air on his face. He blinked his eyes shut.

Instantly, he lost all feeling in his body—except for the damnedest dizzy sensation of rising. And he couldn't swallow.

Upon opening his eyes, he saw that he was rising, being pulled up, weightlessly, jiggling and bobbing, by his hair.

His eyes shifted down to a body falling from his chair and spurting blood from a sheared stump of a thick neck.

The severed head remained conscious only fifteen seconds.

It was a long fifteen seconds.

Nineteen days passed, and time stopped. The last day of Shandee seemed to drag on forever. Layla rapped the hourglass on the table until it broke because it was not moving.

Alihahd still kept Earth time—as valid a schedule as any in this sunless prison. For him the days—Earth days—numbered twenty-four and a half so far. His rituals were rigid and changeless. His patience seemed limitless, his temper ever cool day after day. He was coping best of the group in confinement.

The heat was on again. Harrison Hall took off his coat. He pulled a gold thread from the frayed lining of his vest. Without his heavy rawhide redingote one could see how tight was his waist and flat stomach. He was a powerful man.

"What country is Jerusalem in?" Hall threw out the question casually, all his attention seemingly on the loose threads of his vest.

Alihahd laughed with more bitterness than he had ever

let show. "God knows," he said. Then, "Depends on whom you ask."

Hall knew that. It was why he had asked the question—to discover where Alihahd's loyalties lay. And he'd received his answer: nowhere. Alihahd was not radical anything. His sympathies were everywhere, allegiance nowhere.

"That little shred of land on the coast has always been a hotbed of violence and contention. Whoever has it is perpetually at war to keep it," Alihahd said.

Layla was listening while she combed her hair, ripping out the snarls rather than untangling them. "If the land is so hard to keep, why does not everyone move?" she said.

"Why, indeed?" Alihahd said with a sorrowful laugh, his blue eyes watery, bright, sad, mystified. "It is God's land, you see. Everyone's religion bids him fight to keep that land."

"And what are you?" Hall said. "Religion."

There was a hesitation. "Baha'i," Alihahd said.

"What is that?"

"A renegade branch of Islam, but rather similar to the Na'id without the imperialism and without the armies."

Hall did not believe it. Perhaps—just perhaps—Alihahd was a convert, but Hall was dead certain that Alihahd had not been born into that faith. Alihahd had been in an army. He had been disenchanted with something. Baha'i was a later choice. Or a lie. Hall did not think Alihahd believed in God at all.

Besides, there had been no Baha'i at Jerusalem.

Alihahd had finished drinking two cups of tea. Harrison Hall poured the third round. Alihahd lifted his third cup to drink, looked inside it, and froze. The cup was half full.

All color drained from his face. His lips twitched. Nothing else moved. Some part of him was shredding away behind his glassy blue eyes.

Hall held the kettle with an expression of false innocence: *Is something wrong?*

Alihahd set the cup down clattering, spilling the tea. He

pushed back from the table with quaking hands, stood woodenly, knocking his stool backward, and he stumbled over it to get away. He staggered toward the doorway to the bedchamber. Long arms reached for the lintel to hold himself up and drag himself through.

The others thought he'd been poisoned.

Layla didn't know what had happened or how, but she knew who. She turned on Hall. "What did you do to him? You did something!"

Hall opened his arms with an exaggerated shrug to say, *Who, me?* But his crescent eyes were merry, the sinuous lines of his beautiful wedge-shaped face upswept in barely contained glee.

A guttural cry came from the next room, and a crash and sounds of things being thrown and broken.

Hall had rearranged the cave.

With a groan, Alihahd hurled all the reordered jars against the walls and threw the twice-folded covers onto the floor.

Amerika and Vaslav cringed together at the table in the other room like children whose father was not well. They stared about them, their round eyes begging someone to make everything all right again.

Hall sat himself at the table, satisfied, and took up his pipe.

Alihahd returned, shaken, stiff, his face long and frowning, bloodless. He sat at the table. He clasped his big hands on the table, knuckles white, his back erect, teeth clenched, a muscle twisting over his jaw, eyelids stretched white around staring eyes, looking at no one. A muscle twitched under his eye.

He did not speak again until the days of the Witch Shandee were over.

The days of restraint enshrouded the Aerie, a somber time when the splendid warrior-priests, like drab birds in molt, put away their beautiful clothes for the thirteen days between the leaving of Shandee and New Year's Day. The air was calm. Warm breath still showed in frosty clouds, but the ice on the sunlit slopes was melting at last. Spring had already arrived on the middle slopes in a haze of blue buds on the trees.

Harrison slogged along a path sodden with spring mud and snowmelt. Leathery green shoots of emerald spikes braved the weather and poked through the ice on either side. He felt a cold trickle on his instep and knew that his old boots were finally done for. He turned his foot to find the crack in the thinned sole.

He heard a strange sound. His ear was attuned to patterns by now, and this one was not usual. He straightened and drew his gun from his belt.

As he crested the top, he relaxed and lowered his gun. Alihahd was clad in his red Chesite tunic and red boots. Hall was forming a comment about Alihahd's bony knees being the first sure sign of spring, but he perceived something wrong. Alihahd was smiling. Smiling wrong. Alihahd leaned against the rock face, shiny-eyed and wryly whimsical. His hands flopped strenghthlessly. Footprints in the slushy snow behind him wove on and off the path.

Hall pushed his gun into his belt and stepped down to take Alihahd's head in his hands. He looked into his eyes, searching for signs of fever. "What is wrong with you?" he demanded. Then he got a whiff of his breath.

Alihahd smiled. His hands moved elegantly, almost in caricature of himself. His eyes were pale, drowned sapphires. "Mr. Hall, I am drunk."

Hall's face darkened, and he pushed Alihahd's face aside—the motion was disgust—and he stalked past him in the direction from which Alihahd had come. Hall's head turned left and right with the sharp motions of anger—and searching.

Alihahd scrambled after him. His own blundering foot tracks blazoned a conspicuous trail, and Hall would surely find what he sought.

Alihahd drew himself up on a rocky bluff and thundered at Hall's back in the most commanding voice he could muster. "Mr. Hall."

Alihahd had once been a magnificent man and could still summon power, even drunk. Most of the orders he'd given in the past ten years had been issued in varying states of insobriety, and he still had the voice of absolute command.

"Stop! This is no concern of yours!"

With insistence, his dignity slipped a degree. He took a step forward from the rise and immediately felt his vulnerability increase. "Mr. Hall!"

Hall ignored him and strode away. As he neared his hidden goal, Alihahd became shrill and frantic. He stumbled after Hall. "Mr. Hall! This is none of your affair!"

"I am my brother's keeper," Hall said. "As the Na'id would say."

Alihahd scowled blackly.

Hall found the distillery behind a spreading thorn bush, and Alihahd lunged to put himself between Hall and his lifeline. He spoke in a deep, cultured, angry tremolo, each word precise, if thick. "Leave. Me. Alone."

Hall started forward. Alihahd laid hands on him to restrain him. But at the height of his strength, Alihahd had never been a match for Harrison White Fox Hall. Alihahd felt a shift of balance and a sudden helplessness. *Why is he doing this to me?*

Hall threw Alihahd to the ground. He marched up to the still, ripped out the condenser tube, and threw it at Alihahd as if onto a pile of rubbish. His driving heel came down on the soft copper still pot. Honey water gushed out over the coals. Hall kicked and scattered the painfully collected stack of firewood, and smashed all the clay jars of mead on the rocks.

Alihahd stood up, indignant. "Who do you presume to be? See the lord and master of Eridani. Thou art lord and master of nothing. And not of me!"

Hall rounded on Alihahd and gave him a slap that staggered him. His brain seemed to ricochet inside his skull. Alihahd tasted blood. And he fought, tried to. Alihahd's blows landed uselessly, or did not land at all. Then Hall's fist drove into Alihahd's solar plexus, knocking the wind out of him, and Alihahd crumpled to the ground. Hall picked him up and set him on his feet. Alihahd leaned on him, gasping. Alihahd lifted his head and in the next breath cursed Hall. Hall hit him again, harder, in the same place. Alihahd dropped, doubled over, sick and in pain up to his eyes. Hall stood over him, hands in fists, waiting for Alihahd to get up.

Alihahd crawled to his feet. Hall steadied him, then hit him with his open palm. And kept hitting him after Alihahd ceased to fight. The blows kept falling, and Alihahd could only wonder why.

And he cried, great drunken teardrops rolling down his sunken cheeks.

The blows stopped, and Hall hauled him to an icy steam and made him kneel. "Look at yourself." Hall forced his head down over a reflecting pool. Alihahd resisted with a groan, trying to turn away, but Hall's hands were like a vise holding him over the sotted, blubbering face in the pool.

Alihahd slapped the water with a cry, "I am trying not to!"

After a useless scuffle in the streamside mud, Alihahd was pulled to the rapids. Hall grabbed a fistful of blond hair and pushed Alihahd's head under the icy cataract.

Alihahd's hands scrabbled behind his head at Hall's fingers. Frigid water filled his ears, and sounds were suddenly muffled and singing, otherworldly, like death.

Alihahd was afraid that Hall was trying to drown him. But Hall let him up for air, then pushed him under again.

After the fourth time, Hall pulled Alihahd up by the hair to a kneeling position and searched his red face. Alihahd's eyes were shut and spilling hot tears. "Leave me alone. Leave me alone."

"Shut up and breathe, or you'll be sorry."

Alihahd breathed.

Hall could tell when Alihahd began to sober up. He stopped whimpering in between dunkings. Hall released him and crouched back on his heels.

Alihahd, on hands and knees, hung his head forward, water streaming down his face from his hair. "I don't like you at all," he croaked.

Hall smiled.

Alihahd knelt looking up, teeth chattering, his face scarlet, his tunic soaked darker red down the front. Water drained from his ears and he could hear clearly again. He felt the cold air as if it were blowing through his head. He brought his fingers to his eyes that felt too big for their sockets. "Oh."

"Have you never been in battle, Captain?" Hall asked.

Alihahd answered shakily, "Of course."

"Jerusalem," Hall said.

"I was there," Alihahd said. "If you must know, I ran."

Hall let go of Alihahd with a bark of gleeful surprise. "You deserted!"

"I left," Alihahd said. He put his hand over his eyes. "You're a sadist."

"No, I'm not," Hall said. Then, "Just a little." He helped Alihahd to his feet, like helping up a grimacing doll of wood and rags. Alihahd brushed off the pebbles embedded in his purpled knees.

Hall was looking at the sky. "I think it's time to get dried and presentable, Captain."

Alihahd lifted his head in a mute question. *Why?*

Hall pointed up.

Alihahd narrowed his too-big eyes at the daylight sky, and emotion rushed with sober clarity.

A slow-falling star.

A spaceship descended and sank into the layer of cloud that hung over the valley.

Alihahd went to the Chamber of the Golden Dome to be there when Roniva received her returning warriors.

Alihahd's hair, newly dried, kicked up in wispy cowlicks. He had changed clothes. He wore a dry gray tunic and sandals. His eyes were red and puffed, his face sporting bruises of all colors.

Roniva spoke to him directly. "Art thou ill?"

"He's fine," Harrison Hall said.

Alihahd's teeth clamped tight, and he stood rigid in silence.

Roniva appeared a harsh figure without jewels or soft colors. She wore a dark green robe. Her hair was confined atop her head. She beckoned Alihahd to her with a ringless hand, and he moved around the low lattice barrier onto the dais with her. She took his arm and made him stand beside her throne. "Stay thee here with me. I shall speak through thee."

And when two strange warrior-priests entered and greeted her, she said to Alihahd, "Ask my warriors why they return after a single year. What is wrong?"

In answer, the travelers unfolded a long tale of a series of mysterious attacks on Na'id installations. Reports of a man with a sword and a hawk, who left many dead behind him. The warriors had been following the deadly trail, site to site, but could not catch up with the assassin.

As Roniva listened, her face smoothed in slow-growing shock and dread, then hardened into eaglelike planes. Her long fingers closed around her sword hilt and tightened until her midnight skin paled.

Her warriors opened their arms, powerless in the face of an unacceptable conclusion. "An Itiri."

"A Wolf," Roniva said. "A wolf that walks like a man."

"We would stop him," said one warrior-priest. "But we know not where he is now or whither he will go."

"Has Omonia Station been hit?" Alihahd asked.

Roniva's head turned sharply toward him. Her voice was speaking without her. Roniva looked again to her warriors and bid with voiceless command in her burning onyx eyes: *Answer that.*

The warriors exchanged doubtful looks. "Omonia? Not that we have heard."

Roniva tilted her dark head up to Alihahd, her intermediary who spoke with a mind of his own. "This is significant?" she asked.

"I think so, Fendi," Alihahd said. "There is a pattern to the attacks as they've been reported."

"What pattern?"

"They follow a path a conscript of the Na'id might take from first capture to final assignment. First to a conscription force base for classification. Then to a reloc center and orientation camp. Then to a training center like Alpha 4. All of Alpha 4's trainees begin service in Omonia Station. If the pattern holds, Omonia is where Ben will go next."

"Ben is dead," Roniva said.

"Call him what you like, he will attack Omonia Station," Alihahd said. He was peripherally aware of tawny eyes studying him from a shadowed corner of the Great Chamber. Harrison Hall watched him talk to Roniva as an equal, a contradiction of the sniveling human wreck at the streamside.

"Tell my warriors to take a ship and stop him," Roniva said. "Take *Topaz*. Thou shalt guide them." Her face softened and she gazed up from her throne at Alihahd's bruised face and red-shot blue eyes. She reached up to touch Alihahd's chest. "And I fear I shall lose thee once I let thee aboard one of my spaceships, thou so restless to be gone."

"I shall not return if I have any choice," Alihahd admitted.

"Then I bid thee, once thou art free, leave us lost to humankind, if thou carryest any memory from this Aerie. Bring us no human war."

"It may be too late for that, Fendi," Alihahd said, thinking of Ben-Tairre loose on the Empire, even now on his way to Omonia Station.

"This I fear," Roniva said. She did not look frightened. "Go now."

"Fendi." Alihahd bowed. He turned away in a forceful motion and took long strides to the archway, on fire with mission, freedom, and command. The Itiri warriors fell into step behind him. His sinister shadow, Harrison White Fox Hall, appeared at his flank. Alihahd swept out of the nine-sided chamber into sunlight.

He could not believe he was free. He was actually leaving this alien world after all this time.

He found himself oddly reluctant.

PART FOUR:

True Colors

15. Rogue Wolf

AS THE SPACESHIP *TOPAZ* broke through the ceiling of clouds into bright sunlight, Alihahd glimpsed the twin mountain crest of the Aerie gleaming with ice-glazed brilliance in the snowy sea of vapor. The ship quickened its ascent, and the great mountain became small, then lost entirely. The atmosphere thinned, cleared to black, and the *Topaz* was in space.

With his hand pressed to the viewport, Alihahd watched the blue world dwindle. With a jump to faster-than-light, it was all gone.

He was overcome with sudden déjà vu—the depressing sameness of starships, the isolation of faster-than-light. The familiarity of it overwhelmed. He had for so much of his life been a nomad living onboard one ship or another that coming back to this life was like never leaving it. The short year on Iry was reduced to a dream, as if it had never happened.

He was free at last. Why was he feeling so ill?

He knew what was waiting for him. He wished to anyone's god that Hall had not destroyed his hard-made mead.

He glowered aside at Hall, who lounged easily in the next seat, his feet up on an unoccupied seat across from him. He was puffing Iry weeds in his one-eyed fox-head pipe. He wore his bandana gypsy-fashion. His teeth flashed white in his dark bronze face.

Alihahd wore Na'id type clothing that Amerika had made for him at his instruction. She'd expressed a liking for the design. Hall had told her to bite her tongue.

There were four Itiri warrior-priests aboard *Topaz* along with Alihahd, Hall, Vaslav, and Layla. They had a plan to intercept Ben at Omonia Station, take him back to Iry, and leave Alihahd behind on Omonia under one of his many Na'id guises. An elaborate plan, full of contingencies, it left all kinds of openings to go wrong.

Things went wrong before it had even begun.

Topaz sublighted for its approach to the space station and arrived to silence.

The great polymer triple torus of the station turned in the sunless void, dark as if deserted, without ships coming or going, without radio chatter, without signals of any kind.

There was no question of what had happened. It was only left to wonder if anyone was yet alive on Omonia and if Ben was still there.

The Itiri ship *Topaz* attached itself to a station lock and sealed the passage. *Topaz*'s lock opened. Omonia's lock remained closed against them. The Itiri were about to blast it with their taebens when Alihahd motioned them aside. "Don't do that."

"Canst thou open it?" the eldest warrior asked.

Alihahd moved to the manual access panel at the side of the lock, keyed in an imperative code, then crouched before the sensor and waited for his retina to be scanned. "I can open any lock in the Empire," he said. They were in Alihahd's territory now. Na'id ships were a world he knew.

Harrison Hall came to crouch at his side, his gun drawn and resting across his muscular thighs. "How about the Bel's door?" Hall said. It was supposed to be a joke.

"You want to see the Bel?" Alihahd said very softly and without humor. It was flat affirmative.

Surprise rippled Hall's perennial nonchalance. That level of infiltration into the Na'id security system was beyond belief. That kind of clearance simply could not fall into the hands of an imposter.

Omonia's lock spun in answer to the imperative, and it released. The outer iris dilated. The lead warrior gave the inner hatch a push with his bare foot, and it swung heavily open.

From the first moment of the lock's opening came the assault of wrongness, alarms blaring, miasma of death, smell of blood.

The Itiri bounded through the hatchway like hunting cats and fanned out, listening, looking.

Alihahd followed them aboard. He had originally intended to dye his pale, telltale skin, but there was probably no one left in here he need deceive.

Hall shadowed close behind him with ready weapon.

They came upon the first corpses right away. The slaughter was absolute, the station corridors splattered with blood as far as could be seen.

There was a squeak from Vaslav, who had crept out of the *Topaz* and tripped over a head torn from its body, which lay several paces away from it.

The neck was not severed. It was ripped. The head had come off in the hands of someone of great strength. The wide pool of blood was not yet dry. The killer could have simply choked this man, or broken his neck. This was over-kill, tremendous force used out of no necessity, no reason. The lack of control, the madness of it, was un-Itiri. It was human. The kind of thing humans liked to call inhuman.

Alihahd had backed away and flattened himself against the bulkhead, sweating, face paled to ash, lips bloodless. Something darker than fear haunted his white-ringed eyes. He was shaking, his neck stiff.

Then he steeled himself in a deliberate moment. His head lowered until he was staring out of the tops of his eyes. The crevices in his face deepened, his breath came shallow as if loathing the air, and he moved away from the wall, not talking, meeting no one's gaze, sickened, dangerous. Layla did not know him. Even Hall would not approach him when he looked like that.

The Itiri gave him a wide berth. In search of Jinin-Ben-Tairre—if he was still in the station—the warrior-priests divided and glided down the corridors where they saw the blood was warmest. Sound of life—terrified life—could be heard retreating before them. Children's whispered shrieks and desperate scrambling sounded in the air vents.

Alihahd was eerie, transformed into someone else altogether. He was clad in the dress of an abhorred people that made him appear so strikingly one of them that it was hard to see him otherwise. Na'id square shoulders with epaulets, a tapered waist, full cuffed sleeves and trousers—the clothes made him a hated silhouette, and Alihahd carried himself differently in them.

He opened a wall panel, shut off the clangoring alarm, and turned up the air filters, all with the throwaway ease of one who has handled such controls many times. He swept down a corridor where the Itiri had not gone, stepping wide over the bodies in his path with little pause, wrath growing with each one, and he stalked out of view with the menacing military stride of a new master taking over.

Hall chose a different route, and Vaslav came with him, afraid of Alihahd. Layla struck out on a path of her own.

Claustrophobia and carnage.

Alihahd walked the ravaged corridors. The soft *stick, stick, stick* of blood on his bootsoles sounded loud in the dead quiet. He stepped over more bodies, human bodies, then paused to kneel beside one he thought was still alive. He touched his fingers to the neck.

Not.

He closed another's eyes, rose. The mode of death this time—all down the corridor—was a long blade.

That would be a double curved sword.

Menin aeide Thea . . . He remembered snatches of a song of slaughter. *Sing of the destructive wrath* . . . It ran through his mind in rhythmic chant as he stepped over oozing dead.

. . . *that hurled many brave souls of heroes to Hades and made their bodies a spoil for dogs and carrion birds* . . .

From time to time he heard the scurrying of children. There was only one child's body in the corridor—a little girl with a gun in her hand. The rest of the corpses were adults.

. . . *and so the will of God was done.*

A pain pushed itself into Alihahd's consciousness. His jaw hurt. His teeth were clenched and the muscles in his face had been tensed into a deep, immobile frown for a long time now.

He made his muscles relax. His face ached.

He continued down the passage, paused again to bend over a twitching victim, not sure whether she was alive or this was rigor. An Itiri would have been able to tell at a glance if the body was still giving off heat.

He had just begun to crouch down when he heard heavy running footsteps from father down the curved passage.

A Na'id engineer came stampeding around the bend, then skidded to stop at the sight of a tall, blond figure bending over a bloody corpse. Alihahd looked up at him, showing his white face. The engineer screamed and fled.

Alihahd stood up. His chest felt tight, his breath constricted. The Na'id at his feet—alive or dead—writhed ignored. Alihahd stepped away until his back was against a door.

There were adults alive in this section. In past attacks, Ben killed all the adults. The butchery in Omonia was not finished yet. Alihahd held his breath.

Ben was still here.

Suddenly the door slid open behind Alihahd and he spun.

There was a movement directly before his face—Jinin-Ben-Tairre spinning with his sword raised, the sword striking down on the Na'id-clothed figure in the doorway.

16. Ghosts

THE BLADE DEFLECTED down Alihahd's side in last-instant recognition, slicing flesh and nicking bone at the point of his wide shoulder, slashing open the full sleeve of his Na'id shirt.

Ben coiled back with his sword, and both men froze.

Alihahd gazed into feral eyes—dark pits that went down and down forever. He saw all the horror and hatred in them, and all the pain.

Less a man now than a maddened wild animal, Ben stared with half-sight. His consciousness did not register Alihahd, only a white face, a white man in Na'id dress, and the sight incensed him. His breath came audibly, a rough panting of rage. Then he blinked. His brows tightened together. True realization penetrated that this was Alihahd standing before him—

And Alihahd was not certain that Ben would not kill him anyway.

A trickle of blood wended down from Alihahd's shoulder, prickling at the hair on his arm. The ragged flap of his sleeve hung loose from his cuff. Alihahd couldn't move, couldn't talk, even to save his life.

A movement behind Ben broke Alihahd's trance—a man with a gun shouldering his way through the circulation vent and taking aim at Ben's back. Ben's Itiri awareness must have failed him, for it was Alihahd who sang out, "Behind you!"

Ben dropped into a spinning crouch, drawing and firing his taeben.

The Na'id gun clattered to the deck, and the dead man slid out of the vent and flopped on top of his weapon in a heap. From the narrow passage from which he'd come sounded the hasty scrambling of a companion retreating.

Ben didn't chase the survivor. He turned back to Alihahd, all his weapons lowered, his dark eyes full of wonder, wordlessly asking why Alihahd had warned him.

"I do not know," Alihahd answered harshly as if the question had been spoken aloud. His voice was thick and he was shaking. "I will assume there is a reason for this." The carnage he meant. There had to be a reason. Alihahd gave him the benefit of a gigantic doubt, but let it be known he granted this grudgingly.

Only then did Alihahd look down to inspect his own wound. He touched his cut arm and shoulder with his opposite hand, assessing the extent of the damage, which turned out to be minor. It would leave a pitted scar in his shoulder.

Alihahd turned to go. The light touch of two fingers on his unhurt shoulder stopped him. Alihahd paused, startled by the contact. He turned his head to look back.

Ben sheathed his sword and holstered his taeben. He drew his dagger slowly as if it were painful to him and held it to his own leg. In his pause, Alihahd saw Ben fighting down great fear as if he intended to cut himself. But Ben slashed open his trouser leg and he turned for Alihahd to see.

A blue tattooed number marked his thigh, the brand of a Na'id child conscript.

Bitterness rose in Alihahd's throat. He swallowed. The bitterness stayed.

Why hadn't he guessed? Aliens had not been the ones who taught Ben to kill. They had merely perfected it.

Shock, hatred, and all the rest of it subsided into weary sickness. Alihahd reached back his hand and bade Ben come. "Well, let us be on."

Ben put his bloody hand into Alihahd's and padded after him on silent feet. It was like leading a leopard from its kill on a leash made for toy dogs. The leopard meekly put himself under Alihahd's authority.

What made Ben think he could turn to Alihahd? He could, and knew it. *So you see that in me,* thought Alihahd.

Alihahd wished someone had been there to take *his* bloody hand.

He led Ben back to the *Topaz* and broadcast three words through the space station's public-address system: "I found him."

With that, the Itiri came gliding back like ghosts. Not one of them saluted Ben. One did not talk to the dead.

Layla did. She callously saluted with her dagger. "Good job," she said and boarded *Topaz*. Ben masked reaction if he felt any.

Alihahd took Ben to a solitary unlit compartment on board *Topaz*. Neither of them wanted the light. Ben walked into the cabin slowly, then circled back and abruptly offered his sword to Alihahd, hilt first.

Alihahd regarded the sticky hilt in surprise and quiet distaste. "I do not want it," he said, almost chiding. What was he supposed to do with it?

Ben let it drop at Alihahd's feet, withdrew into the small space, sank to the deck, folded his legs under him, and shut his eyes.

Alihahd closed the door on him and left him there. It occurred to Alihahd only outside that maybe he was supposed to execute Ben. Maybe the Itiri expected it, too.

They were all mistaken.

Alihahd went back through the air lock to re-board Omonia Station.

Vaslav was returning to the lock, a green cast to his face, cringingly following Harrison Hall, who carried himself with the jaunty air of a man taking a stroll on the mountain, no more affected by the mass murder of the Na'id than Layla had been. He stepped over the bodies in his path. Vaslav skirted them.

Corners of a smile disappeared into Hall's mustache on seeing Alihahd. Whatever grim possession had held Alihahd in its grip earlier had released him now. Alihahd looked like Alihahd again.

Hall came to stand with him, his weight casually on one foot. He swept one side of his coat open and back to tuck his hand into his hip pocket. He glanced about him for something he did not actually expect to see. "God damn," he said.

"Mr. Hall?" Alihahd prompted. He pushed back the sweaty bangs that stuck to his forehead, and unfastened some of the buttons of his double-breasted shirt so that the outer flap fell open. Blood still oozed from his shoulder and wetted the tattered edges of his torn sleeve.

"There isn't a damned ship on this station that's flight-worthy," Hall said. "The hangars are a mess. He's blown off half the locks. He hit all the ships—including his own. It seems this was the last stop. There is no way off this station, Captain, except the way we came." He nodded through the lock toward *Topaz*, which would take them straight back to Iry.

Ben had been appallingly thorough. He hadn't even left himself an out. What had he intended to do?

"It looks like I go back to Iry, Captain," Hall sighed. "What about you?"

Alihahd hardly heard him. He was still thinking of Ben. *He wants someone to kill him*. Ben had destroyed his own ship *Singalai* because he intended to die here. Dying was not so easy sometimes. *Now begins the real horror*. Alihahd looked down at his own hands, and marked how easily the blood seemed to get under the nails and stay there. He could not seem to keep it off.

"Captain?"

"What?" Alihahd said, summoned out of his thoughts.

"You coming or staying?"

The Itiri pilot of *Topaz* had come to the hatch and was also waiting for Alihahd's answer.

Alihahd frowned. He was off-planet at last, on familiar if ravaged ground. He could not turn back, having come so far. It was only a matter of time before Na'id ships would come to Omonia. Alihahd might be able to blend into their ranks if . . . there were many ifs.

Alihahd beseeched the Itiri, "Give me a few minutes."

The pilot lifted his chin. "Be thou quick."

Alihahd gave a single nod and ran toward the station dispensary. Up ahead of him all along the way he heard the furtive whispers and scuttling of a flock of preteen girl conscripts taking cover at his approach. One made the wrong move and blundered square into him. She lurched to a flailing halt, a splay of gangly adolescent limbs with distended mouth and eyes. She screamed, "Nazi!" and she sprinted away on her long legs.

No matter who said it, the sound of that epithet never failed to cut like a dull blade.

Alihahd busied himself searching through the dispensary stores for melaninic. Vitiligo was a common condition among the Na'id, and their installations always had a supply of the drug. Alihahd found it and seized up the bottle of pills in his fist with grim relief. Half of his problem was solved. He could melt into the Na'id ranks with his skin a respectable shade of brown. He was not going to be called a nazi again. It was not his fault he was born blond, blue-eyed, and pasty white.

He left the dispensary and quickly made his way over the stiffening bodies in the corridors to the com center. He lifted a corpse out of a chair and sat down at the controls.

He switched on the transceiver without video and immediately received a signal from a ship captain trying to make contact with the silent space station. "This is *Sharru Sennacherib*. Please acknowledge, Omonia. Where is your ID signal? What is your status?"

"*Sharru Sennacherib*. This is Omonia," Alihahd answered. "It's a disaster." That statement carefully told nothing.

"Omonia, elaborate," the captain demanded. "Are you in immediate danger?" The woman's voice was familiar.

"*Sharru*, everyone is dead. When can you be here?" Alihahd infused some calculatedly disjointed panic into his too calm, too military voice. Because he thought he knew the woman, and she might recognize him if he spoke clearly. Wide as the galaxy was, voices such as his that were clear, deep, and cultured with correct speech were rare.

Despite his precaution, the woman's reply was tainted with curiosity. "ETA twenty minutes. Omonia . . . Who is this?"

And all at once Alihahd knew her. No mistake. *This will not work.*

Alihahd disconnected the transmitter and sat back in his seat, his thick lips pressed together in frustrated thought. He could not bring himself to retreat. Not now—when he was actually on board a Na'id station, with melaninic in his hand.

But this ship captain knew him. No matter the disguise, he could not slip past her.

Having the woman eliminated did not even enter consideration. Alihahd would not kill another human being, not in defense, not in war. Never again. He had sworn. He could not do it, or everything he lived for was nothing.

Harrison White Fox Hall came to the com center, paused to make sure Alihahd was not transmitting, then he said, "Time's up, Captain. They want a decision." They, the Itiri.

Alihahd put his hand over his eyes, chasing down every possibility and squeezing his brain for more. So close. The same answer returned again and again. He rose, tapped

Hall's arm, too disappointed to speak, and they ran together back to the *Topaz*.

Alihahd slouched down low in his seat aboard the spaceship, the length of his wounded arm resting flat on the armrest, his other arm flung loosely across his abdomen. Emotions were several and jumbled, fear of the Na'id twined through everything.

Was it possible for the Na'id to figure out what had hit Omonia Station from the tangled evidence left behind? An ungodly hecatomb, the wreck of Ben's two-hundred-year-old ship, a distress call in a voice that sounded like someone it could not be, and Ben's footprints in blood. Those could be identified by the Na'id computer if it searched the database of the dead. Na'id were singularly negligent in checking the rolls of the deceased. They assumed a person could not act simply because the computer thought he was dead. Someday they would learn not to be so certain.

And on top of the physical remains at Omonia would be the stories stricken children told of a semihuman juggernaut, of Itiri warrior-priests, and of a nazi.

Alihahd remembered all the people who had encountered him and had seen his face. There would be other stories, too.

Into his thoughts Harrison White Fox Hall strolled down the aisle of the spaceship that had once been a passenger craft, and he let himself fall into the seat across from Alihahd. He slung one leg over the armrest and took out his pipe. As he lit it, his beautifully sinister orange eyes slid sideways.

Alihahd made an extremely convincing Na'id onboard Omonia. Gone for the time had been the worn-out, pacifistic, sometimes wet rag of a man flagellated with self-doubt and guilt. Left behind had been a soldier to be feared. Hall admitted to being impressed, and even a little frightened — as near to frightened as Hall could feel. There was considerable strength left in Alihahd. And madness.

At this moment, Alihahd was some kind of hybrid creature. He had returned to his customary docile brooding, but he was still in Na'id dress, and some vestige of the commander—the mad one—lurked just below the restored calm. Hall had seen the insanity before, but not its power. And still not its source, the horrible goad from the past that drove Alihahd to heroism and despair. Memory of cowardice? Something was not right with that image.

Hall spoke between languorous puffs on his fox-head pipe. "You're subdued, Captain."

Alihahd sat up. "Should I not be?"

Hall fanned away the gray billows wreathing his head. "Where's your righteous indignation?" Alihahd was always so piously magnanimous to any human foe. He ought to be saying something eloquent for the slaughtered Na'id.

Alihahd shook his head. "No."

Hall pointed at him with his pipe's mouthpiece. "You hate them after all."

"He has a number," Alihahd said, his gaze directed down at the deck between them.

"What was that, Captain?" Hall cocked an ear, better to hear Alihahd's soft murmur.

Blue eyes lifted to Hall's. "Ben-Tairre. He has a number. A blue one."

"That's a boy soldier, isn't it?" Hall said.

"Yes."

This was interesting. "You've forgiven him already," Hall said.

Alihahd slumped back in his seat. His shoulder hurt. "I was thinking."

"Yes," Hall prompted.

"At his age and that number sequence, he would have to have been a trainee roughly sixteen years ago. In fact, he was most likely assigned back there at Omonia."

Alihahd wondered what they'd done to him to make him come back at them like that. "Had he remained with the Na'id, he would have been assigned to an army—in all

probability to one of the three armies that fought the Jeru-
salem campaign. He might have been butchering Jews and
Arabs and Christians for Shad Iliya instead of butchering
Na'id at Omonia today."

"Maybe he was in Shad Iliya's army," Hall said.

Alihahd felt a shock, then reason returned. "No."

"Why not?" Hall said. "Could be why he hates your
looks."

Alihahd was blond, blue-eyed, and fair, like the infamous general.

"He was not in Shad Iliya's army," Alihahd said.

"How do you know?" Hall said. "You left."

Alihahd hesitated, treading around the edges of a nightmare. He answered deliberately, almost as if thinking up
reasons as he spoke. He did not want Ben to be at Jerusalem. "There is no red suffix on his number. He left the Na'id
army when he was still a child." Alihahd's voice dropped
even lower. "What they do to child conscripts is rather
harsh. It washes away their pasts and instills a rabid loyalty.
The conscripts make more enthusiastic soldiers than Na'id
native-borns. But the conditioning methods are extreme.
They backfire sometimes. . . ."

Ben had become a Na'id boomerang. Curious, thought
Alihahd, the boomerang was one weapon the Itiri had
never developed.

"Revenge, Mr. Hall, I understand. Emotion is a human
thing. Blind hatred I understand. It is not my place to forgive or condemn. I simply recognize it. It does not horrify."
And underneath the words his eyes spoke: *That is why I can
endure you, Mr. Hall.*

Then his tone changed again, became distant. "Killing
for an idea. Killing for justice. Killing for the right. That is
horrifying. And that is wrong."

And killing and liking it . . . I don't know what that is. . . .

Guilt. Alihahd felt worse and worse the nearer he came to
Aerie, bringing back Jinin-Ben-Tairre—or whatever the

man was supposed to be called after the Itiri revoked his name. Try as he might, Alihahd could not justify handing over one of his own kind to a race which had made Ben what he was then disowned him and now presumed to decide his fate. And, upon arrival, Alihahd stopped trying to justify it.

The Fendi Roniva was waiting for the crew of the *Topaz* and its cargo—Ben-Tairre—within the Chamber of the Golden Dome. Her sword was drawn and flashing in the light of the newly built fire which crackled in the cold hearth. The Fendi was clothed in midnight colors without ornament in these last somber days before the new year, and the dull gleam of the tungsten-plastic blade seemed very bright against her dark figure. In the frigid air, her breath barely showed a frosty cloud, having little moisture in it—and little warmth, Alihahd thought.

Roniva stepped down from the raised dais and advanced, barefoot on the icy tiled floor, toward the captive warrior Ben. Her black knuckles paled on the hilt of her sword. Ben himself was still. It was an inert kind of stillness, like a pale ivory carving. Someone had cleaned the blood off him. His eyes were unfocused, unless they were looking inward. He appeared unaware of what went on around him, unaware that Roniva meant to kill him. And as Roniva drew close to him, her sword arm beginning to lift, Alihahd stepped in between them, barring the Fendi's way.

Her ebony skin and crimson scars rippled in an expression of disbelief and impending wrath.

Then Roniva's alien face, with its too-keen lines, its hairless brows, its narrow nose and hard, carved cheeks, abruptly snapped to the side and she barked at an attendant, "Tell this man he is to move aside."

"No," Alihahd said with quiet force that gave even the powerful Fendi pause. And he heard himself continue, almost as if someone else were speaking, using his body as an instrument. "It is not your battle."

Roniva's head pivoted back so that she was fully facing

him once again, her expression more and more astonished by degrees. She couldn't even talk, astounded to have heard an Earth man speak Itiri law at her.

Alihahd was at least as surprised as she, but he pressed on. "Jinin-Ben-Tairre is dead. I heard the Fendi say so. This man is a human being, the Fendi made him so. Have the Itiri a war with humankind?"

Roniva struggled for words and someone to speak them to. She would not talk to Alihahd. She presented her back to him and gave her face to her snowy owl, which was perched on her throne. She screamed at the owl, gesturing with her sword, her voice ringing off the domed metal ceiling. "It was not meant that this dead warrior take all that the Aerie taught him and use it in a war that is not of the Aerie. It was meant that he *go home*!"

"The Fendi neglected to consider that perhaps he does not have one," said Alihahd coldly—to the owl.

Roniva wheeled around, her sword hilt in both hands, her eyes flashing rage.

Alihahd went on unwavering, but speaking directly to Roniva again, "The Na'id were there. This home to which he was to return may not exist anymore. This is his battle, his and the Na'id's. I thought that was permitted even under your rules." His tone grew bitter and sarcastic. "But then, who is bound by which law seems to change at the Fendi's convenience. Is this Itiri justice?"

"Justice?" the Fendi said. She turned her head away, addressing herself to her snowy owl. "I have told this one that there is no justice here."

"Yes, I can see that!" Alihahd said, abandoning his stand between Roniva and her intended victim, and making straight for the chamber's exit with long angry strides.

Roniva drew herself erect, extended a pointing arm after the retreating man, and shrilled, "He is to hold!"

Alihahd didn't stop. Even when two armed Itiri warrior-priests stepped into his path, blocking the bronze archway, he pushed through them, buoyant with the death threat.

He was surprised to make it outside to the snapping cold gray dawn. No one had used real force on him yet. The Itiri could afford their customary patience and caution. A thin, aging Earthman wouldn't get far if Roniva invoked her true power. Alihahd kept walking.

Under the golden dome, Roniva stood in rigid, quaking rage.

Suddenly she dropped from her frozen pose, abandoned her attendants, her intermediaries, her victim, and she bolted to the arch. Pushing between the same two warriors Alihahd had passed, she ran out onto the Ledge Path shrieking after him, *to* him. "No one is given what he deserves on the Aerie! *There is no one to decide!*"

Alihahd halted. That sharpest of all thorns stabbed into his most vulnerable point. He who led, who decided so many fates, who was law, judge, and jury, and so often wrong, he had presumed to a wisdom which Roniva never pretended to possess—to be truly just.

Alihahd turned back. He walked to her and spoke quietly. "You took everything from Ben, and you turned him loose with nowhere to go. He is human. He fights a human war. The odds were one against the trained military personnel of four army installations. By any measure, how can you condemn him?" His blond hair kicked across his tall brow that was permanently etched with deep lines.

Roniva sighed. "Ah. I should have killed him at the first, truly killed him. This would never have come to pass. One cannot separate the dead Itiri from the live human as I tried. My mistake. I should have killed him."

"That is beside the point," Alihahd said. "The past is fixed. What will the Fendi do now?"

Roniva brandished her sword. "Correct my mistake."

"He is human," Alihahd said. He raised his voice only slightly. "As I am. You kill him, and we are at war—thou and I."

Roniva stepped backward, her sword before her as if

there were real danger from such a dissipated being. For a while she didn't speak.

Then she sheathed her sword. "O, by the sun, what am I to do with him?"

Alihahd wondered if there was actually anything to be done. He and Roniva were arguing over a man who could decide his own fate. Guilt, Alihahd knew, was the greatest of crippling forces. Alihahd recognized the sudden docility when he found Ben in the space station. After ultimate rage came the mind's death leap. This whole debate could be moot.

"I could resurrect Jinin-Ben-Tairre," Roniva said. "He would be mine again, not thine, and I could do with him as I will." She tilted her head slyly at her human adversary, but then she let her hard shoulders sag and her eyes soften in uselessness. "But I really have not the strength." It had taken everything she had to defeat him the first time.

"You could resurrect Jinin-Ben-Tairre and let him live," Alihahd said.

"Tell me how I could do that, *Fendi* Alihahd," Roniva said ironically.

"Your original reason for killing him was. . .?" He lifted his brows and paused to let her remember for herself before he answered himself. "You feared the Aerie would make him Fendi—or so you told me. Do you think anyone would choose him Fendi, now?"

"No," Roniva conceded. And with the finality of a decision, a reprieve, she said, "No." Then she reached out and held her palm flat to Alihahd's chest as if she could read his heart through her hand. "But, tell me, wherefore this mercy to one who would have seen thee dead?"

"No mercy," Alihahd said. "To let him live with himself? I am being unspeakably cruel, Fendi."

"Ah, thou knowest not our Ben-Tairre." She reclaimed her warrior by the speaking of his name. "Thou speakest not of him." She crossed her arms and moved toward her throne chamber.

Under the archway she stopped, looked over her shoulder, her onyx eyes glinting from under the shadow of her brow. "So who dost thou know who draweth his every breath in pain?"

A silent ghost of the Aerie, his head and broad un-Itiri-like shoulders shrouded in a hermit's hooded black cloak, Ben moved through the halls like one without a soul, having no eyes for the world around him, his sight turned inward, lost and locked there. He drifted, mute, bearded, and strange.

Arilla shaved his face to make him appear more an Itiri, and so that he might know himself when he met his own reflection. She didn't call to him down in the darkness where he was. He would come out when he was ready, when he was healed. Or he would die. Or stay mad forever.

Alihahd passed through an arcade, his gaze chancing inside a stone vault where a shaft of sunlight fell from a single tall window across the hooded figure kneeling in meditation, a sword across his knees. Alihahd knew the shape and the winding of the thick muscles beneath the black pall of the concealing cloak, and was frightened by the sight. Not the sword, but the madness itself terrified. Visions of dreadful memory called to him.

Alihahd shuddered and passed by.

The door to Serra's cave swung in with a swirl of icy air. A shimmering apparition in black and gold extended a long black hand, jeweled and sparkling in starlight. The Fendi never came to Havenside, and all those within the cave, startled by the visitor, were at once on their feet with a kicking back of stools and falling over of cushions.

Gold pendants dangling on delicate chains from many rings were sent into wild pendulum dancing with the slow waving of the beckoning hand that was for Alihahd. "Come know us," Roniva said.

Behind Alihahd, Serra turned over an hourglass, and

Layla whispered to Alihahd as he stood motionless and puzzled, "It is the first of the Sword."

Amerika ran outside to look at the stars, and comprehension came to Alihahd. The Sword was the first sign in the Itiri calendar. The new year had arrived, the year of the Opal Crown.

Alihahd joined the dazzling Fendi on the Ledge Path underneath the glowing field of the Milky Way. Amerika seized his hand and pointed straight up at the sky with a small gasp of discovery at a familiar occultation, a sign of the vernal equinox. And from up on the sentinel's ridges came a crash of bronzes. From all over the Aerie rose a squalling that made Alihahd think of a den of beasts trapped in fire. But the raucous sounds were the alien voice of celebration. Out of all the caves and arcades poured shrieking, bright beings. Torchlight blossomed on every terrace. Alihahd's senses were stunned by the sudden cataract of color after the muted days of restraint. All the ledges filled with the crush of celebrants, and on various levels the lively tap of wooden instruments started up different beats heedless of one another.

Roniva now appeared sedate in her shimmering black robe and gold pendants, standing tall and stately above the mobs of ranga that thronged the paths of Havenside. Her thin fingers closed on Alihahd's upper arm. Her hand was hard, but her grip was not tight. She spoke close to his ear to be heard without raising her voice. "Thou shalt see."

Thou shalt, the Fendi said. It was not invitation. It was mandate. Alihahd yielded to the pressure of her grip.

As he was drawn away with her, he looked back to Amerika, whose hand had slipped from his. He was losing sight of the little girl as the crowd flowed into the widening gap between them. "Are you coming?" He had to shout.

Amerika hung back, her hands clasped in her full skirts, her round cheeks burning in a red blush. He couldn't have heard her had she tried to yell. She motioned no, her head down to the side, and she was enlisted into a gaggle of jubilant ranga to festoon the arcades with flowers and ribbons. Alihahd was pulled in the opposite direction toward the bridge, and he had to turn and watch his own step when he began to cross, starting with his right foot and counting twelve steps.

In the tempest of sound and color and firelight and motion through which he was led, one impression pounded at Alihahd ever louder like a wind brass: *inhuman.*

On one side of the abyss short, stocky cherubs bubbled in an alien speech, their skin white in the night except those closest to the torchfire, who had turned half dark. The ranga were cheerful.

On the other side of the crevasse, the warrior-priests celebrated with more imperative. All impression of humanity they'd ever given Alihahd jangled against what was jumping before his eyes and blaring in his ears. Civilization dissolved into feral howling and dancing. Alihahd's nostrils narrowed in aversion. Everything, down to the smallest details suddenly struck him very wrong—the warriors' nailless fingers, their long toes, their inhumanly lithe, white bodies, their neat white teeth without canines, their hairless limbs, their gem-green eyes, and the crimson burn scars on their smooth faces.

Roniva, as if sensing fear, firmed her grip and led him beyond the Aerie to a place where a bonfire blazed in a great stone pit partly sheltered by a tall, undercut cliff which formed a shallow cave. The smoking, flaming firepit was circled by savages—bright, dancing beings wielding naked blades, screeching wordless cries, and stamping the stony ground with bare feet. It wouldn't have surprised Alihahd at all to be thrown into the pit as sacrifice to some god. But at the pit's edge, Roniva let go of him and he was free to fade back to the fringes of the crowd, away from the fire's heat, into deep shadow, until he backed into a granite wall.

He felt dizzy. He wanted to leave. He wanted the cold, rough-crystalled rock to swallow him up. Whether from something in the smoke or the lateness of the hour or his own imagination run riot, an intoxicated feeling of unreality was overtaking him.

He saw Roniva in flames. She was dancing. Other warrior-priests followed her into the pit, leaping, becoming one entity with the tongues of fire, tearing the last common thread that bound the two species, theirs and Alihahd's. He closed his eyes and tried to breathe without smelling smoke, and to close his ears against the hideous sounds.

The dancers moved out of the fire and into the shadow of the cliff where Alihahd was cornered now. His hiding place reddened with the licking light of firebrands.

At another edge of the throng within the grotto, Alihahd sighted Harrison Hall and Layla. He made his way along the granite wall toward them, proceeding in starts, halting to avoid brushing the violently writhing bodies of the dancers who clawed the air in vicious motions as if tearing unseen enemies.

By the time he reached Hall and Layla, a cold sweat had broken out over his body. He hoped the flickering red firelight would mask his paleness. He swallowed. He hated aliens. And he really hated savages.

The Nwerthan Layla was a little barbaric herself. She was wearing animal skins. She had a gold-fringed shawl tied around her waist and a chain of berinx teeth hung around her neck, but she wasn't swept into the ferocious tide of the dance. She was just watching, her gay smile showing crooked teeth, a shine of exhilaration on her freckled cheeks.

Hall was a pillar of swaggering dignity. His worn, dusty brown redingote and rawhide boots were sober shadows amid the bright dancing colors. He clasped his hands loosely behind his back. The ruddy light played across the planes and hollows of his wedge-shaped face. He surveyed the spectacle, interested but removed from it, a gentle curl on his lips at some secret jest, like the master of the show.

His eyes slid aside toward Alihahd.

All the muscles in Alihahd's face felt slack but for a twitch under one eye.

"Are you unwell?" Layla's voice jarred him, but he couldn't speak.

"I didn't realize our captain was so tender-hearted," Hall said. "It seems we have shocked his finer sensibilities."

Alihahd turned his wide eyes back to the warriors.

Roniva danced in the center of the mob. Her robe was singed. Soot dulled her glossy skin. She circled around a level platform of stones that slowly and awfully took on the aspect of an altar.

Roniva's barking laugh reported above the rest, with no gaiety in it, only lust and cruelty. The sleeves of her robe were torn and they flapped in clawed ribbons from her elbows. Her laugh rose to a shrill scream, carrying a chorus of others up with it, so high it was a siren catching the harmonics of the rock grotto and swelling to a skull-splitting pitch. The sound peaked and shattered into cackles.

Alihahd backed against the granite wall and stiffened, breathing shallowly as if the air itself were poison. He wanted to shut his eyes but couldn't. Through the swirl of black smoke, he witnessed the Itiri descent into the dark elemental side of all that was noble and spiritual in them.

Their voices resolved into a chant. Out of the crowd two celebrants came lugging a spiny-hulled melon that looked like a quilled creature as big as a pig. They hefted the spined thing onto the altar and drew back into the crowd.

The chant grew louder. A sword appeared in Roniva's hands. She screamed a rapish scream. Tungsten-plastic flashed in a lightning strike onto the altar, splitting the melon in two. The pulp oozed out red as blood. The red juice pooled. Roniva dropped the sword and leaped onto the altar. She plunged both hands deep into the spiny hull. She wrenched out fistfuls of stringy, dripping insides and held them up toward the sky. She threw back her head and bayed like a wolf creature in primordial triumph, the red juice dripping onto her face and down her arms.

Alihahd ran away.

*   *   *

He was alone on the windy mountainside, off any track, away from the noise, when finally he stopped.

He hung over a boulder, panting. He groped along the rocks to a rising bank to hold himself on his feet. He'd taken a gash on his shin through his trousers. He'd run away in the dark as if pursued by wolves.

The predator that appeared in his tracks was Harrison Hall, stepping long in leisurely pursuit over the rising ground. Layla trotted after him, two steps to Hall's every one. Layla's impish face was soft in concern and genuine confusion. "What happened? Did it make you sick?"

Alihahd took a few stumbling steps along the embankment, still trying to get away, but they followed him. Hall was grinning. Other people admired Alihahd's horror of violence.

But was it violence that horrified?

Hall moved in. He leaned his hand on the rocks by Alihahd's head. Alihahd turned his face away, one hand holding onto the rocks for balance, one arm circling his stomach.

"No," Hall said slowly and smiled. "That kind of moralistic outrage doesn't come from one who's never known carnage."

Alihahd turned completely around, hugging the rocks, his forehead against stone. Hall leaned in closer, so Alihahd felt his breath on his cheek as Hall spoke. "Captain, you are much too civilized."

Alihahd moaned.

Hall seized his arms and forced him around to face him.

"Leave him alone!" Layla cried.

"Everyone knows that gentleness is the mark of a five-star sadist."

Alihahd lunged free and fled over the rocks, cross-cutting all the twisting paths, making straight for the Aerie. Hall's heavy steps behind him made him run faster.

He came over the last rise to the Aerie's amphitheater, and ran along the Ledge Path to the bridge. Even in his panic he had to stop and begin his traversal carefully with his right foot. He needed to measure and count in shaking breaths twelve steps across—with Hall hounding his tracks, sounding a false count in his ear.

"One, two, three, four—"

"Thirteen, fourteen, five, six, seven—"

Was that ten or eleven? Alihahd became jittery because he wasn't sure now. Or was that twelve? It had to be an even number. Had to be, because he was on his left foot, but he hadn't reached the end of the bridge. He was really too close for it to be ten. This was wrong. It was all wrong. There was a galloping in his stomach. His hands trembled on the guide ropes.

He ran to the other side. "Eleven, twelve."

Hall pursued him into the blackness of his orderly cave.

Hall paused just inside, fists on his hips. He was in no hurry. He towered, a menacing blot in the doorway, until his eyes adjusted. Enough starshine spilled through the opening to allow him to see the quarry he'd run to ground cowering within. He could hear the ragged breathing.

"You've had blood in your mouth, Captain. And the horror is that it did not horrify."

A sound like a swallowed sob choked from the dark. Alihahd tried to rush past Hall to the door, but Hall was everywhere in his path. "Tell me not. Tell me not. Look me in the eyes and tell me not." He backed Alihahd up against the wall, making a cage of his arms around Alihahd's head so Alihahd could look nowhere but at Hall. Silver-blue light from the glowing Milky Way washed all color from his face and paled his eyes, which were wide with echoes of horror.

It hadn't even been true savagery he'd run from. In the Itiri's barbaric celebration there was no pain, no fear, not even terror of a stupid animal. Nothing was tortured, nothing killed. The expression of viciousness was all without true pain. Alihahd ran from phantoms—the mere illusion of savagery. Brutality was not what was actually there. It was what Alihahd saw. He had brought it with him.

Hall had seen a woman splitting a melon. Wide, glassy blue eyes saw something else.

Hall touched his chin lest he look away. "Tell me not."

The eyes lowered and closed. Thin blond lashes quivered, then lifted again as Alihahd's face relaxed and left off its tense trembling. The face smoothed, iced over hard, and the eyes fully opened cold, cold, cold. His demeanor was controlled, unnatural, terrifying. For a moment, even Hall was touched by dread of what he had uncovered.

Resonant voice came from great depth and grew in power. "And so, Mr. Hall, what if you are right?"

"I am," Hall said, absolutely certain. When one set out to corner the devil, one had best be prepared for when he turns around. "You tell me what of it."

Alihahd's face transformed again to a third, unexpected guise, one that was inaccessible, unruffled, and sly. Hall was surprised. Alihahd was many things, but of all traits glimpsed, hinted at, or suspected, cunning was nowhere among them. Alihahd gave a very cool approximation of a smile as if to say this game was over and all that had happened up till this moment was a charade. "I think you are mistaken this time." He ducked under Hall's arm and walked away.

The perplexed hunter pulled in his carefully laid snares and looked for tears that were not there, and he wondered how his prey could possibly have slipped out. Hall sat on the balustrade of the arcade, one foot up, his back against a pillar, and tugged at his mustache.

Ranga with flowers in their red hair were dancing to a gentler music here on Havenside. Simpleminded beings, they had no demons to purge this new year. A ranga woman running through the arcade paused to hug Hall, and ran on. She was hugging everyone.

Across the abyss, Hall spied the lonely figure of Arilla dressed in brown. The fire clan of the carnelian serpent had nothing to celebrate.

A flying bug buzzed at Hall's face, and he snatched at it.

He felt nothing in his closed fist, though he could have sworn he'd caught it. Slowly he uncurled his fingers to look. The bug flew out.

I had him. Hall clicked his tongue against his teeth. Then realization dawned, and he slammed one fist into his opposite palm. *I had him.*

He'd been made to believe his hand was empty, and he'd let his quarry go.

I'll be damned.

Hall swung his leg down from the balustrade and stood up. He'd been right. He had glimpsed Alihahd's true face, the one that belonged to his name.

So mild, so civilized, compassionate to a fault, Alihahd could be nothing but a savage, sickened and afraid of his own soul.

The Itiri warrior-priests were not above recognizing themselves and acting out their own barbaric roots. No species sprang perfect from the head of a god. The Itiri unleashed their barbarism on melons. They could face their baser nature. They had to. They knew what could happen when nature was refused. Locked inside, it could only be held for a time. And then the breaking was unspeakable.

So where had Alihahd met his secret soul and begun to run from it? Had it been something seen or something done? It must be that he'd done something. Alihahd was too contrite to have been a mere witness to horror.

But Alihahd said he'd never fought Na'id. He said he'd run from Jerusalem.

It was Jerusalem, then, that turned him. Sacred duty uncovered what was unholy in him and he ran.

Then which of the three Gods had he deserted? He didn't seem overly attached to any one of them. At first, Hall had been convinced he was a Jew. He was circumcised at least, and he had the attitude of a martyr. But now Hall was thinking Alihahd had to be a Christian. He was too forgiving to be a Jew, too indefinite to be a Muslim. And he had the self-destructive, ox-in-yoke, virtuous servitude of a repentant Christian sinner. He had to be a Christian.

Hall wanted him to be a Christian.

Because there was something else at Jerusalem he could be.

17. Enemies

ALIHAHD WALKED THE LEDGE PATH.
Thawing rocks popped and snapped around him.
Anything above freezing felt mild now, and Alihahd was back to wearing his tunic again. He could see
white, pink, and lavender blossoms on the trees in the valley, and a green-yellow haze of new leaves on all the
branches. Spring had come.

He viewed it darkly. His universe was closing in.

Something nudged at his heels. He glanced down. His
heart skipped in the momentary shock of the unexpected—
a big dark shape, furry and alive. In the following instant, he
realized what it was and he relaxed into disgust. It was a
marlq.

The marlqai had been living on the mountain since before Alihahd had come. They were alien guests of the Itiri,
like Alihahd himself. But he and the marlqai had never
crossed paths before this. They had conspicuously avoided
each other. Alihahd didn't care to be near the marlqai, and
the marlqai had good reason to keep their distance from
humans.

Superficially, the marlqai looked like big rabbits. The size

of a small sow, they had long ears, round, soft eyes, and
brown fur. Their ungainly paws were for locomotion only. A
cluster of slender, hairless, prehensile tentacles were usually
kept hidden in a furry protective pouch in their chests.
Those emerged in a wormy mass to perform delicate work,
such as writing or navigating starships. The marlqai had a
starship on world, but they didn't use it to leave. They preferred to remain as guests of the Aerie. Freeloaders, some
would call them.

The marlq at Alihahd's heels sniffed him, muttering to
itself in the marlqine speech of clicks and whirrs.

Scents were important to the creatures. They had a
highly developed sense of smell and could impart the sensation to other marlqai through their tentacles with perfect
accuracy, bypassing the inadequate medium of speech.

The rabbity nose quivered and snuffled over Alihahd's
leg. Alihahd ignored it, hoping it would go away.

Alihahd had never liked the marlqai—had, in fact, hated
them. He felt nothing now but distaste and mistrust. They
were belligerent, parasitic beasts, repulsive to him for their
incongruous size and their unsightly tentacles. There was
some obscenity in a rabbit that size, and in the naked tentacles coming out of a furred thing so that it looked to be in-
fested with alien worms eating out its chest.

The sapient beings were fellow refugees from Na'id per-
secution. The human rebel runner Alihahd felt no kinship
with them. He regarded the Na'id aggression against the
marlqai the same way the Na'id did: as rodent control.

The marlqai had no homeworld anymore. The Na'id had
eradicated them from the marlqine homeworld and driven
them to near extinction during another of the undefeated
General Shad Iliya's campaigns. The marlqai who managed
to escape the purge of their native planet had quickly re-
plenished their numbers in their spaceships—like rats—and
spread like a plague to other worlds. There were at least two
dozen of them now on the mountain, most of those born
here.

Suddenly, an angry drumming in quick tattoo came, along with pressure like a vise closing around Alihahd's leg, the clacking of tooth on bone and a stab of pain. Alihahd looked down, nauseated more by the sight than the pain, which hadn't yet fully penetrated through his shock. The beast had wound its tentacles around his leg and was shredding his flesh with its teeth, sounding its loud, furious rattle, red froth foaming from its mouth.

All that blood was his.

Alihahd tried to shake the marlq off, but its mass was at least half his own, and everything weighed heavily on this planet. The monster held fast.

Alihahd bent over and pulled, hopped, staggered to the very edge of the Ledge Path, using his hands on the ground to help him, dragging the marlq with him. At the brink, he dropped to his left knee, gripped a granite outcrop with both hands—distantly aware of boundless depth and the far-below rush of wind in a great space—and with a grunt, he heaved his right leg and the grotesque thing over the edge.

Granite bit his palms, his hold slipping with the downward yank of the marlq's weight. The creature held on, dangling into the chasm, still whirring and drumming and chewing. It coughed red bubbles.

Alihahd clawed the rock for a better grip, and he jerked his leg to kick the marlq loose. The tentacles tightened.

Rediscovering the strength of an old fury, Alihahd held tight to the rock spur, swung his leg out, and brought it back in hard. He heard the dull, sick crack of the creature's skull on stone, and he swung out again, his muscles searing, sweat streaming down his sides and beading on his contorted face, his lips pulled back into an agonized snarl, and he beat the thing's head on the stone, again and again.

Finally the drumming stopped. The tentacles loosened. The creature slipped from his bloody leg and dropped into the abyss.

Alihahd collapsed, hugging the granite boulder. His tunic stuck to his sides. Sweat trickled down his scalp under his hair. His leg was an unfocused mass of pain. Then came other marlqai galloping over the summit of Havenside in answer to their comrade's drumming. They stopped at the crest and looked for their relative. They found only blood and Alihahd. They charged down the path, their eyes all arage, seeing murder.

Alihahd lifted himself onto his left leg, staggered, stumbled, then finally crawled to the bridge in swimming pain.

As the angry marlqai reached the Ledge Path with bared teeth, Alihahd's shuddery hands grasped the bridgehook, and he wheeled, rising, throwing his back against a pillar of the arcade, holding the metal barbs out toward the charging animals.

The marlqai bunched to a halt five paces away, noses twitching, eyes wary and malevolent, watching Alihahd and the hook. Muscles beneath their soft brown pelts tensed, untensed. Paws inched forward. They looked as if they might rush him. They smelled weakness. The Earthman looked easy.

Suddenly Alihahd brandished the hook. They flinched. Then they lowered their heads and inched their feet forward.

They were going to try it anyway.

In an instant, an Itiri warrior-priest was standing between them, having leaped down from the higher level to block the attack. The warrior waved the marlqai away with wide sweeps of both his arms. The marlqai shuffled back haltingly before him, furtively shifting their heads to either side, looking for a chance to get around him. One tried, and the warrior caught it by the ears and backed it up with the others, not roughly.

Still gripping the hook in one hand, Alihahd bent down and tugged out a long splinter of bone from his shin. He swayed, dropped the hook, caught himself against the pillar, and slid down, fingers tripping over the stone, his eyes darkening.

Then he was lifted atop firm shoulders—he smelled Hall.

His head hanging upside down, Alihahd was carried across the bridge that swayed in the wind. The crevasse swirled askew in his wavering vision. A thin smear of blood on the rock where Alihahd had beaten the marlq's head wove into view, swam out of view. The world was spinning, the mile-deep abyss at the vortex. He started to retch.

A comfortingly familiar voice growled, and he felt its rumbling vibration beneath him. "You vomit on me, Captain, and I'll drop you." It was Hall.

Alihahd spit up, gagged on it. Hall did not drop him.

At the end of the endless, upside-down journey, Alihahd was laid down in the cave of the physician, who began to tap numbing needles into his pressure points to deaden the pain, but Alihahd saved him the trouble by losing consciousness.

When Alihahd woke, he didn't know where he was. He had seen this cave before, but he didn't know it now. He heard Roniva's voice somewhere outside, but he didn't know her. He didn't know what planet he was on. There was pain in his leg. He didn't know what it was from.

He rose to rest on his elbows, his head clearing. From the distance he heard marlqai drumming in response to something Roniva was saying. He remembered.

He looked down at his throbbing leg. There were stitches in it. *Stitches.* They had *sewn* him shut.

There are stitches *in my leg!*

It had never occurred to him to wonder how primitives closed a wound without pseudo-skin and adhesives. The stitches struck him as absurd. Then funny. It was the natural sequence to being attacked by a giant bunny-rabbit.

His leg hurt to look at. It was discolored purple-red and splashed with the orange stain of a healing herb. Some flesh was missing from his calf, and his shinbone dipped in where pieces had splintered off. His ravaged skin, held shut with zipper-tracks of sutures, was puffed up with outrage but not infection.

He still wore one boot. The other lay on the floor, shredded and caked with brown blood.

Alihahd sat up, swung his legs over the side of the cot,
and rose to stand on his left foot, the ball of his bare right
foot resting on the cold stone floor without weight on it. The
deepest wound in his calf oozed a little. His head throbbed —
or perhaps it was only echoes from his leg. Everything felt
veiled in a haze of pain.

His mouth was dry and coated with a film. His throat
burned acidic. He hopped to a clay storage jug filled with
cool water and drank. Then he hobbled outside to the open
terrace of the second level of Aerieside. The cold air cleared
his senses and swept away some of the misty ache.

He heard Roniva's voice again.

Moving along the narrow path of enameled cobbles at a
painful hop, he followed the sound, steadying himself with
both hands on the mountain's south face.

He came to where the path turned in to the natural amphitheater between the twin crests, and he saw the marlqai,
across the fissure on the first level of Havenside, being
asked to leave.

Roniva was bedecked head to foot in gold, and she
blazed in the meager sunlight. Her hair was twisted into an
intricate crown. A cheela held her familiar, and two other
warriors stood with her.

She didn't address the marlqai directly. She didn't even
face them. She was angry.

No one had ever been asked to leave Iry.

It was not an unreasonable thing to demand. The marlqai
owned a ship. They were able to leave at any time. They
simply hadn't cared to go. They still did not want to go. They
wanted the Itiri to kill Alihahd instead.

Through the warrior-priest who was translating the alien
clacks and mutters to Roniva, the marlqai insisted that Alihahd must have started the fight. Marlqai never attacked
unprovoked, while humans, in contrast, had a history of
wanton aggression against the marlqai.

But all witnesses had reported that the marlq in question had made the first hostile move.

The marlqai whuffled and chittered insinuatingly that all the witnesses were humanoid.

Roniva whirled on them before her interpreter could translate. She understood their language after all. Her teeth flashed white, and she spoke to the outsized rabbits directly. "Get out!"

The creatures hopped back in concert. Then they apologized for their blanket slander against humankind.

Roniva answered coldly through her intermediary, "Tell them I accept their apology. Tell them also to leave."

The scene left Alihahd shaken rather than vindicated. The marlqai shot baleful glances at him across the rift as they prepared to go. What they saw in their turn, if they could read human faces, was madness in the staring blue eyes with white all around. Alihahd's facial muscles stiffened until they trembled.

An old specter loomed. Another break in Utopia. Sanctuary was cracking, and he couldn't hold it together.

Someone came to his side. He didn't look, didn't need to. He knew the pony-trot step. He couldn't face her.

You are not safe anywhere. No matter how far you go, how fast you run. Your furies will find you. There is nowhere to hide.

"They should have made me go. I do not belong here."

Amerika's voice was all hurt disappointment. "You still hate it here."

Alihahd wrapped his hand in her hair and rested it at the nape of her neck in a fist, with great restraint and care, as if the alternative were to strangle her. "No," he said softly, more to the mountain than to the girl. "I should like nothing better than to stay here forever."

Harrison White Fox Hall changed. As the dusk deepened into night, something that started as a gnawing suspicion grew inside and transformed him. Serra watched in alarm.

Something boiled up to a level just short of open violence. She saw it through his eyes. Tiger's eyes. He terrified her.

But the dangerous eyes were not seeing her. They had turned to some inward vision and he paced, prowling in some place other than here.

When he brushed past her and his attention flickered momentarily to recognize her, he beheld her with startled impatience that seemed to demand, *What are you doing here?*

Finally, he stalked out and went to the isolated cave where he stayed when Serra bled.

A little while later, Serra ventured up to bring him some tea before she went to bed, but she turned back at the door.

He was just sitting there polishing his gun.

Hall hummed snatches of a battle tune. He rubbed a soft mhoswool cloth once more over his gun, checked the sight, and holstered it. He felt a vigor he'd almost forgotten in the months of tranquillity. The exhilaration of hatred.

The same puzzles had been running through his head over and over all day.

Marlqai do not attack unprovoked.

Marlqai have long memories.

Hall could read people well and had trouble admitting when he was wrong. His reluctance to back down had blinded him for too long. It was time to make amends.

At first, he'd had Alihahd figured as a onetime coward. He knew Alihahd was a man with a past to be made up for—so moral and self-effacing, with the righteousness of a reformed sinner. It was the kind of self-hatred borne by one who had been in battle and run.

But no. There had been something wrong with that idea from the beginning.

Alihahd had been someone before he was Alihahd. He was not just one of thousands of small cowards who ran at the moment of truth. There was fear in him, true enough. But there was also a streak of sturdier, cruder stuff. And there was blood on his hands, Hall knew that now despite the denial. The mistake had been in assuming that the man had either run or made war. Hall had forgotten that one could do both.

Alihahd had not run—not until after it was over.

That was his sin.

He had stayed and fought. And won.

Dawn's longest rays slanted through the door and cast a warm yellow patch on the cave wall by Alihahd's bed.

He sat up, sick to his stomach. He brushed the sleep from his eyes.

He checked his wound. It had scabbed over quickly and cleanly and hardly swelled. Amerika had brought him a newly made fur-lined boot. He gingerly pulled it on and tried to stand.

If he didn't flex his right ankle and foot at all, and if he kept his weight on his heel, he could manage to move around. He went outside, limped up the mountainside, and found a place to pass water. Steam rose from it in the frigid morning air.

He took a limping walk over the now familiar mountain, even though it was painful. He had a sense that this would be the last time.

Around him, spring was unfolding in earnest. Winter-born mhos cubs mewed in their burrows under budding thickets. A triller tried out its notes as the rising sun softened the brittle air. Underfoot, green shoots thrust up from the hard winter ground and peeked through the dead tatter of last year's brown grasses.

Alihahd sensed the gun at his back before he saw it. A voice sounded behind him. Hall's.

"Alihahd."

Alihahd stopped, rooted to the spot. Never had Hall called him by his false name, and the voice was ironic and deadly. Slowly Alihahd turned. There was the gun, and it was Hall's. Tiger eyes glared behind the barrel. Alihahd returned the gaze with no emotion at all, only weariness. He turned his back again and limped without haste at his same painful, stumbling pace up the grassy scarp and walked away.

Hall lowered the gun. He'd kept his sights on Alihahd, his finger taut on the trigger, until Alihahd disappeared over the rise. Now Hall stared in disbelief at the empty space where Alihahd had been. Did Alihahd think Hall was calling a bluff? Harrison White Fox Hall was not bluffing. He was about to march over the rise after the awkward figure and have it finished, but something was holding him back.

Instinct.

There was something confusing here. Hall could swear Alihahd comprehended the danger he was in. Hall had sensed some fear, seen tension in his shoulders and in his back, braced and waiting for the shot. Alihahd didn't disbelieve the death threat.

Yet he offered no defense. Was that strategy? Did he imagine passivity would earn him pardon? No. Hall thought not. Alihahd was not so deluded. And then Hall realized the answer was right there.

The man wanted him to shoot.

The rains came, freezing at night into icy sheets. Alihahd didn't come back to his cave.

He'd wandered far from the Aerie, slowly, lame and aimless. He didn't take shelter. He slept in the rain. Then the ceiling of the world lowered as the sun began to set. What was left of the clouds sank with the cooling air and settled around the mountain peaks, wrapping everything in damp, blinding whiteness. Alihahd couldn't see past his hands, so he sat in a wet grotto and waited, chill seeping into his bones.

By nightfall, the mountain peaks surfaced, and the sky was revealed cold and icy clear. All below him, the sinking blanket of clouds looked like an arctic wasteland faintly sparkling in the starshine.

The wet ground began to freeze. Alihahd took a few steps into the open and slid a little on the slippery surface. He recognized no landmarks in the jagged black crags. He was alone but for a pair of moving lights—the eyes of a starving meeger aprowl at night.

The wind had stilled. The air was keen. Alihahd's breath drew in, sharp and cutting. It was too cold to stop moving, and dangerous to sleep, but that didn't sound like a good enough reason not to.

Morning came gray. Another cloud layer had formed far above, and the mountaintops were isolated between the two, cut off from both ground and sky in some elsewhere place, a limbo.

The black-hooded warrior came upon the Earthman facedown on the frozen ground.

Alihahd unstuck his eyelids, opened them a crack, and focused on the broad, scarred yellow feet next to his head. Painfully, he lifted his head and looked up.

Ben's black-shrouded figure stood mapped against a bleak sky, at one with the mountains' stark gray solitude. Broad shoulders were slightly forward, his powerfully thewed arms crossed, his shadowed head bowed under the hood. It was said his mind was gone. Ben regarded the half-frozen Earthman curiously. A bird cried in the raw air.

Ben uncrossed his arms and lowered his hood. "Should I summon a healer?" he asked.

"Absolutely not," Alihahd said. He sat up on the ice and touched his numb fingers to his forehead gingerly, as if it might split.

Alihahd had too much conscience for his position, and too much ability for his will. He didn't have enough instinct for self-preservation, but had too much for a man who wanted to die. If only he didn't have a conscience, he would be fine. He would also be the greatest monster the galaxy had ever seen. As it was, he was merely close.

He sighed in sorrow. He was lost. "I really don't know what to do."

Black bangs fluttered over Ben's low forehead in the chill breeze and brushed at the red scars on his cheeks. "Thou might try getting off the ice."

Alihahd held his blue fingernails out before him, frowned, nodded, all in slow motion. "Very practical," he said. When the long view was too overwhelming, look to the small and immediate. That much he could cope with.

With leaden slowness, he brushed off some of the crusty white snow that coated strands of his hair. His tunic was stuck to the ice. He pulled it free and rose stiffly. It was difficult to stand. His joints seemed solidified. He couldn't feel his toes, nor his ears. He ached, weary from shivering. It would be so easy if he could die.

Then he realized he could arrange that very simply.

Sardonic laughter filled his thoughts. *This will be quick.* He would be too cold to feel the sword stroke. He faced Ben. "Do you know who I am?"

"Yes."

Alihahd was dumbstruck. Yes? *Yes?* His neat and certain scheme fizzled out. How was this possible? "Since when?"

"Since first I saw thee," Ben said.

Alihahd remembered the murderous fury in the dark eyes. It had been recognition. *And yet I live?*

Alihahd shook his head. He stared at the young man. He should not be here. He should not be talking. Last time Alihahd had seen him, he had been beyond retrieval. Yet here he was.

Ben turned his back to the breezes and was looking at Alihahd over one massive shoulder. There was a mildness to his mood. Black eyes were neutral despite their fierce narrowness and the oblique angle of his brows and three angry red broken lines on his cheekbones. The ring of the carnelian serpent shone like a drop of blood on his finger. There came the thin sound of the kestrel's cry as it rode the winter air high overhead.

No longer angry, no longer mad, no longer even human, Ben had become truly alien.

Alihahd denied what he saw. There was an ancient expression. "Leopards cannot change their spots."

Ben considered this. He answered with quiet dogma, "Leopards do."

Alihahd echoed softly, "Leopards do." He gazed up at the sunless sky. "One would think there would be hope for me, then, wouldn't one?"

The hide cover over the cave mouth lifted aside with a gust of cold air, then dropped shut again. Harrison White Fox Hall, reclining shirtless and barefoot on his bed, looked up, his eyes heavy and narrow as a sated tiger's.

Alihahd stood in the entranceway.

The small cave was hot. The heat was an assault on Alihahd's eyes, which began to water and kept closing, wanting sleep. His nose thickened and began to run. Coming in from the outside glare, the cave was very dark. Alihahd could hardly see Hall, the faded walls, or anything but the reddish-orange glow from the low hearth. His voice was deep in reluctance, underlaid with embarrassment. "Mr. Hall."

"Captain," Hall said from his bed, low and warm—physically warm if a sound could be so.

"I am cold," Alihahd said.

"Did you come for help or to be shot?"

"Shoot me."

Hall smiled, shook his head. He swung his long legs over the side of the bed and sat up with a grunt. "Come in." He stood, took a towel from his yellowwood chest, and crossed to Alihahd, who was not moving. Hall brushed some of the snow and water beads off his darkened blond hair. "Whistle."

"What?"

"Do it," Hall ordered.

Alihahd tried to round his rubbery purple lips. He puffed out toneless rushes of air, then, barely, a discordant whistle.

Hall's languid eyelids raised slightly in surprise. "I am afraid I think you will live." He pressed the towel to Alihahd's wet hair without rubbing.

Alihahd closed his eyes, felt Hall's hot breath on his face that seemed very fat.

"Take your clothes off. Get in the bed." Hall unclasped Alihahd's belt with a tug and let it fall at his feet.

Teeth chattering, Alihahd pulled his ice-stiffened tunic over his head and limped to the bed. His fingers wouldn't flex to unlace his boots, so he just sat, shaking. Hall put a heavy, coarse blanket around him, and took his boots off for him.

Alihahd's right leg from heel to knee was a solid bruise, but, protected by the thick fleecy boot, the wound was healing, even though lower down his toenails were blue.

Hall put more fuel on the hearthfire, then crawled into bed with Alihahd under a heap of blankets. Hall's hot, dark skin raised in gooseflesh at the touch of Alihahd's own clammy skin against him. He pulled the covers over Alihahd's head, which lay at his shoulder. It was like being in bed with a corpse—a very, very, cold corpse—one that would not stop shivering.

"Ever try to kill yourself before?" Hall asked.

"Several times," came the murmur at his chest under the covers. "Have not gotten the hang of it yet."

"I guess not."

Hall dozed on and off over the hours. Alihahd kept moving, jolting Hall awake.

After a time Alihahd began to thaw and regain feeling. His toes itched fiercely. Clearing nostrils filled with the scent of straw in the mattress and scent of Hall.

Alihahd lifted the covers away, moved to the edge of the mattress, and shakily placed first one foot, then the other on the floor, and he stood. Hall seized his wrist. "Where do you think you're going?"

Alihahd mumbled—he didn't know where he was going—"This is not done where I come from."

"They eat people where you come from," Hall said.

After a dumb pause, the full significance hit Alihahd; he yanked free of Hall's grip and searched for something to wear. He almost bolted out into the icy night naked, just to get away from Hall—no, not really Hall, from himself, the one person above all he could not bear to face.

But why else did I come? Alihahd thought with despair, one of those undeniable truths that shrank from the light.

I knew. I know him. He started to shake again.

He'd come to be destroyed.

He heard Hall's sardonic laughter echo off the close walls. "Nazi."

"You are saying that just to anger me," Alihahd said.

"Succeeding, too," Hall said, and he sat up. "Hey, nazi, you looking for something to cover yourself?"

He didn't mean clothes. The tone was much too insinuating. Alihahd turned.

Hall held up Alihahd's container of melaninic pills. Alihahd hadn't seen them since he'd taken them from Omonia Station. He'd assumed that he'd misplaced them, but he should have known that he hadn't. He valued them much too much. He tried not to let his horror show. Maybe Hall would put them down.

Hall pitched them one by one into the fire. The precious little pills sizzled with tiny sprays of orange sparks. Tawny eyes slid from the fire to Alihahd's stone face. "Oh, don't pretend you don't care." *Phhht* went another pill. "Here, do you want one?" He held one out, then let it drop in the hearth. *Phhht.* "I'm going to burn them all." *Phhht.* "So you may as well fight me for them."

Alihahd trembled. Blue eyes were wary, on the brink of their mad aspect, watching his hopes for brownness and normality go up in orange sparks.

Phhht.

Then Hall grew bored with his game and made to spill the whole bottle into the flames. Alihahd lunged.

The pills were in the fire as Alihahd grasped Hall's wrists. "Too late!" Hall laughed.

"Damn you," Alihahd said, quaking. "God damn you."

"Ah. Ah," Hall said tauntingly and opened his fist. There

were three pills left. Alihahd snatched for them, and Hall snapped his hand shut. Alihahd tried to pry his fingers open, couldn't budge them, so brought his mouth down and bit Hall's hand, hard enough to draw blood.

Hall roared and pushed his fist into Alihahd's face. Alihahd reeled back, blood on his lips. "Well, that's nothing new," Hall said, rubbing his hand. "Go on and lick it."

Alihahd spat in Hall's face. "Sadist."

Hall wiped the blood from his eyelids. "Not half so much as you are."

Alihahd's wan face paled.

"Yes," Hall said. "Come on, now. I have three pills left. You've killed before, what's stopping you now? I swear, as I live, I will burn these. Why don't you come get them, and have some enjoyment of it while you're at it?"

"I do not want to hurt you," Alihahd said. The twitch returned under his eye.

Hall drew a long switch, too green to be kindling, from the firewood pile, and he struck Alihahd across the face with it, raising a red weal on his cheek. Alihahd flinched back in pain and startlement.

"Why not?" Hall said. "You ought to." He hit him again, "Fight me. This gentle son of a bitch is not who you are." He lashed him again, and Alihahd cringed under the stinging whip, and edged, doubled over, toward the bed. When he was near enough, he suddenly uncurled and seized up Hall's gun—Hall had left it by the yellowwood table—and turned it on Hall, threatening. The blows stopped. Something shifted behind the blue eyes, some veil lifted, and there was an insane lucidity upon him, cold, and aware, alive, capable—and reveling in bloodthirst.

"Ah, there he is," Hall said. "The man I wanted to talk to."

And he called him by name.

The cold shattered and crumbled. Alihahd threw the gun away from him and screamed, in Na'id, "Illi! Illi!" *My God! My God!*

Hall dropped the remaining pills in the fire. "Well, hell," he said.

Alihahd woke, pushed away the covers. Alive. He was surprised.

He looked aside. Hall was awake, his eyes shut, resting quietly. His fox-head pipe sat on the yellowwood table. Both opal eyes were gone. Morning light lined the hide cover of the cave that was still warm and stuffy.

Alihahd cleared the phlegm from his throat, brushed fine salt from his eyelids, let go a sigh.

Hall gave him a tap that was a demand for comment.

Alihahd recited, "For I am a shining being who lives in light, who has been created from the limbs of God." A silence followed, then a derisive sound in his throat.

"Is that Na'id scripture?" Hall asked.

"Yes. How glorious humankind." Alihahd sat up. "Might I have something to wear?"

"Yeah," Hall said, reached over to a drawer, pulled out some things, and let them drop on Alihahd.

Alihahd rose unsteadily to his feet and dressed. He touched the welts on his face. "You bastard."

Hall gave a one-shoulder shrug.

Alihahd walked to the door, faced back. Hall lazed in the bed, not ready to stir yet. Alihahd said, "It would have been easier, Mr. Hall, if you had killed me. Then I would not be wondering what I am to do next."

Hall waved his hand idly. "And put you out of your misery? What kind of avenger would I be then?"

Alihahd stepped outside to the bracing cold air that stung his sensitized skin and turned his breath to crystalline clouds.

He went to his own cave to wash, then to Serra's for tea. Serra put something herbal on his welts. She didn't ask where he'd gotten them. Alihahd had never seen any marks on Serra, but he'd seen bruises on Hall. Serra threw things.

Alihahd held the hot cup between his hands and let the

steam unclog his nose. He felt soggy, like the muddy gray mass that was left after pouring water on a bonfire. At the same time he felt light, as if part of him had burned away, no longer weighing him down or giving off choking smoke and sparks.

He went to the door and gazed out, leaning forward with his left hand on the doorjamb, his arm straight, his weight off his bad leg. The tea warmed. The cold air revived. He took no long views, taking each instant as it came, looking no farther than his nose. That was the safe way to go. His furies had broken their leashes and attacked with all their merciless savagery. Now they sat in a corner, all snarled out, doing no more than glare at him, snuffling, not biting.

He hadn't changed his spots. He guessed he might as well claim them like bastard children.

After all, they are my spots.

An outcry of eagles drew him out of the cave. Others of the Aerie, ranga and warrior-priests, came out to the ledges and terraces to look at the sky. A roar on the horizon followed the flight of four low-flying starships, colored electric blue and vivid red, making a low recon pass over the valley.

The next pass would bring them directly over the Aerie.

Hall came out to the ledge and lifted his beam weapon. He took aim along the predicted flight path and waited.

The four ships returned, blazing their twin symbols of Galactic Dominion/Human Supremacy. As they pulled up over the mountain they showed their designations: X99, X37, and X24. Alihahd couldn't see the fourth one but knew it was X48. He reached over and rested his hand on Hall's stabilizer. "Those are mine," he said. Then he clarified. "Alihahd's. I never thought they would come looking here."

"Thou must have been a great leader." The voice was Jinin-Ben-Tairre's. There was a question in his tone, and tentative respect for someone who just might be his better—for all his sins and weaknesses—and an unspoken *Shall I follow thee?*

Another admirer, one who had seen black depths and

the darkest side of his own nature, this one, of all of them, knew what he was admiring. That kind could not be shaken. The rest of them worshipped a graven image.

"Some people were under that impression," Alihahd said.

He turned away and went back inside Serra's cave. Hall leaned in the doorway behind him, his arms crossed. "Well, Captain, since you are alive, what are you going to do next?"

Alihahd picked up his cup where he'd left it. "I am going to finish my tea."

PART FIVE:

Jerusalem Fire

18. Return of a Legend

THE FOUR STARSHIPS X99, X37, X24, and X48 came to rest far from the Aerie on a high narrow plateau wedged between a mountain and the River Ocean. They were Alihahd's ships. They'd found him.

But it hadn't been rebels who'd sighted Alihahd at Omonia Station. *Na'id* had seen him there. It should have been Na'id who came looking here. Alihahd couldn't be sure that these weren't Na'id. There was nothing to say that the four starships hadn't changed hands in the past year. Alihahd needed to identify the ships' personnel before going to them. Jinin-Ben-Tairre sent his familiar ahead to the plateau where the ships had landed and their crews had camped. The kestrel returned screaming.

"The bird sayeth they are Na'id," Ben told Alihahd.

Alihahd absorbed the news with little expression. "Even if they are mine, they are supposed to look like Na'id," he said.

"The bird is not bright," Ben conceded.

The bird squawked.

The only thing to do then was for Alihahd to go and see for himself.

On the far side of the mountain from the starships' encampment lay an Itiri village. Jinin-Ben-Tairre transported Alihahd there aboard a primitive airplane. The antique would be beneath the notice of a starship's scanners. Layla, Harrison Hall, and Vaslav came with him.

They stepped out of the plane within sight of the Itiri village. Its low white buildings, washed golden in the light of the morning sun, were clustered closely along stepped streets, their rooftops mostly flat as they would be in a place where it rarely rained.

"It looks like Jerusalem," Alihahd murmured.

Vaslav spoke at his side, impressed and intrigued. "You've seen Jerusalem?"

Alihahd took a breath. "I saw it."

"Before or after the Fall?" Vaslav asked.

"Both."

The boy paused, then proceeded cautiously, "You saw it twice?"

"No. Once."

Vaslav was in awe.

Alihahd spread his hands, conjuring a picture, his gaze far off. "This is like the Old City. The new city goes on and on over the hills. The slopes were choked with gray limestone blocks of apartment buildings, office skyscrapers, synagogues, churches, mosques, everything of all eras. The Old City was the part the Bel wanted untouched. The rest was expendable, if need be . . . they didn't know that. . . . She burned. All night." He stiffened with an involuntary shudder. "Men and women killing men, women, and children . . . they would not stop. . . .

"There were three armies. The 27th, the 9th, and the 34th." He pointed at the horizons around the village. "The 9th and the 34th had been there for years. The 27th was there to end it. . . ."

Vaslav whispered, "Where was Shad Iliya?"

"Mount of Olives," Alihahd said. "Small for a mountain. No olives. Many graves."

And he described the battle in detail, every tactic. It was a long tale, but no one interrupted. They didn't notice the time passing. Alihahd continued, chillingly photographic, detached and impassioned at once, to the end.

His wide, gaunt shoulders slumped, and he broke from his near-trance. "Jews are the most tenacious people in the known universe," he said tiredly. "You can burn, flay, trample, enslave, outlaw, boil, and eat them, and they remain Jews. They bewilder and humble me.

"And Arabs. They died in droves and still they came — the ones who did not turn and run at the first shot. Those who stayed were the ones who died all night long. They would not surrender."

Vaslav was trying to pinpoint what was odd about Alihahd's account. For the most part it had been a cold, harrowingly factual replay of events. But what was wrong?

"I thought you said you never fought Na'id," Vaslav said.

"I did not," Alihahd agreed.

He hadn't said what he had done in the battle, Vaslav realized. But obviously the man had been there, in the middle of it.

And then Vaslav knew what was wrong with the story. It was the point of view — where he must have been to have seen the battle that way.

Mount of Olives.

Alihahd prepared for his hike down the mountain. He would approach the ships' camp on foot. Before he would make his presence known, he needed to know who was looking for him. Layla, Hall, and Vaslav all insisted on accompanying him. They wouldn't be left behind on Iry. Jinin-Ben-Tairre told the humans, "I shall wait here for three days. Then you are in the hands of your own kind."

But which kind are they? Alihahd thought.

His gaze locked briefly with Ben-Tairre's. Then the warrior lowered his eyes to his own rag-tied feet. A soft black forelock fell across Ben's brow, and Alihahd thought he suddenly looked very human. Alihahd felt he ought to do something, say something.

We have the same soul, you and I. The blood-soaked wretched of this war. But neither of them was the demonstrative breed. They let each other go without a word or gesture to say there was ever any bond between them.

Alihahd, Harrison Hall, Layla, and Vaslav started out. It was to be a steep and brambly trek down. After the dry air of the mountains, the moist lush forest of the windward slope was unbearable to them. They needed to be on guard against a whole different set of hazards in this lower country.

They hadn't gone far when Layla cried out, "Sail snake!" And she pointed up.

Hall grabbed Vaslav and pulled him down. Alihahd and Layla dropped. The four of them crouched into the underbrush as a long, undulating, leaf-green reptilian body glided through the treetops.

The snake passed by without noticing them. The humans stayed in hiding until the inevitable mate appeared and passed over as well.

Complete thine journey before nightfall, Alihahd had been advised. *Sail snakes see heat. In the dark, thou wilt not see them. Thou art too big to eat, but it may strike before it realizes thine size.*

Alihahd stood up. This would prove to be a very long walk.

"Why did they land the ships down there anyway?" Hall said, grumbling. The interior was much cooler and drier.

"Must be my people," Alihahd said and pushed his way ahead through a thicket of willowy saplings. "Na'id plan better."

Alihahd lost his bearings. *How long has it been since I've had to deal with a tree?* His clothes were tough but breathable—sturdy trousers and a dolman-sleeved shirt with its drawstring waist and cuffs loosely tied—but still they stuck to him. The moisture that slicked his skin had nowhere to go.

A leafy branch slapped his face. He pushed it away and tried to find the sun through the verdant screen all around him. Which way?

Down. That much he knew, anyway.

He'd become separated from the others and was about to call out, when he heard shooting—fire and return fire—more than three.

He bounded through the underbrush with clumping leaps, favoring his right foot. He broke into a clearing—

—and came face-to-face with a Na'id lieutenant.

Alihahd and the Na'id officer pointed guns at each other and did not shoot.

The dark young lieutenant gaped and slowly shook his head in disbelief and denial.

Alihahd knew what that look meant, and he felt sick.

The Na'id's expression hardened, and he took aim. Alihahd didn't move, only stared up the barrel in helpless horror.

There was a shot.

The Na'id fell forward. The back of his blue uniform shirt purpled with blood. Behind him in the woods stood Harrison White Fox Hall.

Hall tramped out of the underbrush and came to Alihahd.

Alihahd swayed on his feet, leaned toward Hail, who grabbed him and steadied Alihahd against him.

Alihahd pushed away, staggered to the body, and fell to his knees. He turned the youth over, brushed black hair off the paled face and out of the open black eyes. He touched the chest that was warm but unmoving.

"Know him?" Hall asked.

Alihahd shook his head. *He knew me*.

Hall lifted Alihahd bodily, and Alihahd didn't resist the help this time. He stumbled away from the site, holding on to Hall. Alihahd didn't talk. Couldn't.

In the forest, Vaslav was yelling for them. Harrison Hall

sang out, then crouched down in the ferns, taking Alihahd with him, eyes darting cautiously, gun ready for whoever might answer.

A small, bewildered voice sounded at Hall's side. "Did I shoot?"

"No. I did."

"Didn't think I had," Alihahd mumbled. But he hadn't been certain. He only knew that he'd been facing the young man with his gun. He couldn't remember shooting, but there had been a shot and it was the Na'id, not Alihahd, whose eyes glassed over and who fell facedown in the brush.

Vaslav came crashing out from the trees into the clearing and tripped over the Na'id body. He danced back and called shrilly, "Captain! Harry? Layla?"

Hall hissed, and Vaslav scrambled back to the cover of the wood. He saw Alihahd curled under Hall's arm. "Are you hurt?" Vaslav asked.

Alihahd spoke weakly. "No." Then stronger, "No." He shook himself free of Hall and stood on his own feet. "Where is Layla?"

"Here." Layla came to them quietly as a forest shadow.

"Let us go, then," Alihahd said. "Fast now."

They moved quickly to put distance between themselves and the clearing.

When they paused for breath, Alihahd sat down, his heart pulsing in his wounded leg. He pulled Hall down to him by the arm so he could talk quietly. "How many did you kill?" He hadn't counted the shots.

"I bagged five," Hall said.

Alihahd didn't like that number. "Vaslav?"

"None," Vaslav said.

"Layla?"

"One."

Alihahd relaxed a measure. Six was a good number. "That was probably the whole patrol. We might have an hour before someone becomes alarmed at their failure to report."

Someone. The Na'id base camp couldn't be far.

"Shall we turn back?" Hall said.

Alihahd bowed his head, chin on his chest. If those four ships were manned by Na'id, where were Alihahd's rebels? All two thousand of them. Alihahd lifted his head, level and grim. "You go back. I need to see."

"I can't let you go alone," Hall said.

"I do not need a nursemaid," Alihahd said.

"Yes, you do."

From the mountain—in the direction of the clearing they'd fled—came fighting snarls and yelps and growls. Those would be wolf-hyenas at the bodies of the six Na'id patrollers.

"Yes, I do," Alihahd said, standing. "Shall we get this done?"

The sun was already overhead. They would need to push to reach the coast and get back by nightfall to the place where Ben-Tairre waited.

Alihahd's leg was failing him. He fell into a melancholy brooding as he limped.

"They all come home to roost," he murmured. "It cannot be coincidence. Chance is not so vindictive. Must not Someone be directing events?"

Harrison Hall snorted. "It only looks like someone is in control of this show. When you think of all the trillions of coincidences that *don't* happen, you see how random it all is. Odds are that some coincidences will happen—by chance—even if the odds against any single specific coincidence are a billion to one. It would be odd if there were no coincidences. *That* would be evidence of intervention. As it is, I see none. You're on your own, Captain."

"You're a cynic, Mr. Hall."

"A realistic one. You think too much."

"Only when I'm sober," Alihahd said dryly.

The four spaceships rested on a level area cleared of trees by a fire. The carpet of yellow grass was underlaid by black dust and coal. Charred skeletons of once-tall trees spiked the plain at intervals.

Alihahd, Hall, Layla, and Vaslav stole up to the perimeter of the wide burned clearing and hid behind a mossy boulder at the very edge of the forest. Alihahd peered out cautiously.

Among the ships wandered men and women biding their time in the sweltering heat. Their sweat-patched Na'id uniforms were fleet red, not the army blue of the Na'id patrol Hall and Layla had killed.

A dozen crewmen, seeking the shade of the forest, ambled very near to the boulder where Alihahd hid. From the emotions that played across Alihahd's face as he viewed them, his three companions guessed the worst. But Alihahd exhaled heavily and stood. "Rebels. Those are mine."

He gave Hall his taeben and he walked slowly and loudly into the open, his hands wide and empty.

Twelve guns turned and aimed.

Alihahd's rebels had always been quick to draw their guns. Alihahd never let them use them.

"Put those down," bellowed the strangely dressed, white-skinned, blond man come limping from the forest.

The rebels jumped, stuttered, and stared. They knew the voice. The command was a ghost from the past. What they saw needed reconciling. The Alihahd they remembered was swarthy.

Still they knew him when he spoke again. "It is I."

At once the guns were put up, except for two of the most stunned, who were nudged by their comrades and hastily followed suit.

The thick silence broke. "Alihahd!" someone cried at last.

Exultant and dazed smiles flashed, and one crewman dashed to the ships, yelling, "Alihahd! Alihahd!" And all the rebels gathered around to see.

It was an awkward reunion, with enough excitement, some tears, but no embraces or backslapping, and the welcomes were clumsily expressed.

Then the throng parted for the approach of a stocky woman in Na'id commodore uniform. Blue tribal tattoos around her lips broadened as she smiled, but with no more surprise or jubilation than on recovering a lost nose ring. *So there you are,* said the smile.

The commodore, Musa, took off her broad-brimmed hat, put it on Alihahd's fair head, and said, "What happened to you?" She meant his color, not his disappearance.

"As you see," Alihahd said.

Musa pressed her stout forefinger experimentally to his white cheek. "Is this real?"

Alihahd spoke tautly. "Do you honestly suppose anyone would look like this on purpose?"

"I guess not," Musa said. "Not unless you're trying to be the reincarnation of Shad Iliya."

Alihahd's smile was very thin.

A few grins around him slackened. A fierce, blue-eyed glare from Alihahd silenced any comment.

"You really do have that look," Musa said.

Alihahd told her, "You are aware that there are Na'id on this planet."

"Can't be," Musa said. A whispering wave of consternation passed through the rebel troops.

A strong voice from the woods said, "Are."

That was Hall. And all the rebel guns raised and pointed at him.

"Are," Alihahd said, pushing down the nearest weapon. "But that is not one. Put those things away before you shoot each other."

And when all the weapons were holstered, Hall, Layla, and Vaslav came out of hiding.

Alihahd muttered aside to Musa while the rebels were distracted by the appearance of his companions, "Not battle-ready, Musa. Your ships should be arranged at dome points."

"I didn't think it necessary in uncharted space," Musa said.

"You were followed."

Musa's broad brow creased. "Why would the Na'id follow us? As far as they know, we're a loyal squadron."

"Evidently, you have been discovered. It appears they are tracking you to all your contacts and bases before they make their final strike."

Musa pouted, assessing the dimensions of the disaster. "Shall we make a run for it?"

Alihahd looked up at the sky. There was nothing in it for the moment. "We have to assume they know where we are."

Musa nodded. "How did *you* know where we were?"

"A bird told me."

Musa knew better than to question Alihahd when he was being evasive. She addressed the crisis at hand. "We're sitting ducks down here."

"We are worse if we take off," Alihahd said. Four ships slugging out of a thick atmosphere made a slow, concentrated target. On the ground, even if the Na'id located the ships, they couldn't be certain of where all the people were.

"I would feel much better in a spaceship," Musa said.

"So would most Na'id. I would not," Alihahd said. Harrison Hall came to his side.

"But you're a brilliant spaceship strategist," Musa said.

"I am merely competent in the air," Alihahd said. "I am brilliant on the ground." He glanced to Hall. "I don't lose."

Musa turned with a shrug, clapped her hands, and shouted a command: "Ships on dome points! Now!"

The rebels hurried to obey, and they arranged the ships at optimum angles for their combined force fields to raise a nearly impenetrable energy-shield dome.

"What have you on the scanners, Musa?" Alihahd asked while it was done.

"No ships." Musa opened her thick arms in bafflement. "You say there are Na'id. I don't know where they are."

"It is a metallic planet," Alihahd said.

Musa agreed. "They could hide anything here."

The engines of the repositioned ships were winding

down. They were ready to raise the shield dome on Ali-hahd's command.

Alihahd held his breath. He was inviting direct confrontation if he raised a defensive dome now. If the Na'id were monitoring, they would see the dome on their scanners and would know they'd been detected. "Raise it," Alihahd said and waited for the repercussions. "Is there wine to be had?" he asked Musa.

"Y—"

"No," Hall said.

Musa looked quizzically to Alihahd.

"Never mind," Alihahd said.

Someone gestured skyward and sang out, "Here they come."

All eyes turned up.

Alihahd watched with sinking soul. Twelve ships appeared, not battleships of a space fleet, but troop transports of an army bearing twelve thousand infantry soldiers. The ominous silhouettes of the delta-wing ships flew in the formation of three broken echelons matted against the twilight sky. It was a known pattern, the personal signature of a special army.

Alihahd breathed, "This goes beyond chance and coincidence. This is destiny." *There is a God and He is vengeful.*

It was the 27th Army. The victors of Jerusalem.

Alihahd motioned aside to Vaslav without looking at him. "Vaslav, man a transceiver."

The boy ran to the flagship as the delta-wing transports of the infamous 27th Army were touching down. They came to rest on the burn-cleared plateau a scant kilometer from the rebel camp and set up on defensive points so that their own energy dome nearly overlapped the rebels'. Then uniformed soldiers poured out of the dreadful ships like bottle-blue ants.

"Hm," Alihahd grunted, commenting to himself, noting something interesting.

Hall raised his eyebrows at him questioningly.

"The uniforms," Alihahd said. "They never used to wear those."

The bright metallic blue with red blazons told the galaxy who these soldiers were. The colors reinforced Na'id identity and pride in the Empire. Shad Iliya never used them, preferring less conspicuous battle-drab. But without Shad Iliya, the soldiers of the 27th Army felt increasing need to insist on who they were. They had lost battles since Jerusalem. The blue uniforms were a small sign of slipping morale.

Alihahd touched Musa's sleeve. "I want everyone in battle fatigues and assembled out here inside of four minutes."

"Assembled in what order?" Musa asked.

"No particular order. Just so they take a position and hold it."

"Yes, sir."

If there was one thing Alihahd's rebels were trained to do, it was act as if they knew what they were doing in dangerous places where they had no business being and about which they knew nothing. They were an army of impostors and spies, not soldiers.

As the rebels formed into ranks, the scanner technician came to Alihahd to report that she'd located where the Na'id had been hiding earlier. Their ships had come out of a deep canyon below sea level, between two metallic mountains, less than ten kilometers to the west. Like chameleons, they'd been easily overlooked until they moved. "If we'd taken off, we'd be dead now," the tech said. "It'd be a skeet shoot. You were right, sir."

Alihahd nodded without comfort. There was no pleasure in being right when it meant he had saved himself for a fate worse than death.

The Na'id were assembling by battalions, smart and orderly, each by its ship. They outnumbered the rebels six to one.

For the soldiers of the 27th Army, there was something unsettling in facing an enemy wearing Na'id uniforms—and the drab colors they themselves used to wear when they were still undefeated. The more sensitive of them were aware that hidden things were moving here.

Vaslav came from the flagship to report, "The Na'id opened communications. They demand surrender."

Alihahd's eyes stayed fixed on the ranks across the plateau. "Refuse."

Vaslav ran back to the ship's transceiver to relay the message.

A rebel ship commander beside Alihahd took a quick breath for courage, then spoke. "Do you know what you're doing, sir?"

Alihahd was showing signs of fear. Sweat beaded his tall forehead. His mouth and eyes were lined in white.

"We're not an army," the rebel reminded him.

"They do not know that," Alihahd said.

"They'll find out when they attack," the commander said, suppressed hysteria in his voice.

"If they attack."

The commander licked salt from his upper lip, then caved in to bald fear. "Captain, do you know who they are?" he blurted. "That's Shad Iliya's army. Those people took Jerusalem!"

Blue eyes and white face turned slowly to him. The voice was deep. "I know."

The commander's eyes grew huge, and he backed away, choking on a whimper.

Vaslav came bounding back from the flagship, his face bright red. "Sir, their general calls you a madman and demands that you personally reconfirm your answer. He also wants to know if you realize who they are."

Alihahd put a hand on Vaslav's hard, spare shoulder. "Confirm the refusal for me. And tell the general this verbatim—verbatim, can you?"

Vaslav nodded intently. His hands were furtively making gentle, nervous motions. Alihahd wanted to slap them.

"Tell the general that I am in the habit of studying thoroughly any opponent, knowing his habits, strengths, weaknesses, motives, and all facts available—pertinent and *impertinent*. Do you think you have that?"

Vaslav raised his chin and dashed away, his lips moving, reciting to himself.

"And Vaslav!"

The boy turned.

"Tell him I thought Alihahd was dead."

Vaslav's face blanked in puzzlement. "Sir?"

"Tell him."

Musa offered Alihahd her comlink so that Vaslav wouldn't need to keep shuttling back and forth. Alihahd shook his head. "Let him run. Let them wait."

A fresh sweat broke over his brow in the late heat of the westering sun. The day was never-ending. These kinds of days never did end. The second-worst day in his entire life. Or was it the worst? He closed his eyes, brushed away a buzzing yellow fly. *O God, O God*, he cried inside. And imagined he heard an ironic voice answer, *Yes?*

He opened his eyes, despairing.

Vaslav returned, unnerved. He'd been prepared for anger from the Na'id general at the message, but he hadn't been ready for quite the violence of the reaction. There had been more to that message he recited than was apparent. "Sir, the general is hopping mad. He turned that color." Vaslav pointed at a bright red Na'id badge. Alihahd was the only rebel not in uniform. By now all the rebels, including Vaslav, were in battle drab.

"The general wants to know who you think you are," Vaslav said. "Because you're not the man you're pretending to be. No one ever was or will be. And all Alihahd's cowardly tricks can't change that." Vaslav's voice faltered. His Adam's apple bobbed. "He wants you to quit hiding your face and come to the transceiver and look him in the eyes, because he already knows that yours—your eyes—aren't . . . blue."

Alihahd nodded. He slowly blinked his blue eyes. "Thank you."

"No message?"

"Not for the transceiver."

"Sir?" Vaslav began, bewildered. He was carrying every word that passed between the two leaders, yet he hadn't the least idea what was being said and why their words fell on each other so hard. And besides that, Alihahd's eyes *were* blue. "Who are you pretending to be?"

Alihahd sighed. "Not." He took off the broad-brimmed hat and gave it back to Musa. He limped forward from the ranks in the direction of the Na'id ships, hesitated, then continued out toward the perimeter of the shield dome. His skin tingled as he passed through the force field, his movements slowed, like walking through mud, till he was out of the dome.

The rebels gasped. "Is he mad? He'll be killed!"

Harrison Hall rocked back on his heels, amused. "A little mad, maybe. Killed? Not yet, I think."

He could see Alihahd's white skin even at a distance, and fancied he was even more pale than normal. Alihahd was horrified, and it was not fear of death. He wished he was dead. He could not have been more sickened and terrified walking into a fire and knowing his flesh would burn.

Nothing stirred during his slow progress out to stand between the two armies. Everyone was quiet, watching his painful advance. He forgot to breathe, then breathed too quickly, feeling the pressure of the air now, the effects of descending too far too fast.

I want a drink. He could have in all reality murdered Hall for making him go through this cold sober.

The Na'id didn't shoot him. A murmur rolled back through their ranks. Alihahd didn't dare look at faces. He kept his gaze fixed strictly over their heads. Then, because he could no longer resist, he glanced down once. Their faces, the whole sea of them, read pure shock. Ice trickled through Alihahd's stomach, guts, groin, and into his jellied legs, and he stopped. This was far enough. At the next step he would fall.

He held his position there, midway, and let them stare.

His mouth felt full of bitter pins. His heart wobbled high in his chest. The palms of his hands throbbed. He felt faint. *Not even God can help me.* He forced himself to untense his muscles. *As if God actually would.*

He swallowed, gathered his breath low, and found his voice. "Soldiers of the Empire!" he thundered. The voice carried over the plain and rebounded off the mountains, steady, loud, and resonant.

Alihahd prayed the voice would not break on him. It never had.

He was dying inside, everyone staring at him—those blank, horrified faces. If he looked at them again, he would freeze. He heard their murmurs, the deadly secret spreading.

"Yes, I know who you are!" he shouted at them with a fury that was really fear. *"You are my enemy!"*

The murmurs silenced. Alihahd glanced down quickly at their glassy faces, every one of them unmoving, as if they were watching a special weapon of theirs—a big gun they once had—which had made them feel so powerful and invincible while it was theirs, till this day it turned around and they were looking up its barrel and feeling very small. *You are my enemy.*

He shouldn't have looked. It was some moments before he could speak again. In the silence the Na'id fear mounted to near panic. Alihahd needed to be careful. Cornered beasts bit. *O God, if you get me out of this without a battle, I will never presume to lead a body of your people ever again.*

The Na'id believed themselves cornered. Alihahd would show them an out and hope they ran for it without realizing he was all roar and no teeth.

"If there be a battle today, you will attack. I will not. The decision for bloodshed is yours entirely." He paused, and watched their panic abate a degree. *"But,"* he shouted, and they flinched. "Know it be me you fight, and you know better than anyone that I have never lost a battle."

Even the young soldiers who had never known him were

stunned. His image was aboard every ship. The soldiers of the 27th visited his shrine before every mission.

God had left and joined the other side.

The shift in morale could be felt across the plateau.

Both sides were astounded. Alihahd sensed his rebels behind him reeling, and he was sick again at the prospect of turning around and looking back. His stomach had gone from ice to water.

He saw movement in the Na'id ranks—a single person walking forward out of the camp toward midfield. Alihahd knew him—a broad, stolid bulk in general's uniform, older than Alihahd, with silvering black hair, not much changed from thirteen years ago when everything was normal and this man was his lieutenant commander.

Ra'im Mishari trudged out for conference with the enemy captain. His steps were tired, and a thick forefinger worried at the tight collar of his uniform in the damp heat. For all the years of Ra'im Mishari's service, the computer still could not fit a collar to the general's taurine neck. Even that had not changed.

General Ra'im Mishari came to Alihahd and stopped. He and Alihahd faced each other in silence, awkward as two former lovers.

Alihahd stood at his full height, his eyes turned down to his old second.

Ra'im Mishari's heavy brows contracted. His square jaw moved, grinding. His broad chest expanded. He started to say "General," but blurted out with a cry of pain, "Shadi!" and nothing to follow. Just his name. He felt like shedding tears, but a leader could not before two armies.

Alihahd waited, with no compulsion to say anything.

Ra'im snorted, opened his collar. He looked up. "I worshipped you."

"That was a serious mistake on your part," Alihahd said.

A cloud passed over the sinking sun. Ra'im Mishari glanced toward it in relief, then back to Alihahd to say matter-of-factly, "You realize you just shot our morale to hell."

"That was the idea."

"We wouldn't have a chance if we engaged you now."

Yes, you would. Six to one? Come now, Ra'im, have you deified me? "I realize."

"You leave me no choice."

"That was also the idea."

A glimmer of a sad smile flickered at the corners of Ra'im's eyes. It sounded so familiar—the deft maneuvering, the sure simplicity, ever one step ahead. So it seemed to Ra'im. He frowned. "How could you desert?"

"What else does one do when one is born on the wrong side?" Alihahd said with profound tiredness, his blue eyes skyward and lost. "I do not know if what I did was right—I suspect not. But I did not know what else to do. Suicide, I suppose. But, frankly, I lacked the courage."

A tremor disturbed Ra'im's square, solid chin. The speech sounded exactly like the man Ra'im knew—and he remembered how distressed his general had been the last time he saw him thirteen years ago.

Ra'im spoke low, nearly guttural, emotion-charged and personal. "You should've said something. The Bel would have done anything for you."

"I didn't say anything? I thought I had," Alihahd said airily. "You all treated me as if I had gone mad."

As gently as he could, Ra'im said, "But you had."

Alihahd smiled, eyes shining at the sky. The thought hadn't occurred to him. He found it funny. "But even a madman does not like to be treated like one," he said.

Ra'im Mishari remained grave. "Why did you hit those space stations?"

Ah. Omonia. They suppose that was I? Alihahd sobered. "I did not," he said without explanation, but clearly knowing more than he was offering.

Ra'im spoke slowly, trying to discount the other possibility. "Itiri warrior-priests are legends, of course."

"Of course," Alihahd said curtly and turned away before

Ra'im could ask if the Itiri were allies of his. Let him think. The size of this bluff was staggering.

Alihahd faced his rebel camp, and he paled again. A moment's faintness passed over him, then he started his painful return, his back straight and stiff.

The rebels were silent. What had happened out there, who he was, was still sinking in.

Alihahd was accustomed to having all eyes on him, but he'd never been looked at like this in his life. The stares were tearing his guts out.

When he reached the camp, someone jabbed a gun in his face.

The shock of even that kind of gesture had long ago worn off, and Alihahd didn't blink. He put his hand on the barrel, pushed it away, and announced in a husky growl, "For anyone else contemplating assassination, I suggest you wait for a more advantageous time."

He scanned the sea of eyes, some still denying, some crying. No one moved against him. They may have hated him, but he was still the highest card in the deck, and they wouldn't remove it from play when it was in their hand.

Vaslav was stricken. He was bawling. Only Musa and Harrison White Fox Hall were unaffected.

"Alihahd," Musa said to herself, her brows high. "He left."

"He certainly did," Alihahd said raggedly. He looked to Hall, who was enormously entertained. Alihahd walked past and headed for the forest. Hall fell into step at his flank.

"Do not say anything, Mr. Hall," Alihahd said.

"Not a word," Hall said breezily.

Inside the woods, Alihahd let himself limp as badly as he wanted to. He found a fallen tree trunk and sat heavily. His hands were quaking in aspen-leaf tremors. Lancing pains shot up and down his leg. Every nerve sang in delayed reaction to horror. He cupped his hands over his nose and tried to stop hyperventilating.

In time, he became conscious again of Hall sitting beside him, trying to light his pipe full of soggy tobacco with a moist flint. His muttered imprecations were somehow soothing, and Alihahd gathered strength from his mocking presence.

Noises from the camp filtered into the woods where they were, as the rebels began to thaw from their frozen shock. Only now was their kicked anthill beginning to buzz and scurry and crawl in reaction. Alihahd let it settle itself without him. The rebels would be better by themselves for now, and Alihahd needed to be alone—except for Hall, who did not count.

The woods were shady, deep, and peaceful, cooling with the sun's setting. Alihahd let its damp quietude surround him. He watched a droplet fall from a wet leaf. A creature like a red ant tracked through the moss on the rotting log.

He whispered his own name. It had been so long since he owned it.

"Shad Iliya."

19. Shadow of Masada

SHAD ILIYA WAS BORN INTO a patrician house under the most auspicious circumstances, the second child of two war heroes. His mother was already carrying him at the battle of Antarctica, and it was said later that Shad Iliya had been winning battles before he was born.

Like most prominent Na'id citizens, his mother made a point of being on Earth when her time came so that her child could be called a true native Earthling. And someday when he fought for the Empire to bring all of Earth under Na'id control, he could say he was reclaiming his homeland. He could not be called an invader.

He was bred from the cradle to be a leader, and proved to have a natural ability, but he faced a great struggle to advance to any significant position because of his unpatriotic color. His parents were a typical Na'id mix of racial traits, so their second son was a bewildering embarrassment. He learned guilt early. Even as a child he knew he was evil. He hated his color and all it meant.

So did his peers. He was lucky at least to be highborn and afforded the protection of his patrician heritage. No one dared destroy him. As it was, they were merely unmerciful.

He tried to tan in the sun, but his fair skin only burned. He begged but was refused the use of melanin drugs, for they were deceitful. He was not trying to be deceitful—everyone knew what he was. They called him nazi. He just wanted to look like the others. But he could not.

So he would have to be great instead. Praiseworthy.

He sought refuge in the army, where he was good. He rose to the rank of major and dead-ended there. The rank was plenty high enough for someone who looked like him.

He would have died a major but that the most powerful individual in the Empire had taken a liking to him. The Bel felt for the despised and talented young man, and he married his niece to Shad Iliya.

Shad Iliya's superiors noticed right away that someone was letting the Bel's kin stagnate at his current rank.

But he was still an embarrassment to promote. They couldn't have a blond, blue-eyed Aryan leading battles against other humans. The symbolism was bad. So they sent him to faraway alien lands, where he was simply a human being combating the nonhuman menace. Out of the public eye he could be quietly elevated as his merit dictated. And Shad Iliya advanced rapidly.

In semi-exile all those years, fighting on alien soil, he never lost a battle, and his record grew so astonishing that it reached public view anyway and he became a hero. At long last his name could be spoken aloud. And he was fondly nicknamed the White Na'id, their brilliant oddity.

His victories helped to soothe the Empire's other defeats. His reports could be counted on for good morale. He never failed—still always alien wars. No one realized that keeping him out of sight also kept him blissfully blind.

He would never have run, never have wakened from his illusion of Right, had he not been turned against his own kind.

He could slaughter inhuman aliens till Doomsday without a blush of repentance, as he had slaughtered the marlqai. He still had no regrets about that. But the Empire needed its best to end the century-old battle for Jerusalem.

Shad Iliya did his duty, and Jerusalem fell to him.

And it came to him like a revelation. He held his hands to his face, the truth still blinding thirteen years later in the cool and shadowy Iry forest.

"We were wrong. We were dead wrong."

Gregorian Year 5843 CE

It was hilly country, the land around Jerusalem. The Na'id ships had been landing in the desert hills beyond the city for days until they formed a wide ring with which to raise an enormous energy-shield dome over the top of the defenders' widest dome, cutting the city off from its millions of allies.

Defenders and attackers couldn't see each other yet for the distance and the hills, except atop one hill captured in a surprise thrust during the 27th Army's initial landing—the Mount of Olives. The arriving army set up headquarters there for their general, the new supreme commander of the Jerusalem campaign.

The Mount of Olives was an exposed promontory, but difficult for the defenders to fire upon, for it was actually within their first line of defense.

Jerusalem was encased in energy shields, shells within shells of shields, which kept out electromagnetic radiation of frequencies higher than ultraviolet, as well as n-particles with wavelike properties. The city bristled with antiaircraft and bomb-intercept guns. Its only vulnerable points—so it was believed—were the windows created in the shield domes by the defenders through which to fire their guns. Previous attacking armies and fleets had flown over the city in their spaceships and hammered at those windows with little result.

Now the Na'id were bringing down their ships and ringing the city like a closing noose. An uneasy Jerusalem waited on guard against the new strategy.

Then arrived on the site the famous general, the thirty-four-year-old Shad Iliya. He stood in the open vehicle that shuttled him from his ship, across the Judean desert, toward his new headquarters on the Mount of Olives. The jeep moved fast. Shad Iliya liked the speed. He stood up to survey the land and to be seen. The dry desert wind stung his fair skin and sang in his ears.

At the western foot of the mount, the jeep turned sharply past its center of gravity. It flipped over and spilled its august passenger out to roll in the ancient dust.

The general's waiting aides and horrified driver scurried to pick him up. But Shad Iliya was young, and he was already on his feet by the time they reached him. He shook himself and slapped a yellow coating of dust from his drab gray-green uniform. He spat dust. He would remember the taste for a long time to come.

He looked to his aides easily, his pride only slightly muted, his spirits not at all. "Well. Where are we?"

They directed him up the Mount of Olives.

As he hiked up the slope with an energetic spring to his walk, his aide trotted alongside him, explaining, "There's a twenty-first-century Neo-Hellenistic chapel we've turned into a war office."

"You did not damage it, did you?" Shad Iliya said.

"No, sir!" the aide said with proper reverence for the work of human hands as they reached the summit.

Over the top of the hill, Shad Iliya received his first view of Jerusalem, the golden city. He caught in his breath and felt his destiny whisper to him. The city looked like its pictures and holos, but here, present and living, its majesty spoke. The unmistakable golden Dome of the Rock stood in the foreground, the venerated ruin of the crumbling Western Wall beyond it, within the boundaries of the Old City. The Old City was the enemy prize to be captured, a flag of separation and a place rich in human history. The hearts of three major religions crowded that little space.

"So close," he murmured. "We are here."

"It went just as you said, sir," one of his aides said. "The Resistance didn't expect this line of attack at all. Here's what we're using as headquarters, sir."

The aide directed him to a handsome little chapel high on the eastern slope of the mount. There was nothing higher on the hill left intact after countless interfaith wars through centuries past.

Shad Iliya took a moment to admire the chapel's neat, graceful architecture with its blue tiles, white pillars, and painted entablature. One benefit of religion was that it had spurred humankind to great works of art during the child-hood of the species when Man needed an anthropomorphic divine Father to protect him and tell him right from wrong. And Man built these lovely things for His sake. But the work was human. The achievement was human. The glory was human.

Farther down the mount's slope stood a charming Byz-antine basilica with many-domed roof. Shad Iliya was en-chanted. "Is that ours?"

"Nominally, sir," an aide said.

"Can I see it?"

"Not advisable, sir. It's too dangerous. That's Gethse-mane. Our force field ends right there."

The young general nodded to the disappointing reality. He would have to wait. His blue-eyed gaze lighted on the elegant Dome of the Rock. He drew himself tall, extended a long arm to point, and announced in full voice, "Before the week is out, I shall walk beneath that dome."

Swept along with his emotional tide, the general's knot of aides broke into spontaneous applause. Though the city had withstood an assault of a hundred years, if their Shad Iliya said one week, then the city would fall in one week. The faith of Shad Iliya's followers was absolute. Shad Iliya would not lose.

Shad Iliya smiled at them. He accepted adoration in those days. He actively sought it, and was sometimes given to theatrics.

Drawn by the sound of unrestrained applause, which could signal the arrival of only one person, Lieutenant Colonel Ra'im Mishari came out through the cluster of white pillars that fronted the chapel to greet his general. Ra'im had supervised the taking of the hill as ordered. Shad Iliya could count on Ra'im to follow orders to the letter.

Silently behind Ra'im trailed the morose generals of the 9th and 34th armies, whose command Shad Iliya had assumed. He'd met the generals earlier, on shipboard, to take the command batons from them. They greeted the young usurper sullenly. They regarded his initial success as minor and unpromising. They had been here for years. They knew the intractability of the city.

Shad Iliya returned their salutes, then addressed his lieutenant colonel, "Very good, Ra'im. Any problems?"

Ra'im pointed down the slope to Gethsemane. "The rebels have been trying to move a line of portable projectile artillery into the valley. We've been shelling them before they can set up—those are the craters there—but you can see it's a narrow target."

The craters ran between the wall of the Old City and the Byzantine basilica, both of which the Na'id wanted intact and unblemished. The shelling needed to be precise.

"Where is the Jericho Road?" Shad Iliya asked, trying to orient himself.

"That line of craters."

"I see." The general turned to go into his headquarters but was distracted by the sight of an ugly black tarp spread over a wide lumpy area beside the pretty chapel. "What is that?"

"The dead in stasis, as ordered, sir."

Shad Iliya stared. "So many."

"Theirs, sir."

Theirs. He wasn't accustomed to the enemy dead being human. The fact that he was fighting humans hadn't taken on reality until that moment.

He went inside the chapel.

The place had been readied for him by his alien slave, Pony, and his personal orderly, a boy of thirteen years with the interminable name of Sinikarrabannashi. He was called Sinikar.

The breeze coming through the chapel's windows was dry and surprisingly cool. The faded blue-and-white-tiled floor had been swept clean. The Na'id standard and the flag of the 27th Army flanked the doorway. The blue-and-red Na'id seal hung on the wall.

The curly-haired boy Sinikar saluted his general and, at a nod from Ra'im, put a comlink into his hand.

"What is this?" Shad Iliya asked.

"It was delivered, sir," Sinikar said.

"It's a direct private link to the rebel commander," Ra'im Mishari said.

Shad Iliya looked to Ra'im. "Which?" There were three.

"The Jew," Ra'im said.

It was a Jew who had organized Jerusalem's defense. The command was titularly a three-headed monster composed of one Jew, one Muslim Arab, and one Christian. In reality, there was one acting genius at the helm, and two figureheads for pride's sake, supporting him. The people of Jerusalem had succeeded in the Na'id goal of uniting the impossible trio of Judaism, Christianity, and Islam against a common enemy.

Except that the common enemy was Shad Iliya.

The artificial differences of religions annoyed Shad Iliya—especially these three religions. They professed belief in the same God, the Creator; they all used the same book with the same prophets and angels. Fundamental differences were few. According to two of them, God was sexless but still called "He," while the third gave Him a queen and a son, which did not sit well with the other two, but it was not as if one premised a pantheon, one an Earth Mother, and one fire worship.

In the name of mercy, it's the same damned God!

All three religions were, to Shad Iliya's mind, anachronisms. Born out of early Man's fear of death, they were throwbacks to civilization's early days of infamy, and they perpetuated its slavery, male dominance, superstitions, and intolerance of other creeds—while straight from the Koran came the affirmation: "Mankind were once one nation."

The 27th Army was here to guide these reprobates back to a unified fold.

Shad Iliya strolled outside to the chapel steps, turning the comlink over in his hand. He stopped between two white pillars and clicked on the com. He spoke into it experimentally: "Hello?"

The response was immediate. "Ah, the mighty Philistine general!" The voice was cheerfully mocking and male. "At last. I thought you were sending your toadies to do your dirty work for you."

"No. I am here," Shad Iliya said. "As you can probably see." He took another step out from the pillars and scanned the city whose labyrinthine ways somewhere held the owner of the voice.

A pause preceded the answer. "I thought you people wore blue."

Shad Iliya snapped his heels together and inclined a courtly military bow to his unseen watcher. Then he said, "I detest blue." An absurd answer to an absurd question.

The Jew laughed.

Shad Iliya avoided the traditional blue out of practical considerations. The shiny metallic-blue uniforms were designed to be an instantly recognizable announcement of Na'id loyalty. Shad Iliya didn't like his soldiers to be so highly visible to enemy gunners.

He glanced to the black tarp. He wanted to have this ordeal over, and to take control of the city with the fewest deaths. He'd never fought a campaign like this—trying to preserve both sides. He felt certain of victory but was uncomfortable with these new tactics. It would help if he knew his enemy. And he was discovering quickly that he did not know his enemy this time. Strategically hyperopic, he found that distance made for clarity of vision. Aliens were easy to understand and, therefore, predictable. These people were not predictable in the least.

The inevitability of their defeat and a promise of clemency in surrender were not enough to make them give up their intransigent stand. They were bafflingly illogical.

The two veteran generals, who had joined Shad Iliya on the chapel steps, had reported the same observations many times in past years. They watched the new general grudgingly, waiting for him to fall on his face as they had.

He lifted the comlink again. "Are your Christian and Muslim colleagues with you?"

"They are listening," said the Jew.

"Have you informed them of the terms we offer for surrender, or was the decision to refuse unilaterally yours?" Shad Iliya knew that this was an uneasy alliance at best. If he preyed on the suspicion that the Jew was overstepping his bounds, Shad Iliya might drive a wedge into their fragile unity.

But his opponent was familiar with the methods of propaganda. "Such a bald ploy, Philistine," the Jew said. "My colleagues are not impotent and they can speak for themselves."

The comlink was passed, and the Christian leader, Cardinal Miriam, gave her answer in a florid and prolix diatribe. She spoke in paragraphs of prose.

Shad Iliya cut in, "Your Eminence, I know of only one person who regularly uses lofty rhetoric in private speech, and that is I. Since this is a closed circuit, please speak plainly to me now, human being to human being."

"As you will, General. Go to hell," the cardinal said.

Plain enough.

Just then, from the loudspeaker in the minaret of the near-est mosque erupted a deep ululant *Allaaaaaaaaaaaaaaah Akbaaaaaaaaaaaaaaaaar!*

Shad Iliya took a step back, clicked off the com, and looked to his aides. "What is that?'"

"Muezzin, sir," Ra'im Mishari said. "Muslim prayer call. Five times a day."

"That hideous noise in the name of God?" Shad Iliya said and clicked on the com again. "Are you still there?"

"I am, Philistine." It was the Jew again. "But I fear our Muslim colleague must delay giving you his fond wishes. He goes to pray now."

"Then I shall talk to you later," Shad Iliya said.

"Keep the link with you, Philistine."

"You will be right in my pocket the whole time, Zealot," Shad Iliya said and clicked off.

The prayer call droned on for some minutes more. The crowded city began to crawl.

"Look, General."

Muslims flocked to the mosques, filled them to overflow-ing, spilled out of the courtyards, and bowed down in the streets. Jews and Christians in that quarter walked around them.

Shad Iliya marveled. Religious ardor reached fanatical heights under siege. Yet the conflicting faiths and conflicting sects of the faiths squeezed into the small area seemed to have put their righteous hatred of each other aside for the moment. "They cooperate rather well for avowed enemies," Shad Iliya commented.

"Don't they realize that only proves the Na'id point!" someone said.

"That end of it rather appears not to have entered into their consideration," Shad Iliya said. He didn't understand it either. He beckoned Ra'im to his side. "I require one crack pilot for a possible suicide run."

Twelve officers in and about the war office overheard the quiet request and leaped to volunteer on the spot.

The two veteran generals were gravely disgruntled. This kind of blind loyalty to a leader was unhealthy.

Shad Iliya chose the nearest volunteer and instructed her to take an echelon of eight robot spy planes in a low pass over Jerusalem. "As low as you can manage without burying them."

"I'll wave up to the minarets as I go by, sir," she said. "Purpose of mission, sir?"

"Your ships will be transmitting to this office a computer plot of the trajectories of all enemy fire which you draw. There will be a lot of it. So."

He left off there. The rest of it was understood, and he waited for her to retract her bid.

She saluted, accepting the assignment.

General Shad Iliya saluted, held it a moment longer, as he always did in the face of valor, then barked for a car to take the pilot to her spy planes.

Two computers were activated in the war office to record the planes' signals as they came in. "Don't garble this," Shad Iliya told the technician. "I shall not have this done twice."

He didn't expect to see his pilot again.

He stood out on the chapel steps to watch the pass.

The sleek black planes went into Jerusalem in the 27th Army's characteristic broken echelon.

They came out in perforated echelon. The lead plane crashed into Mount Scopus, failing to pull up steeply enough. Three others fell to ground fire. The four survivors streaked into the desert. The war office waited, hushed, to see if they came back. No one knew which plane had carried the pilot.

"Long live Shad Iliya and the 27th!" crackled over the transceiver.

"She made it!" a technician called out to the steps of the chapel.

The tall white general nodded with an air of near-indifference. But none of his soldiers supposed Shad Iliya indifferent.

He said nothing, did nothing, seemed to be admiring the skyline, until Ra'im Mishari came to him with the tech's report of the lowest angle managed by the defenders' emplaced guns.

Ra'im passed the verdict to him in silence.

Twenty degrees.

Shad Iliya thanked him. Their eyes met. No more words passed. Both knew what the information meant. Ra'im guessed what his general had in mind.

The veterans of the 9th and 34th armies had no idea. All they saw was apparent catastrophe in the half-destroyed squadron of valuable spy planes.

"With the supreme commander's leave," said one. "We told you their ceiling was covered."

Shad Iliya was unconcerned. "We shall not be going in from the air."

Faces slackened. "How, then?"

Shad Iliya became impatient. Blue eyes glittered ice-cold. "Since we are not about to tunnel either, I leave it to you, gentlemen."

Sinikar, the orderly, stepped out of the chapel to inform his general that the Jew was on the radio.

Shad Iliya sighed, expecting this. These taunts would be on an open frequency to advertise the invincible general's disastrous air pass to the populace.

Shad Iliya went inside to the transceiver. "Yes."

"Well, Philistine, give up?"

"No. I was just now telling my colleagues to start digging. We are tunneling in."

The Jew laughed, then said, "No, Shad Iliya. You just found an opening on the horizons. You're coming in with an infantry."

Bald expressions of shock ringed Shad Iliya in the war office. Shad Iliya nodded, accepting the fact that he would get no breaks from this man.

"Yes, Zealot, I am."

"Good. That's where we're strongest. Not those guns." That affirmation was spoken for the benefit of the people of Jerusalem.

"We, too," Shad Iliya said. He turned off the transceiver, looked to the two veterans, of whom he was already thoroughly tired, and said, curtly, "At least someone knows what he is about here. Pity he is on the other side."

The city immediately started bracing for a ground assault. Shad Iliya needed to move fast. The defenders would try to stall for time to redirect some of their guns to ground level—and to the Mount of Olives.

The time-consuming element for Shad Iliya was proper deployment of the weary and dispirited soldiers of the 9th and 34th armies who had been pounding at the gates of Jerusalem for years. And they needed to be accustomed to the idea of an assault without ships, on foot, carrying projectile weapons. Wars simply weren't fought that way anymore.

Jerusalem had the superior numbers. But even had each and every person in the city been a soldier, they only had hand-held projectile weapons for a few—because wars were not fought this way anymore.

Shad Iliya also took care to make wise use of his dregs. In case there actually was a battle, it would be finished quickly and efficiently. He still didn't believe it was going to happen.

While the preparations progressed, the general sent saboteurs into the city to disrupt the defensive measures, while he instructed his own people to challenge any unfamiliar person in their midst to give a password, which was "Shad Iliya is God," in hope that the defenders would be unable to say it even if they happened to learn it.

For himself, Shad Iliya spent the first night rereading the Bible. He sat on a spartan bed under an open window in a small chamber of his war office. He found words that struck him to the heart and that would come back to haunt him later.

If it be possible, let this cup pass from me.

The garden was down there at the foot of the mount.

He closed the book and stepped outside to the chill desert night. He watched the lights of the city spread out at his feet. The dry air carried to him the scent of cypress planted around the chapel. He overheard the exchange of night sentries:

"What is it with these Jerusalemites?"

"They think they're God's chosen people."

"Oh, yeah? Well, if God wants them, let's make sure God gets them." The slapping sound was a palm on a metal weapon butt. "Chosen people. I'll show them chosen people."

Shad Iliya left the temenos of the chapel and strolled over the mount in the dark.

The Mount of Olives was teeming with graves, millennia's worth, sleeping under the fig trees and the pink-flowering oleanders. One could not walk without tripping over the marble fragment of someone's marker.

Shad Iliya did trip and alarmed a sentry at the edge of a stand of pine trees. "Halt!" the girl commanded, and pointed her weapon.

Shad Iliya spoke before she could demand the password. "I shan't call myself God, so do not ask."

"Sir!" The sentry shouldered her gun and snapped to rigid attention. "Sorry, sir."

"No need. Very good"—he squinted at her uniform in the dark—"Sergeant. At ease."

The girl shifted her gun on her shoulder and bowed her head. "Was a hell of a lot easier when the enemy didn't look like us," she said wistfully.

Suddenly sad, Shad Iliya nodded and laid a hand on her close-shorn curls. "Yes, it was."

The muezzin's stentorian wail, distorted through the loud speakers, split the night's peace, and Shad Iliya lifted his hands in dismay.

He had wondered why he hadn't counted five prayer calls during the day. Here was the fifth in the middle of the night. They were going to drive him mad.

Either they or the Jew.

Jerusalem's commander called on the comlink at intervals to harass his adversary. Unlike the muezzin, however, the link could be turned off. Shad Iliya never did turn it off, and realized only too late that he should have. It was the Jew's most powerful weapon.

In the morning Shad Iliya woke, itching from a bout with stinging nettles which he had walked into unawares the night before. The Jew's voice sounded cheerily on his pillow. "Good morning, Philistine."

Shad Iliya rolled to the comlink. "Good morning, Zealot." He cleared his gravelly throat. "Surrender?"

"Never."

Shad Iliya looked to his chronometer and calendar. "Today is my birthday."

"Happy birthday, Philistine."

"Thank you."

"You're welcome. Your sixtieth?"

"Thirty-fifth, villain."

"You will be here for your sixtieth."

"I think not."

"Your army has been rotting outside Jerusalem for a hundred years."

Shad Iliya sat up in bed. "Not my army, Zealot. Not my army."

"Your great alien-killers? You will fare no better than your predecessors."

"How can you even talk like that on a closed circuit? Do you not blush? I know you are lying and you know you are lying."

"Maybe God knows better than both of us, then."

"Oh, no."

"I must say, though, yours is the most thoroughly brainwashed army ever to knock at our gates."

"You mean that your propaganda does not work on my soldiers."

"Exactly."

The propaganda didn't work because it had been aimed at the wrong targets. It attempted to undercut the Empire, the Na'id tenets, the Bel. But the soldiers of the 27th Army weren't fighting for any of that. They fought for love of Shad Iliya. And the sterling Shad Iliya had no vices for a propagandist to use.

"You will find my army immune to your quasi-religious unreason," Shad Iliya said. "So you may as well desist—if you can. Disseminating lies comes naturally to your ilk, does it not?"

"Such insults!" said the Jew. "But what shall I call Shad Iliya? I can say nothing about Shad Iliya. Shad Iliya is perfect."

Shad Iliya smiled. "You have been talking to my soldiers."

"What don't you confess, Philistine? You've no addictions. You drink but a little. You're loyal to your wife even in the field for months on end. You've no strange hobbies. No hobbies at all. You must be a monster. You terrify me."

Oh, but no, Shad Iliya thought. *We have hardly begun with terror.*

The noose of ships and soldiers tightened around Jerusalem's hills, still out of direct sight from the city. Among the Na'id artillery was a great dragon-carved cannon several stories high, an enormous, primitive-looking thing like the figurehead of a bronze-age warship.

The Jew acquired a picture of it from his recon team, broke into disbelieving giggles, and opened his comlink at once in high spirits. "I like your pet, Philistine. It's cute. What's its name?"

"Its name is Ba'al," Shad Iliya said wryly.

The Jew belittled it blithely. At first, Shad Iliya thought his adversary was fishing for confirmation of a suspicion, but as the derision continued, Shad Iliya realized that the Jew had made his first overconfident blunder.

The Jew thought that Shad Iliya was assuming Jerusalem's shields were weak at ground level in the same way the city's offensive guns were lacking at the ground, and that Shad Iliya was basing his attack on that erroneous belief. The Jew thought Ba'al was an n-cannon.

Shad Iliya's fate whispered to him again. No doubt now. No doubt.

You stupid Zealot; dragons breathe fire.

The weapon was actually as primitive as it looked — Man's oldest weapon after the rock.

Perhaps we could use those, too. Shad Iliya thought, ironic.

But fire was the one that had first given humankind supremacy over all life on Earth.

And Shad Iliya went to sleep with a burden on his chest, like something sitting on his heart, cursed with the knowledge that, as a certainty, he could not lose this battle.

The muezzin woke Shad Iliya on the third morning. He rose from bed, dressed quickly without his slave's help, threw open the door of the side chamber that had become his bedroom, and stomped out to the front steps of the war office, where the sentries stood.

"Take out that minaret."

Uncertainly, the sentry changed his grip on his gun. "Really, sir?"

"No." Shad Iliya reached his open hand to the side. His orderly knew the motion and put a cup of coffee into it.

Shad Iliya's brow furrowed with a headache. He hadn't slept well. He marched back to his room and found his alien slave, Pony, making the bed. He chased Pony out and sat on the cot, brooding. His fingers laced around his coffee cup.

God damn you, Jerusalem.

Of the defense, he worried most about the Jewish forces. There was something charming and endearing about the Arab disorder and disunity. He could sometimes count on them to blow up their own weapons because of an incurable tendency to ignore strict directions and maintenance schedules.

But there was something inhuman about the Jewish

unity, precision, and capability. This battle would be a horror. Shad Iliya still refused to believe it would take place. Something would happen to intervene. Surely the leaders would come to their senses. He had given them time to make a patriotic show of defiance. Now it was time to be reasonable.

He rolled onto his back and propped his head up on the pillow against the wall, which was frescoed with faded and chipped Easter lilies. He flipped out the comlink and waited for the inevitable "Good morning, Philistine."

Shad Iliya dispensed with being pleasant and lashed out at the commander for his adherence to and willingness to let a city die for an antiquated religion.

"Antiquated!" the Zealot said. "Old makes it wrong? No, Philistine, old makes it right. Do you think if God were to reveal Himself to Mankind He would wait until now? What of the generations who went before? If there is a Revelation, it is an old one."

"*If*," Shad Iliya said. "The operative word."

"You brought the charge of antiquated against us. Don't change emphasis now because I defeated you on that front, O Ye of the Heathen Name."

Shad Iliya sat up and threw his pillow across the room. "When will you leave off this precious conceit of supposing you have a monopoly on the Supreme Being!"

"When God ceases to be."

That meant never. "I shall hang you from a minaret and use you for target practice."

"Why haven't you attacked yet, General?" the Jew asked, sounding still congenial and tranquil—joyful, in fact. An alarm went off inside Shad Iliya, though he didn't know why. A balance had shifted.

"I shall attack when I am ready," he answered, guarded.

"You're ready," the Jew said, as elated as an unarmed soldier stumbling across a fully stocked weapons cache. "You've been ready."

A lump rose in Shad Iliya's throat. His hands were trembling unaccountably. He was going to say he didn't know what the Jew was talking about. But only the guilty used those words, and of course Shad Iliya was guilty of nothing.

Except that Shad Iliya was afraid to kill. The coming battle terrified him, and the Jew smelled it. And the battle began in earnest. The Jew gave up trying to undermine the faith of the army in its leader and he began to gnaw at the head of the serpent itself.

"It is up to you to stop this war, Shad Iliya. You are the attacker. It is in your hands. You give the word that this atrocity may not be."

"You surrender," Shad Iliya countered.

"It is on your head, Shad Iliya."

And the charge of stalling came home doubly when the general overheard his own soldiers wondering about the delay.

"Are we starving them out?" one asked.

"No. Can't be," another said. "It's not our way."

The thought chilled Shad Iliya. Blockade, starvation, was a messy way to go. It spawned gross inhumanity—or else martyrdom. Either way it was a hideous contemplation.

But Shad Iliya doubted it could even be done here. Any longer delay would allow the defenders to break the blockade. Time was the ally of Jerusalem.

For what am I waiting, then? Shad Iliya thought. Then, in anger, *I am not!*

"Ra'im!" he roared.

"Sir!"

"Twenty-four hours."

"Yes, sir."

All day long the Jew wielded his long knives, and Shad Iliya listened with dread, no longer able to turn off the voice of damnation. The Jew pulled out all holds. But one.

Throughout the campaign, the Jew never called the pale, blue-eyed general a nazi. It was the most obvious shot, and the Jew did not use it, for which Shad Iliya was both grateful and unnerved. Was it mercy?

He doubted it. For when Shad Iliya said, "I shan't glory in destroying your people," the Jew replied, "I shan't glory in destroying you."

You, said the Jew. Singular. Personal. He was not claiming victory. He was claiming destruction of Shad Iliya himself.

Sundown came, the eve of the battle. Jerusalem's guns were not ready despite the borrowed time. The defenders had no chance.

They seem to know. Shad Iliya watched the Arab men flood into their mosques, the women drape their heads and go through their motions outside.

The Na'id soldiers within earshot chanted with the muezzin playfully. They knew, too.

A less certain Ra'im Mishari passed a scan scope to his general and directed his attention to a Jewish station in the new city. Shad Iliya lifted the scope and zoomed in on the group of soldiers. Some of them wore light-benders, which would make them invisible once activated, but that wasn't what was alarming Ra'im. It was their attitude.

Some lounged in groups, joking, passing around their dwindling supply of cigarettes, while others were dancing their circle dances of old—around a fire.

Shad Iliya shuddered and lowered the scope.

"Why are they so confident?" Ra'im said worriedly.

"They are not," Shad Iliya said. "They know."

"I don't understand."

"I do not understand either," Shad Iliya said with a hand on Ra'im's shoulder. "I only know it is so."

Before retiring for the night, Shad Iliya made a last desperate effort to avert the coming massacre. The Na'id supreme commander as a rule never initiated contact on the link. He did so now and asked privately for a surrender.

"Of course not," was the answer.

"What say your Christian and Muslim colleagues?" Shad Iliya asked.

"We are in accord," said the Jew.

"Ask them!" Shad Iliya cried in obvious agony.

The Jew agreed to consult the other two members of the triumvirate, and he relayed their answers an hour later. "The Christian says that the Holy Land is not for the godless. The Muslim says Jihad."

"Shit."

"What means this word 'shit,' Philistine?"

"It is an Anglo-Saxon word meaning excrement, also synonymous with Jihad—so says Shad Iliya."

"Strange. Cardinal Miriam is forever saying that hell is the Anglo-Saxon word for war. Or war is hell. I forget which."

"God damn your flippancy! If you change your mind, this link will be open all night."

"It is a morning assault, then, General?"

"Good night, Zealot."

The defenders were not to spend a peaceful night. Shad Iliya told his own soldiers to get some sleep—real sleep. He bid only a few night officers to keep Jerusalem awake till dawn in readiness. At the places where the guns were being lowered, he ordered heavy salvos and robot flyovers at 0213 hours, and again at 0400 and 0415. "And the moment the muezzin opens his mouth for the 0300 prayer call. Everyone else to bed."

Then he hiked down the far side of the Mount of Olives to his ship for a proper bath. His alien slave, Pony, came along to assist him. The pretty palomino-colored humanoid knew his master's routine and was never too much in the way.

Pony was an androgynous, lithe-bodied, doe-eyed creature with white mane and horsetail. Shad Iliya had named the slave. Shad Iliya was one of those people who called a spotted dog Spot and a red horse Red. Pony's real name had a click in it, and Shad Iliya was not about to torture himself learning to speak clicks in order to pronounce his alien slave's name. Pony was a useful thing, a pretty piece of furniture, better than a robot. Pony would do anything for him.

Shad Iliya pulled Pony's mane and closed both fists in the long, silvery hair, hardly aware of the creature in his hands, his fierce thoughts elsewhere. *By heaven, you cannot fight a war with human beings. Are we not one family?*

Pony waited meekly with bowed head, trying not to wince.

Shad Iliya swallowed hard. *Life goes from my limbs and they sink, and my mouth is sere and dry; a trembling overcomes my body . . . my mind is whirling and wandering. And I see forebodings of evil, Krishna. I cannot foresee any glory if I kill my own kinsmen in the sacrifice of battle. These I do not wish to slay, even if I myself am slain. Shall we not, who see the evil of destruction, shall we not refrain from this terrible deed?*

He released his slave and returned to his room in the chapel on the mount. Pony had already remade the bed and set out his nightclothes and some drinking water. And a shot of whiskey.

Good old Pony.

He lay down, the comlink on the marble-topped nightstand. He lifted his hand to it, wanting to call. But he could not. He had nothing new to say. He would sound very weak and frightened.

The Zealot called in the middle of the night. Shad Iliya rolled to the nightstand and lunged for the com with shaking hands. *Will he surrender and avert this bloodbath?*

No. He said he was lonely.

Shad Iliya was stunned. "So you call *me*?"

"You are the only man in the galaxy who can possibly be as lonely as I."

Shad Iliya fell back on the bed, his eyes directed up at the painted ceiling in the dim light.

Truth.

Cricket sounds and cypress scent drifted through the window. The night was starry.

Shad Iliya checked his chronometer. It was nearly time for the next missile strike.

"You are probably worse off," the Jew said. "Because you are wrong and know it."

"Please."

"Beg with me, Shad Iliya?"

"You know you will be slaughtered."

"I know that?"

"Are you waiting for a miracle?" Shad Iliya rasped savagely.

The Jewish commander was grim. "No. There will be no miracles today."

Shad Iliya closed his eyes tightly.

O gods, there truly will be a battle! The realization sickened him. *That is it. That is it.*

He tried to encourage himself with scriptures:

To forgo this fight for righteousness is to forgo thy duty and honor.

Fighting is obligatory, much as you dislike it.

The latter law the Na'id had taken from the Koran. And, realizing that, Shad Iliya fell deeper into despair. With both sides equally unbending, there was no way out. None at all. Shad Iliya rose before dawn and bawled for Pony to bring his dress uniform from the ship. Pony obeyed and helped him dress, including a bullet plate. Shad Iliya activated the radiation screen in his belt and drank the radiation medicine Pony brought as an extra precaution.

General Shad Iliya appeared on the steps of the war office in high temper, his eyes ringed angry red, his uniform blazing metallic blue. Everyone else was in battle drab.

He marched over the crest of the Mount of Olives to address his troops. A holo transceiver carried his image to his soldiers on all sides of the city. His fury channeled to fervor, and he stirred in them a patriotic spirit he didn't feel. Then, more to encourage himself than them, he read from scripture in a sonorous voice:

" 'No one can bring to an end the Spirit which is everlasting. Therefore, great warrior, carry on thy fight. If any one thinks he slays, and if another thinks he is slain, neither knows the ways of truth. The Eternal in thee cannot kill. The Eternal in thee cannot die. Weapons cannot hurt the spirit and fire cannot burn it. The Spirit that is in all beings is immortal in them all. For the death of what cannot die, cease thou to sorrow. Think thou also of thy duty and do not waver. There is no greater good for a warrior than to fight in a righteous war.'"

He closed, and the army erupted into cheers that resolved into a chant—not the Bel's name, or any of the Empire's catchwords, but his name, *Shad Iliya*.

There remained ten minutes until dawn. Shad Iliya gave the order to mobilize. He climbed back to his observation post on the chapel steps.

The city was quiet. The defenders were in hiding. They would have to be hunted down in the narrow streets and closed buildings, each a kind of fortress in itself with many traps.

The sun rose golden on the ancient town.

O God, save your city.

There were no crickets, no birdsongs this dawn. The muezzin's morning prayer call went unanswered.

I am going to take Jerusalem, and even the God of three peoples cannot stop it.

Not even I can stop it.

The Na'id army appeared on the horizon on all sides at once, a black shroud of soldiers and transport ships and guns drawing in on the city.

A cry rose out of Jerusalem as if the city itself had a voice.

Be frightened, Jerusalem. Be frightened and live.

The tall Na'id standard crested the Mount of Olives behind Shad Iliya and cast a long shadow across the entire city, old and new. Shad Iliya found himself in its shadow.

He scared himself with the sight he had created. He was struck by a strong premonition of death.

Across from him, on the far horizon, the great dragon cannon Ba'al loomed, its mouth gaping at the new city.

This is an abomination. What have I done?

He spoke into the command circuit. "Anthem."

The inciting military music sounded through the tiny speakers each Na'id soldier carried, and the Na'id army charged and opened fire with great noise. Shad Iliya covered his ears with his hands.

Ra'im shouted at his side, "Sir, is all that racket necessary?"

The general nodded. "For the Arabs. If they cannot hear it, they think it will not hurt them."

They were an emotion-led people. Their wailing war cries curdled the blood. Both sides of this conflict were acquainted with the great power of sound.

The defenders had a few surprises. Shad Iliya had anticipated that there would be some. One was a portable scatter-dart cannon that swiveled and felled Na'id ranks on the north side of the city.

Shad Iliya was on the command circuit quickly. "The scatter cannon," he said sharply. "Take that out. Whatever we have to use."

A cluster of twenty-four smart missiles were launched at it en masse. One got through, and Shad Iliya relaxed a measure. The expenditure of precious hardware didn't bother him. What else was it for?

He wished it could all be done with robots. As the battle progressed, he watched, sickened, as each contingency which he had hoped to avoid arose, and blood flowed in answer to it. The soldiers of both sides were heroes all, the best fighters on Earth—the people of Jerusalem fighting for their God, the Na'id fighting for Shad Iliya.

My people can see me, Zealot. Your God is painfully absent here.

A beam ricocheted off his personal n-screen. He wheeled and fired toward the source with a bullet gun.

A child carrying a beam gun reeled back with a high-

pitched grunt and died. It was a barefoot, runny-nosed ur-
chin someone had taken in.

The body was spirited away by Na'id soldiers with hurried, embarrassed apologies.

Shad Iliya was left agitated and ill. The shock was not at
the child's tender age—to Shad Iliya human beings didn't
gain or lose value with age—but that the child was human.
Shad Iliya had never killed a human being with his own
hand. It was too easy. There ought to have been more to it.

He swallowed down a rising gorge, lifted his scan scope
to his eyes, and watched the battle.

An hour passed. He contacted Ra'im, whom he had sent
to supervise the western front. "Pull out of the west quadrant. Stand by with Ba'al."

"General, do you think—?" Ra'im started, stopped, re-
started. "Sir, we're holding our own."

Questioning orders was unlike Ra'im. This battle was
affecting him, too. "This will go on all day," Shad Iliya told
him. "At this rate, the city will fight to the last infant." He
needed to break the back of the defense. Now.

"Yes, sir," Ra'im said, and he initiated the controlled retreat.

Shad Iliya withdrew into the war office and waited out
the evacuation. An officer came to him to report, "We have
a prisoner, sir."

"The Jew?" Shad Iliya asked. He had ordered only one
specific person taken alive.

"His wife," said the officer, and motioned for the woman
to be brought in.

She was young—Shad Iliya's age—with long black hair,
a dirt-smudged face, and blistered hands. Her wrists were
bound behind her back and her ankles were shackled to
restrict her steps to an abbreviated stride.

She knew the White Na'id at once. As she faced him, she
whisked her long ponytail over her shoulder with an impe-
rious toss of her head and spoke coldly in a rough, throaty

voice. "Your wife is said to be the most beautiful woman in the galaxy. What do you want with me, General?"

Shad Iliya was angry. "You are a prisoner of war, not the booty of some pirate raid, so let us not play at that. And, yes, my wife is beautiful. Myself, I would let you go."

"That would be a mistake," she said.

"I fear so."

Jewish women were not gentle things.

"Your soldiers are on the run," she said.

Shad Iliya nodded. His people were efficient in carrying out orders; Ra'im had them evacuating from the cannon's path.

The woman frowned, sensing from his calm something sinister in the ease of the Na'id retreat.

The general's young orderly, Sinikar, came into the room carrying a staple gun and ID with which to tag the prisoner's ear. The woman stiffened like a rod as the boy drew near.

"No," Shad Iliya said. He motioned Sinikar aside, and he removed the gold earrings from the woman's right ear. He slipped them into her hip pocket. She stood rigid at his grazing touch. He took the ID tag from Sinikar and gently laced it through the woman's existing earring holes.

Her eyes slid to the side as if trying to see her own earlobe. "What does it say?" A slight quaver betrayed apprehension.

"It says you are dangerous," he said, then to his aides, "Get her out of here."

They walked her as far as the door, then she suddenly broke away and ran stiff-legged back to him, yanking at her shackles. "General!" she cried.

"Yes."

"Am I to be killed?"

"No."

She breathed in relief. But didn't seem sure if in reality she was better off.

A shout sounded from the portico over a descending-pitched whistle. "Incoming!"

"Get down!"

Shad Iliya dropped to the floor, taking the Jewish woman with him. He covered his head and hers, since her hands were bound, as the shells exploded around the building in thunderclaps. Clods of dirt clattered down on the roof in a dark hailstorm. One shell blasted very near and rang the chapel like a drum, sending down a rain of plaster on their heads and strewing white dust across the time-faded colors of the patterned floor.

Shad Iliya lifted his head, coughed in the dusty, thick, burned air. He checked the woman and then his curly-haired child orderly for injuries. They were unhurt. He looked up at the ceiling. The centuries-old frescoes of his pretty chapel crumbled around his ears.

Suddenly furious, he dragged himself up and outside. The shelling had stopped. He glared at the city in a rage.

He went inside the office and punched on the command circuit. It was still operative. "Are we clear, Ra'im?"

"Yes, sir," Ra'im answered over the circuit. "We are. But a lot of noncombatants have moved into the west quadrant."

"Commence firing."

Ra'im paused. "You don't mean Ba'al, sir?"

"Yes, I mean exactly that!" Shad Iliya cried and punched off the circuit. *Am I speaking Swahili? Is everyone suddenly become deaf?*

He stalked out to the portico.

Jerusalem's layers of radiation shields were impenetrable to any of the empire's sophisticated death rays of a frequency higher than ultraviolet. But simple, primitive fire could pass through as unimpeded as visible light.

The ominous, dragon-faced tower of Ba'al came to life with a roar of flames and sent a long river of fire arching into the new city.

A shudder ran through Shad Iliya with the streaming flames and the long scream of his Jewish captive in the doorway behind him. Tears from some unknown emotion threatened his eyes. He inhaled unevenly, his shoulders, back, and neck taut. The scream from the city reached him even here. He shuddered again.

People flooded out of the western city, fleeing to the un-burned part. They crowded toward the Old City. The Na'id would not destroy that part. There, the fighting would be hand-to-hand.

West Jerusalem was a wall of thick, flickering orange-black fire. Its gutted buildings belched up more hell-hued billows. Shad Iliya watched, wild-eyed, as if mad.

He felt as if this were the first time he had ever really fought a battle. His enemies, dying before his onslaught, were people. Part of him felt sick, part . . . .

His self sickened him.

In extremity, the veneer of humanity disintegrated. Shad Iliya was left facing his essential self and nothing else. And seldom answered in times of rationality was the question of what happens when one cannot live with what he finds. The great flames roared and billowed and snapped like a flag in the wind.

So unfurl our standard and fly our true colors. Flame and death.

The Jew's wife, several paces behind him, cried a con tralto wail over her beloved city, a pure emotion he could never find in himself. Shad Iliya never could act what he felt, and was never sure quite what or if he was feeling.

He beheld the city with his rounded, white-circled eyes, sweat on his brow, a lump risen in his throat. This felt like emotion. And the city burned.

The woman ran to his side with her shortened steps. "Stop it! Stop! I see you loathe it, too! You are dying before my eyes!"

He gestured for her to be taken inside.

A girl soldier came to his shoulder, looked aside at her staring general, then followed his gaze to the burning city. "Terrible, isn't it?" she said.

Shad Iliya couldn't speak. *Terrible.*

He saw the defenders braving the flames. Their heroism never failed. It wasn't simple martyrdom—there was that, too—but these people wanted to live. Their energy, their spirit, their life could not be snuffed out. It put Shad Iliya to shame.

A black cloud drifted over the city and toward the Mount of Olives. Shad Iliya watched it come with detached disbelief. It was on him before he thought to go for a mask, and he was suddenly blinded, choking, and unable to breathe.

Someone groped to his side and pressed a mask to his face. It was the girl soldier, giving her general her own mask. Then she staggered off blindly for another.

Shad Iliya retreated inside the chapel and shut all the windows. He tore off the mask. The air inside was hot and close and hung with floating soot.

The comlink sounded. Shad Iliya grabbed it out of his pocket in surprise. A cold voice said, "You are brutal, Philistine."

"Did you think you had a monopoly on that as well?" said Shad Iliya.

"I did. No. Not a monopoly. A supremacy. We can be ruthless when we need."

"I am aware." He replaced the link in his pocket and turned his eyes to the Jew's wife, crouched in one corner of the war office. He and she were alone in the room.

Why didn't I let them talk?

He knew why. He wanted her. He was alone and he didn't want her to have someone else, least of all the Jew.

He had never wanted a woman so strongly as he suddenly wanted this one. He couldn't say why. *Because she was here? Because she was his?*

"Stop staring at me," she said.

"I like you," he said.

Her back straightened against the wall. "May I say, General, that you revolt me?"

Shad Iliya was stung. He replied wearily, "Why not? You Jews say what you like, to hell with 'may' or 'may not' anyway."

He checked the computer monitors at his station. One was dark. The Na'id fire had taken out one of their own monitors.

He tried to brush soot from his uniform, then gave up. He was very dirty. Only his watery blue eyes were undulled.

"Shad Iliya?"

It was the woman, crouched in the corner.

He turned, mute.

"I didn't mean that," she said.

He shook his head to say it was nothing.

"I had to say that." She stood. "You are my enemy."

"I am only a man," he said, very tired.

She shook her head, her mouth spread into what would have been a smile were it not so sad. "That is a Na'id view. I don't see that way. I am not Na'id."

He crossed to her and seized her shoulders in his big hands, beseeching and insistent. "You are human."

"I am Jewish," she said, helpless before the impasse. She wasn't immune to the syndrome of loving her captor, but she could remind herself that she was a Jew and this poor monster was not.

She did love him. She knew its cause, knew it to be false, but felt it burn regardless, impervious to logic. She was surprised that it had come over her so fast. But that was what came of living at the brink. The law of mayflies. If you have one day to live, you live your whole life in one day, and brightly.

Shad Iliya still held her shoulders. He heard her breath deepen, and on impulse he drew her in to him and kissed her. Her mouth rose and opened to his in startling passion. He put his arms around her, held her, ran his hands over her hard waist and her moving hips that pressed against his groin. He buried his face in her long hair falling loose from its tie, and a deep, sultry voice in his ear said, "Take me."

Shad Iliya laughed weakly. "I can't. Not now. Later."

"I won't want you later," she said. "I need you now."

He covered her mouth with his, and they sank together to their knees as the flames blazed over her city and an all-consuming dark cloud engulfed the landscape and blackened the windows of the chapel.

Armageddon raged outside—the last great battle between good and evil. Except that there was no good and no evil. *Just us.*

And both of them were terrified beyond what the human body and spirit were meant to bear. They pressed together and groaned in animal abandon—the rest outside was madness and this the only sane thing being done in the world.

His passion-clumsied fingers had only begun to fumble at the closings of their clothes when one of his aides cried from outside, "General!"

Shad Iliya scrambled to his feet and ran to the door, forgetting his mask. But the slight wind over Jerusalem had shifted and the air outside was clearing.

The lifting cloud revealed a new scene.

A black-robed troop of Muslim soldiers had moved into the valley at the foot of the mount under cover of the black smoke.

They stormed up the slope with a hideous outcry, dying by the tens and twenties with every step as Shad Iliya's guards cut them down in rows, and still they came with warbling shrieks. The Arabs used the most modern weapons—beams—which reflected off the modern Na'id screens. They themselves fell to simple old-fashioned bullets, their useless radiation screens aglitter, and still they charged as if there were immunity to death in their blood-fierce wails.

Shad Iliya took up a machine gun and mowed them down, row on row as they came at him, right up to his very feet.

When they were all dead, he took a staggering step backward. His hands shook. His eyes stared.

People. These were human. There were hundreds of them. Their blood was spattered on him. He licked sweat from his lips—tasted blood.

Dizzy, he dropped the gun, dead Arabs all around him, some staring glassily back at him, a ghastly mirror. This was what he saw inside Shad Iliya.

Shad Iliya clenched his fists.

It was their own fault they lay all down the slope in heaps. He wanted to scream at them. *Stupid! Stupid!* They carried the best weapons. But the best weapons didn't work here. Rocks would have worked better.

Jerusalem, you are stupid!

Idolatry is worse than carnage—so said the Koran. How was the Empire to absorb such a people? They were oblivious to their human kinship. One could only kill them.

Shad Iliya went back inside the chapel to find the Jewish woman. She was dead—without wound, fallen to a beam shot. She was the only person on the mount downed by the Arab attack.

Shad Iliya knelt with a groan. She appeared to be sleeping, her face relaxed into rough-cut prettiness. He didn't touch her because he was covered with blood.

Wake up, woman. I need you.

He tore himself away from her side and stood.

Who is killing whom and why—does anyone know? Do I?

In the evening, the first faction of the defenders surrendered. The Christians were far and away the most reasonable of the three. Racially, they were the most Na'id-like, a mixture. They knew suicide when they saw it. Not that they hadn't martyrs. Every people had its share of martyrs, thought Shad Iliya, except the Jews, who were made up of nothing but martyrs as far as he could tell.

Once the Na'id forces occupied the Christian quarter, the Muslim resistance collapsed into confusion and left the Jews outflanked.

Shad Iliya climbed to the summit of the mount at day's end. It was a bloody sunset, the sky aflame with tortured hues. The sun's long light cast a red wash over the burning city.

I warned you, Jerusalem. Did you not believe me? You are my city. What did all your blood gain you?

He stood immobile, a tall, angular silhouette against the flames, his straight arms held a little out from his sides, his feet planted wide on the ground, his head thrown back. The wind fluttered his clothes. He tensed and trembled as if in great pain.

This is yours, Shad Iliya.

The recorders, standing ready to immortalize this moment, caught the victorious general so, surveying his conquest; this was the scene that would go over the Net.

Down below, Na'id soldiers poured into all parts of the city. An aide came to his general's side.

Shad Iliya's voice was deep. "Inform the Bel: The city is ours."

The veterans of the 9th and 34th armies ran amok in the streets, wreaking their personal vengeance on the city that had spat at them for so long. Out of control, they killed, raped, and maimed.

"There will be charges filed in cases of excessive violence," Shad Iliya ordered over the command circuit. It was a threat only. He didn't intend to carry it out. "I want this rampage stopped. And I want the Jewish Zealot. Alive."

Then he secured his personal screen, holstered a handgun, and descended into the city on foot, stepping carefully down the slope cluttered with the bodies of Arabs he had killed. He waded through the garden of Gethsemane, muddy with blood of the faithful.

The Lion Gate opened for him, and the supreme commander entered the Old City. Blood flowed down the Via Dolorosa, where the fighting had been close-in with bayonets and scimitars.

Shad Iliya turned into a darkened side street, illuminated his lantern, and proceeded slowly down the crooked way. Moldering walls hugged the avenue. It was strewn with sand and debris, smelling of spice and vegetables and urine. He heard rustling and he halted, lifting his lantern high, expecting snipers.

A herd of mangy goats gazed down at him from a rooftop.

A clothesline stretched across a third-floor balcony, its sooted wash waving in the night wind.

A black kid ran bleating across his path in the stepped, zigzag street, and skirted behind a boarded-up kiosk beside a rickety wooden table on which sat the aluminum keg and three dirty glasses of the water seller. The street's single videophone lay smashed on the concrete.

A jeep whined, careened around the corner, flashing blue-and-red lights. It jounced to a stop and an aide jumped up. "Sir!"

"Yes."

"The Jewish commander, sir. We have him located."

Located, he said. Not *We have him.* "What do you mean, 'located'? Is he dead?"

"No, sir. He's holed up in an alley. He has a weapon and we can't get near. We're afraid to try stun. He's critically wounded. Should we move an armored tank in, sir?"

"No. Take me to him," Shad Iliya said and climbed into the jeep.

The vehicle swerved through the crooked streets, scattering flocks of geese and chickens before its path and avoiding bodies of the dead and groups of prisoners corralled by the occupation force.

They arrived at the entrance to a cul-de-sac where was amassed a broad array of firepower and soldiers hiding behind either corner. Trapped inside the dead-ended alley was one man.

"What kind of weapon has he got in there?" Shad Iliya asked, dismounting the jeep and reviewing the assemblage of arms and artillery that held the Jew at bay. "An atom bomb?"

"No, sir. A pistol, sir. And a knife, we think," the captain said.

"A pistol and a knife," Shad Iliya muttered. "We think." He drifted toward the alley.

The captain gasped and seized his general's shoulders as he wandered too close to the alley's opening. "Stay out of the firing line, sir. He shoots at all comers. He killed our medic."

Shad Iliya shook the captain off and stepped toward the alley.

"Sir, he's a madman!"

"I know that," Shad Iliya said. He walked out into the open and threw his own gun aside.

At the far wall of the cul-de-sac lay the solitary man of about fifty years, short and muscular but not big, his scanty black hair graying, his legs sprawled at odd angles as if his back was broken and he partially paralyzed. He was hardly an impressive figure, and Shad Iliya wondered if this was indeed his adversary. Not that he expected more. He simply realized that he didn't know what his Zealot looked like now that he was unarmed and within this man's range. His gesture had been very rash. *Have I a death wish?*

The wounded man lifted his balding head and saw the White Na'id at the mouth of the alleyway. He smiled as if actually happy to see him. "Ah. Philistine."

Shad Iliya let his hands drop loosely to his sides. He spoke, emotion-choked. "Zealot."

The Jew let him approach. Shad Iliya knelt, lifted the Zealot's head and shoulders off the pavement, and cradled him in his arms. The Zealot let his gun slip from his hand.

Suddenly Na'id soldiers rushed into the alley, but Shad Iliya held up his hand to stay them, and they all froze. "Out," he said.

"But, sir—" the captain started.

"It is not my custom to repeat orders!" Shad Iliya roared, still holding his fallen enemy, and the soldiers hastily backed out of the alley.

The Jew shut his eyes, a faint smile on his lips. "Damn, I could've used a voice like that," he murmured. He was badly hurt, Shad Iliya could see now, some of his bones crushed, his lower organs probably damaged and slow-bleeding. He was dying.

"Our medical technology is better than yours," Shad Iliya said. "You can be revived—"

"I'll cut my throat," the Jew said quickly and gripped the hilt of a knife sheathed at his belt.

"Very well." Shad Iliya had expected that answer. "You are going to die, then."

The Jew winced in pain, but accepted it, his imminent death.

Shad Iliya suddenly could not. He realized that he didn't want the man to die. It frightened him unreasonably.

"If I asked you to live?" Shad Iliya asked.

"Why?" the Jew said. "For you?"

"If I ask as a man?"

"Which is to say, 'as a Na'id.' No, Philistine. I like you well, but the life of a man is not at stake here."

"Then tell me what is, and do not say your damned God!"

Brown eyes opened and gazed up at him. The eyes were large, long-lashed and beguiling, the eyes of someone who enjoyed life, lived it very hard, and loved women. "Do you know what freedom means?"

Shad Iliya sighed. "No. I guess I do not. I don't understand."

"Go to Masada, Shad Iliya, if you would understand Jews."

Brown eyes closed. He wasn't a big man. Then why was he so heavy in his arms?

"Tricks, Philistine," the Jew spoke again, reproaching, his eyes still shut. "You resorted to tricks. I was foolish not to recognize that flamethrower. Who would have thought it? In this century."

"I had to," Shad Iliya said apologetically. "Your soldiers were better than mine."

"They fight like demons—yours. They do all right for not being Jews and having nothing of substance to believe in." He grimaced with a spasm; relaxed again. "Do they really believe so strongly in that Na'id drivel and doubletalk? What makes them go?"

"They believe in me."

The Jew opened his eyes. "You don't worship a heathen god. You are one."

"I begin to think so," Shad Iliya said softly.

The Jew's eyes flitted up and down him, to his sooty hair, dirty face, soiled uniform, and red-brown crusted fingernails. "You're a bloody mess. So how does it feel to kill your fellow humans?"

"What?"

"No *what*, Shad Iliya. This is your day of glory."

"I don't understand," he said, afraid that he actually did.

The Jew moved in for the kill. "Did ever an overwhelming emotion ripple your flat existence before they sent you to kill real men and women?"

Shad Iliya needed to interrupt and shift this line of talk. "And what about you?" he protested.

"No," the Jew said placidly. "I am part of something larger. Something I believed in and still do. You—yours is up in flames." He gestured up to the ash-smeared sky with his eyes. "See there the family of humankind blots out the stars. It's splattered on your face."

An explosion somewhere in the city punctuated the accusation.

"Shad Iliya, I am in a great deal of pain already. Please don't squeeze my ribs so tight."

Shad Iliya loosened his hold mechanically, hardly hearing him with his conscious mind, all the pitiless words driving straight to his heart and into his guts. He stared without real sight.

"Oh, Shad Iliya, you loved it. You were never so alive in your life. The rest is tasteless. You don't even like sex. This is your lust."

Shad Iliya uttered a groaning growl of fury under snapping rein. "You are calling me a pervert."

"You are. The worst kind."

"I fucked your wife."

"No, you didn't," the Jew said as if he really knew. "Here is your ultimate act of love." He slipped his dagger into Shad Iliya's hand. "And you never loved anyone more than me."

Incensed, Shad Iliya took the knife from the Zealot and stabbed into his chest. He didn't know how many times.

Warm blood on his hands, Shad Iliya lowered the body to the ground—or pushed it off his lap. He didn't know exactly what he did. He got up on wobbly legs to stand alone in the alley, not certain who had more thoroughly destroyed whom. The Jew was dead. *But what am I?*

Shad Iliya had only killed the Jew. What the Jew had done to Shad Iliya he didn't yet know. The Jew had done something—irreversible and final as death. He was the last human being Shad Iliya ever killed.

He emerged from the alley badly shaken.

His officers brought to him another prize with which they thought he would be pleased—Her Eminence Cardinal Miriam.

Plodding slowly with swollen ankles, not to be hurried on any account, the stout, white-haired woman let herself be led, sedate and unresisting, but still righteously proud.

Brought before the general, she glanced at him once. "Your hands need washing." And that was all she had to say regarding Shad Iliya.

She had blue eyes.

Two officers assisted the cardinal into a jeep to take her to the prison ship.

Shad Iliya wandered away with aimless, stumbling steps, his aides following uncertainly at a distance.

The crowded buildings opened to a wide way where the dead bestrewed the street, twisted in the shapes of a violent end, fallen over each other.

Shad Iliya stared with unholy awe. There was an obscene beauty in the stillness. He walked softly among the tortured corpses, unblinking.

Black-faced crows sailed out of the night sky and settled on the bodies.

Shad Iliya reached for his gun; didn't have it; seized someone else's—one of his aides'—out of its holster and shot at the birds.

The flock of them rose with a riot of hoarse squawking.

Shad Iliya screamed an order. "Get those things off our dead!"

"Those aren't ours—"

"Keep them off!" He ran up the gradient bricks of a ruined wall and fired at the crows from the top. "Get them off!"

His aides rushed to see the command carried out. "Yes, sir!"

From his vantage atop the wall, Shad Iliya could see the red glow from the western city, and caught glimpses of his soldiers rounding up prisoners in various sectors. Sporadic gunfire marked the clearing out of remaining pockets of resistance.

He climbed down from the wall. He had a vow to keep. He mounted a jeep and ordered the driver to take him to the Dome of the Rock.

His orderly, Sinikar, offered him a gas mask at the door of the mosque. He didn't take it.

He wished he had. Inside was a grisly scene. The fetor of mortification hit him in a suffocating wave. He held his breath. His eyes watered and throat constricted, trying to gag.

It was the same in all the mosques and churches and synagogues. The people had taken refuge in the houses of their God as if He would save them. He hadn't. They died so easily. And He did not strike down Shad Iliya.

Allah had told His people: *Fight for the sake of Allah those that fight against you.*

They had.

Kill them where you find them. Drive them out of the places from which they drove you. Do not fight them in the precinct of the Holy Mosque unless they attack you there; if they attack you, put them to the sword.

The colorful walls of the holy mosque were smeared with blood, the floor piled with bodies wrapped in their prayer rugs because someone had tried to make it neat for him. The air was cooling with nightfall, but the place was still thick with a miasma of rot and rigor from bodies cooking in the ninety-degree heat of day.

Of a sudden, from above, the loud deep prayer call erupted in its changeless refrain. It was a recording. A dead voice calling dead Muslims to pray to an indifferent God.

Is anyone left to answer that?

Shad Iliya beheld all the prostrate bodies, a travesty of adoration in the reeking air. The voice blared and reverberated. Shad Iliya shook.

It's dead! It's dead! It has been dead all along!

He ran outside and put a bullet through the loudspeaker.

His aides came to him, worried. He bent over, hands on his knees, gulping air, his sides heaving. He tried to chase the foulness from his nostrils, his mouth, his throat, but even out here the sticky-sweet, sickening odor of burning human flesh permeated the city.

In a weary, croaking voice, he asked, "Do we have anything that will put out the magnesium fire?"

"Yes, sir, but—"

"Then put it out," he said, lifting his head.

In the distance he heard the sound of human voices, many, chanting in unison.

His aide was speaking. "But, sir, it will burn itself out by morning."

"Put it out!" he shrilled.

The voices in the distance gathered strength and volume. He could make out the words. His name.

"Shad Il-i-ya! Shad Il-i-ya!"

He rubbed his hands against the sides of his uniform, but there was not a part of him clean of blood.

He remembered what the Jew had said. *It is on your head, Shad Iliya.*

In the aftermath, he felt it.

"Shad Il-i-ya! Shad-Il-i-ya!"

It is on your head. Shad Iliya.

He knew it was. There was nothing he could do to change it.

He could only keep silent and wish his station would allow him to cry.

Upon taking the city, Shad Iliya was immediately relieved of supreme command of the combined armed forces at Jerusalem. Someone else was put in charge of normalization. It would not do to have a nazi lord over the city. And Shad Iliya was grateful not to linger over the kill. Later the honors and decorations would be heaped high to bury the implicit slight.

Shad Iliya was uninterested, totally oblivious to the state of his honor. He roamed his ship listlessly. He was bathed and dressed in a fresh uniform of olive drab, his blond hair stripped so clean it drifted up in untamed oilless wisps. Everything around him was scoured and spotless. His bare feet collected no dust on the pristine deck. His fingernails were cut very short, smooth, white, and immaculate. It had taken hours to steam the feel and stench of death from his pores.

Some orderly or officer was always there to wait on his every order and whim. He said, staring, "When you stab someone more than once, it means you are deranged, does it not?"

"Oh, the Zealot, Abram," the adjutant said. Shad Iliya really had made a mess of him. "Don't worry, sir. That part didn't get out to the news Net."

That was hardly the point. Shad Iliya walked away from the adjutant.

He was still in shock, still bewildered. "I don't understand," he murmured. "I don't understand Jews."

Go to Masada, Shad Iliya, if you would understand Jews.

Birds sailed through the canyon, small and swift and smooth, black with dull orange atop their wings. Shad Iliya looked down at them from the top of the massif, a height that was dizzying for its steepness rather than actual elevation.

Desert. All pale brown and white earth surrounded the fortress. No growth but a bare touch of sparse, dull scrub winding along the dried-up wadi far below. Silent but for the wind. Utter silence broken by high lonely cries of the birds sailing through.

Zealot, you are mocking me with this.

He wandered among the ruins alone, sat on a step of a building that was long gone. Bewildered.

Masada was a desolate tell among several other eroded desert mesas banded in brown and lighter brown strata. Piles of scree slipped down the cliff faces and lay in fans at their bases. The air was very dry, making details clear, flattening everything to cartoon unreality.

Shad Iliya brushed away a fly.

This is me, not you, you stupid Jew.

Magnificent, wind-blown waste.

Hard shadows. Sky blue above. Dusty, pale horizons.

On the other side of the tell were more cartoon-stark canyons and the turquoise Dead Sea.

Why must everything be dead?

He had come here for an answer, and there was something here. He wished someone would explain.

The sun rose higher; shadows shrank. The jagged, sharp shadow of the massif drew in toward its western face in the advancing daylight and became something ominous and awesome in Shad Iliya's sight. The shadow of Masada. It did not talk.

I don't understand Jews at all.

* * *

The Bel invited Shad Iliya to a fete in his honor at the palace on Mat Tanatti. Shad Iliya requested time to recover, so the Bel sent him to a villa on the coast of the Levant, a beautiful, relaxing place, and sent Shad Iliya's older brother there personally to ensure his comfort. The hero who brought the hundred-year battle to an end could ask for anything and it would have been granted. He wanted nothing.

One of his aides, a lieutenant, worried that his general was despondent, but he wasn't of a rank to say so and be heard.

Shad Iliya prowled the halls of the villa, not to be consoled by anyone. Neither did Na'id philosophy soothe: *Time destroys all. If you had not fought them, still they would have died.*

Because it wasn't the carnage that haunted him. It was the liking it. He mentioned it in an unguarded moment to his brother.

"Oh, bosh, Shadi. You're the gentlest, most philanthropic person I know."

Shad Iliya whirled on him, eyes ablaze, teeth bared. His brother exited quickly.

He boarded a ship for Mat Tanatti, deciding Shad Iliya needed a few days in relative solitude. His famous brother was simply distraught from the battle and his herculean efforts. And the incident didn't merit repeating.

Shad Iliya sat drinking at a painted wrought-iron table in a chair set out for him on the beach. His aides stayed apart except to replace the bottle and to bring to the table a receiver which would pick up the Bel's speech when it was broadcast over the Net.

This is the hour of humankind's greatest victory....

The air above the water shimmered in the summer heat. Shad Iliya's head lolled onto his shoulder. He poured another glass of cognac—poured twice as much as made it into the glass. No matter. The bottle was always full.

. . . a new nation in which we are all brothers and sisters. And no human being calls anyone Master. . . .

The words shimmered with the air, as if he could see the sound. It was coming from all sides. No. It was inside his head.

. . . Babel refounded. We are one people once more. United we stand and even God shall not sunder us ever again.

Before him the glittering Mediterranean lapped at the brilliant strand. He was hot. His blond hair felt as straw tinder to the touch of his hand.

The water lured. He gravitated toward it. The beach was soft and difficult to walk on. His feet kept sinking in the burning white-gold sand, making his steps more staggering.

At last he slipped into the warm water. Either it was warm or he was drunk. Probably drunk, he concluded, because he had taken his glass with him. He was perplexed to find saltwater in it instead of cognac when he took a drink.

He swam. His thoughts and perceptions ran clear— seemed to. The world was incandescent, the late sun bright upon the water.

Waves rolled in, lifted him, and he rode up with them. The bigger ones swelled over his head and made him sputter and blink.

He saw where the waves were flattened, and he made his way there to the darker water.

Next the world was dark and gritty without sun as he was drawn with a wave that sucked him down and under.

Strengthless against the current, he tumbled like a rag doll in the murky water. He saw himself, as if outside himself, in a dream-vision: his bloodless, pasty, blue-white body flopping backward heels over head, slack limbs floating and twining, doughy-fleshed and dead.

He blundered into a mass of weeds at the bottom, pushed feebly against their slimy leaves, and found his arms tangled in a woven rope net that was pulling him up.

His head broke the surface next to a wooden boat, and he inhaled with a huge gasp.

A voice sounded above him, female and perturbed. "You have torn my net."

"I am sorry." He wiped seaweed from his face. There was no wind. The small fishing boat's single pointed sail hung slack in the still air.

"Hold on to the side of the boat," said the woman. "I will row you ashore."

He grasped the wooden gunwale slick with a thin film of green algae, and let himself be towed. It was marvelous to be breathing and to see the setting sun.

The woman put up her oars, several meters out from shore. "Can you make it from here?" she asked.

"Yes."

He let go the side of the boat and swam in toward the beach.

He gained footing in the shallows and dragged himself out of the water, then dropped to his knees in the deep sand, exhausted.

Suddenly his aides were swarming around him in alarm—in sheer panic—helping him to his feet, staring into his face, and lifting his eyelids with their thumbs.

What is wrong with them?

"Where were you?" they cried. "We thought you were gone for good!"

"Just a swim," he slurred. *Jushaschwim*, he'd actually said, belched, apologized thickly.

And they told him he had gone down and did not come up.

"The woman in the boat," Shad Iliya said, turning back to the water.

There was no woman. No boat. Just red sun on water. He blinked. He turned back to his aides, concerned now. "Did you not see her? Sinikar?"

The young orderly shook his head. Someone else said, "He's drunk."

"I am not drunk!" he bellowed, staggered back, retreating from them. Their faces were full of doubt.

"I am drunk," he admitted in a lower voice. "I am not that drunk."

A dry blanket was placed over his shoulders. A condescending voice said, "Come with us, sir."

A groan rose in his closed throat and opened to a roar. "No!" He threw off the blanket and stumbled in the sinking sand to the water's edge. He raised his puckered hands to his brow and scanned the empty horizon. *Where is she?*

He kept tripping along the waterline in search, only to be cut off and surrounded by coaxing, patronizing voices and reaching hands that closed in on him.

Like wild game cornered by hounds, he roared and snapped to keep his aides away from him. He drew himself up in drunken magnificence and proclaimed himself lucid and them all idiots.

They were embarrassed for him. They wanted to clean him off, get dry clothes on him, and put him to bed. He was weak and drunk and tired, and eventually they managed to take him back to his pleasant-scented, airy room in the spacious villa and coerce him, babbling and objecting, in between the crisp fresh sheets.

Pony brought him some tea with honey, lemon, and whiskey.

A lieutenant slapped Pony's golden hands. "No whiskey!"

Shad Iliya sat up in the bed. "Don't hit my slave!"

An aide pushed him back down.

"Where is the woman?" he said. "A Jew. I bet she was a Jew." He ordered she be brought to him.

"We'll look for her, sir."

They were lying to him. He knew they wouldn't look.

"Pony, find her."

Pony was crying. Why was Pony crying? *Stupid alien.*

In supreme frustration, he closed his eyes and slept for a while, simply to escape the jackasses around him.

He woke in the middle of the night, alone, still drunk. His aides were sleeping in another part of the villa. Pony was out on the beach, looking.

Shad Iliya rose from bed and gazed out the window. The moon was bright. It cast a cold, eerie light on the landscape.

Out on the sand dunes a flock of hooded crows stood, all facing one direction. They were Muslim crows. Facing Mecca.

Shad Iliya turned inside the room. He found a knife and slashed his wrists. He was going to slash more but lost courage.

That was asinine.

He searched for a wrap. He spurted blood all over the room ransacking it for a closure, overturning his nightstand, pulling out drawers and throwing things aside. Finally, he summoned a medirobot, which entered via the service chute and sealed his wounds.

Then Shad Iliya set the machine on a self-destruct sequence, furiously jealous of its mindless ability to destroy itself when he could not. And jealous of its mindlessness.

Before the medirobot could explode, Shad Iliya emptied it of its supply of melaninic. He had always wanted to be dark. Then he climbed out the window—his aides had locked the doors—and wandered away, leaving behind what looked like murder.

20. Jerusalem Stands

HARRISON HALL'S WHISPER called him back. "Captain."

Alihahd sensed strain in the voice, but couldn't answer, staring far away, caught between past and present, wondering what Harrison White Fox Hall was doing on the Mediterranean beach when he hadn't even met him yet.

"You're crushing my hand."

Normality returned to Alihahd's eyes. He released Hall's hand all of a sudden. He couldn't recall having taken it.

It was fully night in the Iry forest. The air was cool and moist, smelling of damp soil, wood, and lush foliage—and the smoky musk of Hall sitting beside him on the rotten log.

From beyond the trees came the subdued sounds of the rebel camp, waiting in standoff with the mighty Na'id 27th Army.

The past had caught up with him. He had always known it must. Something this big could not stay hidden. The universe was not wide enough. And he hadn't exactly been avoiding the Na'id these past thirteen years. He had walked in their very midst—as if he wanted to be caught. It seemed he wanted what he most dreaded. And what he most dreaded had found him.

This was Jerusalem all over again—a great Na'id force facing a hopelessly doomed and cornered resistance—except that he was on the doomed side this time. Cosmic justice? He had made his last possible play, his only chance, to bluff his way out of the impending battle. He had shown his face.

The Na'id were frightened, for certain. But had it been enough? They hadn't retreated. They should have done so by now if they were going to. They were still out there on the plateau as if deep down they suspected that the rebel force was only a paper tiger with a clay general.

Prospects looked bleak. They had to run. They had to. There was no other hope.

Alihahd reflected on the events that had brought him to this pass. He couldn't have done anything differently. All decisions were forced by Fate, despair, ignorance, and cowardice. Had things been different, he could have done differently. But the past was fixed, and hypothetical extrapolations of alternate conditions were futile.

He spoke hypnotically, gazing back at the dream as it faded. "You doggedly execute your duty even though you know you are wrong. You dull your brain with wine to fog the edges of a reality that is too harsh to bear in full light, and still your thoughts will not shut off. There were no choices. It was this or death. And I lacked the courage for an honorable self-execution."

He had spent the two years following the fall of Jerusalem in alcoholic oblivion in the alleys of Cairo, a city that could swallow anyone without a trace. At length he had dared to wake and ask what date it was, and for the first time took a fearful peek over his shoulder to see what he'd been hiding from for two years. It was still there. He was still the man who had taken Jerusalem. And now he was also a deserter from the Na'id army. His name was revered. And in all the universe only he knew it for a lie.

He still couldn't find nerve to kill himself. So he had to figure out how to live.

Henceforth he was *Alihahd*, and never completely sober, though seldom as drunk as in a Cairo street.

He'd tried to make amends with his conscience, doing only what he thought right. But that meant assessing what was right and wrong, what was the measure, and who was the final authority. His ultimate authority used to be the Bel. When he threw off the authority of the Bel by deserting, he kicked the base of his whole life out from under him. The universe was suddenly without direction, confusing and terrifying.

In an almost sober moment he'd taken level stock of his situation and asked of his Furies: *Who is in charge here now?!*

And came the horrifying answer: *You are.*

He had no recourse, even to God. He didn't believe in God—not often. And even if he had, he'd made war on God's people. He couldn't call to God.

He was alone in the universe. Most people had someone to answer to—God, parent, country, leader, law.

I have nothing. He was without country, without law, without God. *And I am the leader.*

And now, thirteen years later, the base had collapsed again and the universe was on its ear once more. The ultimate authority was wrong again. Alihahd was revealed as a fraud. So was the legendary Shad Iliya. He was running circles on an eternal battlefield. Hero, Rebel, Traitor: thrice a legend on both sides of the same war.

In the early-morning hours a messenger ship rolled out of one of the 27th's twelve huge transports, rose from the Na'id camp, and left planet, burning a red streak across the sky. The troubled rebel camp bustled and droned, wondering what the move could portend. Alihahd/Shad Iliya would know. Vaslav was elected to approach him and ask, but no one could find Vaslav. So the rebels drafted another youth to go instead.

The girl came upon the infamous general in the dark of the forest, sitting on a log, talking quietly. The girl didn't know what she had expected of Shad Iliya—a man-eating cyclops perhaps. But despite the horrible white face and eerie blue eyes, he hadn't lost the calm demeanor and personal qualities that made him Alihahd, and the girl dared come near and ask what he thought the Na'id might be doing by sending out the small ship.

Alihahd brushed a bug from his sleeve. He had seen the blazing track overhead, and knew it for a robot ship making deadly haste to Mat Tanatti.

"They are sending to the Bel for advice. They do not want to use the Net, not even in code."

The girl chewed on her peeling lower lip. "What should we do?"

"I would say that until the ship returns with instructions from the Bel, the Na'id will do nothing. So why don't you go to bed?"

The girl smiled nervously. "Really? We're that safe?"

"For the moment."

The girl cast him a grateful look and ran from the forest.

When she was gone, Hall leaned forward to rest his elbows on his knees, turned his head to face Alihahd, and said, "What *does* it mean?"

"It means they are not running," Alihahd said. He tossed a strip of bark away from him. "It means we are dead."

Nocturnal beasts chittered, hooted, and peeped. Insects sang. Trees rustled. In the distance the ocean rushed. They were all lowland sounds, strange to Alihahd's ears.

At length, Alihahd rose, exhaled a voiceless sigh. "I suppose it is my turn now." He quit the forest without further explanation and went to the rebel flagship. Moments later, a second robot messenger ship took off and painted a red trail across the stars, bound to where with what message only Alihahd knew.

When Alihahd reemerged from the flagship, he found Layla sitting cross-legged on the ground at the bottom of the ramp, waiting for him. She had stripped off her shirt. Her chest was beaded with sweat in the sweltering air that didn't cool much with the night as it had on the mountain. She hung her head. Stray hairs stuck to her neck. She moved only to swat at the flying bloodsuckers that lighted on her damp skin.

As Alihahd reached the bottom of the ramp, she looked up at him for a long time, and finally he questioned it. "Layla?"

"You are a traitor?" she said. Her question was not a question — merely incredulity seeking confirmation.

"It seems I am," Alihahd said.

He was surprised to see Layla looking so ill. He beckoned. "Come inside. This ship can readjust your blood. You will feel better."

She reflected on the offer, then reached up her hand to him. He pulled her to her feet.

As she followed him up the ramp, she said, "Do you really think it is a tottering tower of cards?"

"What is?" he said.

"The Na'id Empire."

He had said that once, hadn't he? The woman had a good memory. "Yes," he said. "I am afraid it is."

Layla was reviving when Alihahd was summoned away by one of his rebels shouting from outside, "Captain! Come quick!"

Alihahd descended the ship's ramp at a long-legged trot to find the situation outside radically altered.

Across the plateau, the Na'id had mobilized. Their troops were assembling in the battle order along the perimeter of their defensive energy dome.

Even in the dark, Alihahd could see that their ranks numbered short. At least a quarter of them were missing — presumably wearing activated light-benders and moving God knew where. Alihahd grabbed one of his subordinate commanders by her upper arm. "Tia, get a scanner and find those ghost soldiers. You are looking for maybe three thousand people. Go."

As the young woman ran, Alihahd turned to his second. "Musa, what happened?"

"I don't know. They just decided to move. I've ordered all our people into their ships."

Alihahd nodded, watching the massing enemy troops across the field. With his own people inside their ships, the Na'id couldn't see how frightened and disordered they really were.

"Message for the Na'id?" Musa asked.

"None," Alihahd said.

"Orders?"

"None."

Musa stopped herself from asking, "Do you have a plan at all?" Instead, she withdrew to crouch underneath the flagship and activated her personal radiation screen.

Alihahd walked a few steps away from the ships to stand isolated on the wide plain beneath the black sky. Across the way, like a band of clustered stars, was the enemy's twinkling row of lights and screens, nothing to bar their attack.

Alihahd spoke softly into the empty space around him. "Well, Ra'im?" The humidity seemed to mute the sound.

Any one of the Na'id viewing him through a scope could have read no feeling, no fear on his face or in his loose stance. And perhaps that was what was giving them pause. They didn't advance.

Alihahd heard sauntering footsteps on the grass. They came to a stop behind him. Alihahd didn't turn, keeping his eyes on the army that would not attack.

"Delay and delay," he said in quiet disapproval. "Like Jerusalem."

Harrison Hall's ears pricked. Like Jerusalem. It was not the first parallel.

Was all this intentional? Harrison Hall thought, *We are*

trapped here under the direction of a guilt-ridden, suicidal Na'id general on the wrong side of the battle of Jerusalem.

There was a plan after all.

Hall took a backstep. "Been nice knowing you, Captain."

Alihahd remained as he was. "Good-bye, Mr. Hall."

At his own little camp in the forest, Harrison White Fox Hall gathered up his things—his pipe, a few packages of foodstuff and a water purifier pirated from the rebel ships' stores, a bio scanner, a tinder, and the disparate devices salvaged from his own spaceship, *Nemo*, by the mandesairi—and he fitted them all into a small pack. He stamped out the campfire he'd made for himself, bound back his long graying hair, tied his russet bandana across his brow, slung his pack over his shoulder, tucked his gun in his belt, and hiked up through the trees.

He hadn't gone far up the densely forested slope when Layla came running after him, her form sparkling with a radiation screen, a taeben slung from one shoulder. She closed her hands on Hall's coat and pulled him to a stop. "Where are you going?"

"Anywhere else," Hall said. He tugged free of her and took long strides up the mountain incline.

Layla ran alongside him, two steps for his every one. "There is going to be a battle!" she cried.

"Is that right?" Hall said.

"You are needed!" Layla blazed.

Hall faced her. "Not so."

Layla demanded explanation with a freckled scowl.

Hall let his pack slide down his arm to the ground at his side. "He can kill himself without me."

Layla started to object, but Hall cut her off. "It's Jerusalem, Layla. This time he's on the side he thought was right the first time around—the side that got butchered. Jerusalem never had a prayer, and neither do we. He doesn't intend to win this one. He doesn't want to. This is a setup for a hopeless battle. History repeats itself—especially when the same person is calling the shots."

Layla turned away. She tilted her face up, blinking quickly with gathering pools in her eyes, trying to deny what she heard.

"Vaslav left a long time ago," Hall said. "It's time we did, too. If we stay here, the possibilities are limited—and survival is not among them. He may run away himself."

Layla wheeled with clenched fists. "No!"

"It wouldn't be out of character." He took Layla's small, callused hand, and uncurled her fingers. "He never deserved the kind of loyalty he commands. Come with me. I need you."

Layla pulled her hand away and threw her head back. "I will stay. And if it is to death, I die."

Hall lifted his pack again and started away backward, still facing Layla for his parting. "He hasn't fought in thirteen years. Unlike some of us, he doesn't even remember how to win."

A ship roared overhead, entering Iry's atmosphere. It was another Na'id troop transport bringing reinforcements.

"Sounds like it's starting," Hall said. "You'll be late." He turned and quickened his pace.

Layla ran down the mountain as the ship came to land. She reached the forest edge, dashed across the exposed stretch of plateau, and dived underneath the rebel flagship, where Alihahd and Musa were. No shots had been fired yet. The rebels stayed hidden inside their ships. The Na'id army still held its position as another Na'id transport ship, the *Dayyanu*, came to land on the Na'id side of the field.

"Reinforcements?" Layla asked breathlessly, elbowing her way to crouch between Alihahd and Musa.

"Of a sort," Alihahd said.

Layla lifted the scope of her taeben to watch the debarkation of the new company. Layla was night-sighted and could see well without an infrared filter. "They're all brass and police," she said. "And a general." She quickly groped the ground beside her with a blind hand, keeping her eyes on the scope. "Give me a bolt rifle. I think I can pick him off from here."

"No, Layla." Alihahd stayed her eager hand. "Wait."

Layla straightened and blinked. "Then we are to kidnap him?"

"Wait. Just wait."

Musa pointed. "They're breaking up."

It was true. The Na'id troops had begun to drop back from battle positions along the edge of the shield dome.

"It came over the Net while you were gone," Alihahd told Layla. "A stop order from the *Dayyanu.* The 27th didn't believe it until now. They thought it was a trick of ours." He smiled wryly and revised, "Of mine."

"Why would the *Dayyanu* tell the 27th not to attack us?" Layla asked. Layla thought in black and white. This didn't fit her template.

"There are other ways of winning," Alihahd said. He borrowed Layla's taeben to look at the new general.

Across the plateau, in a small glowtorch-lit ceremony, an honor guard of the dispirited 27th Army relinquished its standard from the flagship *Nashparu* to the *Dayyanu.* General Ra'im Mishari passed the command baton to the new general, an older man unfamiliar to Alihahd on sight.

Damn you, Ra'im. Why did you not run? What an overblown mess this had become.

Ra'im had always been a good soldier. He was not a good leader.

Why did you not stay a lieutenant commander? thought Alihahd. Then, mournfully: *Why did I not stay a general?*

"I can still hit him," Layla insisted.

"Don't hit him," Alihahd said, lacing his long, knobby fingers together. "Where is Mr. Hall?"

"Deserted," Layla said.

Alihahd nodded. "You go, too."

"It is my battle!" Layla cried.

"No battle," Alihahd said. "It is a surrender."

"No," Layla said.

"It has to end somewhere—the blood," Alihahd said.

Layla chewed on her lip, brown eyes welling with tears. Suddenly, she seized his arm and pulled. "Then you come back to Aerie with me and Harry. Let them fight if you cannot. You are not of them anymore. Or them." She threw her hands toward both the Na'id and the rebels.

"Run?" Alihahd said, his brows elevated into his long, unkempt bangs. "That has to end as well." His voice dropped very low, emotion-suffused. "I am Na'id. I have never stopped being a Na'id."

Layla started to speak.

"Do not fight me, Layla. If I have ever made a harder decision, I do not remember." He passed his hand over his eyelids. His eyes hurt. "My army is not an army. They are a mob. They have no training, no discipline, no experience— and little enough luck, it appears. Half of them don't trust me, and—fact is—neither do I. We never had a prayer here. I do not know what possessed Ra'im to make him think we did. Musa, have you delusions of surviving an armed encounter with the 27th Army?"

Musa expelled her breath and admitted realistically, "No." She crossed her arms, still doubting the preferability of surrender. "What kind of terms do you think you'll get?"

She harbored visions of torture and prison and execution.

"What I *have* are: no investigation or prosecution for past crimes against the Empire; no reprisals against any of my rebels for this current action; citizenship for those who do not resist; and no questions."

"How in Creation did you get those?" Musa marveled.

"Those are the terms I offered to the Bel—take or leave. He appears to have taken." Alihahd nodded to indicate the Na'id army dissolving its battlefront.

"How can you trust the Bel, though?" Musa asked.

"The Bel is the only person in this galaxy that I actually do trust," Alihahd said. "If he gives his word to a thing, then it is so. You will all be conscripted, of course, as able Na'id citizens are. But you could fall to a worse army than the 27th. It is not an agreeable prospect, nor even tolerable perhaps. But the alternatives are unthinkable. There really are none."

"What about you? What happens to you?" Musa asked.

"Me, they will eat."

He turned curtly to Layla. "Be off quickly now before they become greedy. I did not surrender my allies. Watch for patrols. They will be combing the woods for deserters. And take Vaslav."

"Vaslav is not here," Layla said.

Alihahd frowned. "Where is he?"

"Gone. He must have run away."

The frown deepened. Alihahd hoped the boy knew what decisions he could live with. Alihahd was not worried about Harrison Hall.

A rebel officer called to Alihahd from inside the flagship, "Captain, there's a message for you from the new commander of the 27th Army. He'll talk only to you."

Alihahd started to rise. He spoke to Layla. "Go now. Surrender will be at first light."

At sunrise, the rebels came out of their ships, weaponless. They deactivated their shield dome.

The 27th Army rushed in.

The sudden charge of soldiers terrified. Their ferocious speed made it seem they would strike down the unarmed rebels, under truce or no. But the Na'id only sought to take control before someone could balk, take out a concealed weapon and start shooting.

There was some brutality, but the old soldiers soon quashed it. Shad Iliya's army still had a tradition of human decency.

A group of young military police grabbed Alihahd roughly and placed him under arrest. No veterans of the 27th Army had volunteered for that task. These MPs were from the *Dayyanu*. The new company with its new leadership was disgusted with the 27th Army for its total lack of initiative in this affair. It became rapidly apparent that this rabble band of rebel malcontents in Na'id dress was not an army at all. The Empire had been had. But there was no turning back on the Bel's word. And that knowledge made the Na'id furious.

One traitorous man spoke, and a whole mighty army had turned into a litter of whimpering cubs. Neither did the one man look like much—spindly, limping, worn, on the downhill slope of middle age. The seventy-year-old Bel looked better than this man. And the Na'id scorn mounted. The great general Shad Iliya's incredible record, seen in this new light, they attributed not to genius but to the machinations of a con artist.

They handled him with more force than they needed— he was not resisting—but not half so much force as they wanted.

Alihahd endured the abuse—which was mostly verbal, with some hard shoves and spits. He welcomed it. It was a thing due. He'd been running from it for years and now felt a perverse relief that it had caught up with him at long last.

And the battle he feared had not happened this time. He'd escaped that trap, the awful circle, with no blood shed but his own. He had revisited Jerusalem and said: *This shall not be.*

Someone slapped his face. He tried not to smile or cry. The MPs chained his hands behind him, then looped the chains around a charred tree, where he was to stand for hours while his rebels were searched, corralled, identified, and their criminal records deleted, to the increased grumbling of the loyal Na'id.

Periodically, young soldiers filed by to gawk at the Traitor with mutters and torment. The veterans of the 27th Army avoided him. Even his rebels, feeling sold, called him Traitor.

The sun beat down on the windless plateau. The dead

tree offered no shade, and Alihahd languished in the stifling air. The afternoon wore on. He felt his skin burn, his joints ache, his muscles cramp with dehydration in the suffocating heat, and he gloried in the pain. *Some kind of deviate you are.*

His perception split onto two levels, one aware in bright detail of the burning in his limbs, the itch from his clothes sticking to his wet skin, the touch of a fly that kept returning to his twitching cheek. On the other level, his mind was detached, and he felt surprisingly well. He was aware that his sense of well-being was symptomatic of serious trouble. But since there was precious little he could do about it and no one around him who could possibly care, he ignored the hazard and enjoyed the alertness.

He recovered some sense of self—or found it. He wasn't sure he'd ever had it to begin with.

After a long while, an MP strutted a slow circuit around the prisoner's tree, his wide chest thrust forward, his fleshy buttocks thrust back. He stopped before Alihahd. Bulging eyes looked down a wide nose. Thick sensual lips formed a sneer. "What's the matter, nazi? Too good for us with your pretty blue eyes and your yellow hair?"

Alihahd gave no answer. There had been no real question.

Another MP circled in from behind, the same curl on her lips. She plucked at Alihahd's loose, rough-weave shirt. She inspected the unfamiliar fabric between her stubby fingers. "What kind of costume is that?" she said.

"Doesn't match your eyes," the man commented on the side.

Alihahd sighed and answered civilly, "It is the dress of people of Iry."

The woman sniffed disdainfully. "There are no people of Iry."

Alihahd wondered how he could have let that slip his mind. Aliens were not people.

I have changed. This place has truly done something to me.

The fleshy man made another remark about his pretty blue eyes.

Alihahd lost patience. He snapped his head around and shot at him, "I think you like my pretty blue eyes."

Thick lips twisted into amazing shapes of outrage. The pulpy face beetled huge in Alihahd's field of vision. The man's breath smelled sickly sweet, and suddenly his knee smashed up into Alihahd's groin with an explosion of pain and nausea. Alihahd folded over, unable to breathe — and he knew the man enjoyed that, too. Alihahd shouldn't have invited it, he thought dimly as he sank down the tree to which he was bound, drawing air in a ragged gasp.

A party of officers marched to the site and dismissed the MPs.

The ranking officer, a lieutenant of the new company, merely stood over him for some moments, watching him retch and gasp at the foot of the blackened tree trunk. Then she pulled him to his feet by his hair and stepped back. She regarded the hand with which she'd grasped his hair curiously and remarked to one of her companions, "Hot."

Alihahd panted, his weight pitched back against the chained post, trying not to pass out, then wondering why he bothered to try. The revilement started up again, slightly more literate than what the MPs served him. The neat and pretty little lieutenant with the blindingly shiny buttons had a big voice and an advanced education, the better with which to recite her creed at him. For her and the young officers, this was a chance to lambaste a general with impunity. One even drew a blade and set it against Alihahd's throat. "You will suffer all the torments of hell for what you've done, Traitor."

Alihahd recovered his breath. "Unless hell is peopled with fools such as you reciting their everlasting twaddle, I would gladly go this very moment, if any of you is willing to send me without an order from your betters." He spat the last word — betters — at them, and his eyes flashed down toward the blade at his neck, daring them.

He could almost hear Harrison Hall chuckling at that speech.

The blade was sheathed.

"Be too merciful," the officer mumbled.

"Then you may stop your threats and posturing and you may shut up. I am not impressed or frightened. I am, however, annoyed."

"You would do well to be fright—"

"Am I then to be killed with the jaw of an ass?" Alihahd roared to the sky. "The glory of the Na'id Empire is its unparalleled ability to vomit back cant."

All six officers at once contested that charge hotly.

Deliverance came at last, painfully, in the form of a veteran officer who walked over to them, attracted by the noise. He observed, quietly appalled. He called off the hecklers, then stood looking at his former general in shame, shook his balding head, and walked away.

Alihahd was sorry. He could have taken the empty insults all day, but that one silent look of shame undid him. His head slumped on his chest. His eyes closed. He listened to the distant tide. It would be going out now. Tides were wonderfully predictable without moons, but not very powerful. He focused on the sound of far-off water. He let the sound rush through his head, until the crunch of a single set of footsteps came very near along with the oscillating beep of a medikit.

Alihahd lifted his head, finding it strange that someone should be interested in his state of health.

Not this man. The medic set the kit down brusquely and dutifully took a sounding of the captive, without one ounce of personal care. He was a coarse, common man wanting to do his job and be done.

"Where've you been?" the medic said gruffly, confounded by the reading. He took off his hat and mussed his already disheveled hair.

"That machine ought to tell you," Alihahd said.

The medic clicked off the scanner dubiously. "A mountain?" Alihahd nodded, his throat too dry for many more words.

"Your heart is bigger."

"Is that a fact?" Alihahd said faintly.

"Strictly literal, sir," the medic said and rummaged through his kit for a diadermic injector, which he brought to Alihahd's chest.

"Poison?" Alihahd asked.

"If it was up to me," said the medic. He gave the injection, and Alihahd immediately felt a few degrees cooler and more comfortable. He was surprised.

"Who ordered this?"

"Supreme Commander General Işşurish," the medic said testily, putting his kit back together. "You've been summoned to his presence." The man snapped his lips shut, reconsidered, and rephrased under strain, "Invited. I'm to ask you."

"Well," Alihahd said lightly, feeling buoyant on his borrowed time. "If it will get me out of the sun, lead on." He shrugged in his chains.

The medic grumbled, let slip a curse, then said, "You won't tell on me, will you, sir?"

Evidently the medic had orders to be polite. "No," Alihahd said.

The medic grunted, took up his kit, and tramped away to send back a six-person escort-guard to collect and deliver the supreme commander's guest.

The cabin inside the Na'id flagship *Dayyanu* was blessedly cool and air-controlled. It took Alihahd's eyes a moment to adjust to the softer light.

The supreme commander, General Işşurish, waved away the six enormous guards in the unhurried way of gentry, leaving him alone with the captive. The general didn't worry that his prize prisoner might bolt or attack him. Alihahd's hands were still bound. That precaution was more than sufficient. Işşurish was a big man, if not nearly as tall as Alihahd. The general was a patrician, full of manners and breeding—one of Alihahd's own kind.

"Shad Iliya," said Işşurish in greeting, swiveling his chair to face him. "And Alihahd also, I believe."

Alihahd stood mute. His silence convicted him.

"You are two men I've always wanted to meet." The general had a long-standing admiration and sense of professional rivalry with the great Shad Iliya, and an obsession with bringing the infamous Alihahd to justice. But since both had been reported dead, Işşurish never dreamed he would actually meet them—and not in the same person.

At first the idea of the two being the same was incomprehensible. How could such an illustrious proponent of the Na'id ideology turn about-face and become such a trenchant foe? But it made more and more sense as he thought about it, and Işşurish began to nod.

Zealots didn't come from nothing. Işşurish remembered the story of the Christian zealot St. Paul, who had been no apathetic unbeliever before his conversion, but rather a notorious, active, fanatical Christian-killer. To Işşurish, there was nothing at all miraculous about a zealot's becoming a zealot. Goals may change. People did not. Great hate could become great love, or love hate. The degree was constant. If Shad Iliya were to transgress, he would transgress hugely—nothing furtive and measly about it.

That Shad Iliya was Alihahd made all the sense in the world.

Işşurish didn't expect to understand Shad Iliya's reasons for betrayal, and he wasn't going to berate him. The prisoner was his honored enemy.

Işşurish had never met a legend before. Strange, this one looked like a man—a battered, outspent one at that—dirty, ragged, tough-knit, and too lean, nothing at all soft but those liquid eyes. There was something very human in his worn, bedraggled features. And something else, the elusive quality of an immortal leader. It couldn't be pinned down, but it was definite in its existence.

"I wish we could have met on the battlefield," Işşurish said. He wanted to do battle with a legend and see who won.

Alihahd did not. There was no more romance in war against his own kind. He'd already had his time to match wits and strengths with a great adversary in a battle to live through the ages. He had his undying fame, and all he could see behind him was a hillside littered with human dead.

It wasn't to be explained. And this man wouldn't understand, even had he been there.

"Your army is a disappointment," Işşurish said. "The 27th."

The brilliance of the 27th Army under Shad Iliya had been that each member worked well in his or her singular capacity. Ra'im Mishari was a perfect second-in-command, and everyone else was perfect in place. But after Shad Iliya had gone, they'd all been promoted to positions in which they didn't belong, and perfection had fallen apart.

"The victories must have been yours, not theirs," Işşurish said. "Such a loss." He shook his head. "You present a sensitive problem, General. I'm not sure yet what I'm going to do with you." Then, as if suddenly realizing that he was remiss as a host, the patrician sat forward and solicitously swept his arm toward a chair. "Sit. Water? Are you hungry?"

Still standing and making no move toward the offered seat, Alihahd spoke for the first time, in a flat tone of injured pride and rebuke. "I have not been given leave to piss since I surrendered."

Işşurish was alarmed at his oversight as only aristocracy could be. There were still manners in the field.

Alihahd's bonds were removed, and he was permitted to go unguarded to the commander's facility. He had, after all, come to them of his own accord.

When he returned to Işşurish, he sat in the chair, his weight to one side, elbow on one chair arm, his feet flat on the deck and spaced wide, relaxed, yet alert and commanding, even as a prisoner. His presence seemed to take over whatever sphere he came into.

"Do you want a change from those barbarous clothes?" Işşurish asked.

"These are fine," Alihahd said. He knew he must smell gamy by now, but he had become attached to this alien garb, and the supreme commander could just endure the stink. Alihahd wasn't feeling as magnanimous as his host.

"Your funeral was very inspiring," Işşurish said, wending his way leisurely to the point of this meeting. "I was profoundly stirred."

Alihahd said quietly, "I saw it."

It had been broadcast over the Net to all parts of Na'id-controlled space, a ceremony of great pomp and solemnity. There had been a long procession with horses and foot soldiers and drums. The Na'id standard had bowed to Shad Iliya's family crest, and flags were lowered to half-mast throughout the Empire.

He remembered now that his daughter, Nikalmati, had been crying.

His beautiful widow, Libbya, had not. She stood, tragic and cold, with her lover standing a few paces in the background. It was a small scandal when she remarried before the official mourning period was done. Alihahd thought it a wise move on her part not to be called Shad Iliya's widow for long.

There was erected a cenotaph, and a shrine in his honor—not as a god, but as a hero. And he had his day of the year when a rite was performed for him. Respect for great men and women did not end at death for the Na'id.

To discover that they had been revering a live traitor for the past thirteen years would be a major scandal.

It was too late to execute him quietly and pretend he'd never surfaced. Too many people already knew.

"It is in the terms of surrender that your life is forfeit," Işşurish said. "But I'm not sure if the Bel wants me to execute you here, or if I'm to bring you back for public trial. He signed it rather peremptorily. He didn't elaborate on his orders. He was quite upset."

He watched Alihahd's face for reaction, saw little that he could read. "He left it up to my discretion—which means I'm to read his mind and do what he wants." Işşurish was talking confidentially to someone who also knew the Bel intimately. "You know how he is."

Alihahd motioned affirmative with a close of his eyes. He knew.

"I would like to be able to tell you exactly what you are in for," Işşurish continued. "I have no desire to make this too bad for you. It will be suitably bad enough as it is. But I haven't yet decided. I am not a mind reader."

"The Bel sent you here to dispose of me for him," Alihahd said. "Of course, he will hold it against you when you return to Mat Tanatti, but it is what he wants. He cannot tell you outright because he needs you to take responsibility for the action."

The general nodded. It sounded in keeping with the Bel's sometimes split character. The Bel's words, thoughts, and actions were not always outwardly in synch. The curse of the Bel's preeminent position was that he was seldom free to speak his mind or heart.

Işşurish was afraid that Shad Iliya was right. Işşurish would bear the brunt of this debacle. The Bel would be furious if he reported Shad Iliya dead, more furious if he brought him home.

But in time, the Bel would forgive and reward those who made hard and ugly decisions for him and saved him from public grief.

Yes, Shad Iliya knew the Bel very well.

Işşurish hadn't actually been asking for help from his prisoner. He was informing him of his status. For the rest, Işşurish had been thinking aloud to someone he knew could appreciate his predicament, talking calmly of deadly concerns, as if they were strolling in one's ornamental garden admiring the blooms and bragging about their children. It was the patrician way—artificial and comical to most, but it was a way Alihahd was bred to, knew, and was at home with—civilized to the last.

"Morning too early for you?" Işşurish asked.

He meant the firing squad.

"Fine," Alihahd said and rose.

Işşurish stood also and paged his orderly. In a sudden surge of bottled-up disappointment, he said, "You never struck me as the venal type, Shad Iliya."

"I was not bought," Alihahd said.

"I was hard put to think so," Işşurish said. "The Bel loved you."

A pang of sadness struck through Alihahd's veil of apathy. It had been a long time since he let himself think about whom he caused pain when first he ran away. "I love the Bel."

"Present tense, sir?"

"Present tense."

Işşurish paused. "Shall I tell him?"

"You may."

He hadn't meant it as a message. It was a statement of fact.

Işşurish's orderly appeared and was given orders to take the prisoner to his quarters.

Alihahd was to spend the night aboard the flagship. The sergeant escorted him to secure quarters inconvenient to any exit. He waved the key, and the doorway's opaque energy barrier disappeared.

The orderly was a reluctant sort, like the medic, unhappy in his present duty of serving an archcriminal of the Empire. But he wasn't above talking to him.

"How long have you been on this steamy rock?" He referred to the planet Iry.

"Best part of a year," Alihahd said, preceding his escort into the cabin.

"Oh. Then you weren't in it." The orderly turned on the light. "Guess you were real happy, though. When we lost Jerusalem again."

Alihahd's limping step hitched midstride. "What?"

The orderly grew uneasy. He licked his lips. "Just how isolated is it out here?"

"Exceedingly," Alihahd growled, turning. "What are you saying?" He stalked back toward the sergeant with demanding steps.

The sergeant drew his weapon. "Don't. Just stay right there," he said, poking the air with his weapon for emphasis. "I meant just what I said. We lost Jerusalem. You didn't know? Now you know. We lost a lot of good Na'id, too. Makes you happy?"

"No," Alihahd said. "I am not happy."

The orderly snarled, "Then what the hell do you want?" He backed out the doorway and reactivated the barrier, cursing.

Alihahd stood motionless in the middle of the cabin, lost in shock.

Jerusalem was free again. What did it mean? What did any of it mean? The historic battle—all the lives—it had been for nothing.

Why did we fight? Why did we fight? Jerusalem stands.

He gazed at the ceiling, chiding himself for trying to make sense of a senseless battle. All human battles were senseless and gainless, given time. It was one of the reasons—one of the good ones—why he couldn't do it anymore.

He broke from his marbled pose in weariness and sat on the cot.

The quarters were spartan, but luxurious next to the Aerie. It was odd to have all the conveniences again. He could easily become soft in conditions such as these, and he realized why he'd almost died on first coming to the mountain.

He was to spend his last hours in comfort. Here was controlled air temperature, pressure, and humidity, a soft bed, a pillow, water on tap, and even the extravagance of a bath and hot water.

And a vial of poison on the nightstand. Very thoughtful.

Alihahd bathed and dressed. He was loath to get into his

soiled clothes again, but did so out of defiance. He'd already turned down the offer of a change and didn't want to reverse his word now. Not that there was anyone to see.

Then he had a visitor.

Alihahd didn't look at the young officer when he came in and wouldn't have recognized him on sight anyway, for he was now a captain and twice as old as he had been at Jerusalem. Neither did Alihahd know the voice since it had dropped and become a man's. Alihahd only knew that the visitor was one of his own from the question: "Why, sir?"

The captain could tell that his former general heard him, though Alihahd didn't acknowledge. Alihahd wasn't quite ignoring him. He was simply elsewhere.

"It wasn't that woman-in-the-boat business, was it?" He hadn't taken the miracle seriously at the time. He worried now that Shad Iliya had.

"No, it was not that," Alihahd said. Even he wasn't certain that the incident had really happened now for all the time between. After a very long pause, he said, "Sinikarra-bannashi."

"Yes, sir," said his former orderly.

"You were at Jerusalem," Alihahd said like an answer.

"Was that it?" Sinikar said.

There was silence. A sigh. "Dead Arabs," Alihahd said.

Sinikar's eyes flickered left and right, searching for a connection—something to make the words make sense. His general was as bewildering as he had been on that last day. "Sir?"

Alihahd turned, his face graven, his stare frightening. "Dead Arabs," he said. Sinikar backed to the door and fled.

The land outside would still be in sunlight. Time yet was left before nightfall. And before sunrise. Alihahd lay lightly drowsing on the bed, dreaming.

He dreamed that he wakened. It was fifteen years ago. He was in bed aboard his own flagship. His slave, Pony, had drawn his bath for him and stood next to the bed, white tail swishing, brown doe eyes gazing attentively down to him.

Soft voice said, "It is 0600, sir." And Pony recited the day's itinerary and asked if he wanted coffee or tea.

He ordered coffee, rose from the bed, thanked Pony, and stepped into the bath. He didn't feel water.

At that point, he realized that he was actually still in bed dreaming.

He also realized that someone really was in his compartment.

He opened his eyes. It was Pony.

The little slave sat on a stool, agitated, blushing, near tears, his hands clasped between his knees, bright eyes fastened on his old master.

It was to be expected, but it had never occurred to Alihahd that Pony would still be attached to the 27th Army.

Alihahd sat up. His muscles had stiffened and shortened during his brief sleep, and he ached all over. He knew he was awake this time, and Pony was truly here.

Pony looked older in the texture of his skin. Fine lines fanned from the corners of his eyes. But his form, face, and musculature were still boyish. His eyes were still innocent— but that was because he was a stupid animal, thought Alihahd. A slavishly devoted slave, Pony had always adored him. But Alihahd was not prepared to find Pony devoted still. Sweet alto said, "I was sent to see if there was anything you require."

Alihahd shook his head. Muscles at the base of his neck knotted and pulled. "No, Pony. Nothing."

Pony was disappointed—devastated. He stood to go. As Pony turned away, Alihahd caught sight of a heavy white scar on the left side of Pony's slender golden neck. His throat had been cut.

Alihahd jumped up, seized Pony's narrow wrist before he could reach the door, and pulled Pony around to face him. "What happened?"

Pony shrank, frightened by his demanding tone and rough hands.

Alihahd pushed Pony's head aside to the right, brushed

away the long snowy hairs of his crested mane, and inspected the deep knife-edge scar.

The first thing that came to mind was that sometimes slaves were killed as grave gifts to their masters. But Alihahd had seen his own funeral, and no slaves' throats had been cut at his cenotaph. And if Pony had been intended as a gift, Pony would be dead. Nobody botched a public sacrifice.

Alihahd took Pony's face in one hand, thumb and fingers on his cheekbones, and brought the enormous eyes around to face him straight. "Who did that to you?" he said.

Small hesitant voice sounded muffled into his big palm, "When I thought you died . . . ." He faltered.

He'd done it himself, Alihahd realized in amazement.

The little fool didn't realize he'd been gashing the wrong place. The human jugular vein was on the left. Pony's was up the back. He'd tried to kill himself.

Alihahd beheld his inhuman slave, mystified. *You did that for me, Pony?*

Alihahd loosed his hold from Pony's face. Reddened prints rose on gold cheeks where his fingers had pressed.

Naturally, Pony had not been allowed to take his own life simply because he wished it. He was too valuable a property for that privilege.

Alihahd then noticed for the first time that the pretty eyes were sick to death of life. It had gone overlooked initially, briefly outshone by Pony's excitement at meeting his beloved master again.

Velvet-soft lower lip quivered. "Sir, will they make you die again?" Pony asked, and his eyes flooded tears.

Alihahd's impulse to comfort him was checked by an old awkwardness. Alihahd couldn't bring himself to take the weeping creature in his arms. He would feel odd and clumsy.

So he gave a command. "Help me to bed, Pony."

Pony's tears stopped at the reassuring sound of order and normality. Pony wanted nothing more than to be allowed to do his job and forget that tomorrow must come.

He laid out nightclothes for his master and helped him undress.

And Alihahd wondered, *Was I always fussed over like this?* He guessed he had been, because Pony was unchanged.

Pony even remembered to bring him a shot of whiskey. Alihahd hesitated—as if Mr. Hall would appear out of vacant air and hit him. Then he swallowed it, felt it warm him, and he gave the glass back to Pony. Pony dimmed the lights and withdrew.

Alone in the almost-dark, Alihahd lay back on the bed. He turned his head on the pillow and looked over to the poison on the nightstand.

General Işşurish came to the prisoner's quarters in the morning.

Alihahd lay stretched out on the bed, the covers thrown off, his arm draped loosely over the pillow.

He was alive.

Blue eyes opened.

"I'm disappointed," Işşurish said.

"So am I, actually," Alihahd said.

He could not do it. Never could. If he could, it would never have come to this. There would've been a body for Shad Iliya's funeral.

The supreme commander's jaw tightened. "Well, then. Come on." He left and sent Shad Iliya's slave in.

Pony laid out Shad Iliya's dress uniform and all his decorations. Alihahd knew what it meant.

"O gods, are we to go through all that?"

This was ugly business. He should have taken the poison.

Pony placed all the ribbons and medals and braids in order—Alihahd didn't remember where all the damn things went—and Pony combed his wayward blond hair.

"I should trim it," Pony said, trying to make the wisps lie down.

"No, you shouldn't," Alihahd said. "Just put on the hat and have done with this."

Shad Iliya always wore his hat dead square regulation, no matter which way the winds of unofficial military fashion blew: slouched, pushed back, or cocked to either side. Pony centered the hat just so, and stepped back. "You look grand, sir."

Alihahd checked in the mirror. He cut a trim figure, appearing not so gaunt as imposingly tall. The uniform could make anyone look good, and it felt right, after all this time, a dark cobalt blue with epaulets on his wide, angular shoulders, and clean-fitted lines down to knee-high black boots.

Pony, can you not guess what I am in for because of this?

Pony did not guess, and Alihahd didn't tell him, not to see his bright admiration fade.

The guards came to fetch him.

"Time, sir."

Shad Iliya was marched out, his hands unbound, in front of the entire assembly of Na'id personnel and the captive rebels as well. It was a long walk, but he didn't limp. The uniform, the moment, his name constrained dignity. He saw his destination—a dead tree that had been trimmed down to a tall, neat post. Alihahd wondered if the proceedings were being recorded.

At the post, he turned smartly to face the multitude. The guards dropped back, and Işşurish stepped up, being the only person of sufficient rank to perform this duty. His face wasn't that of the genial host on the flagship, but of a severe and efficient officer of the Empire, angry at having to do this. He stripped Shad Iliya of his rank, medals, and all the Na'id insignia with which he had just been decorated. It seemed ludicrous. But it hurt. Alihahd was surprised how much it hurt.

Işşurish finished by ripping the twin symbols of Galactic Dominion/Human Supremacy from Shad Iliya's hat and tossing the hat to the ground as trash. The insignia he placed grudgingly in his own breast pocket, a deep frown fissuring his jowls. He spun and marched away.

Left bareheaded, Alihahd felt the pleasant morning air

on his scalp. The sun was rising to a clear sky. The day would be brilliant.

No longer called *sir*, but *you*, Alihahd was backed up to the post and chained there. A firing squad of twenty-one filed into position. The first markswoman asked him ritually if he forgave his executioners.

"Yes," he said.

The butcher waited nearby with a skinning knife with which to carve up the remains into pieces that the ships' food preparers were programmed to handle. The man looked like the kind who enjoyed his work. Alihahd hoped he was not one of those who kept souvenirs—not that Alihahd would know who did what with which part of his carcass, but it bothered him to think that the fleshy MP might come into possession of one of his blue eyes, or whatever else he might want to step on.

The row of marksmen dropped to one knee so as not to obstruct the view of the legion.

Alihahd could look into faces, and he saw more awe than hatred. None of them had a blood score with him. Alihahd had never taken a Na'id life.

Their strained stillness transcended mere military attention. It was an awareness that they witnessed more than a death. The legend had only begun.

A breeze stirred on the plain with the warming air.

Ah. Eaninala.

He smelled charcoal and yellow grasses.

He was offered a blindfold; refused it. He felt the sun on his face. He looked up at the bright sky. *I want to live very much.* He thought of all that was beautiful as the marksmen took aim.

The sun and Amerika.

21. Nemo

THE ORDER TO FIRE hung unspoken, gnawing at the silence like the final resolving note of a melody, which was natural and expected, that didn't come. Alihahd waited for it, became impatient, then alarmed. He lowered his gaze from the sky. The sea of faces before him had all blanched—even those of the firing squad—and all eyes stared past Alihahd, gaping at some horrible vision beyond him, threatening to break ranks. Someone cried, *"Marauder!"*

Alihahd cranked his head around his post to see what they saw.

The ghostly image of a sailing ship. The derelict brigantine coalesced from shimmering air. It raised the hairs on the back of his neck, and he shivered in the heat. Something elemental in the rag sails and rotting timbers never lost power to affect him.

And suddenly all the spaceships imploded—all of them—with a resounding crack and thunder roll as the great engines consumed themselves. Astounded, Alihahd's thoughts flashed like lightning, his heart leaped, and he roared, "Hall!"

Na'id troops cried out and scattered everywhere, trying to stop what had already happened.

And the rebel captives all bolted.

The melee that ensued covered the plateau, spread into the forest as rebels fled or mobbed their guards and seized their weapons. Shots were fired. The unarmed fought with their hands, with rocks, with anything within reach.

Alihahd was in the midst of it, tied to the stake, ignored. He wasn't going anywhere. He couldn't even duck.

The fighting moved away into the jungle. It wasn't a battle. It was a brawl. The Na'id were torn between chasing their stampeding prisoners and fighting the fires around their ruined ships. The ships won the most attention, though there was nothing left to save.

Properly rigged, a Na'id ship could destruct with extreme efficiency.

This was a Na'id nightmare—to be stranded on an uncharted alien world. Alihahd felt a pang of compassion for the panicked troops. He knew their terror.

He heard cries in the jungle, "Get the Marauder! The Marauder has a ship!"

The Marauder does not. It is on the bottom of the ocean, thought Alihahd.

All that was left of the Marauder's ship *Nemo* was "just a gadget"—and a few implosion detonators, it would seem. The fearful specter still loomed over the plain.

Alone and neglected, chained to the stake, Alihahd watched the grass fires switch with the fickle winds, and he wondered vaguely if the flames would come to him.

The fighting moved farther and farther away, until the soldiers were only voices to Alihahd. He still heard their distant shouts among the trees.

Then someone came out of the forest and ran toward him with a drawn dagger. It was Layla. She tried to saw at his metal chains.

"Layla, I surrendered," Alihahd said.

"I did not," Layla said. She looked for a catch, a spring, something to release the chains. "Damn!"

Soldiers were returning. Layla yanked at the chains, gave a grunt of frustration, and scurried back to the jungle at the last possible moment, elusive as an Itiri.

Lost-looking soldiers began to reassemble on the plateau, without orders, without a camp, directionless. At least the ghost image of the *Flying Dutchman* had ceased to menace over the plain by then. Someone else came to Alihahd's stake. Pony. The slender little slave sat at his master's feet, resting his white-maned head against the post to wait until someone came to get him.

Alihahd was thirsty. There was no fresh water. He saw frightened faces among the troops licking their lips and trembling with dehydration on the dusty plateau. Pony was wilted at the bottom of the post.

General Işşurish returned to the plateau, and some small confidence and hope revived in the lost men and women of the Na'id army. Işşurish wiped his brow; he was hot, thirsty, and tired, but not frightened. He moved like a leader who knew what he was about. Like Musa, he was difficult to rattle, even in catastrophe. He organized a few patrols and sent them out in search of water. He sent others to deal with the grass fires, which had almost burned themselves out by then, but it gave the soldiers something to do.

From the jungle, a band of ten soldiers brought a thrashing prisoner, hogtied and gagged with his own bandana. They dropped him at General Işşurish's feet and gave the general a plastic black box they had found on the prisoner's person.

It was a projector. Işşurish turned it on.

The dim outlines of a brigantine ship began to shimmer over the trees. Işşurish turned it off. "Well," said Işşurish and looked down at Harrison White Fox Hall, who was trussed and double-trussed.

"Is all this necessary?" Işşurish asked his soldiers, his voice dripping with tired patience.

"Yes, sir," said the black-and-blue sergeant with teeth marks on his arms.

Işşurish looked down again. Orange eyes slid up slyly, not the least bit frightened or remorseful. Işşurish drew his gun and pointed it at the handsome, wedge-shaped head.

The captive didn't blink. Işşurish guessed that his pulse hadn't even quickened. Işşurish holstered his gun. He could see the man was dangerous—confirming all that the black box implied. The kind with ice in the veins, and no heart— Işşurish wouldn't even bother trying to intimidate him. Vain gestures were a waste of his time.

"Where is your ship?" Işşurish demanded.

Hall snorted a laugh behind his gag.

Işşurish nodded. He'd expected that response.

Torture was yet a possibility, though Işşurish had his doubts even to the efficacy of that. He ordered an organized search begun for the Marauder's ship.

Hall was sniggering at the general's feet.

"Don't look so smug, Marauder," Işşurish said. "I am aware that you have the only working spaceship in the world. And while I would very much like to lay hands on it, it is not imperative. Someone will come looking for us eventually, or we will find your ship for ourselves, and your life and your smug secret will be worth sadly little then." He watched the orange eyes for a reaction.

How could anyone smirk so while gagged?

Işşurish turned away and gave orders to the soldiers who had brought him. "Put him with Shad Iliya. Guard them both closely. And take off that imbecilic gag."

"He bites, sir."

"Take him away."

The guards chained Harrison Hall to the same black, charred post as Alihahd. The two exchanged looks. They'd last seen each other to say farewell.

"Captain."

"Mr. Hall."

"Be quiet," a guard commanded. She chased the little

slave Pony away. Pony skittered off a few yards, then hovered at a respectful distance, tail switching, watching for an opportunity to come back.

The Na'id army had given up trying to recapture their other rebel prisoners. They hadn't the means to keep two thousand people captive. And they turned their energies to survival without prepared food, without pure water, without modern equipment. They couldn't even make Harrison Hall divulge his secrets without the devices and drugs from their ships.

Hall was pleased with himself. He was satisfied with the smoking piles of melted metal that were the Na'id ships. "I like my plan better than yours," he said to Alihahd.

"You have made a liar of me again," Alihahd said. "Caused a melee, stranded all of us on this planet, possibly incited an interstellar purge, and signaled the destruction of this world."

"And I robbed you of your neat and heroic little suicide," Hall said, cutting to the real source of his vexation. "I told you I wanted you alive and stinging."

"You are a devil."

"No. Angel. Who ever heard of an avenging devil?"

"Damn you! Damn you! Damn you!"

"Nothing more eloquent than that for me?"

"No."

"Oh, but I first met you in a spate of elegant fury, Captain."

He still remembered Alihahd exquisitely angry: *For myself, by you or by them, I will be equally dead. I don't very much care. So, please, either shoot, talk, or go away. Or you may go to hell, where I am bound with or without you. Do you want me to repeat any of that?*

"Do you know your buddy talks just like you do?" He meant Işşurish.

He received only a grunt from Alihahd.

Hall grinned. "You're glad to see me." He curled two fingers around Alihahd's wrist behind his back.

"Will you shut up!" a guard snarled.

Time passed slowly. Alihahd and Hall both slid down the post to sit on the ground, still chained. As evening came on, the Na'id were settling. They set up guards against sniping rebels and wild animals from the jungle. They'd built campfires and brought hundreds of animal carcasses to be skinned, gutted, and cooked. They boiled stream water and tested the palatability of jungle fruits on their remaining slaves such as Pony. Once they organized, time was on their side. Eventually, eventually, someone would come looking. The Empire simply did not lose its most famous army, a reinforcement company, and two generals, and not come investigating in time.

"We need allies," Hall mumbled aside to Alihahd.

Alihahd knew of whom he spoke. "It is not their battle," he said.

They both gazed up at the sky, attracted by the sight of an eagle soaring over the mountain.

Their minds ran parallel. Alihahd addressed Hall's unspoken thought: "It would go against conscience."

"Not *mine*," Hall said.

The two guards, who were bragging to each other about their marksmanship, turned back to their captives. "I thought I told you to shut up," said one. She was a tight-lipped, razor-lean sergeant with a pock-scarred face, hatchet features, and a slight curve to her spine. She walked with her shoulders hunched forward, her pelvis tucked under, her sharp hipbones prominent against the fabric of trousers that were too loose on her. She sneered a lot.

The other guard was a beefy young man with peppercorn hair and a walk like a turkey cock. He snarled at the captives and returned his attention to his comrade's high claims regarding her sharpshooting.

Hall said loudly, "I was just saying: Odds say you can't hit that eagle."

Alihahd was horrified. "No!"

The sergeant turned her head back to them and gave a

thin-lipped sneer. "Sure I can." She lifted her gun and took aim at the distant soaring shape.

"They are sapient beings!" Alihahd cried.

The Na'id sergeant looked up from her gunsight and regarded him queerly. It had been a nonsensical thing to say. "Alien's an alien," she said and returned her sights to the target. She took careful aim and fired.

The majestic eagle folded in midair and came fluttering down into the mountain jungle.

Alihahd was stunned. He rasped at Hall, "You don't have a conscience."

"Absolutely none." Hall smiled. "Captain, you surprise me. I didn't think you considered aliens to be on a level with human beings."

"I changed my mind!"

The guard swaggered to Hall and looked down at him with a smirk. "Any more dumb bets?"

"None, ma'am," Hall said. "That was a splendid shot."

And from the sky came a clear, thin cry.

Ki ki ki ki.

Directly overhead the kestrel hovered, suspended on a light breeze, while in the distance droned the engines of rapidly approaching aircraft.

"What's that?" the Na'id cried, and Na'id guns pointed toward the sky.

Işşurish prowled the wide plateau, bellowing at his thousands of soldiers, "For gods' sake, if it's a working vehicle, don't shoot at it!"

And the Itiri came.

The ships landed in the jungle, and in a short time the warrior-priests appeared from the trees, twelve tall alabaster godlings with sunlight hair and eyes of brilliant green. From their midst advanced a midnight figure cradling a great limp feathered body in her wiry arms. Its blood seeped onto her tunic and trousers.

She stepped to the center of the plain and spoke with a

voice like brass. "This is my brother. Who hath done this? This is my battle."

She turned slowly, a complete circuit, then stooped and gently laid the dead eagle on the yellow grass.

The kestrel was hovering above the charred post where Alihahd and Hall were bound. Roniva crossed to them. The two guards moved away at her advance, and the kestrel moved with the sergeant.

Roniva stopped, looked at Hall and Alihahd in chains, looked at the kestrel, looked at the thin, snarling sergeant, whose shoulders hunched defensively as she hugged her gun, her tiny eyes darting.

"Thou?" Roniva demanded of her without an intermediary.

The sergeant's thin upper lip moved in spasms. She wasn't answerable to this *alien*. "What the hell are you?" she sneered.

General Işşurish intervened. To Roniva he said, "Madame, if you have some problem with my soldiers, you will address it to me."

Onyx eyes shifted to him, to his general's insignia. "Thy soldier or thy head," Roniva said.

Işşurish's attitude immediately changed. "Is that a threat, you alien bitch?"

"I decide," Roniva answered herself. Faster than the eye could follow, Roniva had drawn her sword and slashed the sneering sergeant's throat open.

All at once, those Na'id soldiers with a clear shot aimed their weapons at the alien warriors, but in that same instant each Itiri had seized the nearest Na'id soldier as a shield, and no one dared shoot.

Roniva herself had caught Işşurish by the back of his hair and by one thick wrist, which she twisted behind his back.

Twice her bulk, he couldn't move.

"Thou hast come to my home like a great ape," Roniva said. "I will have thee and thine kind gone from here." She had looped his long hair once around the hilt of her sword, and she yanked on it for emphasis. Işşurish ground his teeth in silence.

Roniva took his handgun from him, then unwound her sword hilt from his hair, still keeping hold of his wrist behind his back. She glanced aside at the dead sergeant crumpled in a pool of blood like the eagle. Then she looked to Hall and Alihahd chained to the post. She looked away as if uninterested, then suddenly screamed, swung her tungsten-plastic blade, and slashed down at the post, severing the prisoners' chains in a single stroke. She hadn't let go of Işşurish.

Işşurish nodded, nothing daunted. "We will go. We will destroy your world."

Alihahd, chains hanging from his wrists, came to Roniva's side. "They can do it, Fendi."

Roniva lifted her chin, unafraid.

A deep, groaning rumble and an unfirmness to the ground way down deep like the beginnings of an earthquake unsettled the field.

A great dark mass rising from the horizon slowly eclipsed the setting sun—a leviathan rising out of the River Ocean, spilling water from its crevices—and it kept rising like a continent taking flight.

"What is that?" Işşurish demanded. It was still rising.

"An intergalactic ship—what does it look like?" Roniva said. She was starting to sound like Harrison Hall. She told Alihahd, "Say to this creature he may destroy *that*."

Her snowy owl blinked in above her head and alighted on her hard shoulder. It batted Işşurish's head as it folded its broad white wings.

Roniva spoke sharply to Alihahd. "Now. Say to this one." She twisted Işşurish's wrist. "Say to him: 'Thy Bel hath been notified. Thy people are to be picked up and leave this planet. Not to look back. A ship of the rebel kind will come to collect the fugitives littering my forest. Be gone and continue your fight far away from here.' Am I understood?"

"Have you no concept of justice?" Işşurish asked.

"Oh, yes, justice," Roniva said. "Tell this one that we do not worship that god here."

"I demand—"

"Art thou so stupid? Take what I give thee, or I shall give thee ash!" Roniva cried. "Another Dark Age for thy kind! A long one! Two thousand years was not enough!"

She threw Işşurish away from her. To Alihahd she said, "Stay close to me, in case they shoot."

Alihahd and Hall both drew closer. "You have a shield?" Alihahd asked.

"This creature," she stroked her owl's wing, "can absorb a great deal of energy. Come. I wish to be away from these beings."

Alihahd and Hall followed Roniva into the jungle. None of the Na'id tried to stop them, or fired on any of the warrior-priests.

The intergalactic ship lifted its full bulk from the River Ocean. It now dominated the darkening sky like a close moon.

It occurred to Alihahd that Roniva could have summoned a rescue for him anytime she wanted—had she wanted to lead outsiders to Aerie. As if reading his thoughts, she said in perfect, modern Universal, "I do not like your people."

Alihahd glared at Hall. "At this point neither do I."

As he walked, he nearly tripped over the cut chains which dangled from his wrists. Roniva noticed his difficulty, and she cut the chains off for him and Harrison Hall, leaving them with the metal cuffs.

"And to which side belongest thou?" she asked Alihahd. She already knew Hall's.

"I believe both sides want to kill me, Fendi," Alihahd said.

"I will give thee a ship of thine own," she said.

Alihahd was too surprised even to thank her. Recent events and consequences were still rolling into his brain.

His stare kept returning to the gargantuan, impossible ship in the sky. Its details were difficult to distinguish. If he stared too closely at a point, he could no longer see it, like trying to focus on a single star, and he wondered of what it was made—light?

The thing's existence struck at the very foundation of the Na'id Empire. It represented a superior technology—superior to anything that had ever been known to humankind. The Na'id Empire was founded on the belief that God had created humankind in God's own image to rule over all of lesser Creation. Human Supremacy and Galactic Dominion had become absurd.

Layla appeared from somewhere and pulled on Alihahd's sleeve. "It *is* tottering, is it not? The Empire?"

"It's falling," Alihahd said.

He supposed the clues had been there for any of them to see all along—the Itiri's tungsten-plastic swords, the disappearing, magical-seeming familiars, and constellations that had been given names so long ago they would have to antedate Earth's first infant civilization—why hadn't all that struck him as curious? Thousands of years ago, when men and women were nothing but great apes, someone had been here naming the constellations, naming them after swords, ships—and a Gateway.

He shook his head, feeling blind and stupid. He wondered aloud how the powerful Itiri could have allowed the deluded Na'id to strut and bawl like young bullies for so long, overrunning the galaxy and calling themselves supreme.

Hall's eyes assumed their wicked hunter's gleam. "Yes, how can such an aggressive people bear to watch and do nothing?"

"Aggressive?" Alihahd said.

"The *Itiri*?" Layla said. "The Itiri speak of nothing but peace."

"Ever listen to their music? It's not peaceful," Hall said. "You saw the New Year's celebration." He took a zircon and a turquoise from his pocket and juggled them. "Constant repetition of humbleness and serenity isn't the mark of a peaceful people. What is the need for the constant repetition if they are, in fact, so tranquil?"

Alihahd looked to Roniva. She wasn't angry. She smiled like a master criminal caught by a master detective. "Very astute, Harrison White Fox Hall." She turned to Alihahd. "You wonder at our constant readiness for war and wonder who is the enemy for whom we prepare. Only ourselves."

"But you seem to have the aggressive tendencies conquered," Alihahd said.

Roniva put her spidery hand over his knobby one. "And so do you seem."

Alihahd smiled in rue and irony. They were as savage as he. So they could forgive him, forgive Ben, forgive the Na'id. The guilty did not presume to mete out justice.

"An ancient shame," Alihahd said, remembering her words.

Roniva raised her chin, affirmatively. "That ship," she pointed at the monster from the sea, "is not the one in which our forebears came. Our ancestors were stranded here with nothing. That ship you see was built with redeveloped technology after a long, long time in exile here. And when it was finally built—still a very long time ago—we sank it. We decided we did not want it. We did not want to be what we were, what brought us to this exile in the beginning. We wished to abandon that past and become someone else. You understand, Captain Alihahd? You see, we did not come here by choice, we were not pilgrims. We did not even flee here. This is a penal colony. We do not even know where home is—some place where red birds fly like geese. It could be that we came from another time as well as another galaxy. Once we passed through the Gateway, our ancestors could not know what date it was back home. They could have been millions of years in the passage. That was what our judges intended. They sent us so far away even our familiars could not find the way back."

"But do you know what your ancestors did to deserve this?" Alihahd said.

"I know," said the Fendi. Most Itiri did not know. "We conquered our galaxy. We, the aghara, are natural leaders. Our ranga are a natural army of unquestioning followers. We ruled the universe, we thought. Eventually, we were overthrown and driven out. Now we teach ourselves to own nothing, want nothing, to keep our superiority to ourselves. Humbleness, we still have not. Judge, we must not. It is not for us to check, conquer, or punish the Na'id. We are the Na'id. See you now why we must not take up this sword?" She looked to Alihahd and Hall.

"I see," Hall said.

"Then will you please to shut up?"

Alihahd laughed sadly. *I know these people*. He was suddenly very fond of Roniva.

The ship Roniva gave him was the *Topaz*. He was free to leave whenever he willed. He chose to wait until the rescue ships came to collect both the rebels and the Na'id, so that neither side would see his ascent and wouldn't know to go hunting for him in space. The wait wouldn't be much longer. He could abide awhile yet.

Night fell. Creatures of the darkness were calling within the jungle. Alihahd climbed up to the top of his ship and sat there underneath a wide break in the fringed canopy of tree boughs open to the heavens. He looked at the sky.

Low on the eastern horizon, the Red Geese were rising.

The rebels' rescue ships came first. Layla and Harrison White Fox Hall left the planet with them. The Na'id ships came later. Mustering the means to airlift twelve thousand soldiers on such short notice had been difficult. The humiliation of the mighty human army rocked the Empire. Alihahd wondered how the Bel was dealing with the incredible developments.

Then, before the Na'id ships ascended, a message for

Shad Iliya from the Bel was delivered to Alihahd in the jungle. Pony brought it to him. The Na'id themselves were afraid to go into the night forest.

Alihahd accepted the capsule from Pony's golden hands, and he stared at it a long time before opening it. Something thickened in his throat. He couldn't face the contents.

In that moment, he remembered his youth as a pale oddity in a brown family, a suspected bastard. He remembered that as long as he thought he was a bastard he might as well dream that this man was his real father. Not that the Bel had any more Caucasian traits than his legal father did, but the Bel treated him more like a son than his legal father ever did. Alihahd opened the message capsule and couldn't speak. Whatever he might have said was lost when he read the Bel's single question: *Was it the people?*

Alihahd looked up—lest the tears that were welling in his eyes fall. Second perhaps to Roniva, the Bel was the most powerful individual in the galaxy and close to the wisest. Why was Alihahd surprised that he knew? Was it the people? All those dead at Jerusalem, humans dead at human hands. *Yes, it was the people. Why did you send me there?*

Pony was waiting for a return message, his silvery tail swishing away the winged bugs that plagued him, his great brown eyes timorously scanning the treetops for sail snakes or for those enormous eagles, which terrified him.

Alihahd snapped the capsule shut and buried it in his pocket. Swiftly, he sought out Roniva, while Pony faithfully dogged his footsteps.

He found her in deep jungle shade, seated on a moss-covered boulder. Her long hair, hanging from its topknot, shone glossy blue-black in the winking lights from her nearby airship.

"A going-away present, Fendi," Alihahd announced. He took the startled Pony by his shoulders and presented the little alien to Roniva. "My slave."

Onyx eyes blinked slowly within the frame of the crimson scars on Roniva's high, sharp cheekbones. "We keep no slaves," she said.

"You tell him," Alihahd said, and ran to the *Topaz*.

Pony turned his huge eyes diffidently to his new mistress.

Roniva curled her forefinger on her lips. She didn't know what she was going to do with him. She would think of something.

After the Na'id ships were gone, the *Topaz* took flight. Alihahd was soon in infinite space, free. He had the means to travel anywhere. The autopilot was asking him where he wanted to go.

He'd been flying aimlessly for quite some time before he told it:

Mat Tanatti.

The blue-green world was so familiar that the sight of it hurt. Once in orbit, the starship *Topaz* was challenged for ID and intent by ground control.

Alihahd transmitted an Absolute Priority signal. His message would go straight to the Bel. But when the channel opened for him, he couldn't make himself turn on his audio-visual transmitter. He couldn't trust his voice anymore, and he couldn't face the Bel's image. He could imagine the benign, elderly face with fatherly eyes full of pain and betrayal. He could hear the Bel speaking: *You hurt me, Shad. You have embarrassed me, stabbed me in the back, damaged my Empire beyond repair. What would you have me do now? What would you have me do?*

The image in Alihahd's mind was talking quietly, reasonably, as the Bel did when extremely angry, as Alihahd did. Alihahd had gotten the mannerism from him. He couldn't talk to the man face-to-face. So he encoded his message, requesting permission to land.

Who asks? came the coded reply.

Alihahd had many aliases under which to hide. He answered: *Shad Iliya*.

An eternity passed waiting for the response. It could be

anything, a missile, a refusal, a fleet of police ships, or a cold, cold "Who?" He waited. He died a thousand times. The answer came, the only thing to be said. The rest they could discuss tomorrow.

Come home.

Appendix

The Ring
Signs (Months) of the Year

Equinox
1. The Sword
2. The Ship
3. The Crown
4. The Red Geese

Solstice
5. The Twins
6. The Hexagon
7. The Gateway
8. The Flower

Equinox
9. The Beacon
10. The Serpent
11. The Cross
12. The Triquetra

Solstice
13. The River
14. The Wellspring   Shandee
15. The Veil
16. The Mountain

A sign lasts 10.74 days.

Shandee blows from the second of the River to the seventh of the Veil. The new year begins with the vernal equinox on the Aerie (Northern hemisphere).

Years are named in order for a sign of the Ring. Hexadecades are named in order for a gem in the Gem Cycle, which runs as follows: Topaz, Carnelian, Opal, Jade, Beryl, Onyx, Diamond, Tourmaline, Turquoise, Amethyst, Lapis, Garnet, Zircon, Adularia, Corundum, and Jet.

The present action of this story takes place from the sign of the Red Geese in the Year of the Opal Ship until the sign of the Sword in the Year of the Opal Crown.

The Numbers

Number	Itiri Name	Universal Translation of Name
1	Enna	Sword
2	Shauul	Ship
3	Niaha	Crown
4	Shanwel	Red Geese
5	Bibi	Twins
6	Sorii	Hexagon
7	Dalanai	Gateway
8	Sianasad	Flower
9	Saufer	Beacon
A(10)	Elebanar	Serpent
B(11)	Yxa	Cross
C(12)	Jentas	Triquetra
D(13)	Mandas	River
E(14)	Maeus	Wellspring
F(15)	Ovron	Veil
10(16)	Lodee	Mountain

After sixteen the numbers are named in combinations of the above; for example, seventeen is *endee*—"sixteen and one." And so it goes: *shaudee, niadee, shandee,* etc.

The Hours

First watch	Hour of the Bells	Sunset
	Hour of the wind from the crevasse	
Second watch	Hour of the winged mice	
	Hour of the stars	
Third watch	Hour of the meteors	
	Hour of the berinxes	
Fourth watch	Hour of the sentinels	
	Hour of the dewcatchers	
Fifth watch	Hour of the Sun	Sunrise
	Hour of the eagles (Talassairi)	
Sixth watch	Hour of the waning shadows	
	Hour of the killing light	
Seventh watch	Hour of the lizards	
	Hour of the tide lilies	
Eighth watch	Hour of the waxing shadows	
	Hour of the swifts	

RM Meluch
The Tour of the Merrimack

"This is grand old-fashioned space opera, so toss your
disbelief out the nearest airlock and dive in."
—*Publishers Weekly* (starred review)

The Myriad	978-0-7564-0320-1
Wolf Star	978-0-7564-0383-6
The Sagittarius Command	978-0-7564-0490-1
Strength and Honor	978-0-7564-0578-6
The Ninth Circle	978-0-7564-0764-3
The Twice and Future Caesar	978-0-7564-1085-8

*Now available
in brand new two-in-one omnibus editions!*

Tour of the Merrimack: Volume One
(The Myriad & Wolf Star)
978-0-7564-0954-8

Tour of the Merrimack: Volume Two
(The Sagittarius Command & Strength and Honor)
978-0-7564-0955-5

To Order Call: 1-800-788-6262
www.dawbooks.com

S. Andrew Swann
The Apotheosis Trilogy

It's been nearly two hundred years since the collapse of the Confederacy, the last government to claim humanity's colonies. So when signals come in revealing lost human colonies that could shift the power balance, the race is on between the Caliphate ships and a small team of scientists and mercenaries. But what awaits them all is a threat far beyond the scope of any human government.

PROPHETS
978-0-7564-0541-0

HERETICS
978-0-7564-0613-4

MESSIAH
978-0-7564-0657-8

To Order Call: 1-800-788-6262
www.dawbooks.com

Dave Bara

The Lightship Chronicles

"Totally convincing space navy…check! Perfectly realized characters complete with depth and heroism…check! Plus a fascinating story with an Ahab of a captain determined to complete his mission, and a fledgling lieutenant who comes into his own in the midst of interstellar conflict. Oh yeah: exploding spaceships…double check!"
—Tony Daniel,
author of *Guardian of Night*

"This guy is the next Jack Campbell; it's that good."
—T.C. McCarthy,
author of the *Subterrene War* series

Impulse
978-0-7564-1066-7

Starbound
978-0-7564-0997-5

and coming soon...

Defiant
978-0-7564-0998-2

To Order Call: 1-800-788-6262
www.dawbooks.com

DAW 215